Point of No Return

J L Libstaff

Key Literary Concepts
Washington

For information address Key Literary Concepts, PO Box 925, Vaughn WA 98394

Printed in the United States of America

First Edition December 2014

Libstaff, J L

Point of No Return / Libstaff

Library of Congress Control Number 2014920642

ISBN 978-0-9816065-9-0

10 9 8 7 6 5 4 3 2 1

Also by J L Libstaff

He Shall Appear As
A Morning Star

Farther to Fall

Any Means Will Justify
The Corporate End

To the lights of my life and the hope

for our future

Aubrie, Nathan, and Arloe

Acknowledgements

My dear friends from Watermark Writers who've listened, suggested and corrected. Deanie, who read, helped and encouraged. And my wonderful wife, Pamela, without whom none of this could have been possible

Point of No Return

Each moment passes from our lives
as a
Point of No Return

1

Nashota gathered her baby and held him to her chest. The child, slippery from sweat, evoked the dense, acerbic smells from the tepee. She pushed through the flap and stopped to look across the horizon. Heat rose from the desiccated plains in waves and created the appearance of water in the distance. Air was stagnant, without a breeze. She knew it wouldn't last much longer. Her vision of this day had been the impetus for the men to leave camp in an attempt to alter the inevitable. She'd tried to explain, to stop them, but they wouldn't listen.

The other women and children anxiously milled around in the hot dusty air. They gathered necessities for the possibility of extended travel when the men returned. Everything was gritty and there seemed no end to the heat, although Nashota knew the end would come soon.

As she stared across the sunbaked prairie, the images of water began to roil. The horizon churned yellow and dirty as though the earth itself were rising in the heat. None of the tribe noticed, although the baby seemed to sense the doom and began to cry and wriggle against her hot skin.

Nashota lifted the child to her breast, as much to calm herself as him. The boy began to suckle but it did little to ease the dread they both sensed. He continued to cry with each breath he took.

She bounced him ever so slightly as she watched the cloud of dust grow on the horizon. Still, she was the only one who saw. She should raise an alarm but she knew there was no point, she had watched the entire scene play out in her vision.

Within moments she felt pounding on dry earth, even before the others heard it. Someone finally noticed and shouted an alarm. The entire gathering came alive. Bodies churned in terror and rushed in every direction, each impeding the other's escape.

She ignored the confusion and watched as the rising yellow cloud expelled men on horseback. Images appeared from the dust as ghostly figures, then transformed into a specter as real as the thunder of hooves through the burnt grass.

Yelling and confusion throughout the camp was overpowered by the madness of the pounding hooves and became intertwined with frenzied screams from the attackers and a shrill tone she had never heard before. Nashota stood alone with her child and watched the men and horses approach. The baby stopped suckling and began to shriek but the cacophony overwhelmed his screaming and she stood motionless, surrounded by chaos.

The few remaining elderly men mounted ponies and headed in vain toward inevitable slaughter. Several younger boys and a few of the women rushed in the same direction with sticks and rocks as their only weapons. Those with young children and the infirm began to move away from camp into the brittle grasses of the plains, hoping to escape into the barren, brown fields.

Nashota watched the old men and heard the ponies scream in fear as they met the rushing wall of horses driven by white men dressed in blue. Her people quickly crumbled into the dust. Sounds of rifle fire reached her brief moments later. An Indian pony struggled from under a lifeless rider when a trooper turned and shot it dead.

The men, horses and clouds of mordant filth enveloped the boys and women who comprised the second wave as sharp muzzle flashes confirmed their end.

When soldiers reached the village they continued past her and her son to chase those attempting to escape. She stood immobile as rifle retorts detonated behind her followed by screams and wails from families she had loved.

As quickly as the carnage began, it was over. Riders and horses returned. Several pulled bloated animal skins from their saddles and poured clear liquid over the tepees. She was astonished that these murderers would destroy her people then venerate the village with water. She watched stoically. Her senses were assaulted as caustic fumes filled the air with their hatred. There would be no blessings.

A trooper pulled a branch from his pack, the end was wound with straw. Another rode up beside him. There was a spark and the branch burst into flame. Several other soldiers joined in and each moved away with torches. They proceeded to spread fire throughout the camp until the entire village was engulfed. Screams rose as those hiding inside were met by flames. Waves of heat became exaggerated as the village burned under the scorching sun.

The stench was nearly unbearable but Nashota stood silently with her son who was strangely quiet, held against her chest. She wondered if her vision had also given her a gift of invisibility. She alone, stood among the invaders, amid the fallen and the flames. Possibly her role as prophet had afforded her and her son protection from these evil spirits.

Two soldiers came in from the distance. Before them was a tribal elder, still alive. They prodded him and forced the infirm man to run through the choking dust. As he approached, he looked to her. She realized she could still be seen. When he was near, they pushed him to the ground, hands bound behind him. He fell to his face in the dirt while they shouted unintelligible demands. Then one soldier struck him in the spine with his rifle butt. The old man collapsed, motionless on the hot earth. The others continued to scream at him.

The elder raised his head, looked to her through muddy tears, and began to pray. He asked the spirits to provide for his people. Take them to a cool fertile plain, rich with water and an abundance of food. He begged forgiveness for their misgivings and pleaded for peace and joy in the spirit world.

As soldiers continued to scream, someone pelted him with a rock and he collapsed again, bleeding profusely from his temple. Face down he asked the spirits to allow his blood to enrich the earth and bring forth great bounty. Amid the shouting a rifle fired. The old man twitched and fell still.

Nashota watched in silence. She had seen this fate in the visions. Her baby shifted and she realized he was trying to nurse again. Heat and dryness had sapped the moisture from him. She returned him to her breast.

Approaching horses drew her attention once more. An apparent leader yelled out and soldiers began to drag bodies into a great pile. People she had always known were heaped upon one another and more rancid liquid was poured over them. Moments later the pile was ablaze. She watched in vacant shock as two soldiers retrieved the elder from her feet and threw him on the pyre. The leader shouted again but she no longer heard him. As she gazed at the flames, visions of her people's spirits rose with the smoke.

From somewhere, a strange, piercing sound filled the air again and at once, soldiers mounted their horses and joined in a formation. The man who gave the orders leaned down toward her and screamed once again, spittle sprinkled her face. She stared back without emotion. She could not understand his words and wouldn't respond to his shrieks. His face grew red with anger and he began to dismount when a rider approached and spoke. He looked at her one last time, spit toward her then pulled his horse around and moved off to the front of the column. The sound came again, from a soldier with a shining branch pressed to his lips, and the marauders slowly moved away.

Motionless, she and her child watched them ride off. They were at a distance before she turned to observe the carnage and the funeral pyre again. Her entire way of life rose on the heat with the souls of her people. They escaped the pains of life and joined their ancestors in the spirit world.

She watched the flames subside while smoke thickened then sang a prayer that one day her people could regain power and never again permit this hatred.

The sound of horses faded in the distance and in the near silence of the prairie, she fell to her knees and hugged her child while she continued her songs of hope. From the west, out of the dead grasses, a rider appeared. He cantered past the devastation and noticed her singing, still alive. A sharp retort split her prayers and her head snapped sideways. The world spun in slow motion. She lowered herself to the ground making sure her boy was on top, then rolled slightly away from the burning sun to shade the child. He didn't cry and barely moved. She had no idea if he would join her, since it was not part of her vision. She continued to pray for him and for her people as she drifted away. Her spirit rose with the others in the heat as the sun slowly paled and was gone.

2

Three wagons moved in a line, slowly following deep ruts across the grassland. Heat was intense and the drivers sweltered under straw hats. Wives sat beside them enveloped in sweat, dust and grit.

In the last wagon, a young woman sat beside a much older man and cried softly. Thomas, her husband, tried his best to ignore her as her tears slowly coursed through the dust on her cheeks. Her father had arranged their marriage. Thomas, a widower and a businessman, needed someone to take with him to the Territories. He was leaving his store behind and negotiated a deal with Lanna's father; his business for one of the man's seven daughters.

There was no sign of life in this never ending field of dead grass. No birds sang. Nothing but the sun, the heat and the burnt smell of scorched prairie mixed with the intolerable dust.

In the front wagon road a boy of fourteen who hung his bare feet from the back as he attempted to pencil his thoughts in a leather bound book between bumps. Carson was accompanied by two sisters, both propped against bundles of provisions, and his three year old brother on the wagon floor curled in a ball, sleeping. The Callahan's left Ohio for the promise of green fields, cool water and vast country meadows to farm. Caywood Calahan had convinced eight families to accompany him to California for the good life. They'd left in May and to date, five families had given up and returned to Akron. Caywood and his wife Marie were determined to continue, even when her brother Lawson gave up to turn back the past evening at a way station. Lawson proclaimed his sister crazy to go on in the heat. They argued and she broke into tears when he said she would likely end in Hell.

Caywood lost control and screamed, "Lawson take yer whole damn Fenton clan and go back 'n die workin' somebody else's dirt." He felt personally betrayed by the others who'd left. Now, even his brother-in-law had abandoned him.

The Calahans prayed for guidance that evening and later, through a vision in a dream, Caywood had been assured their path was correct. Marie silently wondered if Caywood really received messages from God or if he was just too bullheaded to admit he'd been wrong.

That morning, just prior to turning back, Lawson gave his little sister the family cross passed to him by their father. He tied the small silver piece to one of the horse bridles for luck. Caywood refused to acknowledge the Fenton family as they left. The remaining three wagons moved on without as much as a glance back.

Marie feared that Lawson may have been right as she wiped grit from her forehead with a rag as hot as the prairie.

The couple in the second wagon had two boys, ages five and seven. Charlie Lake wanted to give his boys a new beginning. He and Darcy had dreams of a fine large ranch with a river running through the middle. Cattle on one side, behind barbwire and farmland on the other, near the house. Darcy dreamed of chickens and rabbits out back in large pens. They would have a homestead big enough for the boys to split when they were grown. They would become right proper young men with their own homes. Girls would fight for a chance to be their wives. However, at the moment, Junior was sick with a fever. Lonnie had become weak and cried constantly in the severe heat.

Sun beat down across the flatlands and there was no relief to be seen as far as they looked; no clouds, no shade and no chance for hope, but they continued on, craving the cool of nighttime.

Caywood squinted at the horizon and almost believed he saw something. It appeared, and then was lost in waves of heat. He tried to determine if his eyes were spotting from sweat or if there was actually something out there. As moments passed, the spot grew larger and appeared to be a rider in the distance. He became animated when he realized his sight was true.

"I think its Horn comin'," he whispered to his wife. She looked in the direction he was staring and said, "I don't see nothin'," then tipped her head back down to shade the sun.

After another moment, Caywood spoke a bit louder, "It is, woman. Look hard. It's Horn. That's his painted horse ridin' toward us, fast. I'll bet he's found the river." She looked again and scarcely saw what he was talking about.

Caywood yelled out, held his right arm to the side and pulled hard on the reins with his left. "It's Horn! He's back! Hold up, Horn's comin', I kin tell his horse." The girls sat up. Carson laid his book inside and jumped from the back of the wagon as the company slowed to a stop.

Charlie shouted, "Think we're near the river? Think he found the river?"

Lanna stopped crying and looked at Thomas with hope in her eyes as he pulled up on the oxen.

The men climbed from their wagons and walked forward to wait for their guide to reach them. As each jumped down, clouds of yellow dust rose from footsteps in the dead grass and enveloped them. They seemed to emerge from a haze as they joined each other to watch the horseman come within sight.

Charlie mumbled, almost to himself, "I need to soak my kids, cool 'em. Think we're close to the river?" No one responded as they watched the approach.

Minutes later, while sun beat down upon them, the guide slowed and came to the three men standing in front of the wagons. He had a scarf over his nose and mouth and as he dismounted he pulled it off leaving a pink area beneath on the lower half of his red, filthy face. He walked his horse to meet the men.

Caywood spoke first, "Did you find it?" and the others joined in, "Are we close?" "How close are we?" "Is it cold? We need something cold."

Horn held his hands in the air. "Wait up, here. Gimme a second." He wiped his forehead and the dust burned against his scorched skin. He took a breath and started, "It ain't as good as we hoped, but it ain't all bad neither." Each man looked panicked and Caywood asked, "How bad is it?"

"This damndable heat's got the Smokey Hill durn near empty. Nothin' but mud and cracks. We might be able to squeeze some water outta some o' the spots, but there ain't no soakin' nor cooling to be done."

Charlie screamed, "You're crazy! You found the wrong place. They said there's a whole wide river up there, not some damned muddy hole. You did bad wrong and you just don't wanna tell us. You got lost, didn' ya!" He started moving forward. The guide made two fists, raised his arms and declined to give way. The other two men grabbed Charlie and pulled him back, "What the hell's wrong wi you," Said Calahan, "Why'd you even think he'd tell us that if it warn't true. Get hold of yourself, man."

Horn lowered his hands and stared at the men in sheer anger. He was about to say something when Thomas let go of Charlie and held up his hands in a gesture of amity, "He don't mean it, Horn. His kids is doing badly and he's awful worried." Thomas looked at the man, contrition in his eyes. The scout took a breath and his look softened a bit.

"You said it warn't all bad, Horn, what's the good you said about?" Caywood let go of Charlie and stepped forward with his hands spread. "Tell us what you got."

Horn looked at the men. Charlie turned his back to them all as Horn spoke of what he'd found. "About a quarter day ahead the road splits. We woulda had ta go way north to cross the river but since it's near dry we can take the road south. It'll cut 'bout five days. We'll be at the foot hills in lessen a week. Means we'll be outta this sun and into some trees." He raised his voice for Charlie who had stepped away, "Man, you tell them kids to hang on a bit. It's gonna get better a lot quicker'n we thought. They're gonna be OK, hear?"

Charlie turned back and lowered his eyes. He nodded his head, embarrassed by his outburst.

***

For three days the wagons continued across the prairie, moving toward the south and west. As the sun lowered toward the horizon each evening, proverbial field bugs began swarming and biting everyone.

On the third sundown Horn decided on a likely spot to spend the night. They formed a triangle with the wagons, tethered the animals and started a fire from scrap cases and wood they had gathered along the way.

The sky became ink black with no moon and although it was filled with stars, darkness seemed to absorb all their light. The women pulled packs from the wagons and started dinner. When the meager provisions were ready, Caywood led them in prayer. Marie, the religious foundation of the family, insisted Caywood give thanks for the group. He did what he could to appease her and although his beliefs were not as fervent, he used prayer and virtue to pacify and at times, manipulate his wife.

After eating, Carson found his book and pencil and pulled his blanket from the wagon. He wrapped himself against the night in the safety of the triangle, near the fire. His sisters and brother slept in the wagon with their parents. There wasn't room for any of them to be comfortable but Marie would not let the young ones away from her side.

The two other families huddled inside for shelter as well. Horn lifted the pack from his horse, removed the saddle and blanket and made his bed opposite the dying embers by which Carson tried to write. He took a bottle from his pack and pulled a huge swig from it. "What are you always puttin' in that there book, boy?"

Carson squinted at the guide as he took another swig from the bottle. "Both my grandpas come across the ocean to get here. They both died before I was born. Mama has some o' their stories about how they got here, but most all they did is gone now." He held up his book. "I got this before we left so's I kin make record of everything we do to get to California. The story's gonna be for my grandkids to know how they got where they are." He smiled, "Yer in here too, Horn. They'll know everthin' you did for us."

Horn sniffed and spit in the fire, "Don't nobody'll care 'bout what I done. I don't expect no grandkids ever." He took another drink.

Carson had watched Horn drink himself to sleep quite often the past few weeks but he kept it a secret from the others after Horn confided, "With all the death and misery I seed out here o'er the years, iffn I don't pull a slug now an' then, I'd go bat crazy." Horn continued drinking as the boy asked, "How'd you get that Indian Pony Horn? You rustle it from them, the Indians?"

Horn shook his head at the boy's ignorance, "The Indians out here ain't that bad, Boy. Fact is they's perty decent." He lifted the bottle and swallowed.

"I run across a camp one time, a bunch a hunters. They was skinning a deer when I come up. Had naught but a broke ol blade that wouldn't cut butter. I had a brand new razor Bowie an' I handed it to one of 'em to use." He held the bottle out near the fire to see how much was left.

"Funny thing is, he thought I give it to him. They was smilin' and laughin' and slicin' skin offen that deer like it was magic.

One o' the young bucks got interested in my saddle 'n bags. He started playin' with 'em an' spooked my horse. The old man got right angry and yelled somethin' horrible at 'em an' that made my ol' horse go nuts. He started to buck an' tripped hard, probly from a woodchuck hole."

Horn took a long drink. "Broke his leg. So the old guy slaps hell outta the buck and goes over 'n gives me the youngin's pony. Had to cart my saddle 'n things back on some branches dragged behind."

The man looked toward the sky and emptied the bottle. "Took me months to break that wild thing to saddle. He's real perty and fast as kin be but he stands out like a black eye."

Horn sucked the bottle dry, burped, threw it far into the grass and laid back. Carson thought about Indians for a while as Horn fell fast asleep. The boy listened to the man's ratcheted, drunken snoring for a while until the noise finally softened. At the same time all sounds ceased from the wagons. The silence overwhelmed him and became nearly unbearable. The final campfire embers died and he felt as though he was drowning in the night. He lay there for what seemed hours until his emptiness was overcome by even deeper shadows. The world faded and the sound of Horn's breathing dissolved until, at last, all was serene.

Carson dreamed of a cat he'd found back home; an old yellow tom with a torn ear and scarred eye. It wouldn't let him near, but still, he continued to feed it every day. He never knew if it was actually male or female since he couldn't get close enough to find out. He decided to just call it "Cat".

Cat came to him every evening when he returned from the field and he secretly shared whatever food he could muster with it. When he was late or when there was nothing to share, Cat would yell at him in a grating whine that drove him crazy. This night he dreamed of the irritating animal yowling until it woke him. He realized where he was and rolled over to go back to sleep when the cat howled again. He opened his eyes but the noise didn't fade. Carson sat up to listen. Could Cat have somehow followed him all this way? It wasn't likely. He strained to hear for some time until he realized the sound seemed more a baby crying somewhere in the distance. Chills ran through him and he sat up to hear, but there was nothing, it was gone. He took a breath, shook his head and lay back down figuring it must have been his imagination, a leftover from his dream, or maybe an animal off somewhere in the grass.

He started to fade back to sleep when the sound seized him once again and jerked him bolt upright. He listened intently. It wasn't a dream. It wasn't a cat. There was no doubt in his mind. It was a baby crying.

He rose quietly and stepped up on the footboard of the wagon. The entire thing shifted and the squeak of wood shredded the night. His mother was the only one to wake. "What? What's goin' on?"

"It's me Momma. I been hearin' somethin'. Stay still a minute and see if you don't hear it too." Marie leaned up, propped on one elbow. "Sorry, boy, You're just spooked. I cain't hear nothin'."

He shushed her and held his finger to his lips. She couldn't see his action in the darkness and began to whisper back when she stopped. From far-off came the faint sound of crying. She raised herself on both elbows and listened carefully to what was apparently the wail of a child. Her heart pounded as the noise slowed for a moment and then came back in force. She sat silent while the pattern repeated several times. Finally, she reached next to her and shook Caywood. He grunted and shifted in the small space. She shook him again and said his name, "Caywood, wake up!" He breathed, yawned and sniffed. "What are you doin', woman? Let me sleep."

Caywood Calahan, you listen to me right this minute. Don't you go fallin' back to sleep, now."

He blinked his eyes but the darkness was still complete. "What is it? Y'all all right?"

"Caywood, just be quiet and listen. You hear that?"

He lay quietly for a few moments then whispered, "What the devil is that? Sounds like a baby. Where the devil'd a baby come from?"

"Caywood, we got to do something. Sounds like that baby's out there all alone. We got to help it."

"Marie, how the devil would a baby get all the way out here by itself? It's gotta be with somebody." He was silent for a moment. In a measured voice he said, "Maybe its Indans. Maybe we're near a camp. We better have Horn check in the morning. We might need to get the devil outta here pretty quick. Maybe that's why everybody goes north."

"Caywood, if it was a' Indian camp there would be someone takin' care of that baby. If they was bad Indians out here they wouldn't have babies with 'em. Somethin's wrong. We got to find that baby, could be somebody's in big trouble."

"Woman, there ain't a thing we can do in this dark. Come light, I'll tell Horn. See what he says. Then we'll do all we can. Right now, cain't even find my hand on my arm. It'll have to wait till morning.

Marie spoke severely, "In the morning we're gonna find that cryin' baby in help 'em. It's what God would have us to do. I ain't goin' an inch further till we find that baby and her people."

The decision made, Carson climbed down in the darkness and found his blanket again. The three of them lay awake listening to the distant wailing until the black sky paled in the east.

3

Marie stood next to the cold fire, a shawl wrapped snugly in the dim morning light and watched Carson fold his blanket. The crying still came and went, although it was less apparent and more sporadic. "We gotta hurry. Sounds like she's gettin' more weaker every time she hollers."

Caywood came from behind the wagon closing his pant buttons to join his wife and son. Marie pushed him toward the sleeping guide, "Wake 'em. We need 'em, right now."

Carson put his hand on his father's arm, "He mightn't be too eager. He had a bit of medicine last night."

"Caywood, we can't go out there alone. Somebody's gotta get that baby and we need Horn to take us."

Calahan stopped and looked at his wife in the pale light, "You didn't say 'take us' did ya? I won't have you out there with maybe indans all over."

Marie looked sternly at her husband, moved to Horn, bent down and shook his shoulder, "Someone's goin' and it best be quick."

Horn didn't budge. He exhaled and rolled over. Marie smelled his liquored breath. She became instantly angry and shouted his name as she shook him again.

Lanna poked her head from her wagon, "What's wrong? What's goin' on?"

Marie shook Horn once more and barked his name again. He finally rolled toward her and looked through one bloodshot eye, "What the hell?"

Lanna cried louder this time, panic inching into her voice. "What's happenin'? What's wrong?" All three wagons began to shift and squeak as the occupants woke to her concerns.

Calahan shouted at her, "Lanna, would you shut it up! You're the problem here, awakin everbody!" He turned back to Horn, "Missus heard what sounds like a kid out there. Not far away. She's been obstinate we got to go find it. Durned thing been cryin' most the night. We need to find iffin it's someone in trouble or iffin we should hightail it outta here cause we're in the wrong place. You did check things out round here didn' ya?"

Horn squeezed his eyes, sat up, snorted prairie dust and spit toward the fire, "They cain't be no baby out there. I know they's an Indian camp somewheres around, but they's friendly. I met 'em on the trails lots o' times and they just lookin' to trade and talk. As long as we keep movin' they don't mind if we pass by." He sniffed again, turned his head and spit then dragged a crust out of his left nostril with his thumb and flicked it away. "If you been hearin' a baby it could be more people who decided to turn back. Lotsa folks think they just follow the trails and get where they's goin'. Then when they get lost they decide to go back home. Could be that."

The others climbed from their wagons and came to the cold fire ashes. Lanna hid back inside, crying. Marie offered a stern glance to Caywood and spoke, "We gotta find where this baby is. It's our God given duty to save her."

Caywood took her shoulder, "You ain't goin' nowheres, woman. You're gonna stay right here with the train. Iffin anybody's going with Horn, it's gonna be me.

Horn pushed himself from the ground and walked to the outside of the wagons.

Charlie came forward, looked into Calahan's eyes, noses nearly touching, and whispered, "What the Hades are you all a talkin' 'bout? Babies an' such. Caywood, you think we're in trouble? If they's Indians out there I gotta get my kids somewhere else. We cain't be chasin' no Indian babies. We'll likely all end up dead and scalped." He looked back at Darcy and smiled, then returned to Caywood. "Let's don't be crazy, Caywood. We go lookin' for some kid and we're all gonna pay for it."

Although he thought no one could hear, Marie pulled his arm and spoke in disgusted tones. Her eyes squinted with anger, "Charlie Lake! It ain't no Indian baby out here all alone! What if it were one a your boys out there, hurt? What if somebody could save 'em? Would you and Darcy want 'em to run away and leave your kids to die in this heat? Where's your Christianity? Is that what you lernt in Church?"

Horn returned to the group and spoke, "Look! It's probably people such as you, that couldn't make it and has turned back. I'll ride out and follow the sound then come back to let ya know what I found."

Marie looked at the man and spoke with clenched jaws, "Horn, I ain't sayin' you won't do right, I'm just tellin' you I'm going too and I'm gonna bring that baby back." She stepped forward and her husband grabbed her arm. "Woman, you'll do no such. You'll stay here with the young'uns and take care of 'em. I ain't sending their momma out to maybe disappear and leave 'em all alone. "He looked at Horn, "If anybody goes with ya it'll be me."

The others murmured in the background as Horn looked at all of them. "Looky here Caywood, if you take one o' your wagon horses it's gonna be forever to git where I'm goin'. Jus' let me go see what the business is and I'll come back with the news."

Marie stepped forward again, "Not on yer life, Horn. What if yer out there alone and you need some help with something? What if there's more than just a baby? What ya gonna do then? You need somebody with you, Somebody to hold that baby. You cain't decide to leave it there if you cain't bring it with you."

Horn became irritated at the woman's insistence. He glared at her for what seemed forever then spoke, "O K, I'll make a deal, you send this boy with me, on the back o' my horse and if we find a child, he can carry it. In the meantime, you folks git some food in ya and hitch up the wagons. I'll be back before it gets too hot. We need to move out. We gotta get to the foot hills by tomorrow night." Marie took a breath to speak but Horn cut her off, "I won't take no. If you want me to spend time lookin' for some kid, we're doin' it my way. Boy, let's us get ready."

Half an hour later a man and a boy rode across the plains together on the small, painted horse. Every several minutes, Horn pulled on the reins and stood quietly listening. "You hear anythin', boy?" The sound came after a moment and Horn turned his horse slightly south from the trail and continued through the tall, dead grass. They stopped and adjusted direction a few times until they came upon trodden prairie in a wide swath. Smells of burned remains combined with death confronted them; began to envelop them.

Horn pulled the horse to a stop, "There's somethin' bad wrong out here, boy. We need to be careful. You hear or see anythin', and I mean anythin', you tell me, understand?"

He turned to the boy whose eyes were as large as dollars. Carson nodded.

They moved onto the trail of flattened grass and rode forward slowly holding to the outer edge. The trail opened to what might have been a camp so Horn pulled up the horse and they dismounted. A sickening sweet stench of death filled the air and Carson was glad he hadn't had breakfast. Horn told him to remain quiet and still and keep the horse as calm as possible. He bent down, crept into the high grass and disappeared.

It was questionable who was more nervous. The horse kept clubbing the ground with his hoof and pulling erratically. Carson shushed him and rubbed his nose. The thick odor made it difficult to breath. The sudden, overwhelming silence and the thought of somehow ending up alone was unnerving. He fought the urge to jump up and ride back to the train but instead stood fast and continued to calm the animal.

"Besides," he thought, "If I leave Horn out with a bunch of devils, I'd be responsible for killing the man." He knew he couldn't live with that. Yet, even worse, if he returned to the wagons without Horn and a baby, he'd have to face his mother. She'd drag him back with the rest of the train, regardless of the situation. She'd insist they do the right thing.

Carson searched the surroundings and listened for any sounds. The sun rose higher in the morning sky and with increased heat, the odor became thicker each passing minute. He glanced back and ached to break off and return to the wagons.

With no warning, the horse nearly pulled him over and snorted in fear as it balked. Frightened, Carson pulled back and tried to move into the tall grass to hide. In front of him, the prairie began to part as someone or something approached. He dropped the reins and froze, tried to call out, but words stuck like phlegm in his throat. The horse moved away and he stood frozen and watched the form draw closer. Fear clawed up his spine, left him helpless, when a baby began to cry. Moments later Horn came through to the clearing nearly crawling, carrying a child.

He moved rapidly to the horse and Carson followed in fear.

Horn was deeply distressed and out of breath. He whispered, "Take this damned cryin' baby, we gotta git hell outta here. Now!" The child, wrapped in a skin, was crusted with dried blood. The man passed the infant to Carson and jumped up on his horse. The boy, appalled by the scabs covering the baby, held the package at arm's length and gaped. Without a word, Horn grabbed the child by its leg then pulled the boy up with his free hand and kicked the horse hard. The pony broke into a run. Carson bounced behind and tried to find balance. When he settled, he reached for the baby, still hanging by a leg, and took him to his lap.

Horn rode hard, Carson struggled on the back of the horse, worried he might fall or crush the screaming child.

In the far distance, a man in blue watched through a scope. He collapsed the glass, placed it in a leather scabbard, mounted his horse and rode east.

4

The entire group gathered around Marie as she held the baby and fed it dried bread thinned to a liquid with water. Darcy had carried her nursing can west. Since she'd not been able to breast feed her boys it had been a necessity and she couldn't leave it behind in case her sons might need it for their children one day. She chewed a small piece of jerky to break it up and soften it into mush for the baby.

Lanna brushed the child's hair with her hand and said, "It's a dark little devil, ain't it? Careful, it'll probly bite."

Thomas glanced at her and she cowered. He'd struck her before for saying something he felt inappropriate. From the look in his eyes she fully expected another lashing although she didn't know why.

As Marie rocked the child and the others looked on, one of the girls asked, "What we gonna name her, Momma?"

Marie looked around. "I think we might call her Mercy. Since she come to us by God's mercy. What y'all think?"

Horn pulled Caywood away and explained what he'd found, "It was a massacre. Everybody at the camp dead, even horses. I don't know who did it but I know I don't wanna find out. They burned everthin' and everbody. We need to git movin'. I'd near say we turn back and go north but we're too close to the foothills. If we kin get there, we kin protect ourselves better than here on the bare flat. I ain't meanin' to scare nobody but what I seen was awful. There's gotta be some devil mad Indians out there and Lord knows who else that coudda done that. We need to git outta here is all I'm saying. "

"Keep this to ourself, Horn. I'll tell the others that someone died of heat or some such. They don't need to know. It'd be enough to scare em' back home an' we come too far for that."

A short while later the wagons moved west toward the foothills with their new passenger. Horn rode forward a mile or so to be certain they wouldn't be ambushed and to verify the way was clear. The sun reached its peak and the heat was nearly unbearable. Carson rode up front, next to his father, while Marie tried to keep the baby alive. From the back she shouted, "Caywood! Caywood, are you hearin' me?"

What is it woman? Is it the baby? Is she alright?"

"Caywood, that's the thing, the baby ain't a she. It's a boy baby! I don't think Mercy would fit for a name."

As the train followed the never ending wagon ruts, heat and dust grew more intense. A wind came from the north but rather than cooling the air, it carried hot plains dirt and whipped the skin of the drivers. The two other women retreated inside their wagons to escape the sanding of dirt. Inside it was nearly 20 degrees hotter than on the front seat, but while inside, the dust pummeled canvas rather than their faces. The drivers wore scarves so just their eyes were thrashed by the wind. It was at times like these that Charlie was happy to wear spectacles.

Hours later, as the sun moved toward the horizon, they finally saw foothills in the distance. The monotonous, flat landscape of the past month was about to recede. The country finally offered a bit of character. They kept moving toward the hills in the distance as Horn had instructed and watched as the setting sun created multiple shades of purple across the skyline. Since they'd found an Indian child, the men were told to watch intently for anyone who might approach. Thomas looked south, Charlie north, Caywood studied the west and Lanna was forced to ride backward, something she despised, and focus her attention east. All day, there seemed nothing out of the ordinary, only dead grass, sun and dust.

Horn told Caywood the massacre was less than a day old when he found the child, so the perpetrators might still be fairly close. His hope had been, whoever they were, they'd gone in a direction other than the one the train was headed. Though not sure, he encouraged them to watch for anything unusual and revisited their instructions for protection should any danger arise.

The sun finally began to fade and hordes of bugs joined them when Horn appeared in the distance, riding hard. Caywood saw him coming, held his hand out to the side and shouted to stop the train. Moments later the drivers stepped down to stretch their sore legs. Carson joined them.

Horn rode up at full speed, pulled up just short of the three men and jumped from his horse. He walked it to them. Out of breath and nearly crazy he spoke, "We gotta git rid of that baby. Gotta dump it or sumtin."

The men looked at one another and Caywood spoke, "What's up Horn? Why you wanna git rid o' the kid? What the devil's wrong?"

Horn took a breath and explained, "I run into the Indians. They are pissin' fire. I thought they's gonna cut me up when they saw me. I stood in my saddle an' put my hands down, that means friend or talk or some such. They saw I got a' Indian pony and I knowed how to talk to 'em. I don't get much, but all's I know's it saved me from getting' kilt."

The women climbed from the wagons and gathered behind the men as Horn continued, no longer withholding information, "They saw the village, saw what happened. They was askin' if I knowed who did it. I let 'em know, best I could, that it warn't us. I tol 'em we was just passin' by and we couldn't any way do what was done."

Darcy spoke first, "What was it they was angry about? You said some Indian died from the heat frustration and you took the kid. That warn't bad was it? Let's just give it back."

Horn looked at her, said nothing and turned to Marie who held the baby, "All's I know is we gotta git rid o' that kid. Bury it or something. If they find it with us they gonna think we had something to do with killin' all their women folk. We got no hope to get to the hills if we got that kid with us."

He stepped toward Marie who looked at him in shock, "Killed their women? What are you sayin'. Who killed who?"

"I'm sayin' I don't know who done it. All's I'm sayin' is we got to get rid o' that baby. Ain't no sense in any of us dying for an injun kid." He reached toward Marie but she spun away,

"You'll not touch this boy. God sent him to us. We got all the means to care for him. You cain't kill him and you ain't givin' 'em to a bunch o' mad savages with no women folk. He's mine now and I'm sure gonna help him."

Horn jumped toward her and both Caywood and Carson pushed him away. "Dammit woman, you don't understand. Them Indians is gonna check us out probly at daylight. If they find this Indian kid they ain't only gonna take 'em, there gonna kill us all. You can't have him less you wanna see the rest of your kids dead here on this prairie."

Lanna began to sob and fell to her knees. Thomas slapped her across the back of her head and demanded she shut up but she only sobbed louder. He spoke, "There's gotta be something we kin do rather than killin' the baby. I'm with Marie on that, we'd all go to hell for killin' a baby."

Horn shook his head and looked to the sky, "Dear God, why'd you ever talk me into leadin' these people to your wilderness? What horrible things did I ever do to you? I thought you was spose to hep me." He looked back at the group, "OK, OK. All's I knows is we cain't have that baby on the train if they get here. You tell me what we gonna do!"

They were all silent for several moments, except for Lanna who wept softly with Thomas standing next to her, his hand on her head. Marie finally broke the stillness, "Horn, kin you find the foothills in the night?"

He looked around and replied, "There's a sliver o' moon startin' to break sometime after dark. The tracks are deep enough I kin follow 'em. What you thinking woman?"

"You say the Indians'll find us in the morning? Kin you get to the hills and back before daylight?"

"I might if I ride hard. If you think I'm gonna take that baby an' stash it somewhere till the wagons get to it, you're crazy. It'll be dead long afore you find it. Sompins gonna eat it in them woods."

Caywood looked at his wife with uncertainty, "Where you goin' with this, woman?"

Marie turned to him, "Horn could take Carson an' the baby. We could send a pack with them. He'll just have to spend the last part o' the night an' tomorrow by hisself with the child." She looked at Carson, "You could do that, couldn't ya' hon? If the Indians come to find us there won't be no baby. Everthing'll be fine and we'll come get ya by tomorrow night. That way no one has to die."

***

The camp fire burned within the triangle of wagons and with the evening meal finished, two riders and a baby moved off into darkness and disappeared into the night.

5

The sun rose, cold, through the trees. Carson wrapped himself in a blanket and rocked the child, who hadn't slept since the scout quickly set up a haphazard camp in the dark before he returned to the wagons. It had taken all his strength to fight back utter panic as he listened to fading hoof beats when Horn left him alone with the baby. He cried silently as the horse rode into the distance and wished they had agreed to bury the child and move on.

The baby's constant, shallow breathing had only increased his terror. The only things that prevented him from dropping the boy and running, were the darkness and strange sounds that filled the night. At one point, he laid the baby on the ground and stood to leave then realized he was blind to his surroundings and had no idea which way to go. The slight moon and the stars were hidden beyond tree branches so no light reached the forest floor.

There was nothing but emptiness, filled with sounds of God knows what scurrying through the underbrush. Winds or wings or ghosts rustled the branches above and each noise increased his terror. He finally sat down, found the child where he'd left him and held him to his chest. The baby who had been strangely quiet on the ground, began to whimper, then cried until the entire forest echoed with his screams. Carson tried to shush the boy, rocked him like his mother did with his sisters but the crying persisted. It began to rattle his nerves. Thoughts of animals eating the helpless infant were almost welcome. He sat down and continued to rock back and forth. His attempts to quiet the boy seemed to soothe his own fears and he hoped the movement and noise would scare away any vermin.

Throughout the night, he imagined angry Indians everywhere, thirsting for revenge while he harbored their stolen child. He felt the breath of vicious animals or maybe even spirits of lost souls all around him, so he rocked even more fiercely and continued to hush the boy and listen for movement in the darkness.

The black seemed eternal as he sat wide-eyed, and stared into the night. He strained to hear as the boy first calmed then jerked awake and screamed again and again.

Exhaustion besieged him. He sobbed quietly and continued to move back and forth. The boy was finally silent, breathing regular, when he noticed faint shadows appear around him and the forest began to reveal itself in the dim light. He now saw where he was and began to feel a modicum of relief. He'd survived the terrors of night and the wagons would come to rescue him in the better part of a day.

For the first time in hours he began to relax when he realized the child reeked of urine. Although he'd been there when the girls and his brother were babies, he'd never been expected to perform nursing duties. As the oldest and a boy, he'd accompanied his father to the fields and played the part of a farmer since he was seven.

He picked up the bundle his mother packed and moved slowly to let the baby sleep. It contained two rags, a few hunks of jerky, a lump of dried bread, a handkerchief filled with dry beans, a canteen of water and Darcy's nursing can. He found the pencil and his book he'd grabbed before he left camp.

Carson looked around and chuckled to himself, "Good ol' Momma. Givin' me beans so's I don't starve. With nuthin' to soak 'em in nor cook 'em with. I guess they'll do in a pinch."

He looked at the baby, "I spose I'll have to do this whether either of us likes it or not." He laid the sleeping child on some leaves and rolled him over to find the brooch that his mother used to fasten the rag on the boy, undid the clasp and let the wet material fall away. Carson winced, took a deep breath, and held the rag at arm's length as a large, sticky lump peeled away and plopped onto the forest floor. "Dear Lord boy, why you got to do that to yourself? How am I 'spose to get the rest off ya'? I do believe this camp is now safe from wild Indians, wolves or even demons."

He wiped the crying boy the best he could with a corner of the soiled rag then proceeded to do his best to wrap him with a fresh one. As he pushed the brooch through the material he pricked the baby's skin and there was instant chaos. He lifted the child to his shoulder and patted him, apologizing for his incompetence. After the boy settled he made several more attempts to get the rag to stay on. It hung loosely from the tiny body and when he held the boy at arm's length to look at his work, the weight of the brooch nearly pulled the bungled diaper off.

He laid the boy on the ground to prepare breakfast, crumbled some of the bread into the nursing can and added water. He found a stick, peeled the bark then used it to crush the bread to a loose paste, then replaced the top and picked up the boy.

Shocked by the smell he shouted, "Boy! What the heck are you doin'? I ain't got but one more rag for the day and no way to clean the ones you mess in. I'm sorry but your just gonna have to wait till later to get another one. We both got to sacrifice here today."

He proceeded to feed the child who did his best to eat between sobs.

***

Heat intensified as the sun rose in the East despite the trees and shade. The air was parched and the forest almost seemed to smolder. Smells here were vastly different from those on the plains. For weeks there'd been the stench of burnt grass and dust. It encompassed everything and scorched the lungs with every breath. Here the smell consisted of pine needles and moldy earth. Although it was still hot in the lungs, the evergreen was almost soothing. Still, Carson longed for the moisture he'd inhaled when they'd barged the Mississippi. The fresh, cool smell of water was a promise of hope. Horn assured everyone they would find it again near the foothills. He'd been wrong about that. He also told them the mountain coolness was something they would experience the rest of the trip. Carson hoped he was right and that they just hadn't reached the point where the days would be pleasant again. He so looked forward to the time he would not only smell the water but bathe in it. He planned to swim for a week as soon as they found a home. He wouldn't come out of the water until his skin started to peel away.

Nervous and afraid, he picked up the baby and wandered in ever growing circles to explore his surroundings but didn't stray too far in case the train arrived early. He finally came across the trail about a hundred yards from where he'd camped, found a patch of thick brush and sat out of sight to listen and wait.

The sour diaper grew steadily more rancid with the heat, but he explained to the baby, "You only got one skiv left 'til the train gets here. You're gonna have to deal with it."

But sometime after noon, when the sun was moving lower in the west, he returned to the camp and removed the rancid rag. He threw it on top of the first.

"I guess you can sit nekkid for a while and pee all over the ground. Soon as I hear horses comin', I'll strap that last skiv on you and make it look as you and I both been takin' care of things."

Carson chewed a piece of jerky for the baby. It took all the strength he had not to swallow. The juices just made him more hungry. He chewed it to mush then continued until there was nearly nothing left, then fed the remainder to the boy and followed it with water from the nursing can. There seemed enough bread and jerky to have a meal himself but he had no idea how much the baby would need and so he refrained. In Ohio he'd spent several days in the fields, working without food and was used to getting home famished. Momma always had a huge supper on the table for him and his father, and he was sure she would feed him well when she arrived. He sucked on a mouthful of dried beans until the skins came off, chewed them and kept sucking with hope the beans would finally soften.

The baby began to fuss and wiggle so Carson laid him on the ground and walked a few yards to a log to write in his journal. Crying became more incessant as he wrote so Carson did his best to become lost in thought. He had completed one page and started on the other side when the baby suddenly screamed. It was a new sound, not just aggravation. Shivers filled him and he dropped his book and rushed to the child, concerned an animal had taken a bite. He knew he'd never pacify his mother if something had eaten the baby.

He scooped the child in the air to find a pine needle stuck in his thigh, pulled it free and sat down with the naked baby in his lap. He held the crying child out in front of him and spun him around to look for more needles or bites when he realized the boy's skin was sticky, that he'd been lying in pine pitch. Beads and smears of clear glue covered his back.

The sun was beginning to dip behind the mountains. Shadows grew and began to fade together. He knew the train wasn't far. In a panic, he decided to clean the boy and put the last rag on him. He tried to wipe the pine pitch off but it smeared. He spit on the boy's back and rubbed to no avail.

He finally retrieved a soiled diaper as he checked for prying eyes, attempted to wipe the mess off. The rag stuck to the baby's skin and as he pulled away and his hand slipped into the waste, still soft and wet. He threw the diaper and cursed beneath his breath. Carson nearly dropped the boy but held on and placed him back on the forest floor. He dug into the dirt in an attempt to clean his hand.

The feces seemed gone so he picked up the baby again and attempted to wipe away the pitch, but dirt spread in brown stains across the boy's back and wouldn't come off.

With darkness approaching once more, mountains in the distance hid the sunset much earlier, so Carson decided it was time to act. He wrapped the baby in the last rag and carefully hooked it with the brooch. It was tighter and more proper this time. He picked up the boy, retrieved his pencil and book then returned to the camp and fed the child once more before the light faded.

6

Night came quickly and the baby, at last, was quiet. He slept the first time in more than a day. Carson believed it was exhaustion, but continuously placed a hand on the boy's chest to be sure he was still breathing. Each time he did, he was relieved to feel body warmth.

Worried about the train, he convinced himself travel wasn't always as predicted. Several things might delay progress. The scout might have estimated the distance wrong since a man alone could travel much further on horseback than the wagons. If the train hadn't found the hills before nightfall they would have had to stop and set up camp. Maybe Horn was worried the Indians were watching so he couldn't come for him and the baby.

Now, a bit familiar with the surroundings unlike the night before, he was slightly more at ease. There was still food and water and he felt somewhat safe in his location. Indians on the trail, even if they were searching for him, would never find him in the dark, especially with the baby quiet. And who would ride the trail into the hills at night other than Horn? He lay awake, huddled next to the child and listened for a horse. Since the

Indians had not found their baby with the train and the wagons still hadn't reached him, he was sure Horn would come for him, if he could.

During the night, questions arose; could Horn find him in the dark? Would he even know where he'd left them? Could the Indians have taken revenge after all? He fought that consideration and assured himself everyone was safe and the train would arrive by morning.

Tomorrow he would reunite with his family and continue the journey west.

He listened intently for the sound of Horn's horse until exhaustion overcame. The next he knew, sun was again highlighting the tops of the trees.

He fed the baby once more and this time his own hunger was worse than he remembered from the fields, but he convinced himself he would be well fed soon.

He removed the baby's rag, shook out what he could and decided his Momma would have to understand why the boy was naked. Sure she would feel guilty for leaving them alone an additional night, she'd also forgive the pitch and dirt stains on the baby's back. The child was unusually quiet after being fed and it worried him so he looked the boy over to be sure there was nothing wrong. He saw what looked like an hour glass stain just under dark hair at the base of the skull and rubbed the spot softly to remove pitch or maybe a bug. The child suddenly smiled then broke into a ringing giggle. Carson snorted. He realized he was rubbing a birthmark and became amazed when the boy laughed again as he rubbed the spot once more. The baby cooed at him and bubbled. "I'll be durned. Yer' just like a dog and I found yer' spot. Looks like you got some happier times ahead, young'un."

Carson pulled out another handful of beans and put them in his mouth, "We best get ready cause we're gonna be on our way soon now." He mumbled as he packed everything back. He kept the pencil and book to write in his journal while he waited.

During the course of the day he pulled food from his pack for the baby two more times. The beans were becoming very old and it was harder and harder to refrain from swallowing the jerky. He took to holding beans in his cheek while chewing the meat so they might absorb some flavor.

As night again began to fall, Carson became determined to take action. Food was running out and there was only enough water left for the baby. He decided to search for the train, although he hesitated several times during the afternoon remembering Horn's warning, "If the Indians find us with that baby we'll all be dead."

Thoughts previously cast aside returned and scratched the door of his consciousness, demanding entry. He realized he had to act, if not for himself, to save the baby, and to find what had delayed his family.

He packed his belongings, picked up the child and found his way to the trail. As he started east, the sun began to dip behind the mountains again. Darkness was upon him in no time and though the trail was lost in shadows, he continued along the rocky way through tracks worn deep. Several times he nearly went down but was able to maintain balance. He began to slide his feet to steady himself but when he slid into a deep hole, his ankle twisted and he fell. He swiveled as he went down to protect the baby and hit the road hard. The back of his head slammed something solid.

From the darkness, a child's screams floated to him as if from a great distance. He blinked his eyes and for a moment, thought he was blind. The screaming grew louder with each passing moment when he realized it was dark and the baby was half on and half off his body.

His head throbbed horribly with each wail. He pushed the child aside to sit up. A cool breeze caressed his forehead and neck. When he reached back he found a huge lump on his skull. It stung and felt unusually damp. A few moments of confusion passed before he remembered where he was. The boy's screams brought him around even more and he rolled to his knees to stand but ended on all four and hung his throbbing head to vomit.

When the confusion had subsided a bit, he crawled toward the cries, picked up the boy and rubbed the birthmark. The screaming quieted.

Carson sat on the trail with the infant in his arms and looked for a point of light. A decision forced upon him, he clambered a few yards into the trees and settled to spend the night. He spoke to the baby who was now quiet, "It's alright boy. In the morning we'll have the whole of daylight to find everyone. They'll be plenty o' food and water and actual beds to sleep in. And my Momma kin clean that nasty crust off your bottom. You'll see, everthings gonna be alright in the morning." He continued to stroke the baby's birthmark and soon, the boy fell asleep.

Carson huddled down and lay awake in fear. His head throbbed, he didn't know how far he'd come and terror began to overwhelm him. Finally, the pounding ache combined with exhaustion overcame and he slept a restless night filled with dreams of the demons and death. Several times he woke as he cried out in the darkness.

7

Night dragged on forever but just before dawn he finally gained a remnant of peace and slept; slept late into the morning. When he finally woke, drenched in sweat from growing heat, his head still pounded and his thoughts were confused. He sat up and looked around in an attempt to determine his location. Everything seemed blurred and indistinct so he wiped his eyes to get the dust out. Several moments passed before he recalled where he was and why.

In the confusion he remembered the baby, looked around in fear and breathed a sigh of relief when he found the child lying quietly on the blanket next to him. A bit too quietly. His heart pounded and he reached across and placed a hand on him. The boy was still warm and his chest rose and fell with each tiny breath.

He released a weak gasp as Carson lifted him from the ground. His eyes remained closed and he no longer cried. The naked baby had wet the blanket during the night but there was almost no moisture.

Carson sat up, crossed his legs and cradled the boy in his lap. He rubbed the back of his own head and found a scabbing wound over a huge knot. He tried to shake the soreness away but it felt like his brain might explode.

After a few moments, the pain subsided slightly so he reached for the pack to retrieve the last of the bread and the nursing can. From the canteen he added the final ounce of water, placed the top on the can and shook it hard to liquefy the contents. When clanging stopped and it sounded soft, he tried to feed the child who seemed indifferent. Worried that it might be too late he pleaded, "Come on boy, you've gotta keep goin'. I'll get ya' help, I promise."

He forced the end of the can into the boy's mouth and the child finally began to cry. "Hush it up and eat! The sooner you get fed the sooner we kin get back to the train."

Eventually the boy began to suck, but as he did he yelled even louder. Carson opened the can and saw the lump of bread nearly whole. "Yer just gonna have to live with that for the time, boy. We gotta move so we kin get some real food."

He put the last handful of beans in his mouth, packed up his belongings and started toward the trail with renewed passion. At the ruts he turned east and proceeded. Though the headache and dry, bitter beans turned his stomach, he pushed on until he was forced to stop and gag. He bent full over, still holding the boy, and somehow held what was left inside. He wanted to spit but kept the beans in his mouth. When he was finally able to continue, confusion nearly overwhelmed him. He had no idea how late it was although it seemed much hotter than it should be. The morning sun was still in front of him, so he hurried as quickly as he could.

He became confounded. He seemed to move upward for the most part rather than down toward the plains. He continued along on the wagon ruts realizing these were foothills and foothills went both up and down. Each time he started downward he gained a bit of confidence until the trail rose up again.

He continued at a near run despite his aches, for more than an hour. Throbbing and thirst began to get the better of him. He'd swallowed the hard beans after his mouth dried too much to soften them any more with hope they might settle his stomach and offer some energy. The baby had been quiet for quite some time. He hoped to find the wagons before it became dark. He continued for another half hour while he thought what he'd write in his journal.

The hills seemed to grow steeper as he traveled and confusion mounted. Since his arrival the first dark night, he had no idea how many hills Horn's horse had climbed and descended. He hurried faster since light was beginning to ebb.

Exhaustion began to prevail so he stopped to rest. As he sat to recover, he realized the sun was dipping in front of him. Darkness began to overcome as the sun started to set in the direction he'd been traveling. Something was desperately wrong, his concerns had been correct. It suddenly struck him he was moving away from his family, not toward them.

The fall the previous night had turned him around. He hadn't camped on the south side of the trail as he'd thought. He'd inadvertently ended up on the north side, and then spent the afternoon headed west. He'd gone a good part of a day in the wrong direction, nearly running most of the time, away from his family.

In the twilight, nothing seemed right. He didn't know what to do. Panic overwhelmed him and he turned to go back the way he'd come. He tripped again, in the fading light, but this time recovered. Tears welled up and he collapsed in frustration at the side of the trail and wept.

He reasoned, if the train had come for him while he was gone they'd certainly be worried. They would have spent the day searching near the camp to find him. They'd probably think the Indians had discovered him. He wailed but there was barely moisture to feed his tears. He slapped himself on the forehead and set the headache alive. Looking in circles, he tried to figure his next step.

After a few moments, he placed the baby on the ground, stepped off the road into the trees. There he found dead branches took them to place on the trail in the shape of an arrow, pointing east; the direction he needed to go.

He finally picked up the weakened baby, found a small clearing just off the road and sat to wait. The child began to whimper softly and Carson knew he had to feed it. He pulled the nursing can from his pack and removed the top. Inside was damp, crumbling bread. It wasn't soft enough so he found a stick to mash what was left, pulled it from the can with his fingers and placed bits of the mush in the boy's mouth. The baby winced but did what he could to eat. Darkness came quickly and Carson sat against a tree and spent the night rocking the boy in his lap. The child was still and fairly silent. Between occasional small bouts of whimpering, fear for his family and his personal admonishment for going the wrong direction, Carson found small crumbs of troubled sleep.

8

Day broke and the sun rose, this time on the correct horizon. Carson grabbed the baby and his pack and began the return trek. He followed the point of his arrow, assured he was traveling east this time, toward the sunrise.

He kept a steady pace, now too weak and thirsty to run. The baby somehow found heightened energy, became fussy and cried often. Even rubbing his birthmark did nothing to calm him. As Carson made his way back toward the wagons, the sun grew hotter and thirst began to overpower him.

Eventually, the baby grew quieter. He realized the boy hadn't peed since the previous night. Desperate, Carson stopped at the side of the trail, plucked some leaves from what looked to be a berry bush, and sucked them. Stricken by an intense bitterness, he immediately spit them out. Rather than add moisture, they seemed to have absorb what little was left in his mouth. He wiped his tongue on his sleeve in the event the bush was poison.

Nothing in these hills was familiar. His throat ached. It was dry as the dust on the plains, so he focused on the baby. In all the heat, they were both becoming completely parched, the baby more than him. He had to get back, there was little time left.

He forced himself up, to continue at a steady pace through the pain and the heat. After an hour he was no longer aware of his motion. Instinct kicked in and he just continued to move on.

When he recognized the place of his original camp, his spirit grew. He left the trail and searched the area for anything he might have left behind. There was nothing.

Even the dirty rags were gone. "I can't believe anythin' would take them nasty things." That's when it came to him, Horn might have been there.

He sat on a fallen log to think. If Horn had come and he was gone, would the scout have ridden back to tell everyone he was missing? They'd be worried sick that he'd been killed.

Reality struck, if they hadn't passed him on the trail they would have gone on looking for him, or at least, sent Horn out.

He should have seen someone over the past two days. But what about when he slept till nearly midday? Might they have passed him then? He realized he would surely have caught up with the train when he ran west. Chills knifed his spine. Thoughts he'd tried to drive off, those that had encroached into his dreams came back to haunt him again. What if the Indians had taken revenge?

He sat on the log rocking the baby and tried to cry but his tears were dry. The only logical answer was the Indians had either slaughtered the entire train or taken them hostage. He looked at the baby in his arms and was overcome with rage. "If they're dead because a you, I'll kill you right in front of your people. They'll watch me stomp your head in and there'll be nothing they can do to stop me.

If they killed my Daddy an' Momma they're gonna have to kill me too, but no matter what. They ain't getting you back alive. We should've listened to Horn and buried you right there on the prairie."

The baby watched as Carson spoke and smiled at him as though he'd whispered a lullaby. Carson saw the boy's weak grin and felt instant guilt about what had just come from his mouth. God knew what happened at the Indian village and this baby was no more a part of that horror than he was. He put his head down and prayed for forgiveness for threatening the boy's life. He heard his Momma's voice as she read Bible verses about doing unto others and turning cheeks. He so wanted to see his family again.

He sat quietly for a while, the baby in his arms, when he thought he heard a noise. He perked up and listened a moment. It was there again, mixed with wind in the branches. He stood to hear. Nothing for a moment, then again came the faint sound of a woman's voice. Under that he heard the squeaking of wheels and the heavy, nearly imperceptible sound of horse hooves.

His heart began to pound. It was the train, they'd come. It wasn't Indians, there were wheels. He could hear the voice again. He moved from the camp back toward the trail as the sounds gradually grew louder. When he reached the ruts he looked east but there was no one there. They'd passed him and were coming back. They were coming back. Carson found new energy and began to run toward the wagons. He shouted as loud as he could, "Momma, I'm here! Here I am Momma." As he ran, the sounds stopped so he ran harder and yelled louder, "It's me Momma, I'm here. Here I am!"

As he crested a small hill he stopped fast. In front of him was an open buckboard pulled by a single horse. Three women sat in the front. Those on either side were frozen with fear surrounding the third who stood with a rifle aimed directly at him. They all stared at one another for what seemed an eternity, fear in their eyes while a finger slowly squeezed the rifle trigger.

9

Bonnie

"And so, we commit the body of Johannes Copholeito back to the Earth. From dust we come and to dust we shall return. May he forever rest in peace at the right hand of God and may the Lord have mercy on his soul."

The undertaker nodded to Bonnie. She dropped a handful of soil on the casket and turned away as the grave digger began to shovel. The sound of gravel clattering on the wooden shell sent chills through her and tears silently dripped from her chin as she walked away, depressed by the gray morning light and the totality of her isolation.

Johannes Copholeito had been well liked and respected in the town, but his murderer Lord Vincent, quite literally owned the town's people and nearly all they had. When Johannes was killed, the sheriff had no choice but to declared him in the wrong and from that moment, Bonnie had become a virtual outcast.

The Vincents settled the area nearly 20 years before. Leonard Vincent laid claim to nearly a thousand acres of river valley that no one wanted. The area was too high to grow anything, the air too thin for a decent breath and the land too rocky for livestock.

The site became a way station on the trail west and was so inhospitable travelers coined the name, Pariah. It was a huge hardship for the Vincents until the discovery of gold in the river. Settlers traveling west began to stop and stay. Prospectors created an influx of humanity and the area began to take shape.

Rather than sell pieces of his claim, knowing he could never work the entire river himself, Leonard developed an elaborate plan. He surveyed three acres on the west side of his property for a town and sold plots for a hotel, a general store, a saloon, a livery and a school house.

The remainder of the 1,000 acres was divided into claims and homesteads then leased to the settlers and prospectors for a fee and percentage of their take. Aside from the buildings in the town, Leonard owned every home and every claim throughout the valley. He was rather fair in his dealings although extremely demanding of his payments. He personally hired the sheriff and paid the man for his services.

Locals began calling Leonard, "Lord" Vincent both from respect and from fear of losing his graces. Vincent drew so much gratification from the title, when his son was born he named the boy Royal.

Pariah took hold and prospered. The town did a strong business and the valley filled with people all indebted to Vincent. His wealth grew exponentially from every pan that glistened with flakes of gold and from every person who signed a pact with the Lord.

Johannes and Bonfilia Copholeito were on their way west when they stayed a night at the hotel in Pariah. At the saloon that evening Johannes found there to be a great need for a man of medicine. That night, after an enthusiastic conversation with Bonfilia, Johannes negotiated with the hotel owner to set up a barbershop/apothecary in a room just off the lobby. The room had a wood stove and was large enough for a counter and a chair. Behind the counter, screened by a curtain, was room for their bed and dresser. The Copholeitos had found a new home and were assigned new names. Townspeople began to call them John and Bonnie Coffer.

Pariah grew and so did the businesses built there. John treated the many mining accidents, broken limbs and cut flesh. With potions and remedies for colds, fevers and every kind of sickness, he attended to births and declared deaths. When prospectors wanted to keep going through sleep deprivation and exhaustion,

John provided remedies to extend their energy and allow them to forget the pain.

During the next several years, John treated everyone in Pariah, some on a more regular basis as needed due to his powders.

But as years faded, so did the gold. Many prospectors quietly stole away heading for the new fields discovered in Northern California.

Some left owing Lord Vincent large debts. Occasionally the sheriff would deputize a few men, capture deserters and bring them back. Lord Vincent made examples of them on the main street. As the wealth and work moved west, the saloon did a rousing business with stragglers who stayed behind due to liability owed Vincent and fear of the sheriff.

Public fighting and gunplay became common. More and more families, those who were able, departed for their original destinations leaving Pariah with the dregs, debtors and addicts. As time passed, the town developed a reputation as a place to avoid on the trail west.

The hotel stood nearly empty but for John and Bonnie so the owner turned its upper rooms over to three professional women. When even that didn't support him he decided to head out for the new gold fields. Rather than turn his "bought and paid for" building back to the Vincent family, he contracted John as manager and allowed him to continue his medical business in exchange for running the hotel and collecting a percentage of the income from the "Upstairs Ladies". In return for living there, all he asked of John was to forward whatever cash that was earned each month, a deal John Coffer was happy to agree to.

***

Lord Vincent, a regular visitor of the Upstairs Ladies, decided to honor his son on the occasion of Royal's 16th birthday. The two walked to the saloon and stood at the bar where Lord ordered two shots of whiskey. The barkeep poured abundant shots and refilled several times. "Ya ain't brung the boy in here afore, Lord. There a special cause?"

Lord smiled and slapped Royal on the back, "Boy's 16 years old today. He's a true man."

With that everyone in the saloon cheered and toasted Royal and the barkeep sent him off with a full bottle as a gift.

Lord decided to give the boy a real present and took him to meet the Upstairs Ladies at the hotel. Gathered in one room, Lord introduced his son and instructed the women to provide the boy a memorable birthday. "I'm goin' back to the saloon for a bit. If I hear y'all screamin' with pleasure, I'll know you're doin' my boy good." Before he left, he wished Royal well, "I don't expect to see you till morning, boy" With that, he winked at the Ladies and exited the room.

Royal was already an extreme distance from sober but pulled the cork and took another large swig of whiskey. He offered the bottle around and when it reached him again he proceeded to gulp another vast portion. The Ladies thought it extremely entertaining to watch the young boy become uselessly drunk. They encouraged him to have more, knowing that their agenda would consist of waking the boy at daylight to send him home with wild stories of his randy night.

However, as he nearly finished the bottle he was still conscious. "I want all three o' you whores all over me right now!" he shouted. "We *let* you all whore here and daddy paid a hunk o' money to do what I say, so quit yer pissin' around and get to it." They looked at him in silence wondering how long it would be before he passed out, but, instead Royal grabbed one woman by the breast and attempted to bite her. The three wrestled him off, threw him out of the room and blocked the door.

Although excessive noise wasn't uncommon from the second floor, Bonnie woke from the shouting and door pounding. She got up, pulled on her robe and left John asleep in the bed to see if all was well. She watched from the lobby as Royal tripped down the stairs holding himself up by the rail.

Bonnie rushed to help him as he reached the bottom. She took his arm to steady him and led him toward a chair. "Royal, you look a might troubled. Are you alright?" He muffled something in response and spun sideways. She pulled him back around and nearly held him up, then continued, "You want me to get John to take you home?"

Royal looked at her through half closed, hazy eyes and replied, "I ain't leavin' here till I get what Paw paid fer. Get them bloomers off ya damned whore."

Bonnie let go but the boy began to fall so she grabbed his arm again, "Just a minute here, Royal. I think you had a bit too much liquor tonight. You aren't talking straight. Look at me, it's Bonnie."

With that Royal twisted hard and knocked Bonnie back. He swung his right fist and caught her on the ear, knocking her to the floor. He shouted, "Get them bloomers off, whore. I'm going home a man!" He fell on top of her and tore her robe open. Bonnie screamed waking John, who rushed from their room as Royal ripped into her bed clothes, "Come on whore, gimmy my money's worth."

John acted blindly in the dim light. He pulled the boy off by the hair and proceeded to drag him across the lobby and out the door onto the porch. All the while Royal screamed in pain. He pushed the boy into the street as large tufts of hair fell to the wooden steps. John ran to the boy and began to pummel him in front of a gathering crowd.

From the saloon, the sheriff came to see what the new ruckus was, accompanied by Lord Vincent. Both had been drinking and were somewhat unsteady.

The crowd formed a circle around the two as the man punched the boy repeatedly. The boy curled into a ball and was finally quiet. The sheriff pushed through the spectators followed by Lord and watched for a few moments, "I never thought that barber fella could get so pissed off. He must of taken some of his own drugs." The two men chuckled until one of the observers tapped Lord, "That's yer boy ain't it, Lord?" Vincent's eyes grew huge as realization set in that it was his flesh and blood getting beaten while he and the town enjoyed the show.

"God damn it. Stop 'em sheriff. Stop that crazy guinea right now 'for he kills my boy."

The sheriff pushed through the crowd, grabbed John by the shoulder and tried to pull him off but he kept flailing the boy so the sheriff kicked him hard in the kidney. "What the hell you doin' Coffer?" John lay in the street next to the balled up boy and tried to catch his breath. Lord ran over and punched him with a glancing blow that slid off the side of his head. "It's my boy's god dammed birthday, what the hell's wrong with you?"

John looked up, breathing heavily, then looked back at the hotel where Bonnie peeked through the curtains.

"I asked you a question, guinea. You'd damned well better talk to me."

John looked to the sheriff, "That boy hit my Bonnie an' tried to rape her, that's what he did." He took a few breaths, "I pulled him off her. He tore her bed clothes and called her filthy names."

The sheriff turned to Lord who was straightening his boy out in the street. "He might be dead. You coulda' killed him, you bastard. His eyes are closed and he's hardly breathin'." He slapped the boy on the face several times and Royal just moaned and tried to curl back up.

"He's just drunk. He's not even hurt. He's just drunk and he tried to rape my wife."

John stood and walked to the sheriff, "Sheriff, this man beat up Bonnie and tried to rape her. I want him arrested. Do your job!"

From behind, Lord shouted, "Arrested? You stupid guinea, you damn near kill my son and you want *him* arrested? I'll see you rot in jail for beatin' an innocent kid" Lord moved toward John and the sheriff. "Take this boy beater to jail sheriff. I want him locked up now, this minute."

The sheriff held his hands up to Lord and looked at John, "I think we need to talk to Bonnie first, see what she's got to say 'bout all this."

Lord exploded, "Talk to Bonnie? Talk to Bonnie? She ain't no more than one of those whores here in this hotel. For all we know she does her duty upstairs with the rest of 'em. An' you want her side of it, a common whore?"

John exploded with anger, lunged forward and grabbed Lord by the hair. He attempted to drag him to the street. In a flash, blood splattered everywhere. John released Lord, grabbed his thigh, looked at the faces around him and fell to the ground.

Moments later Bonnie knelt beside him, in a tattered robe, and held him as he died.

The following day, the sheriff declared the killing self-defense.

Bonnie found herself widowed, forsaken by the townspeople and stranded alone in Pariah at age 26.

10

For several months Bonnie Coffer sold medications to maintain her livelihood. Though the townspeople were afraid to associate with her since Lord Vincent made it clear she was guilty of wrongly accusing his son, they still needed to renew the drugs John had provided.

The Upstairs Ladies did brisk business and Bonnie collected the shares and faithfully sent them by what would one day become the Pony Express. She didn't know if the owner of the hotel even existed any longer, or if he ever received the funds, however, since John agreed to send them, she would honor that contract.

For the following few months, with no one to associate, Bonnie became closer to the women upstairs. It was a natural progression since they were all outcasts. The Upstairs Ladies weren't the least bit evil; they could be quite delightful and funny and were always honest in their dealings with Bonnie. Although they were kept separate from the rest of the town, they quite often had company. Even their clients would shun Bonnie since Lord had decreed she was no longer acceptable. Bonnie almost felt that if she joined the Upstairs Ladies her fate would actually improve in Pariah.

One late April afternoon, someone knocked at the front door of the Hotel. Bonnie thought it strange since the door had no lock. She walked from her room to answer. A short, stocky man stood in the darkened doorway with a young girl in tow. Dressed in worn overalls and a faded shirt with frayed holes at the elbows, he asked, "This here the house o' sin?"

Bonnie looked at him and saw the girl try to hide behind him.

"Actually, it's the hotel, but things do go on upstairs." She wondered what the man had planned, if he'd brought his own concubine with him. Bonnie decided immediately she would not let this happen. "What did you have in mind, sir?"

The man looked inside the lobby to see if they were alone, then pulled the girl from behind him. She was young, maybe 15, and obviously pregnant.

"This was my daughter. Her name is Ruby." He pushed her toward Bonnie, "She is a sinner and a harlot. She has fornicated and got herself pregnant with the spawn of Satan." Bonnie stood in shock and looked at the man as though he were mad as he continued, "She has disgraced her father, the memory of her mother and I will no longer have her parading that belly around the little one. I condemn her to this house of evil. I no longer know this harlot. She *was* my daughter but is now the devil's whore from this day on."

He turned and stomped out the door leaving the girl crying behind him.

Bonnie rushed to her side as she collapsed and helped her into her room and through the curtain. There she lay the girl on the bed and soothed her the best she could. "I'm going to get you some tea, darlin'. You just lay here and I'll be right back. It's gonna be alright, you just wait an' see. I'll be right outside the curtain.

An iron pot already heated water on the stove so Bonnie poured some over herbs in a cup. When it was steeped she sprinkled a few grains of opium in the warm water and took the cup to the girl. A short time later, crying subsided and the girl slept.

When the upstairs Ladies found that a girl had been abandoned at the hotel, they came to meet her. She was starved and frail. The three Ladies and Bonnie befriended and helped her and per her request, kept her hidden from the town. Over the next two months, Ruby's depression over her growing size began to diminish. The women assured her she was still a good person and encouraged her. They told her how wonderful it would be to become a mother and have a child she could love.

When there were no clients, Ruby joined the Upstairs Ladies on the second floor and they played games as though they were all children.

Early one morning, while Ruby visited upstairs, Bonnie heard a faint tapping somewhere behind the lobby desk in the back of the hotel. She ignored it at first believing it might be a rat or other critter, but the noise grew louder. When it sounded like glass was about to break, she went to investigate. A small window overlooked the alley between the hotel and general store.

She found a young girl knocking on the glass. She thought it was Ruby and wondered why the girl was in the alley. Maybe it was part of a game she was playing. But as she drew closer, wiping her hands on her apron, she realized the child was younger. She walked to the window and the girl cupped her hands to the glass then spoke through them as though they could evaporate the barrier. Bonnie motioned her back, undid the latch and pushed the casement open. "What can I do for you, little one?"

The girl looked around, leaned in and whispered, "I come to see my sister. I heard she is here." The girl began to tear up, "Papa told me she went to hell but a lady up the way says she could be here." She looked at Bonnie with moist blue eyes, "Is Ruby here? Kin I see her?"

Bonnie reached a hand through the window and caressed the girl's hair. "It's all right little one, Ruby's not in hell. She's doing just fine." She glanced up toward the ceiling and continued, "Does your Papa know you're here? Does he know you're gone from home?"

"Naw. He goes off to pray every morning then goes to work the river. He don't come home 'til after dark these days. I snuck out to find if Ruby is burning in Hell or not."

Bonnie smiled, "I can assure you that there is no burning goin' on, in Hell or otherwise. Let me help you in here," She reached through the window and the girl locked her arms around Bonnie's neck as she lifted her through. "What's your name, little one? "

"Bea. They call me Bea but my real name is Beatrice."

"Well Bea, you stay right here for a minute and I'll find Ruby."

A few moments later the girls sat on the floor in an embrace, crying together in joy. Papa's really mad at you for some reason. He says the devil's gonna burn you on a 'pick fork'. He said I could never see you again."

Ruby began to bawl and through fear Bea joined in. Bonnie hugged them both and spoke softly, "There are no fires and no forks. Ruby is living here now and she has new friends. Everything is going to be all right. In fact, pretty soon there will be a new baby around for her to play with. It's an exciting time.

The girls stopped crying, "Maybe if I tell Papa that you're here and you ain't with no devil, he'll let you come home again."

Bonnie took Bea by the shoulders, "Little one. You can't talk to your Papa about Ruby or this place or no babies. This is all a special secret that only we can know. Someday it'll be fine to talk about it all, but if you want to see Ruby again, you got to promise that you won't say a word to no one. Can you do that?"

Bea was overcome by fear again. She looked at her older sister. "For me, Bea. Keep it secret for me. Please?" The little girl looked back and forth at the two in front of her and slowly shook her head yes.

"Maybe in the fall, Ruby and you can go visit your Papa together and he'll see he thought wrong. If you kin keep the secret till then, you kin come an' visit Ruby. You just watch, It's all gonna be back the way it was when summer's over."

During the following two months Bea visited Ruby a few times a week and they played with the Upstairs Ladies when they could. During all the time and the bonding, Ruby refused to talk about the pregnancy although she was sure the boy she'd been with truly loved her.

11

An early afternoon in late June brought pleasant sun. Wild flowers perfumed the valley. The girl's father was spending long days at the river attempting to eke out enough gold to pay his rent and feed himself and his daughter. He'd lost his wife here while he searched for riches and was determined to stay until he found the mother lode to justify his choices.

Bea snuck away to the hotel where she and Ruby played hide and go seek with the Upstairs Ladies. Ruby had hidden behind a dressing screen and Bea snuggled quietly under the bed. The three women had just returned to the room to search for the hidden girls when an irksome voice bellowed up the stairway. They stopped their search and the girls froze in their hiding places as Royal thundered up the stairs and burst through the door. "Surprise Ladies, your Royal stallion is here fer a dip. " He held a half empty bottle in his hand.

One of the women spoke, "Well, if it ain't our favorite stud. What brings you here in the middle o' the day?"

"I jes stopped in at the saloon and after a belly warmer or two, decided you needed a surprise social call."

One of the women moved in close and grabbed his butt, "What say we go to my room and I'll show *you* a surprise or two."

He laughed, "No, no, no. Today I'm a randy son of a bitch. I want y'all, I want ya' here and I want ya' now."

Another woman spoke, "We got a bigger bed next room. Let's go where we got space to tussle without fallin' on the floor."

Royal's smile faded and his eyes tightened, "Listen whores, I don't want to go nowhere. I'm ready now and what I say goes. Unnerstand?"

The room became silent as Royal moved toward the bed. "Come on Ladies, don't make me get mad an' do something I'll regret. Right now I love all y'all. I don't want to have…"

At that moment, Ruby jumped from behind the screen. "You what? What do you mean you love them? You said you loved me. You promised you loved me. You said you 'd come get me an' the baby when it was time."

Royal jumped back with an expression as though a skunk had appeared. He looked to the three women then back at Ruby, shook his head and laughed. He took a deep pull from the bottle but as he did, Ruby slapped his hand, drenching him in whiskey.

Royal looked on in shock as anger fired in his eyes. He threw the bottle against the wall and screamed as glass shattered, "You little bitch!"

Ruby's anger rose as quickly and she rushed him. Instinctively he pulled back and punched her stomach with a fist. She fell back against the bed, curled over and coughed hard as she tried to catch wind. The others recoiled in shock, frozen by the sudden violent response.

Eyes wide, he growled through clenched teeth, "I warn't never comin' fer you and your bastard. You ain't nuthin' but river trash. I got too big a standin' here in Pariah to be stuck with the likes o' you."

She forced herself to stand and blindly rushed forward, hands like talons aimed at his face, eyes glazed with pain. He raised his knee and caught her again. This time she fell to the floor and he kicked her in the midsection.

The Ladies screamed, one pushed him away, another rushed to help Ruby and the third ran into the hallway to go for the sheriff.

Royal froze a moment then turned toward the third, "Go ahead, get who you want. I'm Royal Vincent. It's my town an' I kin do anythin'. Who's gonna believe a bunch o' whores?" He sauntered out to the stairway and stood glaring at the woman as she ran down the steps.

He walked to the edge to see Bonnie appear from her room and grab the woman in confusion. A smile came over Royal's face, "I got some business to finish with you too, whore. Looks like all of ya's here for ol' Royal."

He laughed hard when from behind, Bea jumped on his back. Royal lost balance and slid down the stairs head first with Bea riding his shoulders, yanking his hair as though she were trying to stay on a running horse. Royal's face caught every step and when he came to the bottom a pool of blood began to flow from beneath him.

Bea got up, unharmed and looked at him in shock. Bonnie immediately enveloped her in her skirts so she couldn't see. "Ruby!" She shouted, whisked Bea in her arms and ran up the stairs followed by the Lady.

They all helped Ruby up and to the bed. She was in severe pain. "It's the baby," said one, and Bonnie ran back down to get John's medical bag. She stepped around Royal's body, got what was needed and returned upstairs.

***

Several days later Bonnie, Ruby and Bea traveled east in John's old buckboard. They made a pact with the Ladies who promised they wouldn't go for help until the next day. They agreed to clean the room and linens and leave Royal where he lay. The story was, Royal came and spent the night with a bottle of whiskey. Everyone passed out about midnight but apparently Royal decided to go home and in his drunken stupor, he must have fallen down the stairs and died. They didn't find him until late morning and immediately reported the horrible tragedy to the sheriff.

As far as they knew, Bonnie had hitched a ride West a week prior with one of the passing wagon trains. No one had seen her for some time.

As the buckboard rounded a sharp curve in the trail, Bonnie heard a voice shouting ahead. Terrified that Lord Vincent had found the truth, she pulled the horse to a stop and told the girls to be quiet. She stood, took a rifle from its scabbard, cocked and aimed it at the trail ahead to wait as the shouting grew louder.

12

Carson stood transfixed as the rifle fired. The baby screamed at both the noise and the sudden tightening of arms around it. Carson hesitated a moment then fell backward in what seemed like slow motion, just barely aware when he hit the ground. Somewhere, the baby continued to scream but the sound echoed distant in his ears. Then all was black.

***

Hearing returned first. Several voices floated over him. Gentle and hushed, female voices mixed together, almost in harmony, filled his senses with a chorus singing on the wind. He laid there and listened, relaxed and at ease, the first time in recent memory.

Everything seemed soft and warm until he realized the baby was no longer in his arms. He opened his eyes slightly to a light so bright it burned. Above him, in the harsh glow, hovered an angel. Long black hair surrounded her olive face and trailed to his cheek as she came close. "Odd," he thought, "I kin feel her hair, it tickles." He smiled softly and closed his eyes again.

Suddenly he was shaken by a brutal slap to the face. He opened his eyes, wide with fear. Before him knelt the woman who'd shot him. She slapped him again and he pulled his arms over his head.

"I said wake up, you're all right." The voices became more prominent, coarse and jagged. He peeked through his arms to see his attacker. A woman leaned over him, prepared to slap him again. Another stood close by rocking the baby, whispering to it. The third walked in circles, mumbling incessantly, and from what he could hear she said nothing that made sense.

The first raised her hand again and Carson attempted to push himself away with the heels of his feet. "Stop hittin' me." He shouted, and the woman lowered her hand.

She yelled in his face, enraged by fear, "Who the hell are you and what're you doing out here in the middle of nowhere with a naked baby?"

The one holding the baby spoke up, "Bonnie, he ain't from town. I never did see him before."

Bonnie looked at the girl, "Ruby, I want to know what this boy is doin' out here and where they came from. He's gonna tell us or I will shoot him dead this time."

The one with the child replied, almost in tears, "If he was after us, why would he have this baby with him?" She rocked back and forth and looked at the bundle in her arms, "This here boy is in mighty poor condition. We got to help."

The woman above him stood, "We'll surely help that baby but I need to know where it came from. We might be hunted and he now's seen us."

At that, the third began to chant louder, still saying nothing. She hugged herself and tightened the circles as she moved.

"Beatrice!" The woman shouted, "Will you quit that incessant racket and stop dancing 'round!" The girl froze and stood wide eyed.

"Go sit in the buckboard and be still! Now!"

She moved back toward the wagon, climbed up to the seat and sat in silence, hands between her knees.

Bonnie bent down, grabbed Carson by the collar and pulled him upward, "Now I'll ask you again, who are you, where'd you come from and what're you doing out here with that baby?" She looked around, picked up a small rock with her left hand and raised it above Carson's head. It was barely a threat but all Carson saw was a boulder about to crush his skull. He began to blubber his story with barely a breath until he had told her everything from the day he left Ohio to being dropped off alone with the baby in the woods because his Momma wanted to protect it from the Indians. He told her how he'd become lost in the foothills and ran in the wrong direction.

The woman dropped him to the ground and threw the stone in the bushes. "Stay still," she demanded. I gotta think about this." She turned and walked back to the wagon where Beatrice sat quietly.

Relieved, Carson suddenly remembered the child and desperately looked for him and the other woman. To his surprise, he saw her sitting on a downed tree with her blouse open, breast feeding the hungry boy. He looked back at the others, then to her and the baby again. For the first time he actually saw her. She was not much older than he, but it was apparent she was much more a woman than most girls his age, and she was feeding the baby. He didn't know they could just do that. He watched for a few moments then embarrassed, looked toward the others, hoping they hadn't noticed his indiscretion.

The older woman, Bonnie, hugged the younger girl, spoke softly to her and stroked her hair. Bonnie seemed to be somewhere in her twenties, somewhat attractive but with the hardness of a man. She was olive skinned, like the Cartaglias who ran the butcher shop in Ohio, but didn't have their accent. The girl next to her looked to be his age or younger. She was lighter skinned with muddy colored hair, a smaller, version of Ruby but much more frail. Bonnie was definitely not part of the family, too young to be their mother and too different to be a sister.

Carson rolled over and sat up, caught the attention of Bonnie, who turned toward him and pulled the rifle from beside her.

He threw both hands in the air when Ruby looked up and shouted, "Bonnie, stop! That boy ain't here to get us. You heard him; he's in a bind, just as we are. You would of killed him and this baby if I hadn't pushed you. Now leave him be. He needs us to help them too."

Bonnie lowered the rifle, "So you think it's a wise thing to take 'em? You sure about that? Think about it, they already slowed us down and they're gonna eat our food and water. What then?"

"Take them at least till we find their family. Get 'em back to their wagons before they starve to death. If his people are decent they'll make up for what he eats. And this here baby needs me or it's gonna die. We cain't just leave 'em here. Besides, we ain't passed no wagons so we should come upon 'em soon. They're coming towards us and we're goin' towards them. Cain't be long till we cross paths."

Bonnie, rubbed her forehead and looked at Beatrice, "Bea, what do you think? Should we keep 'em?"

The youngest looked at her sister with the baby, then the boy. She sat silent for several moments then turned to Bonnie. "I don't want no one else dead cause of me."

She leaned into Bonnie and began to cry.

Bonnie released a huge sigh and shook her head. "When you're done nourishing that child we'll go. Boy! You can come but you'll ride in the far back. Any fuss and I'll dump you on the road in an instant. And don't even think I'll leave that baby with you. We'll drop him with your wagons; you surely ain't able to care for him. If I throw you out it's just you. Understand?"

Carson nodded agreement, got up, walked to the back of the wagon and climbed on. Ruby carried the child to the buckboard, handed him up to Bonnie, climbed aboard and took the boy back into her arms.

Bonnie picked up the reins, snapped them and the horse moved forward. They traveled for nearly an hour while Bonnie looked all around and listened intently for anything on the air, either in front or behind. The buckboard moved on in silence.

13

Carson rode in quiet fear, facing behind, as the buckboard made its way down the foothills toward the plains and his family. The severe heat intensified as they descended to the flatlands. Grasses seemed to swallow everything as land leveled and trees became sparse. The three in front were virtually silent, with only an occasional comment about the heat or the condition of the baby. Carson glanced forward on several occasions to look for the train and each time he found himself gazing at the three in wonder until his neck became sore.

He wanted to talk with them, to find out who they were and why they were traveling east. Once he started to raise the question and the older woman told him to hold his mouth and keep quiet. After a time, the sun crested and began its journey toward the mountains when they were accosted by a heavy, sour smell that tainted the air.

"What in the Lord's name might that be? Any other body smell that?" Carson looked forward as both girls answered they did.

"I kin smell it. It's awful."

Bonnie finally acknowledged the boy's presence. "You run across this on your way to the hills?"

Carson pulled his legs up and turned forward, "No ma'am, it was all grass 'n dust but none like this."

Bonnie fell silent again. After a few moments of anticipation, Carson reluctantly turned toward the back of the wagon once more. As he swung his legs around, he noticed something in the distance, far to the south. It was hard to determine what it was through waves of heat that diffracted his view. He wondered if he truly saw anything, wiped sweat from his eyes and squinted. The images didn't fade but grew slightly larger as he watched. He finally took the initiative and spoke, "Ma'am, I kin see…"

Bonnie reacted sternly, "I told you to keep it quiet. You talk if you're asked, not the other wise."

"But…"

"Did you hear me boy, I'll ask for your thoughts when I want 'em."

Carson turned back in anger and complied. There seemed more than one rider so he hoped it was someone from the train along with Horn, searching for him. They would give this obstinate woman her due.

The riders drew closer and images became more distinct. There were actually four horses and as the distance diminished, his hopes perished in the heat. They kept to the south and although they came closer, they seemed to maintain a space.

Carson held his tongue for a time until he was sure it was not his family and they were being followed.

He could no longer be silent, "Ma'am, I got to tell you. There's someone followin' us. They been there for a bit. There's four of 'em kinda' keepin' a distance."

Bonnie pulled up the horse, swung around and glanced at the boy. Her gaze followed where he looked and she scanned the horizon. When she saw them, color drained from her dark skin.

She swung back, snapped the reins to push the horse to a trot and shouted," Keep an eye on 'em and let me know should they come closer."

They traveled that way for nearly half an hour. Carson kept watch as the riders maintained nearly the same distance and kept pace with the buckboard. They all traveled in unison.

The horse became hot and lathered as it pulled deeper and deeper breaths from the ever more rancid air. The entire world took on a yellow haze and the smell made breathing consistently more difficult. Bonnie figured if it bothered her, it must be hurting the horse as it ran with the weight of the wagon.

She looked again and realized the others hadn't gotten closer so held the horse back to allow it to catch some breath. As they slowed the riders began to close the gap.

When they were closer, Carson shouted, "They're Indians! I can see 'em, they are truly Indians. We might want to get out a here with that baby. Horn said they'd kill us all if they found us with that baby."

The two girls looked back in shock. Bonnie turned and shouted, "What are you talkin' about? What about this here baby?"

Carson turned to her, "I was afraid to tell you that part. I thought you might throw us out if you knew."

"Knew what, Boy? Now ain't the time to keep it buttoned. Tell me what we should know. Now!"

Carson started breathing hard and the caustic air burned his lungs.

"*Now*, I said." Bonnie demanded.

He spoke quietly at first, "He's the only one left from a massacre at an Indian village."

What! Did I hear you right? Say again, dammit!"

"He's an Indian baby, Ma'am. Someone killed his people. I was hidin' 'em so they wouldn't kill us. Horn wanted to bury 'em but my Momma wouldn't hear of it. They sent me off to care for him till they could come get us."

"You tellin' me your Momma stole an Indian baby? Stole 'em from them?"

"No! Don't be crazy, My Momma wouldn't steal nothin'. She's a good woman. She sent me and Horn to save the boy."

Bonnie looked back at the four riders as they drew closer. "You better talk quick boy, or I'll put you both out right here, right now. How'd you get this Indian baby?"

"We found 'em, I swear." Carson's voice broke as he spoke, "A few nights back I heard the boy wailin' in the dark. The next day, Momma sent me and Horn out to find him. We found a camp, burned to the ground with everyone killed but the baby. We took it back to the train to save it."

The baby began to cry and gasp. Bonnie realized the air had gotten so bad none of them could catch a decent breath.

"Ruby, put a cloth over that baby's face, careful you don't hurt him; we just want him to breath clean." Ruby covered the baby's face with a corner of cloth he was wrapped in. The child wriggled and cried even louder.

Bonnie searched again for the riders and noticed they were closing the distance. Carson had crawled over the few supplies and huddled against the back of the wooden seat. Bea joined with the baby and began to cry as well.

Bonnie began to panic and tried figure out what she could do. To Ruby she said, "Take the blanket and keep that boy covered. When they get here, don't let them see him if you can help it.

Boy!" she shouted to Carson, "Do the Indians know you? Did they see this baby with you?"

"No Ma'am. They weren't around when we found the boy. Horn run into their warriors on the trail next day. He never said nuthin' about we had the baby. He rode us out o' there that night 'cause he was sure they would check the train next morning. None of them ever knew about me nor the baby."

Bonnie turned toward Carson and watched as the Indians slowly closed the distance. She no longer noticed the smell and filth in the air until she choked.

Bea and the baby both cried while Ruby sang something beneath her breath, taking ragged gulps of tainted air as she did. Bonnie wondered if the Indians had tortured information from his family about the child. Thoughts flashed of horrors stories she'd heard of travelers and some of the tribes on the trail.

The horse suddenly jumped, hesitated, then tried to circle back. She spun around to take control and pulled the wagon to an abrupt halt while Carson watched the four horsemen suddenly pull up as well.

He stared in wonder as they swung around and rode back toward the southwest.

When he turned back to Bonnie, he realized why she had stopped and saw where the smell originated. The plain's grasses ahead were blackened by a fire in a swath half a mile wide. The burn started somewhere in front of them and winds had carried the flames south. Bonnie stood in shock and was joined by the others as they looked at what seemed a river of ash stretching to the horizon. The flames were gone but the odor of burnt grass and everything in it permeated every breath they took. The horse danced nervously. The only sound on the prairie was the baby's cry. Ruby hugged the child to her chest and rocked slightly for comfort. Bea sat frozen, in shock as she scanned the destruction.

Carson turned back but the riders were gone, nowhere to be seen. "They're vanished," he said to no one.

"I think we're in Hell," Bonnie whispered, "Can't even imagine what those Indians are thinkin'."

Finally, she snapped the reins and forced the horse forward. As the wagon lurched, Carson grabbed for the seat to keep from falling and inadvertently found Ruby's shoulder. He rested his head on his arm and held on to the girl. They all stared in disbelief as the wagon moved forward. The horse hooves and the wheels threw up a cloud of black dust as they rolled through the ash. They buried their faces into shirt sleeves and skirts to breath. The baby finally quieted.

They continued across the blackened landscape following wagon tracks nearly hidden beneath several inches burned grass. Ahead, Bonnie spied something unusual on the barren, empty landscape. A mound stood out; a slight prominence on the flat horizon. She couldn't make out what it might be but her senses told her it was not right. As they approached, it became apparent it wasn't a natural occurrence. She said nothing but her stomach began to churn and she assumed the worse. She hesitated to speak out until sure and when they were within a hundred yards she gently requested Carson's attention. "I think you need to take a breath, boy."

"I'm breathin' Ma'am. It just smells so awful."

"No, Carson. I mean..." She couldn't imagine what to say. "I mean, I think there's something really bad up here and you need to be ready." She pulled the horse up again and stopped the wagon.

Carson sat up, glanced at her, then looked ahead. He froze and stared in shock. It was the site where the grass fire had begun. Before him were the charred remains of three wagons, steel wheel rims and collapsed frames, still in a triangle. They stood out above the ashes. North and east of the wagons grasses remained high and brown, waving on the breeze. This indeed was the point the devastation started.

He spoke in a strained, halted voice, "They're probably on their way back to the fort for help."

He said softly, "They couldn't come for me 'cause of the fire."

"Look! The horses an' oxes are gone." He assured himself, "They took 'em and rode back to the fort." He began to laugh through his gathering fear, jumped from the wagon and ran toward the site.

Bonnie called out, "Carson, wait, wait for me." She crawled past Ruby and jumped down but he was half way to the burned wrecks before she could start after him. She followed through the ash as a thick slate cloud surrounded both of them. When she neared, she reached to stop him and nearly lost balance. Her fingers found his shirt; she seized him and pulled him to a halt before he reached the first wagon. They froze in place as the haze of dust and ash surrounding them floated past.

Neither breathed as they witnessed several bodies in heaps, piled atop one another beside the ashes of the wagon. The bodies were charred but whole, not burned like everything else.

Carson inhaled a lungful of soot that etched his throat and made him gag. He coughed deeply and covered his mouth as the filth gritted on his teeth.

Bonnie tried to pull him back, back to the buckboard, away from the agony. He yanked his arm from her and stepped forward to see more closely. At the lead wagon, three children were piled across two adults like cordwood. He froze in shock, nearly comatose, and wavered on legs that barely supported him. The gagging stopped; he could no longer breathe, he couldn't move.

Bonnie grasped his arm again, to hold him, offer support. He stood motionless like a pillar of stone. She gripped hugged his shoulders to let him know she was there when he suddenly spun toward her, searing rage in his eyes. She raised her hands in submission, stepped back, tripped and fell to the ground. Ashes puffed and surrounded her in a heavy cloud. She coughed and choked for breath as she watched him silently turn and continue to the wagon. At the wreckage, he gently lifted the topmost body.

Bonnie watched in terror as he carried a small child 30 feet away to lay it in the unburned grass. She wondered at the child's hair as it flowed back and forth with each step. "There shouldn't be no hair." she thought, and the entire situation seemed a nightmare she couldn't wake from.

The world seemed to stop as he repeated the action four additional times, struggling with the final two.

The girls sat motionless in the buckboard and watched in shock as the scene unfolded. Bonnie didn't move from her spot in the ashes. The cloud had finally settled and tears washed streaks down her cheeks.

Carson silently and tenderly finished moving his family, laid them side by side in the dry grass then collapsed to the ground beside them. He gasped as though it were his final breath, sucked the sickened air and released a mournful sound Bonnie had never heard. It tortured her and through the anguish, she wanted to join him, to help him, to hold him, but she knew she shouldn't.

As she watched his agony, all of the events of Pariah flooded in and overwhelmed her and sucked her dry. She lay in the ashes and the filth ash swirled around her like a halo.

Sometime later, Carson rose and moved toward another wagon. Bonnie stood and joined him. He said nothing but accepted her presence as they removed all the remaining bodies, carried and dragged them to the grass near his family.

When at last, all the dead were together, Carson reached to Bonnie. He collapsed into her arms and wailed aloud. They slowly fell together and sat in the grass.

Bonnie waved to the girls who hesitated but finally stepped down from the wagon and joined them. Both Bonnie and Carson reached out as one, pulled them into a huddle and surrounded them with hugs. The silent prairie was permeated with sound as the four embraced their suffering and filled the air with moaning and wailing until they were all spent.

Carson eventually collapsed and cried softly into the grass, his life energy nearly exhausted. Bonnie reached to him and began to stroke his hair. "I'm so sorry dear boy. I'm so, so sorry."

14

The evening continued in silence. With pieces of steel frame recovered from the rubble, Carson and Bonnie proceeded to dig shallow graves while the girls searched for rocks and gathered unburned pieces from the wagons. When the bodies were covered, no words were said over them. Bonnie left that to Carson out of respect, and he decided no prayers were appropriate. She honored his wishes. The only thing he whispered to the graves, as they left, was a solemn vow that those responsible would suffer the same fate.

Bonnie insisted they return to the buckboard and travel away before sun set. She didn't want to sleep in the presence of the dead. In truth, she needed to leave the burned wagons, grass and bodies as far behind as possible before dark.

At the wagon, Ruby held the baby up to Carson so she could climb aboard. He just looked at her and turned his back. "I got nuthin' to do with that Indian no more. You took 'em. You keep 'em. If I get 'em back, there ain't no tellin' what's gonna happen'."

They traveled in silence for another 40 minutes until it became too dark to traverse the trail then pulled up for the night. Bonnie felt extremely vulnerable in the open prairie after her years in the mountain forests. She slept sporadically. Both the girls and the baby breathed heavily and she thanked the Lord that they survived all the tragedies they had experienced. In contrast, Carson rose and walked away several times during the night.

At first, she worried he might leave or worse, do something to the baby. But when she heard him in the distance sobbing she understood. Her heart wrenched with pain and although she was empty with nearly nothing left to offer, she wanted to go to him and hold him, to assure him he was not alone. But each time, he returned and she faded into fitful a sleep, only to awaken as he wandered off again.

The night wore on forever and Bonnie prayed for the sun to rise. She knew she would be exhausted but within another day and a half they would reach the fort, safety, and the possibility of true rest.

When the sun finally broke, Bonnie dug provisions from the wagon and they ate in silence. She glanced at the boy they had found two days before. Carson was no longer the innocent youngster. His trauma, as well as layers of ash and grit, caused him to appear drained, broken and weary. She had witnessed his youth and innocence dissolve in less than 48 hours.

After eating and attending to the baby, they broke camp and resumed travel. Carson remained in the back of the buckboard and spoke to no one. They continued for hours as the sun reached its peak and baked the land as well as everything upon it.

The day was total monotony. The entire world seemed to consist of interminable grass and sun without end.

Carson could think of nothing but the fact that he was now alone. After all the trials and hardships, after all the arguments and abandonment, he was returning to where he'd started, but this time without family or friends. He'd hoped to never cast eyes on Ohio again. He shared his father's dream of a huge, prolific ranch in paradise, a life of "Milk and Honey" promised by the Bible. But they'd been defeated, the dream crushed.

In Akron he'd be an indentured slave to his father's scoffers. To the visionless slugs that refused to budge from the winters, the droughts, the floods and especially the banality of living in unbearable boredom with nothing to show but tedium and death in someone else's sodden field.

As the sun lowered in the west, bugs began to attack. Carson sighed deeply as he tried to accept the fact he was returning to a life he hated, when he was startled as Bea yelled out, frightened, "It's Indians, Indians are comin'."

Bonnie pulled up on the reins and stopped the buckboard. There in the grass, several hundred yards to the north was a lone rider, not actually riding but sitting still, leaning forward on a painted horse.

Carson, spoke for the first time that day, "That ain't no Indian. That's Horn! By God, that's Horn!"

He jumped from the buckboard and ran through the chest high grasses as the dry blades caught and cut his skin. Minutes later he was beside the horse that pranced and attempted to turn away from him. He grabbed the bridle and pulled the animal back. Horn, still astride the horse, had his hands lashed to the saddle horn to keep him from falling off. Blood crusted his side and he appeared nearly dead. Carson yelled at him but received no response.

He pulled the horse forward and shouted to Bonnie, "He's hurt bad. They got him too but he musta' got away. He needs help." Carson led the horse back toward the trail and although it fought a bit, it followed the boy to the wagon.

Bonnie stopped the buckboard in the road and she helped Carson untie the man and lay him on the ground. She unbuttoned his shirt to find a bullet had pierced his chest just below the collar bone on the left side. But when she gently wiped crusted blood from the wound, it began to bleed again, heavily. Bea arrived with John's bag and Bonnie rummaged through to find some powders that she sprinkled on the injury. It was something John used for several of the miners when they were cut. Horn cringed and began to struggle.

"Just hang on. It's some medicine to stop the bleeding and I got a poultice to draw out the poisons. I think there's a bullet inside. My husband could of got it out but I'm afraid it ain't in my ability. I can give you something to ease your pain and tomorrow we can get you back to the fort. They got ..."

When she mentioned the fort, his eyes sprung open. He forced a guttural sound deep in his throat and began to thrash again.

"Lay still, you're hurt bad. I'm gonna give you something to help you sleep 'til morning then we'll get you to a doctor."

Horn tried to move again. His voice wouldn't come though he did his best to speak. Bonnie mixed several grains of opium in some water and forced him to drink.

He stopped thrashing, became calm, closed his eyes and slowly faded to sleep. She covered the wound with a poultice, wrapped his chest in a bandage, wiped his forehead, then covered him in blankets. As she tended to Horn, Carson tied his horse to the back to the wagon and rushed back to offer any help he could.

Bonnie looked up, "You're friend is in dire shape. He needs a doctor bad. He'll keep peaceful tonight but first thing in the morning we need to get him back to the fort. He ain't gonna make it if we stay out here. Especially with Indians still about."

"We got to help him. He's the only one knows what truly happened. He needs to tell who killed my family. Maybe we should try to move in the dark. We could get him to a doctor faster."

Bonnie looked into his desperate eyes, "We won't make it in the dark. We got to wait till morning. If we hit a hole or something, it could kill the man. He'll be good till daybreak, then we'll move when we can see the road."

"But what if he ain't? What if he don't make it through the night." Carson was beginning to panic, I'll walk the trail. I'll walk in front of the wagon and lead the horse. It'll be safe, I promise.

Bonnie looked at him and noticed the boy coming out again. She decided to act on that and spoke sternly, "Listen to me. All we need is for you to break a leg, or maybe you walk the side of a rock and our horse breaks a leg. Don't be crazy, we ain't going tonight." She toned her voice a bit and touched his shoulder, "I know how important it all is to you, this man, your friend, what he knows. Believe me, he needs a good rest and I provided him that. In the morning we'll all be feeling better, including your friend." She took both shoulders in her hands and looked into his eyes, "I tell you, tomorrow you'll be ridin' in the back of the buckboard with him, He'll be talking and tellin' all the stories you need. It's gonna be OK, Carson. I promise." She pulled him to her and hugged him as though she were his mother. He was nearly limp in her arms.

"I know you didn't sleep much last night so why don't you try in do better tonight. Your friend's gonna need you tomorrow. He'll be alright but he's gonna hurt with every rut we drive over. Get some rest, please?" She let him go.

Carson pulled his blanket from the buckboard and settled down for the night.

Bonnie checked Horn one more time before settling in herself, all the while praying he would still be alive at daybreak.

15

When the sun rose, Horn was still breathing. Carson gently shook him as the darkness faded, in an attempt to get him to talk. Although he still drew breath, Horn was no more conscious than the night before and didn't respond.

Bonnie woke from a feeble sleep to hear Carson's growing demand on his friend to answer. She jumped up and rushed to their side to stop him from shaking the man. "Boy, don't you do that, you're gonna hurt him worse."

Carson stopped and looked into her eyes. In the dim light, his were so wide, they nearly glowed, "Ma'am, I gotta talk to him. He's gotta tell me what happened. I gotta know what went wrong. He said the Indians wouldn't hurt nobody if the baby weren't there."

She pleaded, "Boy, he's still hanging on but it won't do him no good if you shake him. You'll start him bleedin' again and that would kill him quick." She reached for Carson's shoulder and encouraged him to back away. We're less than half a day from the fort and a true doctor. We'll find out what happened before nightfall if you don't shake him to death first."

True morning light found the buckboard moving east toward the fort. Together the four travelers had lifted Horn to the back of the wagon. They moved supplies to the sides and made a reasonably soft foundation for him to rest on so he would, hopefully, survive the jarring from ruts in the trail. As they moved on toward their destination and the doctor, Bonnie drove carefully. Each time the buckboard struck a rut, a slight moan came from the back of the wagon.

Carson grew more and more concerned and suggested he take Horn's horse and go for the doctor. Bonnie finally convinced him the round trip would take as long as their one way journey. If he brought the doctor back they would still have to reach the fort before Horn would have a real bed and a place to recover.

In truth, she was concerned that they were still being followed by Indians. She didn't know if their observers had just been curious or were scouts who rode off to bring others. She worried that she could be caught with two girls, an Indian baby and a dying man that they might well be looking for. She was also concerned that Carson, riding alone, might become a target himself and felt slightly more at ease, although no safer, with the entire group together.

The sun grew higher in the sky and the temperature began to spike again. Their progress was slowed by the fact that the road was much too rough for a wounded man. They put a light blanket over him and pulled it tight around some of the supplies as though it were a tent, so he could have shade with a bit of air. Everyone kept look out in all directions and Carson checked beneath the blanket on occasion to be sure Horn was still alive. He hadn't regained consciousness and had quieted but was still breathing.

By evening, as the air began to cool slightly and the bugs appeared, Bonnie saw the silhouette of the fort on the horizon. "We're here!" she shouted, "It's up there!"

Carson demanded she stop and when she did, he jumped from the wagon, untied Horn's horse and mounted. In a moment he was fading into the shadow of the fort ahead. Bonnie snapped the reins and moved the wagon forward. Horn didn't complain with the new speed so she moved the horse a bit more quickly to close the distance as fast as safely possible.

As the wagon approached the fort, several men rode out on horseback to meet them. Carson was not to be seen as they neared, and Bonnie wondered if he were helping the doctor prepare for their arrival. As the riders came closer the girls began to cheer and clap. Bonnie slowed the horse to a walk at their onslaught. The men whooped and shouted as they waved their hats in the air.

When the first reached the wagon he pulled the reins from Bonnie's hands and began to lead the horse toward the gates at a gallop. Bonnie shouted to him, "We have a bad, wounded man in the back. Go easy!" But through the noise of horses circling the wagon, the men shouting and the girls clapping and laughing, her words never reached the rider. The baby began to scream and added to the confusion.

As the rowdy group moved nearer the fort, amid the cheering and shouting, Bonnie became overwhelmed by feelings of impending catastrophe. She attempted to turn around to check Horn and nearly fell from the buckboard, so she sat tight and held on.

Inside the fort as the gate was closed, the riders settled some. They dismounted and tethered their horses while a huge wooden post dropped with a heavy thud behind them. The girls, though excited, sensed Bonnie's fear and quieted as well. For the first time the baby could be heard over the air of celebration from the soldiers.

A man appeared from the barracks and sauntered toward the wagon. Unlike the others, his uniform was clean and crisp. Bonnie watched as he approached and smiled, "Madam, you are in the presence of Captain Landon Flowers." He bowed slightly, "I am the superior officer here at Fort Larned and I officially welcome you and yours to my home."

Bonnie nodded but sensed something gravely wrong. She attempted a smile then stood to look around, "Where is the boy who rode in here? I don't see him nor his horse."

"Have no concerns Madam. The boy took a fall when he reached our gate, hit his head and got knocked a bit silly. He and his horse are in the stable where it's cool, being cared after. He'll be just fine."

Bonnie turned to the back of the wagon as she spoke, "We got a wounded man here. He needs a doctor, bad. The boy rode ahead to get the doctor ready. You got a doctor here, don't ya?" Before she could move, a soldier pulled the blanket from the wagon. "Looky here Captn'. It's as she says. Man's been shot. But I don't think he needs the doc no more. I'd say he could do with a buryin' instead."

Bonnie climbed to the back of the buckboard and lifted Horn's head. There was no response. She listened for breathing but heard none. The body was still. The girls leaned into one another and fell silent. The baby's cries seemed to echo from the walls of the fort.

"Your men did this." She glared at Flowers, "I told them to stop but they ran the buckboard here. They wouldn't listen."

Flowers walked to the side of the wagon and looked at Horn. He reached across to the body and placed the back of his hand on the man's face. "My men can become a bit exuberant Madam, but I can assure you they weren't the cause of this man's passing. He's too cold. He's been dead for a bit, I'm sorry to say." He reached for her hand and spoke with an insincere sadness in his demeanor, "Was he kin of yours? The baby's father?" His expression developed an air of suspicion as he raised an eyebrow and continued to question her. "Why don't you introduce your little band to us? What in the world brings you this far into the wilderness with these children and a wounded husband?"

She turned from the captain, looked at Horn's body and spoke intently. "We found him on the trail, hurt, he's not my husband."

Her intuition screamed, something here was direly wrong. She decided it wise to keep as much information from him as possible. "None of us knows him." She reached forward and put a hand on each girl's shoulder and squeezed hard, "We come from Denver, when my husband passed. On our way back to family."

Flowers looked at the baby, "And who's the mother of this child?"

"That's my baby. This here is my wet nurse and her little sister."

The captain turned his gaze back to the body and nodded.

Bonnie looked back to Horn's corpse, "We found this here man by the trail, already shot. The boy started talkin' crazy, said he'd seen 'em before, but I think he'd just been too long in the sun." She turned and stared directly into the captain's eyes, smiled slightly, then continued, "Don't pay no mind to that boy. He's been near senseless since we came through a burn in the prairie. We was being followed by Indians when we come across some wagons full of dead folks out there. It spooked him bad. We think this man was…"

Flowers interrupted, "Indians? You saw them? They followed you?" She nodded, "When, when did you see them? How far back? How many were there?"

His focus turned rapidly as he insisted on information about the Indians.

"There was just four of them," Bonnie saw excitement and anger rise in the man. He leaned into her as she continued, "When we came to the burn they turned and went west, that was day before yesterday. We didn't see them again."

Flowers raised a hand and motioned for one of his men to join him. He spoke quietly. The soldier called two others and they rushed to the store. Bonnie watched them leave then continued, "We found this here dying man yesterday. Suddenly the boy knows 'em all, the people in the burn and the man back here." She pointed to Horn's body. Flowers studied her intently. Though she was extremely uneasy, she made a demand, "I need to see our boy to find how he is doing," she was adamant. Flowers stared at her as though she had just slapped him. Bonnie allayed her insistent manner, "If he's hurt, he'll need me. Please, I got to see if he's gonna be alright. You can understand that." Her tone became almost submissive, "If I kin get the boy, we can bury this here man. Then if we can rest here tonight we'll be on our way by morning. Won't cause you no effort at all."

Flowers humbled his demeanor again, "You'll do nothing of the sort. My men will tend to this man. You and the children are welcome to stay as long as you choose. I'll provide comfortable lodging for the four of you." As he spoke, three soldiers appeared with packs from the store and ran to the stable. Both Bonnie and Flowers watched as they rode wildly from the stable toward the gate which was swung open just as they reached it. They rode off at a fevered pace and the huge gate was closed and latched behind them.

Flowers smiled again, "We will bury the body this afternoon out back in our cemetery. If you'd like, our Reverend Wilkinson can say a few words over him to hasten his journey. I'll let you know when it's time. In the interim, you and these children can rest and freshen up."

Flowers bowed slightly again, turned and walked off, waving for one of his men to follow.

Bonnie shouted after him, "What about our boy? I need to see our boy."

Flowers continued as though he hadn't heard a word. Two men escorted the women and the baby from the wagon and led them to the barracks.

16

Carson opened his eyes to a shadowy darkness. His head throbbed and as he felt for injuries, he found another large lump on the back of his skull. It hadn't healed since the last time and was again bloodied and extremely sore. He tried to sit up but became instantly dizzy and fell back onto a mud floor. The smell of the hay mixed with urine and feces caused his stomach to churn. He rolled over and threw up. Dizziness overcame him again and he lay back in the mud in an attempt to gain some sort of balance.

He tried to remember where he was and how he'd arrived. In the shadows he could hear horses, several horses. Horses! He'd been riding a horse, riding to a fort. He was outside a large gate, sitting horseback. A wave of nausea came over him again and he rolled to his side and vomited once more. As he laid back in the coolness of the damp earth, he attempted to recall events.

He was outside a large gate, on horseback, yelling for someone to open up. He'd come for help. Faces looked down from the top of the wall and he pleaded with them to open the gate. That was the last he could remember. He was asking for help when everything went gray. His stomach churned again, he took a deep breath, rolled to his side and attempted to spit the sour taste from his mouth. The wave of nausea subsided and Carson rested his cheek in the cool mud of the floor.

Exhaustion finally overwhelmed him and he drifted into an aberrant sleep. In the world of his dreams he was visited by a vision of burning bodies. They were everywhere. He didn't recognize them as he wandered through a vast plain of death. He wanted to cry out but couldn't make a sound. His voice fell silent in the devastation surrounding him. He tried to escape but with every effort he continuously found himself still in the center of the remains. Somewhere in the emptiness of his dream he heard a baby cry. It terrified him and he tried harder to run away but with every step he was still surrounded by the burned bodies. The crying scratched his ears and tore at his heart. Unable to get away, he gave up, sat down in the middle of the carnage and covered his eyes. Surrounded by blackness, the crying continued and grew ever louder. He squeezed his eyes shut and covered his ears with his hands to smother the sound.

Something touched him and he looked in terror to see his mother's burned body standing over him. He seized and shook himself awake. He was back in the stable on his hands and knees consumed by dry heaves.

Gasping for breath, he fell back to the ground and attempted to remember what was of the dream and what was real. His mind would not focus and he could confirm nothing.

A thought flashed and he suddenly realized where he was, he concluded he was in Hell. This was the terror his mother had warned him of, the punishment for not listening to his parents and the penalty he earned for not following rules. He began to cry and tears rolled across and down his cheeks.

Slowly, thoughts of a baby began to filter in. He lay there and tried to force his memory to return, so he might escape from this place. After a time, other phantom memories, those of a woman and girls swirled through his mind intermingled with thoughts of the baby. The memories were fractured by empty spaces and nothing made sense although he remained convinced his mother was no longer alive. He lay there quite some time until he finally felt able to sit up. Slowly he rose without feeling sick and sat fairly steady. Though he didn't lose balance, he began to weave back and forth and felt the nausea rise again. He crawled to a wall and sat against it while he attempted in vain to remember. Still unable to determine where he was or how long he'd been here, he finally concluded he was still alive. There were horses all around and he knew from Bible training that horses or dogs or cats didn't go to Heaven, or he imagined, Hell for that matter. He was sure he was still alive on earth, just trapped in some wretched situation.

He tried to stand but fell back so he just sat still and waited. Things seemed to be improving and he was finally able to gather ghosts of memories.

Suddenly, the darkness split and light nearly blinded him, causing a surge of pain. He threw his arms over his eyes. Voices shattered the stillness and the horses began to stir. Sounds all echoed hollow and liquid, almost like when his father called to him while he was under water in the pond. The voices approached and Carson squinted in the burning light to see who they might be.

Someone grabbed his arm, "Air ya' still alive boy?" Carson continued to block his eyes with his other arm to shade the light. "Come on 'n git up. We got some talkin' to do." The man pulled him to his feet and his vision began to swim along with the sounds. He started to heave again, but received a sharp slap on the jaw. "You puke on me an' I'll knock your ass out agin, ya little tweed." The blow caused his headache to expand and his thoughts and memories faded into a red fog.

"The doc wants to talk to ya' now. We all need to get some things straight afore ya' talks t' the Cap'n."

Carson was led to a small building attached to the side of the store by two men. One opened the door as the other pushed him through. "Here 'e be doc. He's still kickin'."

They pulled the door behind them and in the dimmer light Carson was able to open his eyes again.

"Have a seat boy, I don't want you fallin' down in here." Carson looked around, saw a bench against the wall and sat. His stomach was queasy and he wavered back and forth slightly. Swells of pain surged through his head.

The doctor spoke, "You remember anythin', bout when you got here, Boy?" Carson attempted to pull his thoughts together again when the doctor continued, "You was at the gate yellin' and when we opened it yer horse bucked and you went down hard. Remember that?"

Carson shook his head, "no". The pain intensified when he did and he squeezed his eyes shut.

"Just sit still, open yer damn mouth, yer head ain't good for shakin', yet." Carson opened his eyes to see the chubby, grizzled man with a huge mustache looking at him from behind a small table. "What is it ya' do remember? Tell me everthin'. I want to be sure yer brain ain't squashed in there. Ya' won't do nobody no good iffin they scrampeled yer head. Dumb asses, they don't never listen to me."

Carson couldn't understand what the doctor was telling him. He tried to grasp who the 'dumb asses' might be. They said he'd fallen. Who tried to scramble his head? He sat quietly as he tried to comprehend.

The doctor asked more questions but the boy's memories were too scattered for him to make sense. He then had Carson perform a few tests to see if he was able to focus his eyes, touch his nose and count to ten.

"I believe you're gonna be O.K. Hey, you're young and strong, just what the doctor ordered!" And he laughed a bubbly chuckle at his own humor. "I'm gonna take you to the barracks and get you some clothes. Yours is filthy, bloody and covered in horse shit. I cain't take you to the captain like that. We'll get ya' cleaned up and ready to go afore I present ya' to Captain Flowers." He turned his head sideways, smiled and said, "That's Captain Land o Flowers," and he bubbled laughter again. "Don't tell him I said that, He'll shoot us both." He smiled and winked at Carson who now felt even more confused than when he entered the room.

Twenty minutes later, Carson stood before a glass mirror in the captain's quarters and surveyed the blue uniform he was clothed in.

17

As the sun faded, Bonnie, the girls and the baby were led out the gate and to the back of the fort by a soldier. They rounded the corner of the building when Bonnie stopped. In front of her were nearly 20 white crosses protruding from the prairie. At the side was a freshly dug grave and two soldiers standing next to Horn's body. Their coats lay in the grass near a dirt pile. Bathed in sweat they breathed heavily as darkness approached. One rested a shovel on his shoulder while the other leaned on his handle, blade planted in the hill of dirt. They both swiped at the growing swarm of insects.

They looked to Bonnie and snapped to attention as the procession came closer. She almost felt honored at their consideration.

The sentiment faded as a voice from behind proved to be the focus of their respect, "I'm glad to see we're all here. Let's get this over so we can stop feeding these interminable insects."

The captain stepped forward and nodded to Bonnie, "Happy you decided to join us. We hold quite a reverence for the scriptures here at Fort Larned. Please say hello to our religious guide, The Reverend Artimus Wilkinson."

A tall, slender man with a gray shirt and white collar stepped forward. His salt and pepper hair was cropped very short and though the cut was done badly, probably by knife, he presented an air of esteem. Bonnie thought of John and how his talents might have made this man look almost regal if he were still alive.

The Reverend nodded to the woman and girls then offered a saddened smile of contrition as he slapped at something on his neck. His expression then turned to rage and he demanded, "Let's get on with it! This could have waited until morning, the man isn't going anywhere." Bonnie realized the reverend was very British.

Flowers interjected, "You know what the smell would have been if we let him lay here through the night. But to your point, let's put the man to rest so we might get some ourselves."

The Reverend stepped to the body, knelt down and said a few words. As he stood and turned away he displayed an exaggerated wince that inferred it was indeed, best to bury the man as soon as possible. He nodded to the soldiers and the two grave diggers rolled Horn into the hole.

As they began to back fill the grave, Reverend Wilkinson spoke for the small gathering to hear, "We commend this body to you oh Lord, so that you may guide him to your spiritual realm. Receive him oh Lord God and forgive him whatever sins he's committed against you. And dear Lord God, help us to find the savages that killed this man and by your hand, lead us to the complete annihilation of those devils that swarm this land like the locusts of Israel. Lead us to the cleansing of this wilderness in your name, Dear God. Amen."

The reverend turned and walked back toward the front of the fort.

Captain Flowers took Bonnie by the arm and led her away from the graveyard, Ruby and Bea followed with the child. "Now that that's all taken care of and you folks have had a chance to rest a bit, I would be delighted if you would accompany me to the mess hall so we might fill this emptiness that has developed." He stopped and smiled at her, "The doctor has released your young companion and he will join us, so please don't deny me your company." His manner seemed foreboding "I'd love to hear your whole story, how you all came to be here together."

Bonnie became anxious. She wanted to see Carson, find out what actually happened and to know what he'd shared with the soldiers. "How is the boy? Was he able to remember anything?" She tried not to sound as though she was interrogating the captain, but she didn't want to step blindly into a trap if he had an inkling she had lied to him.

"He's doing much better. Apparently he's still a bit confused but we'll have him back to normal by morning, I'm sure." They walked through the gate and it thudded shut behind them. "Sentry, keep your ears open for the search party. It's going to be dark and you'll need to open the gate for them."

Flowers patted Bonnie's hand and continued, "I have a surprise for you. I believe you'll be delighted. "

She looked at him and smiled although inside she had the anticipation of doom. They walked on in silence.

In the mess, the captain had four more chairs added to his table and asked the girls to sit. When they were seated he joined them and said something quietly to one of the men. "I'm afraid our wares might not be quite what you've anticipated, although we tend to do rather well with what we have."

Two more soldiers approached the table with plates. "We have a Mick here that I sequestered as my cook. He assisted his mother, a servant to one of my brothers. I sent off for him after I arrived here and found the food deplorable. It's nothing like New York but it's exceedingly better than it was."

As the servers left, two other soldiers approached. Bonnie looked at her plate and wondered what the meal might be. The chair beside her was pulled out and she turned to see Carson sit next to her, dressed in the uniform of a Cavalry Soldier. She gasped. The girls eyes grew wide and the captain chuckled quietly.

Carson looked at her and seemed confused. Flowers broke the shock, "I told you I had a surprise for you. Doesn't he cut an impressive image?"

Bonnie tried to talk but her words wouldn't form. Flowers continued, "Don't fear, he hasn't joined up... yet. "He chuckled again, "His clothes were covered with filth so I provided something clean for the boy to wear. Fits him well, don't you think?"

Carson looked at Bonnie as though he'd done something wrong. Her expression both bothered him and increased his confusion.

She finally spoke, "Are you all right? I was worried sick, they said you'd hurt yourself."

They looked at one another for several moments until Bonnie could take no more, "Carson, talk to me!"

He just looked at her and tried to remember, "Ma'am?"

Bonnie turned to Flowers, "What have you done to 'em? What's wrong with 'em?"

Carson looked to Flowers, back to Bonnie and then Flowers again.

"I told you, he hit his head. He's a bit scattered still but our Doctor says it will all pass in time and he'll be good as new." The captain put his arm around the boy's shoulder, "You'll be just fine, Carson is it? First I've heard your name. I won't have to call you boy any longer." He looked at Bonnie, "He'll be just fine. Now, maybe we can have a pleasant meal and you can relate just who you are and how you came to be here. I am truly interested."

18

Bonnie pulled a harsh wool blanket up to Bea's chin and kissed her on the forehead. "How come we're not tellin' that man the truth, Bonnie?" Bea raised and propped herself on one elbow.

Ruby rolled over and whispered from the other side of the bed, "You want the soldiers to know we killed a man? You want them to send us back to Pariah for hangin'?"

Bea looked toward her in the darkness and took a breath in shock.

"Be easy Ruby, don't scare yer sister." She ran her fingers through Bea's hair as the girl lay back. "We just don't know these people yet Bea. Sometimes it's better to give 'em a few white lies till we kin figure where we stand."

She reached across and rubbed Ruby's arm, "I sorely appreciate you girls going with the story. We need to keep up the pretenses for a bit longer. Right now they got Carson and won't let us alone together. We don't really know what happened to him or what's planned. But I kin tell you, I don't like none of it."

Bea lifted up again, "They seem perty nice Bonnie. They gave us a real good dinner and they got Carson some new clothes."

Ruby sat up, pulling the blanket with her, "Bea, them clothes could mean Carson's now a soldier and he's got to stay here with them. It might not be so nice if they keep 'em an' won't let him go along with us tomorrow."

Bonnie patted Ruby, "I got to tell you Ruby, Carson is still harmed, he might not be able to leave tomorrow. But don't you worry; we ain't leavin' here without him. If we got to stay a few days till he's fit, we might have to. In the meantime, we gotta find a way to talk to him so when he remembers he'll know not to make us out as tellin' falsehoods."

Ruby fell back in the bed, "I don't want to stay here, Bonnie. I don't like this place."

"Shush now, you're gonna wake the baby and that's the last thing we need." Ruby rolled over and Bonnie gently pushed Bea, "Scooch, little one. We all three got to fit in this bed." She slid in beside Bea and pulled the blanket up over the three of them.

***

Bonnie woke early the next morning to the sound of horses leaving the fort. She got up and relieved herself in the jar from under the bed. The girls still slept and she decided to let them rest.

After pulling on her pants and struggling with her boots, she quietly opened the door and stepped out into the morning.

Across the compound, a young soldier returned from the gate. She hastened toward him and he stopped when he saw her. "Hey there boy. Where'd everbody go in such a hurry? Is everything OK?"

The young man watched Bonnie approach in silence. When she got closer she realized the soldier was a young boy, probably not as old as Bea. "I asked you, where'd everbody go. You got a voice?"

The boy looked at her intently, "I heard they was womenfolk about. It's really true!"

Bonnie became agitated, "I'll ask you once again, and I expect an answer. What is goin' on around here? Where'd everbody go?"

The boy sprung to a feeble attention, "I'm sorry Ma'am, Field cook Brighton McGinnis to your service, Ma'am. Three scouts come back this mornin' sayin' dey tink dey know where the Indin Renegades is hidin'. Da Cap'n took da men to hunt 'em down 'n kill 'em, Ma'am."

Bonnie looked around, "Are you the only one left here with us?"

"No Ma'am, Doc Dibbins and da Reverend is still here." He paused, "Oh yah, an' da new recruit. He got sick again last night and couldn't stay onna horse dis mornin."

The boy stepped closer and smiled, "I hear there's three o ya anna baby?"

Bonnie nodded.

"Ma'am, I got a mess a oats boilin' onna fire. More than enough fer all o' us still here. If you and your party are hungry, I'd be obliged to feed ya all."

Bonnie looked back at the room she'd come from, 'That's kind of you, Brighton is it?"

"Yes Ma'am."

"I'll get the others and we'll take you up on your offer."

"Thank ya Ma'am. I'll let de udders know de foods to be served an' we're havin' guests."

Bonnie rushed back to wake Ruby and Bea while the boy shuffled off to the kitchen.

Several minutes later, the three women and the baby entered the mess. The doctor saw them as they arrived, stood from his chair and greeted them, "My oh my, what a beautiful day we're havin'. The sunlight is very much brighter this morning." He pulled a chair out beside him and motioned for Bonnie to sit, "I kin actually hear the birds singin' the songs of the angels." He looked to Reverend Wilkinson who hoarded a table to himself. "Don't you hear 'em too, Reverend?" He released a small bubbly laugh.

The Reverend didn't look up, "They're not interested in you, Dibbins. Leave them be."

Ruby looked around, then sat next to Bonnie followed by Bea who'd taken a turn with the baby. "Where do we get something to eat? I'm hungry."

The doctor answered, "The boy will be right back. He went to bring your fella to the table. Yer boy got sick all over the barracks floor last night; he had to clean it up then got sick again. I'll bet he's a-starvin' 'bout now." He chuckled again.

The door opened and Brighten led Carson in. Bonnie jumped up to help.

"Seat the boy here, McGinnis. Give him some room to breathe." The reverend studied Carson as he entered.

"If you don't mind, Reverend, we've not talked to him since night before last. I've been worried sick he's OK. I'd truly like to have him at our table so we kin have some time."

The Reverend glared at Bonnie, "No, I believe he could do with some space. Come sit by me, boy. McGinnis!" he demanded, "bring him to me!"

The doctor chimed in, "He'll need some space if he vomits again. Hope you won't mind some lumps in yer meal." He bubbled at his joke.

The Reverend looked at the doctor then at his plate. "Damned frontier." He stood, kicked his chair and stomped away. "Have it your way. I'm fed up with this empty wilderness." As he burst through the door he mumbled something about "never leaving god damned Boston," and slammed the door behind him.

Ruby moved to the other side of Bea and the boy helped Bonnie seat Carson next to her. He went off to get breakfast for the new arrivals.

"Carson, you look awful. Have they been treatin' you?" She looked at the doctor, "What have you done for this boy?"

The doctor looked somewhat bothered, "I've done my best. I tried to tell Flowers that the boy needed a few days rest so's he kin get back his strength and his memories. But Flowers..." Plates were set in front of Bonnie and Carson, "Flowers won't hear of it. He runs these men to death, won't give 'em a proper break for rest. You seen that graveyard out back. That's filled up since June, month after we got the Reverend assigned."

McGinnis brought dishes to the girls, then started back, slightly dragging his left foot. The doctor grabbed his arm, "Since there's so much left an' those troupes won't get back for a time, git me another helpin' boy, I'm famished." He grinned and winked at Ruby.

The cook nodded and went back to the stove. He returned with two bowls and sat to join them.

Bonnie looked at Carson, "What can I do to make sure Carson gets better?" The boy sat quietly and looked around the table. The women were beginning to seem familiar. The baby captured his interest most as he tried to organize his memories of the entire group.

The doctor shook his head, "As long as he keeps getting sick and fallin' off his horse, it's a bet he won't be pushed too far. But Flowers is gonna get him out there sooner or later and if he ain't ready, who knows what's gonna happen."

Bonnie looked at Carson, "What if we just leave, right now, today? We just pack up and get outta here? Ain't nobody around to stop us, unless you or the reverend has a mind to."

The Doctor looked concerned, "Don't be silly woman. You'd be ridin' a buckboard with one horse an' five people. How long do you think it would take men on horseback to catch ya? I can guarantee you don't want to piss the captain off." His seriousness softened as he continued, "They might call him Land O' Flowers but them flowers is full of nasty bees." The doctor and the cook both laughed and the girls joined in.

The boy noticed their laughter and froze, "Whataver you do, don't say none o' that to the captain. He goes mad if you tease his name. His brudders usta to tease him unmercifully and dey was bigger 'n 'em. Dats why he's a cap'n here in tha middle o' noplace. His Da had him sent here after what he done to his oldest brudder. It ain't no laughin' matter."

The doctor spoke with remorse, "I shouldn't say those things after I seen what it'll make him do. Brighton's mother was a cook for the family oldest, Richard. When the captain got here he sent people back to bring her. When Richard wouldn't let her go, the men stole her boy. After Brighton got here," he reached over and tussled the boy's hair, 'he jokingly called the captain by his tease name in front of the men. Captain had the boy lashed to an inch of his life. Hurt his back, that's why the limp. Took two weeks of work to get him to even walk again in the first place."

Bonnie looked on in terror, "And you've stayed? Why haven't you run away?"

"Ma'am, if the captain wants someone out here in dis wilderness, you ain't goin' noplace."

Bonnie looked at Carson who was beginning to realize his fate.

"Just be pleasant and try not to irritate the man, nor his Right Reverend Wilkinson for that matter. They are a power to be feared." The doctor leaned close to Bonnie, "I can continue to give the boy a tincture that keeps him from being too well. It'll allow him rest and recuperation. If the captain figures he's damaged and too much trouble he might send him off with you in a week or so." He looked around, "In the meantime, Brighton here will help me nurse him. There'll be plenty time for you to get together."

She looked at Carson as she responded, "I'm obliged doctor, much obliged."

The Doctor smiled and spoke joyfully, "In the meantime, you will surely brighten my life with your presence and make this place worth livin' in. We do have some comfort here," He smiled at the cook, "Brighton don't brighten much but he's the best damn cook this side of the Mississip." The doctor laughed out loud.

Bea looked at the boy, "Dinner was great last night. What was it?"

The boy swelled with pride and smiled at the girl, "Thank you kindly. We don't get dat too much here. It was fresh Ox meat. N' don't you worry, we got anudder one getting fat in da stable."

19

Carson spent the day with Bonnie. They talked in detail about their time together, although she avoided their encounter with the bodies and the burned wagons. As hours wore on, flickers of memories began to return and solidify.

By the time the evening meal came around, Carson recognized all three of the women again and began to remember his relationship with the baby. As they sat together, the doctor explained how a blow the boy had received might cause his thoughts to be amiss for weeks, "but he's a strong young man and he seems to be comin' along pretty quick." He smiled at Bonnie as he pretended to knock Carson's head with his fist, "Must be near solid bone in there," followed by his bubbling laughter.

Alone, at a separate table, Reverend Wilkinson shook his head in disgust, "Doctor, your sense of humor eludes me, as I'm sure it does everyone else here. Please, try to control yourself and refrain from your attempts at levity. It's truly boring."

He pushed his chair away from the table with a loud grating sound of wood against wood to emphasize his displeasure. He scowled at the doctor as he exited, turned to Carson and commented, "God will be your recovery, boy. I'll see to it!" he nodded to Carson and left the building.

The doctor shook his head, "Seems God's been challenging that one. Got him all up in a tizzy."

He offered a hurt smile to no one in particular then spoke to Brighton, "A job well done as usual, my boy. Ya make this place nearly bearable." He quickly turned to Bonnie, "Not to say it wouldn't be near Heaven with you an' yer girls here."

Brighton turned to Bea, "The rest o' da Ox is salted 'n smoking. It'll be ready 'n a week. If ya kin stay till din I'll have some good tings cooked up." He smiled with a hopeful look and turned to Bonnie, "If you could stay fer a few weeks, we could have da fresh ox again after dat."

He looked to Bea, eyes wide in anticipation. Bea smiled and swung her gaze to Bonnie.

"I can't say how long we'll be here. It'll all depend on how Carson does. Soon as he's able to travel, we'll probably be headin' back to Philadelphia."

Ruby looked at her with a question when Bonnie continued, "Sure as rain these kids miss our old home in Philadelphia. Dontcha, girls?"

Ruby caught on and shook her head 'yes' a bit too rapidly. Bea just stared for a moment, confused. "Eat up Bea, we need to walk Carson around a bit and get his blood flowin' so he kin get better."

Bea looked quizzically at Bonnie, then Ruby. Still confused, she finished her meal.

When they were done, Brighton picked up the empty dishes and began to carry them away when Carson spoke up, "Brighton." The boy stopped and looked at Carson, "Where did you get the oxes?"

The young cook smiled at everyone, "Troops found dem about four days ago 'n brought dem in with some work horses. Great find out here in da wilderness. Said they musta been cut loose by da Indans in a raid."

Carson said no more. He looked as though he was becoming confused again so the doctor offered to walk with the group around the compound.

Walls of the fort offered shade from the setting sun but the heat was still persistent. The bugs had begun to swarm. "As much as I hate to say good evening, you ladies should get back to your room and get some rest. No tellin' when them men will be back and when they come it's gonna be a lotta noise and confusion.

They'll be no getting any sleep for anybody then. So you might want to do what ya' can before."

Bonnie hugged Carson and the Doctor led him toward the barracks, "I'll take good care of him, Ma'am. They won't have him 'til he's strong enough," he paused, "maybe not at all. "

The soldiers returned late in the night. Someone fired a rifle to waken Brighton, who ran out to open the gate. The baby began to cry and the three women sat up, wide awake. Confusion reigned as men shouted and dismounted. Horses were stripped of their gear and taken to the stable. Flowers screamed orders and made multiple demands at the top of his lungs.

Bonnie heard Reverend Wilkinson shout amid the turmoil, "Did you find them? Did you finish them? Are they done?"

Bonnie strained to hear Flower's answer. It was muffled but through it all she could sense he was furious, "...to be seen. Nothing!" he shouted, "....those men in chains. I'll flog them myself! Taking us out there for nothing!"

The confusion went on for nearly an hour, curses and blasphemes filled the darkness, nearly all presented by Captain Flowers.

"Thorson, Adams and the other one, Get your asses over here, now!" As the remainder of the confusion quieted down, it nearly sounded as though the captain was standing next to the bed in her room, "I want you men to get fresh horses and get back out there. I know those savages are somewhere to be found and I want them located. You'll leave here tonight and you won't come back until you know where they are. When you find them, one of you will stay and watch their movement, one of you will report back to me and the other will be God Damned sure we don't lose track of anything. Do you understand?"

One of the men spoke softly, "Captain, the only horses we got are them fat ol' wagon horses. They're too..."

Flowers erupted, "I don't give a damn if you have to crawl on broken legs. Get the hell out of my sight and don't return until you have Indians for me to kill. Now get out of here before I shoot you myself!"

There was a sound of boots running and the captain shouted again, "Boy! Cook! Where the hell is that Mick? "

A faint voice returned, followed by the captain again, "Tell him to get his ass busy. I'm hungry and I want something to eat twenty minutes ago. If he doesn't hustle, I'll break his back again!" As he walked away he added, "And shut that damn baby up or I'll throw you all out of here tonight."

The compound quieted as the men filtered away but neither Bonnie nor the girls could sleep.

From the barracks, Carson listened to the ruckus. When he heard of the wagon horses something began to jell. "Oxes, wagon horses, the baby." It all came flooding in at once: the wagon train, the Indian village, the baby and above all, his family. He remembered burying them with his own hands; laying them in the dirt and covering them. He began to moan and sob uncontrollably. He rolled back and forth in the bunk trying to clear his thoughts. Still cloudy were the Indians and Horn. Horn said they wouldn't kill his family if the baby was gone. He rolled over, buried his face in the mattress and screamed until his throat was raw. He cursed and cried for nearly half an hour until exhaustion began to overtake him. Others began to return to the barracks so he quieted and lay there fully spent. He decided then and there to join the captain in his quest to destroy the savages. Tomorrow he would become a soldier.

20

The next morning Carson rose early, dressed and was off to the mess before the troops were awake. He found Bonnie and the girls at a table alone and joined them. "I got some news for ya Bonnie. I remember!"

She looked at him with concern, he was acting erratic and his voice was rather horse. "Carson," she began, "We need to do more talkin' about..."

Brighton walked in yawning, "Dis cookin' ain't hard but da hours is awful." He smiled and moved toward the stove.

"Listen for a minute. I remember. They killed my Momma and Pa, my sisters and brother too." He looked at her with steely reserve, "I'm joining this group to make 'em pay."

Bonnie was shocked, "Carson, wait. Please. I know how you feel but..."

"Bonnie, don't say any more. I swore on my Momma's grave I would see the same happened to those what killed her. You can't do anything to stop me."

They argued for a time, Brighton returned with cooked oats but when he saw the intensity of their conversation and the look on Bea's face, he set the plates down and went to a table by himself.

Bonnie, finally convinced she couldn't change the boy's mind, explained her situation,

"If you let on that we didn't come together, if you tell that it was your family in those wagons and that's a Indian baby, you might as well take a gun and shoot all of us." She took his hand in hers, "You got to do what you promised, I know that. But please keep our story so you don't get the rest of us beat or worse. It won't do your family any different to get us killed along with them."

Carson looked blankly at her as she continued, "All he wants is you to fight with him. All you want is to revenge your folks. Please let me take these girls and the baby away from here safe. Just keep our story with that man. He's crazy and he don't care who he hurts."

Later that morning, Carson paced outside the captain's quarters, waiting for the man to awaken. When the door eventually opened, the boy rushed to him.

"What the hell do you want, young man? If it's leaving, I don't think the doctor will…"

No, Sir. No, that ain't it. I want to join with you, Sir. I want them Indians to pay for what they did."

Flowers stopped and stared at the boy before responding. A slight smile came upon his lips, "You want to kill the savages, boy? You sure you'll be able to do that?"

Carson stood at an awkward attention, "Yes Sir."

"You ever shoot anyone before?"

"No sir, but I know I can without a doubt."

Flowers put an arm around the boy's shoulder and walked him toward the mess, "Even though they aren't truly people, it's almost like killing a person. It's a responsibility. If you want to go out with us, I want you to spend time with the Reverend first. He can provide you with a moral compass and remove any doubts you might have."

Carson tightened his shoulders and snapped, "Yes Sir."

The captain laughed and said, "Good boy, I'll tell Wilkerson to expect you. You can spend the rest of the day with him."

The remainder of the afternoon, Carson sat with Reverend Wilkinson as he read passages from his Bible. None applied to the savages but there was great emphasis on smiting and revenge. Wilkinson became quite animated at times, even to the point of hugging the boy fairly close. He demanded that Carson kneel in front of him several times, while the Reverend stood and held him. A musty odor arose after a while and Wilkinson explained it was the smell of Carson's sins passing into and through the holy man, preparing him for battle.

That evening, sitting together at a table, the captain joined them. "How's your new recruit coming along, Reverend?"

"I think the boy is a good addition, Captain. He's on path to become a good soldier."

The doctor, watched in silence as long as he could, finally stood and left the mess.

"Looks like he's lost his sense of humor," the Reverend said sarcastically and the two men snorted.

With the doctor gone, Bonnie watched the other table deeply saddened by the events.

The Reverend lowered his voice but could still be heard, "When you get those devils, bring me evidence. A finger, an ear or something grander. Bring me a gift and we'll pray together all night." They leaned into each other and their voices became too muted to hear. Bonnie could take no more; she gathered Ruby and Bea and walked out shortly behind the Doctor.

Everything was wrong. The boy was being groomed to be a murderer and there was nothing she could do to stop it. She lay there in the darkness praying for guidance and hope for Carson.

The following morning the captain took Carson to the stable so he could prepare Horn's horse. "I think it ironic that you'll ride one of their animals into battle against them. It's good that the horse is too stupid to understand. I'd hate to have to shoot your animal. As he spoke there was a noise at the gate. The captain told him to get the pony ready because he might get the chance to prove himself sooner that he'd hoped.

As Carson grabbed a blanket he noticed something shining faintly in the dimmed light. There, lying in the hay where the wagon horses had been stalled, he found a small silver cross. When he turned it over the name 'Baker' was scratched on the back. It was his mother's family cross. It had come from their train. Carson wanted to tell someone. He rushed from the stable and into the compound but the captain was talking to a scout who sat on one of the wagon horses. He shouted a command, a trumpet sounded and soldiers poured out from every building to gather in formation.

From across the yard, Brighton came shuffling toward the stable. When he reached Carson he said, "Looks like dis is it. I heard they found the marauders. You gonna go wit' dim?"

Carson just held out the cross.

"What's dat ya got der?" Brighton took the cross in his hands, turning it over and over. "Perty nice. Take it wit' ya, worse happens ya' can bargain wit' the Indans. They'd give their own fadder fer somtin' like dat. I hear they loves da shiny tings." He handed the cross back to Carson and ran into the stable to help with the horses.

Carson looked at the cross. "Why would the Indians burn everything and not take the teams. Even if they abandoned the teams, wouldn't they take something like this?"

It suddenly struck him. When he pulled the families from the wagon, everything was gone, the wagons were emptied; dishes, pots, pans all of the barrels, food and hard goods. Indians would have no need for most of it."

Before he could wonder further, a rush of soldiers picked him up and carried him back into the stable. The next thing he knew he was saddled up, in the back of a formation in the compound. Two soldiers tied water bags to the last six horses then proceeded to their mounts. The captain raised his saber in the front of the group and the formation galloped out with Carson and another younger solder bringing up the rear.

The scout led the formation at a rapid pace having traded the wagon horse for one his own. They rode two by two and as the fort disappeared behind them Carson realized he hadn't seen Bonnie before he left. He wished he had been able to talk to her, to tell her what he'd found. Now he was going off to fight a people who might be guilty of nothing. He realized he could possibly die for no reason.

He'd been assigned to the rear of the formation next to a young recruit he'd seen around the compound who had shouted improper things at Ruby. This boy soldier apparently wasn't well liked since he had seen an older man slap him to the ground while several others stood around and laughed.

They were both forced to ride in the least likely position for battle; the back of the column. They were apparently not considered essential to the campaign.

The trooper shouted over, "You one lucky devil to be travelin' w' all them beautiful wermen. Must keep you real busy at night." He bellowed an obnoxious cackle.

Carson looked at him in anger but he still continued, "I'm Scancy. That's my name, not what I am." He cackled again,

"When we git back you gonna have to introduce me to one 'er two o' those wermen, can't keep 'em all fer yourself."

The young soldier continued, "This here's my second time fighting these bastards." He smiled wide, "We run up on their stinkin' camp a while back, surprised 'em and killed ever one of 'em dead."

Carson looked at him in shock. The boy continued, "Oh, don't you worry none, they's still plenty left. Most of 'em warn't even home fer the party. We been huntin' 'em since." He wiped his nose on his sleeve, "This time they's all gonna get their due. Cap'n says we get to cut parts off after we kill 'em. Says it's somtin' we kin look back with 'n be proud, like medals."

Carson rode in silence. All the while the soldier next to him reveled in the coming confrontation.

Feeling as though he should have some response he finally asked, "Do they think this here water is enough to put out fires if those Indians start burnin' again?

The soldier laughed wildly and slapped his leg, "They said you might still be a bit teched after we hit you the other night. Stupid boy, Indians don't do fires. Cap'n does. These is full o' kerosene." He laughed again, "I'd surely like to see ya try 'n drink from one o' these skins." He nearly lost control as he cackled.

Carson's thoughts reeled. The statement repeated in his mind over and over, "Indians don't do fires. Cap'n does."

He began to panic. He needed to stop this somehow. He wouldn't be part of this madness. It couldn't have been the Indians who killed his family, ransacked and burned the wagons. It must have been the soldiers who did it, then burned the prairie. Who the hell were the savages here? He attempted to put all the scenarios together but his thoughts were still grainy and confusion burdened him. He knew time was running out and he needed to understand what was truly about to happen.

21

Bonnie marched across the compound. Brighton was leaving the stable and waved to her, she ignored him and headed straight to the doctor's quarters. She pushed the door open and shouted, "What the hell? I thought you were going to stop this!"

The doctor sat at his desk with a half empty bottle of bourbon and a nearly empty glass. He looked at her, poured a drink and held it out, "Can I interest you in a bit of morning sunshine?" His laugh was subdued by the liquor.

She slapped his hand and spilled the drink across his desk, although he held fast to the glass, "Now look what you did." He wiped at the mess with his sleeve, "There ain't much of this left and it'll be a damn site before I get more."

"What about the boy, you said you'd keep him sick so he couldn't go with that mad man."

"Now, listen lady, I believe I said I'd try. But if the boy won't take what I give 'em, there ain't much I kin do. He wanted to go! How the hell am I supposed to change that? I'm just a doctor, Ma'am, not God. If you want to talk to God, go find the Reverend.

He's around somewhere and you kin bet he's havin' himself one o' his little prayer parties in anticipation of the killin'."

The doctor shook his head as he refilled his glass, "I'm shore he's got God scared silly, hidin' under the bed." He downed the contents, "That man is to be feared," He poured more.

Bonnie turned and stomped out, slamming the door behind. She marched to the barracks, stormed in and shouted for Brighton. When she received no response she nearly screamed his name. After a moment she exited and made her way to the mess. As she approached, Brighton came to the door wiping his hands on a towel. His eyes widened as she closed on him, "Ma'am?" He began to back up.

"I need you to go the stable and get me a horse ready!" she scowled, "Nobody in this God forsaken place will do nothin'. I guess it's up to me."

"Ma'am?" He nearly fell backwards as she came within an inch of his face.

"A horse! I need a horse to stop this craziness. That boy's out there to get himself killed and I won't have it." She took a breath and yelled, "Go saddle me a horse!"

She was so close, Brighton wondered if his hair moved from her breath. Her voice stung his ears and he stood frozen.

The doctor stumbled from his office, empty bottle in his hand. He saw Bonnie face to face with the cook. The boy looked terrified but didn't move. "Wait one minute here," The doctor slurred, "What are you yellin' at that kid for? He ain't done nuthin." He came to them nearly walking sideways, reached the boy and put an arm around his shoulder, "This here's a good boy. No need to give him grief. He gets enough o' that from the captain. He don't deserve any o' that."

Bonnie backed away and focused on the Doctor, "I want a horse made ready. You'd just as soon let Carson die but I refuse. I'm goin' out there 'n bring him back, you hear me. Boy" she shouted again, "Get me a horse!"

The doctor's anger faded into misery. He took a drunken breath and exhaled toward Bonnie, stinging her nose, "Look here Missy," He took an awkward step toward her, "You cain't get a horse. You ain't goin' out there by yourself."

Bonnie took a step forward and started to demand a horse again. The doctor placed his chubby hand on her mouth and shushed her. Her eyes sparked and she grabbed his arm. She looked at Brighton and saw him with his mouth wide, staring at the doctor. When she turned back she could see tears rolling down and dripping from his great mustache. She dropped his arm and it fell limp, "Ma'am," he said softly, "I been here for two an' a half years, six months afore the captain. It's always been a hard life for a doctor, patchin' up all the breaks and cuts." He looked at the ground, "That man is a terror. He done more harm to these men than anything else out here."

He reached across to Brighton, "For God sake, look what he did to this boy here," He pulled Brighton around and lifted his shirt. Bonnie gasped. The boy's back was like the bark of a tree, swathed in scars. "Flowers ain't right. He's got the soul of the Devil. It turned bad here when he took over. I patched more soldiers hurt by his hand than anything else."

He turned and looked toward the Reverend's quarters, "When that man got here, last spring, that's when all hell broke loose." The doctor tipped up the bottle and sucked the last few drops, "That's when men started comin' up dead. Every once in a while, a man gets hisself killed somehow. But we've had more than 10 over the last seven months. That just ain't right."

Brighton shot a glance across the compound and grabbed the doctor's arm. The other two looked around and saw Reverend Wilkinson walking toward them. The doctor leaned toward the door and dropped the empty bottle inside. He nearly fell but the boy helped him stay on his feet.

"Is there an issue here? Is this gathering for a reason?"

The doctor began to speak but his words were jumbled. Bonnie cut in, "There's no problem Reverend, We were talkin' about getting some lunch."

Wilkinson came up to them and continued, "I thought I heard shouting. I finished my prayers for our boys and came to see..." He turned toward the doctor, "Dibbins, are you soused again?" He didn't wait for a response, "Damn you, you pathetic, fat drunk. If we need you after the men return, you'd better be sober."

He turned to Brighton, "Boy, take this sot for a walk around the compound a few times. Maybe get him some coffee after that." He turned back to the doctor, "You might consider forcing a stick down your throat to get some of that poison out of your system." He pushed the doctor away and shouted, "Get moving, man! If any of the men need you and you're not capable, I'll personally hang you for treason."

He continued to Bonnie, "I must apologize for the stupidity of our doctor. Although I don't imagine any true resistance from the savages, one never knows. They can be tricky but I'm sure they will be overwhelmed by our troops in no time at all and with little effort. It will be like spanking children," He paused and smiled slightly, "but they'll all be dead."

Bonnie looked at the man in horror,

"Go now. Get some rest. When the troops return it could be rather chaotic for some time. Landon, rather, Captain Flowers, is sure they have the pack this time and it will be an occasion for celebration."

He turned away from her to return to his quarters. As he strutted back, he watched Brighton lead the doctor in a slow, undulating lope around the inner fence. "Pick up the pace, boy. If he's not ready by the time the troops return, it'll be the lash for you as well."

Bonnie turned back to join the girls and the baby.

22

The formation reached the second scout. Flowers held up his hand and stopped the band of soldiers. "Report private."

"Thompson, Sir."

"What?" Flowers was instantly enraged, "I don't give a damn who you are soldier. I told you to report and if you don't do so immediately, I'll shoot you on the spot!"

The private sat straight and began to natter so fast he was difficult to understand, "...followed 'em to the river. They went down to bank 'n it seems they's settin' up camp for the night. They's all getting offa the horses an unpackin'. Humphry is still above a watchin' and since they warn't goin' no further, I come back to lead ya there."

Flowers sneered toward the rise.

Thompson smiled, "I bet this time we got 'em, Captain. They be sittin' ducks."

The captain turned to the man, "Better be right soldier, or I'll have your ass."

The scout still sat astride the lumbering wagon horse. Flowers called another man forward, "You two trade mounts. This man needs a capable horse to lead us to the battle. Take that work horse and fall to the rear. I don't want you holding us up."

Minutes later the man Adams, now riding the wagon horse commanded Carson to drop behind and yield his place in formation. Carson obliged and fell in, alone, behind the others.

Forty minutes on, the captain raised his hand to silently stop the group. The lead scout, Thompson, dismounted and moved forward on foot. The sun was beginning to set and shadows stretched in the plains behind each man and horse as Thompson disappeared in the tall grass.

He returned, stepped next to Flowers and smiled.

"Report," the captain demanded in a whisper.

"They's just waitin' for us, Captain." He spoke with nearly a giggle, "I didn't find Humphrey out there but I did find his horse, tied. He's likely circled around 'em. They got some teepees raised down on the river bank. Their ponies is all tied next to 'em. It's perty dry so's we can come at 'em durn near any way you want."

Flowers turned to the men who were becoming restless in anticipation and spoke quietly to those in the lead, "Clear your bladders boys, I don't want anyone pissing themselves when we do this. This will be our greatest hour and I want to be proud." He told them to pass the information back, dismounted and followed his scout toward the encampment to design the trap.

A few men took advantage of his offer, dismounted for a moment then returned to their saddles. Carson watched from behind the formation as the men jumped from their horses disappeared into the grass, then returned and spoke to those behind them.

When word reached the two in front of him, the younger trooper, Skansie, dismounted, undid his pants and urinated. When he finished he walked back to Carson, "Hold that ugly horse still a bit." He proceeded to the skins filled with kerosene and unstrapped them from behind Carson's saddle. "These is goin' to a real soldier who's been awaitin' to use 'em. You'll jus have to get yer turn some other time."

He ordered Carson to get down and help. As they carried the skins to Adams on the wagon horse, the captain returned. Both he and Thompson mounted up, he waved for the troops to follow and they all began to move out. Skansy, Carson and Adams were still tying the bags to the wagon horse. In the excitement, no one noticed they were being left behind.

"Hurry up, ya damned pup. I ain't about to miss this." Skansy jumped up in his saddle and he and Adams moved out, even while Carson finished a knot. When it was done, he was 20 feet from his horse.

The two rode off to catch the formation while Carson stepped into the high grass to relieve himself. When he returned, the entire cavalry was out of sight. He mounted and sat there, trying to decide.

***

At the edge of the riverbank, overlooking the camp, the captain motioned for half the squad to go to the north while he led the remainder to the south. Both groups found passage to the bank below and when they were in place, the captain fired his rifle in the air. The men started screaming and riding toward the camp from both sides, with a trumpet blaring. As they approached, firing their weapons into the teepees, a half naked man, hands behind his back, ran from a tent. Flowers was there first and fired into the man's chest. He flew back and the captain cheered.

The entire camp was torn by bullets. Men on horseback threw ropes over the tops of tents and dragged them to the ground. As the two latecomers came upon the extermination, Skansy rode up to the only body he could see, to shoot it again. When he got beside the dead man and aimed his rifle he froze. "Humphrey," was all he had the chance to say before an arrow pierced his throat.

At once, the air filled with arrows and shots rang out from above, from both sides of the river bed. Men were riding in circles with nowhere to go, all falling to the ground. Flower's horse screamed and fell. He lost his rifle when he hit and scrambled, crab-like to find safety. Bullets peppered the earth all around him and followed him as he scuttled along. The scout on the wagon horse fell from his mount and landed next to the captain. He pulled the man over and lay behind him for cover. The scout was still alive but when Flowers yanked him on his side to hide behind, Adams was hit by an arrow and released a final scream.

Flowers lay still for several minutes as the chaos grew, then quieted. He heard the Indians climbing down the sides of the river bank and realized he must attempt an escape. The huge wagon horse was still next to him so he stood, clambered up its side and lay across the saddle as though he were dead. He tried to get the horse to move when it whinnied and stomped its feet. One of the warriors saw the attempt and shot from the bank as the horse turned. His bullet passed through the front of Flowers thigh and penetrated the horse's chest. It bucked, rolled and fell on top of the captain's torso, crushing him on the hard ground. The Indian dismounted and drew a knife. As the brave approached to be certain of his kill Flowers played dead.

Gun fire filled the air again and distracted him. He turned back to his horse, jumped up and rode off toward the shooting.

The Captain pulled and scraped on the ground until his fingers bled. He could not free himself from the dead horse. He knew he'd been wounded in the leg but the weight of the huge wagon animal had already cut off enough blood to cause his legs to go numb.

A short time later, there was nothing but the sound of a hundred horses riding away. A few of the Indians visited the carnage to verify all the soldiers were dead. Flowers spread blood over his face and lay still until they all rode off.

***

Carson heard the soldiers whooping as the gunfire began. He knew it would be a slaughter and the remains would be desecrated then burned. As he listened to the insanity in voices from the soldiers, he decided he could have no part of it. His Indian horse was smaller and much faster than the military mounts. He knew he could outrun them if he had to. He removed his uniform coat, shirt and hat and threw them into the grass; he was dressed only in boots and blue pants and decided to go west to somehow accomplish his parent's dreams.

He started to ride north, to find the wagon trail. Travel would be much quicker and because it was a trail, they might not see his tracks. He thought about Bonnie, the girls and the Indian baby and realized how much he would miss them, but figured there only hope would be for him to disappear and leave them be.

As he moved on, gunfire and the yelling diminished, then after several moments ceased altogether.

He made his way, listening for the soldiers, ready to run. Although he knew they would be busy taking souvenirs and torching the camp. He tried to move quietly and remain inconspicuous. As rode solwly, he heard a noise from behind, stopped to look back but saw nothing. When he turned forward in his saddle, before him were four Indians on horseback stretched across his path. He froze, they all had rifles and two were aimed at him.

Carson remembered Horn's story. He stood in the stirrups and placed his hands down at his sides. Horn never knew what it meant, only that it worked to save him.

The Indians rode forward. One jumped down from his mount and examined Carson's pony. He walked around it, patted its side and shouted something to the others. Carson stood silent.

Without further comment, rifles were lowered and as the warrior jumped back on his horse he smiled. He said something in his guttural language but to Carson it was like a song. He was almost sure he heard the word, "Horn" mixed in.

They moved on, and as they did, more horses joined from the direction of the battle. Carson sat as though in a dream and watched them gather, by the hundreds. Many looked at him as they passed but others acted as though he were invisible. Several led military horses, all with empty saddles, many damp with blood.

When they were all together, they rode off leaving him alone on the trail. His legs began to cramp and he realized he still stood in his stirrups. He finally released a breath and sat.

After a time, attempting to make sense of what he'd just witnessed, curiosity overwhelmed him so he turned his horse toward the dry river bed and followed it to the battlefield.

In the distance he saw torn teepees and as he got closer, bodies of soldiers lay everywhere, strewn across the river bed and up and down the banks. A few dead cavalry horses littered the bed as well, but there was no sign of Indian causalities. He dismounted and his horse spooked so he tied it to a broken tent post forced in the dry mud and walked through the carnage to search for life. He wandered through the bodies and became sickened by the slaughter. He'd seen far too much death. He wanted no more.

Half way through his search, he collapsed on the ground and sobbed. As he took a breath, a faint noise came to him through the silence. In the fading light and the waning heat, chills caused him to shiver and he looked around.

It was quiet again so he stood and turned a circle, listening. As he slowly spun he heard it once more; the sound of someone groaning, and begging for help. Someone still alive.

He followed the sound to the body of large horse, one of the draft horses from the train. He walked to it and saw it was dead, but there, half covered by the huge body lay the captain. He approached and knelt down. The man was still breathing. Flowers opened one eye slightly, saw who it was and demanded, "Where were you?"

He raised his head slightly and spoke, "Those bastards tricked us, attacked us. Killed my men."

He looked at Carson and both eyes opened wide, "You did this. You were in it with them. You and your damned Indian horse."

Carson was stunned. He didn't know what to say to these ravings.

"Get me out of here you son of a bitch. I'll see you hanged for treason. I'll hang you with my own hands. Get this damned horse off of me, soldier, that's an order."

Carson looked at the man, pinned beneath the horse and couldn't believe his audacity. "Before I do anything, Captain, I've got a question for you."

"Get me out of here. I don't answer to traitors.

Carson leaned close to him, "Answer a question or I ride away."

The captain's face reddened, he began to shriek manically, "I'll not address you until you're hanging dead from the gallows, you traitor, bastard." His voice intensified "Get me out of here, that's an order!

Get me out of here now soldier!"

Carson leaned over and looked into his eyes, "I don't think you've got much behind your orders. I believe you could stand to give me an answer before I make a move for you." He leaned to the captain's ear and whispered while the man shook his head to no avail, "You're not givin' orders here. I don't take orders from a dead man. Answer me this and we can talk."

The captain puffed with rage as he attempted to move. When he finally realized he had no choice, he took a breath and nodded.

"Alright, Sir. That's better. Carson backed up to watch the man's face, to see if he lied. "The wagons that was burned up on the trail. Did Indians do that or was it soldiers? Think hard if you have to. All I want is an answer to that question and we kin be done here."

Flowers laughed painfully, "You mean those dumb ass sod kickers? They saw what we did to the Indian village. They went there. All we wanted was to talk with them, to offer them protection. But the bitch of a woman wouldn't hear of it." He swallowed deeply, "She threatened me! Can you believe it? She threatened ME!'

"So, it was you that killed them, burned the wagons and the prairie. You, not the Indians?"

"Nobody threatens me, boy. Nobody. She screeched about God and called me a murderer. When I grabbed her husband, she begged me for mercy. I showed her mercy. I killed them all in front of her, her friends, her husband and her children so they wouldn't have to watch her die. Now, that's mercy." He snorted. "There, you got your damned answer. Now get me out from under this horse."

Carson moved to the back of the stallion and worked there for a few moments.

"What the hell are you doing, boy? Get something to dig me out."

"Almost there Captain."

A minute later he appeared with a full bladder skin in his hands.

"What the hell is that? Get something to dig with you halfwit. That's an order. Do you hear me, soldier?"

Carson reached to his side and took a knife from its sheath. He pierced the skin and poured the kerosene over the captain's head and shoulders.

Flowers sputtered and spit, his eyes burned he couldn't breathe through the pungent odor. Carson laid the empty bag on the man's chest, knelt beside and pulled a leather pouch from his pocket. He removed two stones; a flint and a striker. The captain's eyes grew wide and the caustic oil stung even more. "What the hell are you doing, boy? I'm an officer, you'll do what I say or I'll have your ass shot at sunrise!"

Carson leaned forward, a stone in each hand, ready to strike and looked into the man's eyes for what seemed an eternity. The trapped man grew pale and his demands moderated as he finally realized he had no escape. He was quiet for several moments before he began to plead, "Please. Boy. Please don't. I beg of you."

Carson turned his head slightly and held eye contact as his anger grew. He snarled "I swore on my Momma's grave that I would visit the same end to the man that killed her."

Flowers stopped breathing. He swallowed in and began choking on kerosene as the words registered and he finally realized who the boy actually was.

Carson continued, "I've seen what a hateful wretched man you are. I'm sure you're gonna' burn in Hell by God's hand." He leaned forward, hovering over the man, holding the flint.

The captain whimpered, sniffed his nose and closed his eyes to the inevitable.

Something heavy fell against his chest; he gasped and turned his head away.

"I ain't like you." Carson rose and stood over him, "No matter what I promised my Momma. She did have mercy. She'd want me to do what's right."

He turned and began to walk away, "you like to burn things so much, I'll let you to your joy."

He stopped and looked back at the trapped man, "I imagine all the blood's gonna draw a whole bunch o' hungry animals out tonight. Water's most dried up so they'd love a nice warm, juicy body. I leave you with a choice Captain, burn or be food."

Carson mounted and rode off to the sound of cursing and screaming. It filled the air more than ten minutes until prairie winds and the buzz of bugs were all he could hear.

23

The following morning, Bonnie heard shouting in the compound. She glanced through the door to see Brighton rushing toward the gate. There was no gunfire, no whooping. She feared the worse, turned back in and closed the door behind her. Ruby looked up in fear as Bea rocked the quiet child, and started to softly cry.

When the gate thudded shut, there was no cheering, no celebration. The three women rose and went to the door. The baby woke and began to fuss. Bonnie watched as a lone rider on a painted horse entered the courtyard. Her heart jumped when she realized it was Carson and the three ran into the compound overwhelmed by both joy and fear.

Brighton took the reins of the painted horse and Carson climbed down as the doctor came from his room, holding his forehead and rushed toward them shouting, "What happened? Where's everbody else?"

Before he was able to answer, Carson was caught in a wave of hugs from Bonnie and Ruby. Bea was there with the baby who began to cry. The doctor reached the boy, pulled Ruby away and demanded, "What are you doin' here alone, out of uniform? Where's everybody else?"

Carson didn't respond. He just looked across the compound. The doctor turned to see Wilkinson rushing to them. He seemed infuriated and when he reached the tiny crowd he began pulling everyone away. "Where's the captain?" He took a breath and screamed into Carson's face, "Why are you here? What the hell have you done" If you deserted Captain Flowers during battle you'll hang before the sun goes down." The Reverend grabbed Carson by the shoulders and pulled him forward violently, "Speak up you damndable coward, what have you done?"

The Doctor grabbed the reverend's shoulder and tried to draw him back. He was met by a backhand to the face. Wilkinson took the boy with both hands again, shook him and continued screaming.

Bonnie jumped at him and demanded he let Carson answer, Wilkinson tried to backhand her but she ducked and he missed.

Carson, who to this point had given no resistance, grabbed both the Reverend's wrists, pulled him even nearer and returned a scream directly into his face, "DEAD! That son of a bitch is dead! All of them are dead!"

Wilkinson froze as if the words had struck him dumb. He let go of the boy, although Carson still held his wrists, he said softly, "The Indians, right? The Indians are dead?"

Carson felt tears well in his eyes and became even angrier, "The son of a bitch that killed my family is dead. He's layin' out there under a horse and I can only pray he's naught but ashes by now."

Bonnie looked at Carson in terror, "What did you do?"

The Reverend just looked down at the ground, Carson released his wrists and the man's arms fell limp.

Wilkinson's thoughts seemed to reel and he sparked back, "Why are you still alive? What did you do, Boy? Tell me, did you run away and leave my Landon? Did you leave him to save your own skin? Where is he you little bastard. Take me to him!"

There ain't nuthin to take you to. He's dead. They're all dead, Indians killed 'em, all 'n every one. I was there, I seen 'em."

Bonnie took his shoulder, "Carson?"

He looked at her, "I was there, Bonnie. I seen it all." He turned and hugged her, "It's over now. It's all over. We kin go back home, all of us, even that baby too."

The doctor looked curiously as the two talked.

The Reverend was still filled with disbelief. He spoke in rapid shallow breaths, "No one will leave this fort until there's an examination of the facts. First, I need to find the captain and bring him back. Then we will determine if you are at all responsible for the events."

Carson looked at the man as though her were mad, "There was near a hundred Indians at the fight. They must of come from all over the plains. A hundred Indians to 23 soldiers. They had no chance. If you want to go back and retrieve your Captain, you'll do it alone. Chances are they're still out there lookin' to kill anyone in any uniform. They know what the captain did to them and I know what he did to my family. I'm pretty sure you know all of it too. Captain brought it all on himself. I got away once, but I'll not try it again. You go by yourself. It'll serve ya good."

The Reverend turned and walked briskly to his quarters. The doctor seemed distressed and went toward the mess. A moment later, Wilkinson came across the compound with a revolver. As he approached he raised the gun, steadied it with both hands and took aim. At that moment, the doctor came from the door of the mess and slammed an iron skillet down on the back of the Reverend's head. The man dropped to the ground before he could fire.

As the small group rushed to the doctor, he knelt down and checked the man lying in the dirt. He looked up and smiled as they approached, "Hard as rock, this man's head is." He offered a muted laugh; "He's goin' to be just fine, I'll see to it."

A short time later, Carson searched Flower's room for anything that might have belonged to his family while Bonnie and the doctor drank coffee in the mess. "So that there is an Indian baby? Quite a dilemma. What do ya' plan to do with it when ya' get back to Philadelphia?" He leaned toward her, "It'll be darned hard to get people to tolerate an Indian baby or you either for that matter, tryin' to raise it."

Bonnie thought for a moment, "You all believed it to be my kin. I can't see where it would be a problem back east where they don't often even see western Indians." She hesitated, "And by the way I'm not from Philadelphia. I said that to keep everyone from knowin' much. I figured it would sound better if these children and the baby were all from the same place." She sighed, "Truth is, I don't know where I'll go. I was a servant when Johannes married me. He was new from Italy and we just run off together. I've got nobody."

Carson walked through the door, "We might have nobody but look what we do have." He held up a small steel box and lifted the top. It was filled with currency. "It was Flowers'. There's enough here to get us back to Akron in style, then we kin figure something out. My uncle is there. Maybe he'd take us in?"

Bonnie shook her head, "I thought your uncle farmed someone else's land for 'em. Is he gonna be able to take three strangers and a baby along with you?"

Brighton poured another cup of coffee and brought it to the table.

The doctor nodded to the boy, sat silently for a few moments, then held up his hand and excused himself, "You all three wait here a couple a minutes. I got an idea. I'll be right back."

He rushed out of the mess.

Bonnie turned to Brighton, "You heard 'em. Sit down here and take some coffee. Doctor's orders." She smiled all around looking for acknowledgment.

Several minutes later, the doctor rushed in with several papers in hand, "Here we go. Look at this." He bent over and spread the pages across the table. "I assume you all want to stay together, and I assume you'd like a good life for that baby." He looked at Bonnie then Carson. They shared glances and both nodded in agreement.

The Doctor pointed to the first page, "This here is your marriage certificate to Landon Flowers, dated two years ago. Wilkinson actually had one in his desk." Bonnie looked at the doctor, startled, as he continued, "Here is the birth certificate of little Landon Flowers Junior as of January 10, this year," He smiled brightly, "and here's the best one, Land o Flower's death certificate." He laughed aloud. "This last one is a will, certified by his doctor, namely me, leavin' all his worldly goods to you and askin' his family to care for you and your whole entourage."

Bonnie looked at Carson then to the doctor. She was speechless as she reached for the papers.

The doctor grasped her hand and stopped her, "They's only one condition to this whole deception. You agree and it's good. You don't and we forget the whole thing."

Her eyes widened as fear grew throughout her. She nodded and waited for his demand.

"You got to agree to return Brighton here, to his Momma. You got to take him home."

***

The next morning, the buckboard packed full, Bonnie Flowers, Landon Flowers II, Ruby the nursemaid and her sister Bea, departed toward the east in route to New York. Carson rode the paint, leading the group as their guide and Brighton sat on the back of the wagon with a huge smile and waved enthusiastically to the doctor as he pushed the huge gate behind them. It echoed shut with a dull thud that made each one shudder.

24

When the wooden stock was dropped in place, the rotund man released a quiet giggle that was closer to a cry. He made his way to the barracks and began to rummage the soldier's lockers for whiskey and anything else that might be of use. He found a small bottle of brown liquid, pulled the cork and sniffed. "Damned rot gut," he sneered, "I thought I set you boys a better example." He tilted the bottle up and choked down a gulp.

That evening, he attended to Reverend Wilkinson who still lay unconscious. His head swollen quite large from the blow, the man was drained of all color. "I don't know why I'm doin' it. 'Cause I know for fact you'll get me hanged if you get better. But it's my solemn oath to get you back from dyin', and maybe it's got something to do with me putting you there the first place."

He went to the fireplace and stoked the coals under a pot of water. "I should be tryin' to cool that head down but I got no way to do it. We'll just have to hot soak that ball you got growin' on back o' your skull. I got some powders to make ya feel better...If ya can feel anything at all."

He washed and cleaned the wound, wrapped Wilkinson's head with a bandage and placed a small amount of dried coca leaves under his tongue. "That's the best I can do for you at the moment. It's getting late and I'm growin' a bit famished."

The doctor went to his cabinet and took out his last bottle of good whiskey. He checked the Reverend a final time and proceeded to the mess.

***

Carson located one of the way stations. They were far more plentiful east of the fort. He returned to the wagon and informed the group they could stop for rest before sundown. That evening they sat around a camp fire. Bea and Brighton had become fast friends. They whispered and giggled while Ruby assumed the duties of cook. The weather had cooled a bit as they traveled and dusk was almost pleasant.

"I know you got kin in Ohio but I'd truly like to see you stay with us. I know you had dreams of California but we might just do pretty well in New York. Ruby and Bea would be pleased if you went with us."

Carson looked at the sky and sat silent a few moments. "I sorely don't want to be a tenant farmer again. My Daddy dreamed we'd own our own land, run our own life, beholdin' to no other man. I'd really like to make that true for him. But..." He hesitated, "How's that gonna happen in New York? How is it I won't be just someone else's servant?"

Bonnie started to answer when Ruby passed her a plate with pan bread and beans. Carson looked at her and she offered him a proud smile. "I hope ya like it." She grinned and proceeded to dish up plates for the other two.

When Bonnie bit the pan bread, it cracked loud and crunched as she chewed.

She watched Carson as he tried the beans. He pulled a piece of grass from his mouth and continued to grind the leathery fare. They both looked at each other and said nothing. The two younger children just sneered as they attempted to eat. It wasn't until Ruby took a bite and scowled that Brighton finally spoke. "That's a wonnerful dinner ya cooked up fer us. But iffin ya don't mind, I'd be honored to do cookin' 'round here." Bonnie looked away as Bea laughed.

Ruby studied everyone, placed her plate on the ground and stood up. She lifted her head and stepped away from the fire.

Bonnie started to go after her when Carson spoke up, "I'll go. It'll be

O. K"

The next morning Carson rode alongside the wagon, "By night we'll be getting near Kansas City if you want to go there, but if you want to catch a train from Chicago we should head north toward St Joe just ahead. It'll cut off a couple a days."

Bonnie looked back at Brighton in the rear of the buckboard. He'd been joined by Bea and neither was paying attention to anything else. "I suppose it would be best to get to Chicago as quick as possible. It'd be grand to take a train. If the doctor sends word with the mail rider end week, the Flowers should get a wire an' know we're comin'. I'd like to get to the train as soon as we can. I've had enough of this buckboard."

"I agree. Besides, when the Army gets word all the soldiers been killed by Indians, I don't want to be anywhere close to this place. They'd be obliged to conscript anyone in sight for their war. I'd rather not be nowhere near where they can find me."

A short time later the buckboard turned along a trail to the northeast heading toward Chicago.

25

Sun gave way to heavy winds from the North, followed by unrelenting, torrential rains. Everything was slogged with water and became nearly useless. Fortunately, with a much greater population as they approached Chicago, they encountered roadhouses along the trail to take meals and dry out a bit. The captain's tin of money provided for provisions. The cost of tickets for the entire group took a greater amount of their new fortune.

Upon arrival in Chicago, the buckboard and horse added several dollars to their cache. They sold them at a livery near the yards. As Bonnie talked with the owner, a man in a striped suit and bowler hat stopped to admire Horn's horse. Carson told the man the story of how the scout had been given the pony by a Kiowa hunting party in trade for a Bowie knife. He vaguely explained Horn's death, leaving the pony to him.

The gentleman pleaded a price for the "Indian Pony" and gave Carson a $20 dollar gold piece for his property. When the deal was complete and a scrap of paper signed, the man exclaimed, "A true Indian pony that's saddle broken. My daughter will be the pride of Brighton Park." Bea's eyes widened and she pushed

Brighton, laughing, "They named a park for ya. I'm pleased to know such an important boy." With that she bowed to Brighton and he pushed her back.

The morning following their arrival, they rode the train eastward, out of the city. Travel was like Heaven after weeks in the open air behind a horse. Bonnie watched absently as rain obscured the city in the windows. She dried an occasional drip that found its way inside and down the wall to dampen the floor. Next to her feet lay a canvas valise she'd purchased from a street vendor, stocked with necessities for the trip. She moved it closer to the aisle to keep it dry.

The train drove east toward New York and the trials of the past month finally seemed behind her. Bonnie was both excited and worried at the thought of her new life. She wondered aloud if the rest of the Flowers family were anything like Landon. Brighton assured her than they were not. He explained, "Sir Richard is a good man. He named his first boy Richard II and his second Charles. My mather works in Sir's household. Dat's where I learned to cook." He smiled proudly,

"We was happy dare except being around that nasty o' Landon. Sir Richard raised up da first two to put da family in front of everyting. Landon was like he come from somebody else.

He was always a mean devil." He reached to rub his back, "but you know all dat.

"He didn't like nobody and let em' all know. When I was little, he finally met up with somebody an da whole o' da family rode him bad. His brothers started callin 'em 'Land o Flower'. When dey did, he just went crazy. His Momma cried a lot an' Sir told him to stop what he was doin'. We never did see who he was sweet on, day wouldn't let em' bring her to da house. I think dey paid her to go north to Massachusetts an' disappear.

"One day Richard II was teasin' 'em at dinner. I was bringin' in plates. Land'o took da plate, trew it at his brudder's head and ran out. Me an' Momma cleaned up da blood an mess while everbody else left, yellin' an cryin'.

"Dat night, curtains in II's room caught fire and burned a big part o' da roof. II got 'is face burned to blisters. Lost all his hair too. He was a real mess.

"Sheriff come out an' took Land'o ta jail. His Momma cried and Sir yelled a lot at her. When the doctor brought II home it was more constant cryin' an yellin'. A few days later, some soldiers come to da house. Most stayed outside but one went in an' had a long talk with Sir an' da Mrs. After dat, Sir went to town, got Land'o from jail and put him onna next train on account a he was goin' out west. I was right happy to be done with him, or so I tought."

***

A wire was delivered to the Doctor, explaining that Army investigators would arrive soon to determine losses and prepare the fort for a new complement. Doctor Dibbins was told to have a full report prepared upon their arrival and any other pertinent information at the ready.

The doctor looked down at Wilkinson who was beginning to recover. The swelling had diminished and he was becoming lucid again. He realized it was just a matter of time before the Reverend's cognizance returned. It was very possible he would be able to relate that the doctor, the women and boys were somehow responsible. He had to do something, short of taking the man's life, to prevent the Reverend from placing everyone in jeopardy. Wilkinson had proven to be truly evil.

In the mess that evening Dibbins prepared supper and brewed a cup of strong tea. To it he added several grains of powder given to him by Bonnie.

He carried a tray back to Wilkinson's bedside and placed it on a side table. After assisting the reverend to a sitting position he fed the man then held the cup and watched as he drank the tea.

A short while later, the doctor rummaged under the bed and found what he was looking for, an Indian arrow that had been retrieved from a dead soldier as one of Wilkinson's souvenirs. Dibbins set about his plan of protection.

***

A fresh Lieutenant sat across from the doctor at a table in the mess and read the report that had been hand written on several pages. He still wore his long leather gloves and seemed to have difficulty shuffling the papers. "Is there a problem Lieutenant? I know these dry plains can have a harsh effect on skin." Doctor Dibbins waited for the man to respond but instead was addressed by one of his aides.

"The Lieutenant is never without full uniform. If he has a problem, he will address you. Understand?"

They sat quietly for some time while the officer read and absorbed the content of the report. "So you would have us believe

Captain Flowers and his entire compliment of armed soldiers were slaughtered by a few Indians out there in the grass?"

The doctor looked concerned about the beginning interrogation, "Sir, as it says in my report, word has it that several groups of Indians banded together and surprised the soldiers."

"Word has it? Whose word might that be, Doctor?"

"Sir, we get riders through here nearly every week. That's how I got news to the Army through Wichita. The man said he saw hundreds of Indians riding together a couple weeks back. Said they had Cavalry horses too."

"How do you know, Doctor? How do you know that the entire company was killed? Could there have been survivors out there who needed you? Maybe, just maybe you're to be held responsible for some of those deaths. What do you have to say for yourself?"

"Sir, Captain Flowers went out to exterminate the natives. He was a very capable and brave man. If he were defeated by the savages, there is nothing an ageing, overweight, unarmed doctor could have done to save him from the scourge. Besides, I was sequestered here with our Reverend Wilkinson. The captain gave me explicit orders to care for and resuscitate the good Reverend after he had been attacked by renegades. It's all there in my report."

The Lieutenant looked to his second in command, "Have someone bring Nilsson in here. I want his opinion on this Reverend." The man rushed from the mess as the Lieutenant turned back to the doctor. His eyes were ice and Dibbins fought off a chill of fear.

The man made no effort to hide his contempt, "I'll have my man's assessment here in a just a moment; confirm your evaluation. Two heads are better than one, isn't that what they say, Doctor?"

Moments later the soldier returned followed by an older man in uniform who addressed the Lieutenant, "Sir, what is your request?"

The Lieutenant asked him to step in and introduced him to Doctor Dibbins who held out a hand. The other gentleman just nodded and remained still, hands laced behind him. The doctor retrieved his offer of courtesy as his face reddened.

"The good doctor says that he's been tending to the fort Reverend on orders. He says the Reverend was attacked by savages. I'd like you're input on those claims, Nilsson."

The man raised an eyebrow, studied the doctor in silence, then turned to the Lieutenant, "It's apparent the patient was struck in the shoulder by a native arrow. I assume the doctor had to force it through to remove it. The surgery is well done for such a rustic setting."

He nodded sideways to Dibbins and continued, "What I *don't* understand is why the man seems to be drugged so heavily?" He faced Dibbins and demanded, "Doctor, can you explain that?"

All eyes focused on Dibbins who stood in silence, overwhelmed by the weight of his accuser. His cheeks nearly glowed and sweat began to bead on his temples. Heat rising from his collar seemed to blur his vision and he hoped they didn't notice. He inadvertently released a slight, bubbly chuckle and threw his hand to his mouth to try to cover his nervousness.

"Do you find something funny here, Doctor?"

The Lieutenant's long hair swung into his face as he turned in anger.

The doctor bit his own finger to refrain from giggling again, "No sir, not funny at all. It's a nervous fit I have. Sorry Sir, won't happen again."

The Lieutenant squinted, took a breath in anger and nearly shouted, "Continue!"

"Yes Sir." Dibbins deigned in compliance, "Yes sir, Lieutenant." He bent his head and continued, "As I was about to tell, Reverend Wilkinson came in with a head injury as well as the arrow in him. He was unconscious and his head was swelled huge. I tried to fix both but when he came to he started screamin', shakin' around and drooling. I believe he had a bruised brain so I gave him some medicine to stop him from hurtin' himself even more. I tried to cut back on the powders yesterday so he could be lucid before you got here but he started seizing again. Hopefully we can get him off medicine in another week or so, before you leave. Then he can tell you just what I told you." The doctor looked at the older man to see if he had accepted the story.

The Lieutenant turned his back, "Nilsson?"

"I suppose the doctor took correct steps to save the man, Sir. If what he says is true, it looks to be a proper procedure"

"Thank you Nilsson, you're free to go," and he waved the man off.

"Sir." Nilsson responded, then exited leaving the others.

Dibbins took a deep breath as innocuously as he could. He straightened and feigned an air of confidence, "Sir. I can give you a basic idea where the massacre took place. It's said to be somewhere along the Smokey Hill River, south of the trail up to Pariah. River's damn near dry this year."

The Lieutenant turned away, took a paper from the desk and spoke to no one, "When the replacements arrive we'll retrieve the soldiers. You'll lead us to them." He stepped around the desk and without looking up said, "Dismissed."

Dibbins, eyes wide, began to respond but a soldier took his arm and pulled him from the office.

Outside, the doctor pleaded with the man, "I ain't no a soldier. Hell, I've never been west of the fort. How the hell am I supposed to guide an army? I might get us all killed out there."

The soldier closed in face to face, "Shut the hell up. Lieutenant ain't gonna get nobody killed 'cept maybe some Indins. Hell man, he's the best there is. That man's gonna run this whole country one day after he cleans it up of Indins. You're just talkin' to Lieutenant George A. Custer. You'd best be ready to stand behind him all the way to Hell if you got any sense. Now shut up and get outta here."

26

Bonnie watched trees pass as the train continued east. She held baby Landon while he slept and wondered what the future might bring to an Italian widow with an Indian child and four teenagers. It was difficult to believe a well-to-do family would accept six strangers into their fold. She racked her brain to think of alternatives for their little band of misfits should plans fall apart.

Bea ran up the aisle with Brighton shuffling behind her. Bonnie held out her arm to stop them, "Are you two ever gonna 'light?"

"It's a big train Bonnie, an' Brighty needs to keep movin', don't ya, or he gets real sore." Brighton smiled at Bonnie as she lowered her arm.

Alright, but you best be careful goin' between cars and don't be botherin' anybody. Ya hear? Keep it quiet and get back here for some dinner before it starts to get dark." The two ran off to the next car laughing. Bonnie hadn't heard Bea's laughter since she played games with Ruby and the Upstairs Ladies. It had been far too long and she didn't want it to stop.

Carson was in the row behind her, writing in his journal, Ruby beside him. "Kin ya read it to me? Kin ya?" He looked up and shook his head, 'no', then returned to his writing. "If it's about what's been happenin' did you write something 'bout me? Am I in yer story?"

He kept writing as though she hadn't spoken, "If you wrote my name kin you show me? I never seen 'Ruby' spelt out before. What's it look like?"

He looked at her, feigned bother, then smiled, "You can't read 'n write?"

She was hurt by his statement and sat back in silence.

He realized he'd embarrased her and attempted to reconcile, "I didn't mean anything. There's lots of folks who was never taught. Ain't their fault. You've got to be taught." He lifted the book, held it open to her and pointed, "Here it is, this says 'Ruby'."

She reached over and touched the lines.

"It's a pretty name with the swirls 'n such but it can be done different ways." He wrote 'Ruby' in block letters and showed it to her.

"That's my name too? It looks like somethin' different." She smiled at him.

"Here," He handed her the pencil, "You hold it like this." He took her hand and placed the pencil between her thumb and fingers. Her eyes widened slightly as she looked at it. Carson placed the book in her lap and took her hand in his. He began to move the pencil on the paper and as the lead left swirls he realized he was breathing harder. "This is a 'R'. This one is a 'u' then a tall one being a 'b' and last, a low one being a 'y'.

She was thrilled with the pencil marks and with his hand on hers. "That's my name? I spelt my name on the book?" She laughed softly, "Kin you teach me how to do it myself? I want to know more. Will ya' teach me?"

Bonnie glanced back between the seats and saw the excitement on both their faces. She sensed it to be much more than teacher and student and looked at Landon as he breathed peacefully. She whispered to the air, "I think those two will be alright, no matter."

***

Doctor Dibbins cringed as a rifle fired in the dusk. The smell was hideous as the wagon filled with bodies and body parts waited outside the gate. The corporal in charge motioned for the driver to go around back to the graveyard as the gate opened and the mounted soldiers entered.

The complement had arrived the evening before and the Lieutenant demanded they retrieve the dead at the first suggestion of daylight. Despite his opposition, the doctor had been forced to accompany them since none knew where the Smokey Hill River might be. The doctor hadn't been much help. He seldom strayed from the safety and confines of the fort and had never gone further west. The group spent the morning following the wagon trail to the banks of the river then riders separated and rode in both directions in an attempt to locate the bodies.

All afternoon Dibbins sat in the wagon, terrified. He watched the horizon all around and listened for anything unusual. Several times he believed he heard thousands of savages sneaking through the grasses to kill him. He'd taken a few powders to placate his fear, just enough to calm his nerves. But in the field he worried that deadened senses may, instead, make him an unwitting victim.

Concern of his inability to respond to an emergency stopped him from indulging further as the afternoon went on. The accompanying paranoia, he didn't know if it was from the powders or lack of them, frayed his nerves even more. Anxiety grew with each passing moment. He knew he could becalm the terror but only at the sacrifice of his ability to escape.

When the wagon of bodies was finally parked behind the fort, he jumped down and joined the driver as they unhitched the horses and walked them around front. They entered and the gates were secured behind them. Only then, Dibbins reached in his vest pocket and fingered the vial he'd brought along. He proceeded to his quarters when Nilsson came from the mess to intercept him. "Doctor, welcome back. Great news, you found the dead. Glad you're all safe." he said as he approached.

Dibbins smiled, nodded and continued walking with the small container now in his hand.

"One moment doctor." Nilsson stepped faster and caught the man by the arm, "I've got more good news."

The Doctor stopped and looked with new fear at his counterpart. He regretted not having the chance to empty his vial before dealing with the next bit of 'good news'.

He said nothing but waited for Nilsson to release the trigger.

"When you left this morning I stopped medicating Wilkinson."

Dibbins forced a spurious smile as panic began to take over. He was about to down the contents of the vial right then and there when Nilsson continued, "He hasn't had a fit the whole day and he seems to be coming out of his stupor this evening. He can even talk a bit. He wants to see you." The man smiled and patted Dibbins on the back, "I believe he wants to thank you for saving him."

The doctor broke loose and set a rapid pace toward his quarters. "Don't be long Doctor. He's still not well and he might not be conscious for long."

***

Dibbins ambled in a soft haze toward the Reverend's quarters in the darkness. The edge was off his fear since he'd stopped long enough for the drugs to quiet his concern. He found the door and stepped in. Wilkinson lay in his bunk with eyes wide open. He didn't seem to notice when the doctor entered.

Dibbins held a small box of pills in his hand. He had decided if worse came to worse he could claim he found the reverend already cold. As he approached the bed the Reverend turned toward him and oddly enough, smiled. When he got closer he noticed tears in the man's eyes.

"Wilkinson? Are you…." His voice faded off, not knowing what to say.

The once cold, rock hard fiend seemed to have been replaced by a man. Wilkinson spoke hesitantly in a soft voice the doctor never knew he was capable of, "It's all my fault."

He looked into the doctor's eyes as though begging for help, "Sorry. So sorry. My fault, all my fau…." His eyes closed and he said no more. Dibbins checked his breathing and found that the man had fallen asleep.

With a great breath of relief, he studied the box of pills in his hand. After a moment he moved the box to his vest pocket and turned to leave. At the door he looked back across the darkened room and considered his next step, placed his hand over the pocket and exited.

27

Two days later the train pulled into the yards in New York. The speed had slowed to a crawl and Bonnie's nerves began to creep as well. She had gathered the others and prepared for the worst. They had cleaned up and changed to their best clothes at the last way station while water tanks were filled. As the train crept along through a railroad yard that made Chicago look like Pariah, Bonnie closed her eyes and said a prayer. The sound of the tracks faded as she concentrated on her hopes for her and the children. A sharp explosion of breaking glass startled her and she nearly wet herself. She immediately took account of the others to be sure everyone was alright. The baby broke instantly into tears and Ruby rocked him to try and soothe his nerves.

"It's alright folks." A voice from the front of the car shouted, "Somebody threw a rock at the window. Nothin' to worry about."

Bonnie took a breath and hoped that wasn't the answer to her prayer. She looked at her group, "Now when we get off the train, I want us to all stay close together. Please don't go nowhere. I don't know how we're gonna get to the Flowers house. They should know we're comin' but we don't know how they'll take to us all."

She almost felt embarrassed at her directions, sounding to herself like a schoolmarm.

She looked at Brighton, "You say you'll know 'em if you see 'em?"

He puffed up and smiled, "I'll sure know dem but I don't tink dey'll know me. I got grown a bit in da last year anna half. You don't worry Bonnie, I'll get us to da house an' I'll be sure dare happy to see us."

The train came to an abrupt stop and everyone lurched forward. People began to exit the cars. Bonnie hesitated, took a huge breath and reminded the others, "Remember who we are now, me an' the baby are Flowers. Stay together and don't say nuthin' unless yer asked. When we get to the house, you be as polite as you know how." She straightened Bea's collar and smiled at them all, "Let's go. Brighton says he can get us there even if we have to walk. If we do, it might take a bit but we'll get there together and it will all be O.K. I promise. No matter."

As she exited the door and stepped to the platform, she was enveloped by a massive wave of humanity. There were more people here than she'd seen in one place in her entire life. She hesitantly moved away from the steps to a space between some columns to allow the others to disembark. Her heart felt as though it could burst from her chest as she watched Carson and Ruby come out holding the baby. Bea followed and stopped to look around at the wonder of New York. From behind, Brighton pushed her softly, "Come on Beaty," His response to Brighty, "Let me offen dis train." Bea smiled at him and moved forward as he followed close behind.

There was suddenly a scream from the platform and Bonnie moved forward to protect the group when someone nearly knocked her over. She became instantly primed to fight. The platform was a chaos of bodies that rushed in all directions. Brighton started running and Bonnie tried to intercept him when he ran into a rather large woman.

She screamed, "My boy! My boy has come back to me!" Brighton disappeared into huge arms and the folds of a billowy dress. He squealed a muffled, "Momma, Momma," over and over again. Bonnie stopped and watched in wonder. Tears filled her eyes and she reached for Bea and put her arms around the girl who had been pushed aside and was obviously frightened.

"It's alright Bea, the boy's found his mama."

After several moments the two parted hugs. His mother refused to let the boy go, and held him close as she turned toward the others. "Which of you brought my Brighton back to me?" The boy pulled her to Bonnie, "Dis is da lady what got me back here Momma. Dis is," he swelled with pride and smiled to Bonnie, "Dis is Bonnie Flowers, Momma."

The woman held tight to Brighton's arm, threw her other around Bonnie and pulled her close, "God bless ya Ma'am. I'm forever yer servant fer bringing my boy back to me."

As she squeezed Bonnie, an extremely well dressed gentleman placed a hand gently on the woman's shoulder. "Cleona, I know how appreciative you are but you must let our new Mrs. Flowers breathe."

"Yes Sir, certainly Sir." She released Bonnie and bowed slightly as she backed up with her son still in hand.

"The man dipped his hat, "Richard Flowers my dear. I understand you are part of my family."

Bonnie stood awestruck. An older woman rushed forward, "My grandson. Please, may I see my grandson? Oh dear, my dear. Is this him? Is this Landon junior? " She moved toward Ruby who looked to Bonnie for direction. Bonnie nodded and she passed the boy to the woman.

"Mother! Have patience. We haven't yet had proper introductions. Mind your conduct." He looked to Bonnie, "I do apologize, my dear. This must be quite overwhelming after all you've been through. We're just so thrilled to have you both here. Mother has been beside herself since we received word. I hope you'll understand."

Bonnie nodded and tried to smile.

"Mother, bring the child, come over here so we can have these formalities out of the way and get these poor people home."

***

Doctor Dibbins quietly read his old, dog-eared book for the fifth time as he waited for Wilkerson to wake again. The man seemed to become more aware each time he regained consciousness and was able to carry on short conversations now. The improvements were offset by a mild slur and Nilsson agreed that swelling may have caused some brain damage. There was no way to know how it might turn as things progressed. "Time and patience will be the telling."

When he was awake, Wilkerson vaguely remembered the doctor but nothing of the night Carson returned. He apparently had no memory at all of either Bonnie or Carson but asked after the captain. When told of his death, he wept openly before, once again, withdrawing into sleep.

The doctor became dedicated to monitoring the improvements in the Reverend, something Nilsson admired as deep commitment. In his pocket, however, Dibbins kept the box of pills constantly at hand, in the event the Reverend remembered his attacker. He would not let this vile man destroy any more lives. He believed he could administer the pills if it became necessary to protect himself and the others.

Daily routine at the fort progressed back to a norm, although this time, the mission was more protection than destruction. Since Flowers and his band were eliminated the natives seemed satisfied and had apparently returned to what was left of their lives.

Dibbins was astonished that these people could go through the devastation they'd experienced, then continue at any measure without the slightest animosity to anyone. Once they'd satisfied revenge on Flowers, they seemed fulfilled.

Both Flowers and Wilkinson had questioned Indian humanity. The doctor laid his book in his lap and considered, "Maybe they were right. The Indians aren't human. They're much more than that. Especially if Flowers and his like are what humans should be."

Wilkinson stirred and interrupted the thought. He opened his eyes and looked straight at the Doctor, "Dibbins? Is it you?"

The doctor took a breath and moved his hand to the pills in his vest pocket, "It's me, Reverend." He waited for a response and prepared for the worse.

Wilkinson tried to sit up, "Where am... That's right. I know. I remember." He dropped back to the bed and rolled away from Dibbins.

The doctor's breathing became rapid and shallow. He nearly panicked at the possibility he might have to take a life and doubts filled his jumbled thoughts. "Now, dammit, now!" his mind screamed, "Kill the son of a bitch before he turns on ya. He deserves it. He deserves to be gone."

Dibbins reached for a glass of water on the desk near the bed and took the box from his pocket.

Wilkinson rolled back toward him and saw the glass, "Thank you. I'm as dry as a stone." He reached for the glass and took a drink. "How long have I been like this?" He took another sip. "It's coming back to me. The memories. They're all coming back." He took another drink from the glass and handed it back to the Doctor. "Thank you, thank you."

The Doctor took the glass and looked into the empty vessel, then back at the Reverend. "What do you remember? How much do you remember?" His teeth clenched.

The Reverend looked up at the ceiling, "It's all there, everything, all there." His voice began to fade slightly.

"What!" Dibbins shouted, "Tell me!"

Tears appeared in the corner of the Reverend's eyes, "I remember New York. I remember the money they paid me to leave. I remember the pain I caused and still, he found me again. He sent for me. His family made him hate, made him crazy." He rolled over and sobbed into his pillow. The Doctor watched wide eyed as the sobbing slowed and finally ceased. The man lay there still, breathing gently into the pad. Dibbins looked at the unopened box in his hand and sighed.

28

Bonnie couldn't believe the opulence of the Flowers home. They arrived in a coach then she was escorted to her room. It was larger than the last house she had lived in. There she found an ornate, hand carved crib for the baby. As she laid the boy on the cotton pad, she ran her fingers over ivory inlay. Landon fussed a bit but she rubbed his birthmark as Carson had explained and he smiled at her.

Ruby was guided to an attached room with an adjoining door to allow access to care for the baby. The room was furnished with a bunk for Bea as well.

When they had been delivered to the front entry, Brighton went with his mother to his old cottage and a foot servant took Carson across the huge landing to another entrance.

Mrs. Flowers assured everyone they would gather again for a homecoming supper that evening after they were able to clean up and settle in.

Bonnie continued to marvel at the size of her room and the fact that it had a basin and dressing table as well as a great bed with a headboard and posts. In the corner was a fireplace and behind a screen was a white tub on lion's feet. Beyond that, a door lead to a wardrobe larger than her sleeping area in Pariah. As she fell back on the bed, a knock came from the ajoining room. She opened the door to wide eyes and huge smiles from the two girls. Ruby and Bea danced in, covering their mouths in attempt to stifle giggles.

"Can you believe this?" Bonnie looked around and waved her arm in a sweeping arch, "I feel like I'm gonna wake up and be in Periah again."

The girls hugged her and proceeded to drag Bonnie to their room to share their excitement.

The evening meal proved to be much more than Bonnie could have envisioned. The table was adorned with incredible linens and fine china such as she had never known. She was seated at the head of the table surrounded by the rest of her ensemble. Landon was positioned in another ornate crib placed between her and Ruby. Next to Ruby sat Bea and across from them was Carson beside Brighton who seemed both excited and rather embarrassed to sit at the main table while being served.

Sir Richard stood and tapped his Champagne glass, bringing the attention to him. "Tonight I would like to welcome the newest members of our family, home to our table at Arrow House. Please allow me to go around and present every one.

Bonnie and Landon were first, followed by their colleagues. When he came to Brighton he offered a heartfelt welcome, bowed to the others and thanked them for bringing the boy back to the fold.

An attractive blond woman with a shy smile was second from last, "I regret your youngest brother in law, Charles is not here to join us. He is in Washington DC meeting future colleagues at the House of Representatives. In his absence, I would like to introduce his beautiful wife, Amanda." She smiled and nodded her head.

"Last but most possibly best, is your other brother in law, Richard II." He held his hand out to the man sitting to his right and II, as he was called, nodded politely.

His face was mildly scarred and his hair was combed to cover patches that never grew back after the attack by his brother.

Bonnie's smile faded and she looked down, "It's an honor to be here. I thank you for your kindness to all of us."

The meal was extravagant and when it was done they all retired to a library where others were waiting. Sir led, with Bonnie on his arm and Mrs. Flowers behind carrying the child. As they entered, Sir presented Bonnie to the attendees and they applauded. "I hope I don't embarrass you, however, these people are here to document your arrival for tomorrow's edition. They have a few questions and would like a photograph or two, if you wouldn't mind." He released Bonnie to the waiting group then spoke to all, "Please make this prompt. Our family has much to catch up on and we would like all the time we can secure. Thank you."

They were directed to a corner of the room where large cameras had been arranged and the process began. Family photos were completed and each waited in turn for separate portraits while reporters questioned and recorded responses.

The newspaper people were finally shuffled on their way and after dinner drinks were poured. The women retreated to their sitting room and the men proceeded to light cigars. Brighton excused himself and went to join his mother and the other help in the kitchen.

"So, Carson, just what is your relationship to these women? How did you come to be part of this entourage?" Carson looked at II and tried to talk to his eyes rather than his scars. They had anticipated questions and practiced responses so all would offer the same story.

Sir relit his cigar, shook the match flame out and dropped the stick in a pewter ash tray. "Yes son, how is it you came to be with my daughter-in-law and her child?"

Carson's heart beat harder as now both men looked to him for information. His mind raced with the answers as he began, in an attempt to keep the story straight.

"I was goin' West with my family on a three-wagon train. Most had turned back cause of the heat and misery. I spent a lot of time ridin' with our guide, Horn, tryin' to find the quickest way outta the prairie."

He took a breath and tried to remember the story and keep his thoughts away from the burned wagons and his family. When he gathered his strength, he continued with a quavering voice, "We come back from the foothills to find the wagons had been attacked with everybody killed."

The two audience members leaned in, "I'm so sorry my boy. It must have been awful. Please, don't even attempt to recall that piece. Go on to my son and his wife."

Carson breathed again and hesitated. II put a hand on his shoulder, "I know this must be difficult, but it means so much to know what happened to my brother." He took a puff on his cigar and let out a long slow trail of smoke that blurred his image.

"After we did what needed to be done, Horn decided it'd be best to go back to the fort and get help."

He gazed at the two men again. Burning in his throat caused his eyes to water and he did his best to continue. "When we got to the fort, the captain sent men out to look for the renegades but they come back with nothing that night."

He hoped his strained concentration wasn't apparent as he tried to keep the story separated from reality. Bonnie had assured him the truth would be of no advantage to them and of no solace to the Flowers family.

He continued, recalling in fabricated detail how the captain united his troops and together, with Horn, pursued and fought the renegades. Carson explained how safe the captain made him feel at the fort. He told of how Horn returned alone and nearly dead, to report of the ambush and the captain's bravery to his very death.

When he described Horn's dying scene, all three men were gathered together in tears.

***

The doctor was Wilkerson's constant companion now. The lieutenant had moved Dibbins into the Reverend's quarters and given the doctor's office to Nilsson. Arrangements were made for Dibbins to escort the Reverend back to Kansas City since he was no longer welcome at the fort.

"He's a distraction to the men." Custer explained. "Every time they see him and his tears, they believe they could be the next casualty. I can't have that impeding the morale of my soldiers. We need to get that man away of here."

Dibbins had actually grown to almost like the new Wilkerson as he explained in a letter to his brother in Virginia:

"Sure he cries a lot, but the man has just become damn polite. He's a proper gentleman these days."

He bubbled a laugh as he read what he'd written:

"So I'll drop the Reverend off at the hospital in Kansas City and make my way home. It'll be true pleasure to get the hell away from this endless prairie. The lieutenant says he can give me a good word for a hospital spot there. It'll keep me busy. I only just hope I can deal with real people again after these years of naught but crazy soldiers."

He put his quill down and watched through the window at uniformed troops walking across the compound then glanced back at a sleeping Wilkinson before he continued:

"I should be relieved from this place in the week. It will be a few days in travel to get 'ol brain pan settled in Kansas City and then I'll make my way home. Hope all is well.

Your brother, Donald."

29

The following morning, Bonnie woke to sunshine and realized day break was well behind her. She hurried her dress and made herself reasonably presentable before she rushed from her room and down to the dining area. The house seemed all but empty. As she stopped to wonder what she should do, a house servant entered behind her, "Good Morning, Madam. What is your wish this fine day?"

Bonnie spun in surprise and looked at the woman. "Excuse me?"

"Breakfast, Madam. If you're hungry, that is. Can I get you someting for your Breakfast? What might you like this fine morning?"

Bonnie blinked and looked around, "I'm sorry. Where is everyone? Did I sleep too late?"

The woman walked to the table and pulled out a chair, "No Madam, not at all. After your long journey, the Mrs. asked that you be allowed to catch your rest. Please, sit."

Bonnie walked to the table and took the seat. "Mrs. took the baby to the doctor to be sure he doesn't need anything after your ordeal. Your girls went with her."

"And the others?"

"Sir had business and your boy went with Richard II to see the newspaper office. Our dear Amanda is probably still asleep in her cottage." She smiled maliciously and changed the subject, "Speaking of the newspaper," The woman went to a side table, picked up a paper and handed it to her. "There's a mighty interesting piece about your arrival, Madam. It has pictures and all. You can read it while I get your meal. What would you be havin'?"

Bonnie looked at the front page and saw a photo of her and the Flowers family. Mrs. held the baby center and her smile drew all focus.

Bonnie looked up, "Ah, what was yer name again?"

"Doneath, Madam, though they call me Donna."

"Donna, what've ya got?"

"Whatever you're desire. Steak, ham, oats or eggs. It's all here, Madam."

"Just bread and coffee, is that alright?"

Certainly, Madam." She smiled and retreated to the kitchen.

Bonnie read the headline:

"Mrs. Landon Flowers and son return from the Wild West"

She snickered at the 'wild west' reference and read on about Landon Flowers untimely death while saving settlers from marauding savages. The man had apparently been a hero and a benevolent soul who gave his life in service to others. She shook her head at the exaggeration of the fiction she'd imparted the night before.

Near the end, the message turned to her and the baby:

"The widow, Mrs. Flowers, arrived yesterday with their son, Landon Flowers II. Mrs. Flowers, formerly Bonfilia Verga, daughter of Giovanni Battista Catalano Verga and Catalina di Mauro, a principal Sicilian family, is the sister of well known Italian author Giovanni Verga."

"A memorial for the late Landon Flowers will be held at the Arrow House chapel on Saturday. A reception for the bereaved arrivals will follow. Invitation is by request."

Bonnie was perturbed at the falsehoods written about her heritage. She'd been born and lived her entire life in poverty near Baltimore, until Johannes. Their marriage was arranged but when she refused to travel to Italy, Johannes worked passage to the United States on a steamer.

Three months after they wed, Johannes decided to search for fortune in the West. His small savings had faded and with her diminutive dowry, he and Bonfilia packed a wagon and left for the land of sunshine and streams of gold. His hope for riches ended in Pariah as other opportunities kept them in the small town. Her hope for the future seemed to end when he was murdered.

Now, presented as the daughter of a wealthy landowner from southern Italy, she found herself in a New York mansion with a new family and a child she believed would be difficult to pass as her own.

Somehow, they had seemed to become fully accepted. She set the newspaper aside as Donna placed a plate of bread, toasted and buttered, next to a cup of dark coffee. She thanked the attendant who excused herself, picked up a slice of toast and looked at the coffee cup, "Maybe the stories aren't all that bad." She took a bite, tasted the warm butter, rich on her palate, smiled and whispered, "Bonfilia Verga." Took a sip of coffee and quietly said, "Bonnie Flowers."

It felt comfortable. It felt right.

***

Carson rode with II in a coach driven by boy a few years older than he. "Stop at the door Laurence. Mr. Calahan and I will get out here."

"Certainly, Sir." The driver pulled to the curb as a doorman rushed over to help II down. "Morning Sir. Fine day it is. Is this one of your guests?" He smiled as he took Carson's arm and guided him to the ground. Although he felt awkward at being assisted, Carson smiled and nodded 'thanks' before the man rushed to the huge door of the building and pulled it open for II.

"This is Mr. Calahan, George. He accompanied my sister-in-law and her child here after their horrible loss. You'll probably see much more of him. He's quite a hand with a story and this morning he's agreed to talk with one of our writers to bring some of his experiences to life for publication."

"Outstanding Sir." George nodded and as the door began to close, II passed instructions for the driver, "Please tell Laurence to return for us at two."

"Certainly sir. Pleasure to meet you Mr. Calahan." II made his way across the marble floor with Carson close behind. An odd, steel lattice door divided the center wall where a man in uniform greeted them. He pulled against the steel and it contracted to one side.

"After you Carson," II held out his hand and motioned for the boy to enter what resembled a small prison cell. Though concerned, he continued forward. II followed. The uniformed man joined them and stretched the door closed again.

Carson looked around in wonder as II smiled. Moments later the cage jerked and began moving upwards, causing the boy to grab the rails.

"Pretty amazing, isn't it? One of the first in New York. It's an Otis safety elevator. Something of the future. It takes you where you want without stairs."

The cage door was opened again to an expansive room cluttered with desks and crowded with people who seemed to all be talking in unison. Their movements ebbed and flowed with no reason. It seemed absolute confusion.

"Welcome to the news room, Carson. This is where the Free Press is born."

They walked through utter commotion; each person II passed stopped and acknowledged him then continued as though he hadn't been there. On the far side they entered a small, windowed office that looked out over the workers. II settled into a leather button chair behind a massive desk and motioned for Carson to shut the thick oak door.

The chaos outside was instantly muted as they became isolated.

II picked up a horn attached to a tube and spoke into it, "Maddy, Are you there?" A moment later Carson heard a tinny, small voice and II continued, "Please find Berkeley or Leak and have one of them join me." Another sound came from the horn and II thanked the invisible 'Maddy'.

"Sit. Sit young man. I have some things to catch up on. One of my reporters will be here momentarily and you can adjourn to a quieter location to relate some of your stories."

30

Bonnie sat in a wicker chair on the huge porch. The late summer sun was high in a clear sky and breezes here were filled with moisture. She inhaled deeply, closed her eyes to the sun and marveled at the experience. Her world had turned around and presented something she never could have even imagined. She prayed that the fabrication could continue for at least a short while before anyone became the wiser. As the sun warmed her face the sound of an approaching horse and coach drew her attention.

She watched as it enterd the drive. When it stopped she stood and walked down the stairs to greet The Mrs., the girls and Landon II as they exited. The girls giggled as they jumped down, laden with large boxes. The driver appeared at the step to help the Mrs. who cradled Landon, wrapped in a gauzy silken blanket. Bonnie was shocked at how dark the boy's skin appeared against stark white material. Another woman, a stranger, stepped from the carriage and joined the The Mrs.

"My dear, I hope you had a pleasant rest this morning? I told Donna to allow time for you to recover from your journey. How are you?"

Before she could respond, Ruby and Bea surrounded her. Bea placed her boxes on the drive and began to open them, "Look Bonnie, look what I got."

Mrs. Stepped up and placed a hand on Bea's head, "Not here my dear. We'll have plenty of time to share later. Please take your things to your room."

Bea retrieved the boxes then she and Ruby ran up the steps and into the house.

"Bonfilia, this is my dress maker. She's come to measure you for an appropriate gown for the memorial. I assumed you had no need for formal wear in the wilderness.

"I also took the liberty to purchase accessories since we were in town. I hope they'll be acceptable." She asked to driver to have the extra boxes delivered to Bonnie's room and the three women retired to the fitting room.

After the dressmaker had gone, Bonnie and the Mrs. sat in the dining room with afternoon tea. "You read the article?" she picked up the newspaper, "I hope you weren't upset with the liberties I took?"

"To be honest, at first, I was a bit shocked. I never even heard of the people you said I'm related to."

The Mrs. became solemn as she continued. "We need to have a little talk, my dear." She hesitated, "I have an extremely serious proposition for you and I need your total concurrence. If you'll agree to my wishes, there can be huge advantages for all of us."

Bonnie swallowed as fear began to overtake her. She inadvertently looked toward the door for an escape.

The Mrs. placed her hand on Bonnie's and continued, "Relax my dear. This will be painless, I promise." She took a sip from her cup while still firmly holding Bonnie's hand.

It was almost as though she were preventing her from running as she continued,

"As far as your background is concerned," she squeezed tighter, "please don't be offended when I say, most Italian families here are in service positions. After a doctor wired us information that you were coming, I was curious. Since he included your previous name in the information, I quietly began a search."

Bonnie pulled back but The Mrs. held tight to her hand, "I have no issues with your heritage. I've traveled throughout Italy and have known some fine and honorable families such as the Vergas. I found record of your wedding in the Baltimore Sun. My husband's paper has long arms and I have the ability to use them in confidence.

In the end, it all comes down to appearances. Let me explain." She put down the cup and took Bonnie's hand with both of hers, "My Landon was always an extreme problem, even as a child. He was cruel and so problematic we had to nearly isolate him. We hired several private instructors and despite their compensation, none lasted more than a few months." Depression seemed to pervade as she continued, "My Richard is a very influential man and this family has a crucial position to maintain. All of my sons were intended to distinguish this family as government servants to this nation.

"As Landon grew, he chose and followed very misbegotten paths. Near his end here, he took up with a Reverend in a...," she searched for words, "in an unnatural way. We attempted to stop him, explain what his choices were doing to the family. When that failed, his brothers tried to shame him. Nothing seemed to work so my husband paid the man to go away."

Desperation filled her eyes as she continued, "Landon became incensed and committed a horrible act. It was by his own hand that Richard II received his deformities. Landon might have killed his own brother and even the rest of our family. We could not endure the boy any longer so my husband sent Landon away with a singular hope the military might reform him and help him find his place."

She cleared her throat and straightened her back, "You see my dear, I lost Landon long ago. He was a huge disruption to everything this family holds sacred. There seemed no possibility of redemption so we sent him away. Now, Richard II is relegated to the newspaper and Charles is our only hope in Washington. My Landon has finally met his destiny. So you see, you my dear, you and Landon II, have resurrected a portion of this family we believed was gone from us forever."

She became resolute as she took a breath and continued, "You may have to adopt a certain level of imagination should we take this forward. But trust me my dear, I will provide complete support for you and the child as I already have." Bonnie's eyes widened and her heart pounded, "If we both agree to support one another, you will have cleared my son's name. In return, you and the baby will live a grand life as members of this family. Your future and that of the baby holds no restrictions."

She released Bonnie's hand for her decision when a sudden noise drew her attention away. Bonnie turned to see Donna come through the doorway, "Is there anything at all I can get for you ladies before we prepare the evening meal?"

Bonnie shook her head 'no' then glanced back with a subdued smile and tipped her head slightly to agree to the conditions.

The Mrs. offered a broad grin of acknowledgement then responded to the servant, "Thank you Donna, we're fine for now." She held out both hands to Bonnie and they squeezed in conspiratorial agreement.

***

"It's Leak, Gonto Leak Jr." He reached a ham fist to Carson and shook, nearly crushing the boy's hand.

"Don't break him, Leak. I think he's going to be a valuable asset to the Free Press. I want you to spend a bit of time with him and see if you can put something together that will convey to our readers what it is to journey west. We might find a regular feature in this. The boy has quite the ability with a story."

Leak smiled at II and nodded although his teeth were grinding. He thought to himself as he waved for the boy to follow and exited, "Where the hell is that ass, Berkley when he's needed? Probably out chasing a skirt while I have to babysit for the Boss."

Carson followed the man from the office into the confusion on the floor. Leak placed his hand near the boy's ear and shouted, "Let's go somewhere a bit more quiet. Follow me."

They proceeded to a corner of the room and through a door that led to a closed stairway. Carson nearly ran to keep up.

Three floors down, they came to the lobby then exited through a side door. Gonto carried a thick pad of paper and had several pencils in his jacket pocket. Carson was thrilled to be with someone who wrote for a living. He followed the stocky man through an alley and to the door of a tavern. He stopped as the big man continued in.

"You back already, Leak?" The bartender said smiling, "When da you find time to get da stories ya write? Yer here so much I believe ya must make all 'at stuff up."

"Careful Charley," Leak stopped and pointed at the man. He turned to Carson, "Get your tail in here boy," then turned back to the bartender, "Two beers or I'll be doing my next exposé on you and your waitress. I could make your Mrs.' eyes spin. Have you living the rest of your life behind that bar."

"It's a might early fer beer, Leak. An' that boy looks a might young." He watched as Leak shuffled the boy along, ignoring his statements. "But if ya behave I'll have da new girl honor ya wit a couple tall 'uns."

They made their way to a back table where the reporter dropped his paper and lined up the series of pencils. "Wait here boy; I have to get rid of some so I'll have room for more. I'll be right back."

As he disappeared through the back door, the waitress, a young red haired woman with a lacy blouse came from the bar with two beers. She bent down and placed them on the table and asked, "Dese both fer you? Ya' sure you're old enough?" She paused, "Ya' got any money for dis?"

Carson had never seen a blouse quite so revealing and he stared at her cleavage as he absently answered, "They're not for me, they're for that reporter... Leak." He looked up, into her eyes.

She nearly laughed, "Reporter, huh? I din't see no reporter. Where's da reporter, big eyes?"

Carson felt his face burning in the subdued light and couldn't bring himself to say anything. He just stammered until the back door opened and Leak returned.

"Hey gorgeous. My boy's a bit young for you isn't he? How about a grown man?"

She turned to him, "I's just bein sure da kid's got a couple nickels fer da beers."

Leak laughed, "Don't worry yourself. I have an account here and it's never been neglected." He patted her on the butt, "Now get along with you, we have business to take care of. Just keep your eyes open and if you see this glass near empty, bring me another."

Carson talked and Leak wrote for better than an hour. The waitress brought three more beers for Leak and finally a second for Carson. When it was half gone, Carson found the nerve to ask if he could use some of the paper and write a bit. Leak obliged and after fifteen minutes he sat with a fresh beer and read what the boy had written.

"This is outstanding. Where'd you learn to write like this?"

"I been doing it all my life, far back as I can remember."

Leak looked up and laughed, "It's a damn site better than your talk. Did this truly happen? It's gripping."

"No sir. I just made it up while we were sitting here. It's got facts about where I was but it's all just made up."

Leak folded the paper and slid it in his coat pocket. "I like it. Can you do more of these stories?"

"I'm sure I can. Been doin' 'em all my life."

"You mind if I show this to the boss? Take no offense, but I'd rather write police reports. If this does turn into a regular feature we'd have to spend a lot of time together and you're far too young to spend your days in a tavern. Besides, I'm just not too fond of the Wild West. If you can write more stories like this, I might be able to convince the boss to print them under your name. What do you think about being a paid reporter?"

"Sure, give it to yer boss." Carson became excited, "Get paid to write stories? That would be... Damn!" His smile faded as the beer hit, "Before we go back, I gotta pee bad. It's back there?"

Carson was slightly unsteady as he exited. Several moments later, when he returned to the tavern, Leak was shouting at the red haired waitress, "No! It's Gonto! Gonto! Like Pronto but a G."

The waitress stood between him and the door to block his exit. The bartender was closing on them, "Leak, it's OK." He moved between the two and held up his hands, "Persy, dis guy's good. I got track of everting. Da man's spent more time here than me."

He turned to Gonto, "Come on Leak, she's new an' doin' what I taught her. Bet she remembers yer name from here on."

Leak dropped his defenses and released a full laugh, "Charley, at least you hire the good looking ones. Never mind their manners." He turned to the waitress, "Sweet thing, you can wait on me any time, forgive my brashness."

Carson caught up with him and as they left, Leak patted the waitress on the butt again.

Her red hair seemed as though it would burst into flames from anger.

31

The Memorial service at the chapel was over and the few guests adjourned to the ballroom at Arrow House. Although she'd known Landon, Bonnie was still surprised by the limited number of people who attended. Most seemed to be the wealthy and powerful, there not from loss but respect for the Flowers family.

At the house there were considerably more people, apparently attending to celebrate. Landon hadn't had a large assemblage of friends but it was apparent his enemies were plentiful. Bonnie sat with the rest of the family, all in black, as guests passed by and offered condolences to each. Two reporters took notes in a corner and cameras had been located in several parts of the ballroom to record the event. The room continually brightened with flashes of light.

Charles had arrived that morning and Bonnie was pleasantly surprised at his charm. He had a slight resemblance to Landon but the effect of his appeal was nearly breathtaking. When they were introduced, he bowed at the waist and kissed her hand causing her to tremble with chills. He, like Richard II and Landon, was well over six feet tall. He sported thick hair and large sideburns that framed a chiseled face.

Amanda placed herself between the two as quickly as politeness allowed and whisked him off. He glanced over his shoulder and smiled at Bonnie just before he entered the library.

Now, Bonnie sat with Landon II in her lap at the end of the reception line. Although Charles and Amanda should have been to her left, Charles was missing and Amanda sat third, after Richard and The Mrs. leaving Richard II as a barrier between her and Bonnie.

Feeling extremely awkward and alone, as the line thinned Bonnie attempted a conversation with II. He responded politely with yes or no answers but refused any social involvement.

When at last, the line ended and the gentlemen went to acquire punch for their wives, II walked to the table, picked up a glass and proceeded to join his reporters.

Charles delivered punch to Amanda when he noticed Bonnie alone with the baby.

He excused himself from his wife, despite her apparent umbrage, and moved close to Bonnie.

"I see you've been abandoned. You'll have to forgive my brother. It might take a while for him to warm to Landon's family."

Amanda stepped beside Charles and took his arm. He offered a brief glance and returned to his conversation, "Don't be concerned, he'll come around. He knows you and the child have no fault in what happened."

He smiled as he looked into her eyes, "Richard's still torn that our brother found such an attractive wife while he feels forever destined to be alone."

Charles felt a tug on his arm but continued, "I know this must be a difficult time for you. May I bring you something? Punch? A sandwich?"

Bonnie noticed Amanda's irritation, "No thank you. I'm fine." She felt it best for all if Charles moved on.

Sir Richard led the Mrs. To Bonnie as their son was dragged away by his wife.

"How are you Bonfilia? I hope this isn't too painful. I realize it hasn't yet been a month and you've been traveling since. That, in itself, must be dreadful."

I'm doin' alright Sir. Please, call me Bonnie. I was only Bonfilia when I was a girl and my parents were angry with me." She forced a smile.

"Don't worry, dear, we're taking great care of our new daughter. As soon as these formalities are over we will have her well occupied." Mrs. placed an arm around Bonnie and with the other hand smoothed the baby's hair. "It will be an adjustment but a very pleasant one." She smiled at Bonnie, "Richard, why don't you make sure your friends are comfortable while I formally introduce our daughter and grandson to the ladies."

As the evening progressed, Bonnie looked repeatedly for Charles but couldn't find him. She searched the reception several times during the night until at last, she noticed him in a crowded corner and gazed for a time. When he finally turned toward her, she realized it was actually II.

She turned away, startled at the similarities between the brothers and realized she hadn't looked beyond II's ragged hair and ruddy skin. Across the distance, she could see the man Richard II had once been. She watched him talk and laugh with his guests and she wondered what he might be like to know. As she watched, he glanced in her direction. His demeanor seemed to change as their eyes met. His smile vanished and he quickly turned away.

***

It was a warm evening so Ruby decided to wander the grounds.

Bea had pleaded to help in the kitchen since Brighton was there with his mother. Mrs. Flowers could see the delight the two children held for one another and felt her approval was the least she could do for the boy.

In less than a week, Ruby was feeling nearly abandoned. The baby had become a focal point for the Mrs. She and Bonnie doted on the child and one or the other attended to him whenever they weren't otherwise occupied. Each night they assigned him to Ruby. Bea was forever hovering around Brighton and although Ruby hoped Carson might become her beau, he was never there. He had spent the past few days with II at the paper and was apparently becoming a journalist, leaving Ruby home by herself.

Bonnie's attitude seemed to change as well. Although Ruby enjoyed the new clothing, the house and the lifestyle she'd been thrown into, it seemed to be much more important to Bonnie. In the past few days Bonnie began to act quite differently; as though she had actually been married to that captain. She carried herself as if she had always dressed in fancy clothes and actually deserved her status. All four had agreed to accept their new identities but it was almost as though Bonnie believed the story.

Instead of friends in a stage play, Ruby felt their performance was something more. She started to feel that she was truly seen as Bonnie's servant and it wounded her pride.

Her father had called her names, screamed at her and thrown her out, but he never treated her as mere property. She'd been his daughter; then she wasn't. That was horridly painful, but in a much different way. She tried to understand her feelings as she walked the grounds alone.

When she rounded the house near the stables, she came upon several buggies and coaches gathered together. The horses were boarded and several men and boys were collected there. They talked noisily and laughed too loud. Some smoked and threw coins against a wall.

She turned to leave when someone called her name. "Ruby, is that you? Don't run away. Just a minute."

She looked back to see a young man break from the crowd and rush toward her.

She backed away as he came close, when he spoke, "Don't go. It's me, Laurence, the coachman."

She stopped when she recognized him but she was still wary.

"I've been waiting to see you by yourself. I wanted to tell you, I think it's great you're here."

He came to her and some of the others started to follow. They drew Ruby's attention. When she looked past him, Laurence turned to see them approaching and held up his hand. The procession stopped.

He turned back to Ruby, "Sorry about them. I told some of 'em about you and they'd like to meet you too. Just not tonight."

She smiled and stood quietly as he continued, "I'm eighteen years old and I run my own carriage." He pointed his thumb over his shoulder, "Some of those guys are more than thirty and they just got to where I am already." He lifted his head and smiled at her. "Problem is," he confided, "I need to be here and ready for the Flowers any time they need me. They count on me so I don't get occasion to meet many people that aren't drivers. Most of the others here are married or old so it was a ray of sun when you showed up the other day." He squinted one eye and gave her his most alluring smile.

She said nothing but her eyes smiled back.

"Maybe one day Sir Richard will let me take the coach out and I can take you for our own ride. Wherever you want. How's that sound?"

Ruby's eyes widened and she glanced over his shoulder to see the entire assembly of drivers smiling as they watched intently. All activity had come to a halt and all eyes were on Laurence and Ruby.

Ruby looked back to him, "I have to go." She whispered, then turned and rushed back toward the front of the house. Behind her several of the drivers were laughing. Comments were shouted but she couldn't make out what was said.

***

Ruby spent the evening wandering, away from the house, away from the stables, away from everyone. She came upon a gazebo, climbed the steps and sat down in the darkness to consider the events. Carson didn't seem to care anymore. He just neglected her after everything they'd been through. She liked him but each time they were together he talked of nothing but the newspaper. She'd been confused when II called the Free Press his mistress, but she was beginning to understand what he meant since Carson had all but forgotten her.

Now an older, successful boy wanted to know her. Her heart pounded when she thought of what Laurence said. He wasn't an awful looking boy and he seemed nice enough. As she considered the driver for a boyfriend, she remembered the lies Royal had told her and what that led to; disowned by her father, a lost baby and the lying boy's death.

She didn't know if she could ever start over with Laurence. He might possibly be the liar that Royal had been. Everyone she'd known had promised to care for her and then they all deserted her. Besides, if she gave herself to this boy, what would he think when he learned her truth; knew what she'd been and what she'd done? He'd surely leave her too. She lay on the bench in the dark and sobbed until she eventually fell asleep from exhaustion.

Sometime later she woke to the sound of horse hooves moving away, up the drive. She had no idea what time it might be but the ballroom was darkened and the guests had gone.

From the darkness, Ruby climbed the steps to the house, hidden by the night. She opened the huge door as quietly as possible, entered, then pulled it shut behind her. The click of the latch seemed to echo from the walls and she waited a moment to hear if anyone might stir.

She removed her shoes and walked across the foyer and up the stairway to her room. Before entering, she stopped again to listen for anyone that might have wakened. When she was sure she was alone, she went in to find a sliver of light coming from the adjoining room. Bea lay asleep in bed but the crib was empty. Ruby closed the door to the hallway and stepped quietly across the room to shut Bonnie's door. As she pushed, it suddenly stopped and pushed back.

"Where the hell have you been?" Bonnie whispered as she entered the room, Landon in her arms, "I've been worried sick about you." Ruby was about to apologize, to explain when Bonnie continued, "The memorial was over hours ago and I've been here waiting for you with this baby."

Ruby looked at the child then directly into Bonnie's eyes, "That's it? You worried that I wasn't here to take care of that baby? You got important things to do? You need your servant girl to take care of your 'Son'?" she shot back sarcastically.

Bonnie stood silent a moment, then stepped toward Ruby in the dim light. "What the hell are you mad at? You're the one's been missing."

Bea awakened and sat up in bed, "What? What's wrong?"

Bonnie softly snapped at her, "Nothing, Bea. Lay down and go back to sleep,"

She moved forward as Ruby stepped away, eyes wide in anger.

"I asked where you've been." She was determined but still whispered.

Silence became an intense presence as Bonnie glared at the girl, waiting for a response.

Bea sat up in bed, "Ruby?" she asked and looked back and forth between the two as she attempted to understand.

Bonnie looked at the youngest and demanded, "I said lay down and go back to sleep. This doesn't concern you." Then to Ruby, "You were supposed to be here with the baby. If I hadn't checked, he would have been alone all this time. What if something had happened?"

Ruby stared at her and her expression hardened. She began to breathe rapidly and as Bonnie started to speak again, Ruby shouted, "That baby? Your baby? You want me to give up my entire life for that baby?"

The child startled awake and began to cry.

"Now look what you've done." Bonnie's voice grew louder. "What are you thinking?"

Ruby stepped forward, fists clenched, "That ain't my baby, remember? Mine is dead. You just took that one and called him yours. I ain't gonna give up my whole life to be a slave to you and that Indian. You want me to lay down and die so you kin act like some sort of rich queen? You ain't no better than the Vincents and remember, one o' them's dead cause of it."

At that point, Bea joined the baby and began to wail out loud. She rolled over and buried her face in the pillow.

Bonnie felt as though she'd been hit by an ocean wave, as if her nose were filled with water. She had no response and just stared at Ruby, mouth open, as a tide of anguish filled the room to submerge everyone. She struggled to regain her breath when Ruby ran to her own bed, fell into it and joined in the cacophony.

Bonnie turned in silence, overwhelmed by the reality of what had been said, and returned to her room. She collapsed onto her own bed, held the crying child tight and listened as the weeping continued in the adjoining quarters. Her own eyes filled with tears.

After time, when everything had quieted, Bonnie fell into a fitful sleep. Her dreams were riddled with visions of guilt. Royal

Vincent lying dead at the bottom of the hotel stairway; Bea on his back still pounding his lifeless body; Ruby beaten and bruised, agonizing in premature labor. She'd hoped those images had long faded but they rushed back in force to haunt her again. This time, however, she equated herself to the monster.

32

Although Bonnie made a decision to show Ruby greater respect in her new role as nursemaid, the Mrs. made it imperative that Ruby spend much more time with Landon II than either Ruby or Bonnie were comfortable with.

For the next several weeks Bonfilia was instructed daily in manners, speech and social graces. She became a project for the Mrs. who then took her to community teas and events to introduce her to the affluent of New York City. Occasionally Landon II accompanied them for an initial introduction but more often he was left with Ruby.

Each time Bonnie apologized and promised Ruby things would improve in time and the girl would benefit from the new surroundings, but each time she would drive away in the coach and leave Ruby to mother the child.

As Bonnie left for every social event, dressed in elegant clothing, Ruby became more incensed with her own position. Impatience grew deeper each day and with every incident. As the weeks passed she became more remote and disconnected, oft times leaving the baby to cry in his crib while she took solace in the garden.

What bothered her even more was Bea's relationship with Brighton. Her younger sister was free to spend time with the boy she liked and follow her path while Ruby seemed destined to mind the child for the remainder of her life.

A month on, Bonnie could no longer ignore the resentment. She worried about Ruby's demeanor and the effect it might have on the baby. She request the Mrs. allow Laurence to take Bonnie for a coach ride and picnic that Sunday afternoon.

The two young people were informed on Wednesday evening that they would have two hours together on the back division of the property. Although they would be alone, the location was still visible from the house and they could be monitored from a distance.

The entire house seemed brighter the days following the announcement; Ruby laughed and danced with the baby in her arms as she made plans for the event. Brighton's mother listed items from the pantry so Ruby might plan a menu.

With Sunday morning worship complete in the Flowers' chapel, the entire family returned to the house. Ruby and Bea ran to their room to change from church clothes while Bonnie sat on the porch and rocked Landon in the early sun.

A short time later, the two girls rushed down to the pantry where Brighton joined them. The kitchen was filled with a party tone as they assembled the basket that Ruby had promised, "Laurence will never forget."

Bonnie felt warmth from both summer breezes and the joy she'd seen in Ruby the past days. She wanted the girl to fit in and pledged to herself that things would be better now that her own tutoring was nearing an end. She would see that Ruby receive instruction to become a proper young lady along with the freedom to enjoy that status.

In the pantry, the three young people worked excitedly and soon the wicker basket was filled with what would be a picnic lunch to remember. Ruby closed the lid and hefted the basket. Bea lifted a crock of iced tea but Brighton tried to take it, "Let me." He said. He reached for the container and fumbled it as Bea turned away. The crock fell to the floor and shattered, spilling liquid everywhere.

Brighton stepped forward, slipped in the tea and fell backward against a butcher block. His head slammed the sharp corner and he collapsed to the floor. The spilled tea was blended with a dark veil of red running through it.

Bea screamed and fell to her knees on the broken pieces of crock. Ruby backed toward the wall and watched the scene as though it were a nightmare from the past.

Brighton's mother rushed in from the kitchen and saw her son lying there surrounded by red, not realizing most of it was tea. She screamed, crossed herself and fell to her knees beside Bea.

Bonnie who was next on the scene with the baby in her arms, handed Landon to Ruby who was backed against the wall shaking, then joined the others to help Brighton.

***

As the coach drove away up the road, The Mrs. watched from the porch and assured Cleona, "The doctor assured us it's only a minor scalp wound. They tend to bleed excessively. Your son will be fine with a few day's rest. He should have no more than a headache and the doctor left some powders to help with that." She put her arms around the rotund woman and hugged her.

256

"All I cud see was losin' da boy so soon after I jus' got 'em back." She leaned into The Mrs. and let go a huge breath. They turned and walked back into the house.

Ruby stood alone on the porch holding the squirming child and watched the coach disappear up the road as Laurence drove the doctor back to his home.

She remained for some time until the baby became too heavy, then sat in a chair another hour as the sky darkened and the air cooled.

***

At breakfast the following morning, Bea sat at the table with the baby rather than attending in the kitchen with Cleona. Carson smiled to her, "How's your beau this morning? Have you seen him?"

Bea bounced the child in her lap and offered a halfhearted smile. She said nothing. Carson spoke to Bonnie, "They said Brighton is all right, didn't they?"

Bonnie looked down and took a breath before she spoke, "It's not Brighton I'm worried about. I left Ruby alone last night. After all her anticipation she was devastated when her picnic didn't happen. We all attended to the boy and left her by herself with the baby. She wasn't in her room this morning." She paused and took another breath, "I've been so unthoughtful lately. I'm afraid she might have run off."

A tear ran down Bea's cheek, "I run away from my Papa to be with Ruby and now she's gone off without me." The tears expanded as she tried in vain to hold back her fear.

Carson put his hand on Bea's shoulder, "Don't you worry, little one. I'm sure she didn't leave you. People get upset. Sometimes they need a bit of time to think things over. Ruby is just off sorting everything out. She'll be back when she's ready. Last she'd ever do is leave her little sister."

He hugged the girl, smiled to Bonnie and spoke, "No time for breakfast, I'm late to the paper. I'll ask Laurence if he knows where she is when he drives me. I think he keeps pretty close tabs on Ruby. I don't believe she'd run off without him. I'm sure she just needs to figure it all out."

Carson left the two alone at the table. Bonnie rose and went to Bea's side, "Let me take Landon. You need to be with Brighton. He'll cheer you up until Ruby gets back." She took the baby and smiled, "She'll return before you know it. There's nothing at all to worry about."

Bea handed the boy over, wiped her eyes on her dress sleeve and swallowed before she spoke, "I think Ruby is going to get herself in trouble again, Bonnie." Her voice rose to nearly a squeak, "You ain't gonna make her leave like Papa did, are you? You're not gonna pretend she's dead now, are you?"

Bonnie ran her fingers through Bea's hair, "Listen to me, little one, I truly care about Ruby and there isn't anything she could do that could change that." She held the baby in one arm and hugged Bea with the other, "Ruby's pretty sad right now and it's up to us to let her know we're fond of her." She put her arm back under the baby, "Now you run along and see to Brighton. I suspect he's worried about you too."

On the porch Carson, pulled his new watch to check the time as he waited for the carriage to come around. He now rode separately from Richard II. As a writer, his hours were far less intense than those of the editor. He'd become a regular contributor to the Free Press with stories about "Horn of the West". Several fan letters came to the paper so II found it appropriate to give him his own desk.

The carriage stopped in front of the house and Carson walked down the porch steps, opened the door and entered. Ruby sat across from him. He looked at her in wonder as he knocked on the cabin to let Laurence know he was settled. The coach lurched forward.

They rode in silence, each waiting for the other to begin.

33

"Charley!" Gonto sat across the table from Sir, II and Carson. "Set 'em up again and hurry it up. We don't have long before the train."

The bartender poured four beers in large glasses and the red haired waitress placed each on a tray.

"Charley, bring two more. I want you and Persy to join us for a toast to bid these two adieu." As the waitress approached, II stood, pulled another chair and placed it next to Leak.

Gonto slid his chair back and as the woman sat the tray on the table he pulled her into his lap. "We only need one extra chair at this table, boss."

The woman giggled as Charley crossed the room with two more glasses. "Member, Leak, ya' break it, ya' buy it." Persy flipped a hand at the bartender as he sat.

"I think I already paid for this one, bucco." And he kissed her neck.

Sir cleared his throat to draw attention, "I'd like to make a toast to my two favorite reporters." He raised his glass, "May your notebooks stay dry, your pencils stay sharp and your reports sell newspapers."

Everyone at the table tapped glasses together and downed their beers. Leak released a huge burp causing Persy to wriggle in his lap. "Quick, barkeep, get me another beer. I don't want this to end."

"Easy lad, we got a innocent boyo sittin' here. Yer gonna frighten' 'em." With that the waitress attempted to stand but was immediately pulled back. Carson shook his head as II slapped him on the back.

Charley stood, "Ya boys need to get goin'. Ya miss da train an' ya jus might miss dis here war. Ya need ta get some stories back afore dim rebels get chased to da hills with der tails twix der legs."

Sir spoke, "Charley, let's all hope it will be that quick. I'm afraid there are some very angry and determined people down there. When folks have a lot to lose they tend to sacrifice quite a bit."

As the group rose and moved toward the door, the bartender questioned Sir, "Ya ain't sayin' ya agree wit' dim crazy rebels?"

"Oh, dear no. I'm just saying these two may be in for much more than what many people expect." He stopped and turned to

Leak and Carson, "We've kept the two of you from combat, I'd say an extremely good investment, but I caution you both. It might not be easy and it might not be safe. Please," he smiled as he continued, "for the sake of this paper's expenditure, come home whole and healthy." With that he shook both their hands.

II stepped out to the sidewalk raised a hand, then whistled for the carriage. When he turned back he said, "I'll accompany them to the station, father."

Charley slapped Leak on the back as he stepped through the door, "You'd better get back 'ere soon, bucco, yer my bread 'n butter. I'll like to go broke iffin you ain't here drinkin'." He turned to Carson, "Yer a healthy young buck, be sure to watch out fer dis here old man." They shook hands and Carson nodded.

"The carriage is here, time to go." II opened the door and held it, waiting.

Without warning, Leak turned, rushed back into the bar, grabbed Persy, bent her back and kissed her long and hard. "That's so you won't forget me, Red." He lifted her upright and gave her a quick slap on the rear before he turned and walked out the door.

***

The sentiment on the train south was exuberant. The soldiers acted as though they were going to a celebration rather than war. Most of the first wave of volunteers was sure the battle would be swift and complete and there would be little resistance from the loose band of rebels who had somehow taken Fort Sumter.

Despite the festivities, Gonto somehow fell asleep leaving Carson the lone reporter among hundreds of soldiers preparing for battle. Feeling rather isolated, he pulled his notebook and began to record the experience as he had each day for the past several years.

After he tired of documenting the merriment of the troops, he peeled a piece of paper from the book and began to fulfill a promise to young Landon. The boy was now six years old and had become extremely close to Carson. He wanted to be a reporter as well and worked diligently to learn how to read and write. Carson promised to correspond with the boy at least once a week and the boy promised to "report" what was happening with everyone at Arrow House.

34

Six months had passed and the war wasn't going well. All available young men were conscripted to fight the deepening conflict. Looking for leverage over other correspondents, Leak requested the Free Press pay another government stipend to have their best photographer exempted from combat. Douglas Murphy then joined Carson and Leak as November winds began to freeze New York. Although most correspondents often arrived at the carnage after the fact, it was not uncommon for these three to be on the line as battles raged.

From Washington DC, a new Senator was appointed junior member of the War Department, conversant to high level decisions, troop movements and battle plans.

Charles Flowers took the opportunity to anonymously release information to the Free Press about events other newspapers were not privy to. The conditions he made were that Sir agree to delay articles until each battle began and keep all tactical information and troops movements classified.

Sir agreed, allowing his reporters the rare opportunity to be at the forefront of each confrontation and his paper the opportunity to be first with war news. The three men followed, reported and photographed some of the bloodiest battles over the next two and a half years.   Their information was devoured by a country hungry to know the fate of an entire generation of men. Calahan, Leak and Murphy became synonymous with details about the war and The New York Free Press became the channel for that news throughout the north.

Three years on, the war had become what Sir had feared, devastation to the highest degree. By 1864, body count for the Union Army alone, had reached nearly 150,000.

Articles were telegraphed and photographs mailed or sent by horseback. Sir's pages teemed with actual pictures from the battles and, unlike other papers that offered only vague artist's renderings, the Free Press provided color etchings of gritty scenes taken directly at the front.   The advantage brought massive readership and huge sales.

Richard Flowers Sr. invested a fortune to make The New York Free Press the "world's greatest informer and the high priest of public opinion," and his investments returned great treasure.

***

"June 4, 1864, Doggetts Fork, Virginia

Byline, Calahan

In one of the most ruthless confrontations this reporter has yet seen, the battle of Cold Harbor is still progressing. I am writing this report as I accompany my co-correspondent, Gonto Leak at a field hospital. Leak received a severe wound to his left hand in a mortar blast during the battle. He shall live to write another day but without several left digits which were lost to the explosion.

On May 31, two opposing armies faced one another in warfare. As Union battalions moved into the area, trenched Confederate rebels slaughtered thousands of our brave men. The Union Army bombarded the rebels with mortars to weaken their resolve but rebels persevered. Union forces dug in and fought a mighty battle for three days. The trenches were hot and miserable. Between the lines, thousands of brave Federal Soldiers suffered horribly as southern forces refused their deliverance.

Without food, water or medical assistance, our valiant wounded began to succumb to the tortures of the rebel army.

When Union reinforcements attempted to assist in vanquishing the rabble, a new barrage of confederate artillery went awry and wounded my cohort.

Our third member stayed behind to follow up on a hoped for victory by the Union Army while I brought my wounded comrade behind lines for medical assistance."

***

Carson sat at the end of a cot, waiting for someone to help and writing while Gonto slept under a morphine haze; a crusted bandage bound his hand. Carson recorded the experience of the past days and Gonto's wounds with hope that he could locate a teletype office near this remote outpost.

As he wrote he heard footsteps approaching through the gravel outside the tent. The flap opened and a rotund man in bloodied clothing came in. "What do we have here?" He placed a leather bag next to a tin bowl of water on the floor and proceeded to roll Gonto around, assessing him.

"Hey! Just a moment." Carson knitted his brow in anger. "He's got a wounded hand. No need to roughhouse the man."

The doctor glanced up for a second and went back to work. "Take it easy, I've seen every kind of shit ya' can imagine this past few days. Gotta be sure there isn't something worse than his hand. Don't want to just fix a finger if his guts is drippin' out." The man released a tired giggle.

Carson stared at him. Something felt familiar, something from far away. "I brought him here and I can tell you it's just his hand that needs mending. Please take care of that."

"I'll take care of 'em. He's got one of the most reasonable wounds I seen today. I understand we're gonna be busy as summer bees around here for the next month or so. What with those Union devils acting like they came out to be target practice." He removed the rancid bandage to inspect the extent of the wound. Leak moaned in his stupor as windings pulled away from flesh.

"Easy man! Can't you see he's hurting?"

The round man looked up at Carson, "He's hurting less than a lot of others and if I don't do something quick it might be more than a couple fingers he loses. I got to take care of these minor injuries fast as I can. The real damage is on its way soon as the shootin' is over."

With a wet rag from the bowl on the floor, he washed the finger stumps as Gonto tried to pull away then reached in his bag and found a sack of sulfur. "He's probably gonna shout a bit but this here powder will keep him his hand so we don't have to cut off any more." He looked at Carson again, "Ya' ready? Brace yourself." And he sprinkled the yellow powder on the wound.

Even in his daze, Gonto screamed. The doctor released a high pitched nervous laugh and quickly looked toward Carson. "Calm down Mr. He's fine and I promise you, he won't remember none of this in the morning." He laughed again, "He'll end up thrilled we made him squeal in his sleep instead of havin' his arm cut off like all them other boys that come through here." He giggled again.

Carson's eyes grew wide and his mouth fell open. The doctor became concerned and began to stand. "I ain't makin fun, Mr. It's just a nervous tick I got. Not right for a doctor, I know, but I never been able to help it."

"Dibbins?"   Carson stood as the doctor backed away. "Dr. Dibbins?"

They looked at each other for a moment and the doctor raised an eyebrow. "Do I know you?"

"Dibbins, it's me, Carson Calahan." He moved forward.

The doctor tried to make sense of what he was saying and prepared to skirt by him and run out of the tent.

"Carson Calahan, from Fort Larned. You saved my life. You sent me and Brighton McGuiness back to New York with three women and a baby. Don't you remember?"

The doctor thought for a moment and he released a huge bubbly giggle. "My God, boy, it really is you. I wouldn't a recognized you at all. You're all growed up." He relaxed, smiled and walked toward Carson with a hand raised. The two clasped and Dibbins nearly lifted Carson's feet from the ground he shook his hand so hard. When they were done he reached up and rustled the boy's hair, "Getting a bit thin up there. I still remember a thick patch of sandy fur." He released another familiar giggle and Carson smiled back at him.

"How'd you get back here? They find out what happened in Kansas?"

The Doctor became serious and spoke in quiet steady terms, "That preacher never got his full brains back. They had me take him to a special home in Kansas City so's he would no more be a distraction to the soldiers. If he's still livin' it's no worry. They were gonna keep him drugged 'n happy in his own little room the remainder of his days."

The doctor proceeded to place fresh bandages on Leak's hand. As he wrapped the cloth he continued, "I come back home and settled into a nice little practice here in Fredericksburg." He rolled his eyes as he tied the ends of the cloth, "Everythin' was just peachy when that damndable Lincoln took over. He started these scare tactics and got the whole country crazy." He shook his head as he stood, "Now I'm livin' in a lousy tent out here in nowhere, working 20 hours a day fixing blowed off arms an' legs and trying to sew guts back in dyin' men. It just ain't right, none of it."

Someone called from outside, "Another group of wounded, Doc. Front an' center."

The doctor shouted, "I'm here. I'm comin'," He hastily shook Carson's hand again as he rushed toward the flap. "You gonna be around a bit longer for yer friend? Maybe we can talk more afor ya' go. Tell me what brought you here without a uniform." A voice called again. "I'm here dammit," and he rushed out of the tent. His voice faded as footsteps led away.

***

Carson was left to keep track of Gonto who was moved to a blanket beneath some trees. More and more mutilated soldiers poured in from the field and space was needed for the seriously wounded. He saw Dibbins in passing but there was never time for words. Nurses occasionally changed the dressing on Leak's hand and administered morphine to keep him quiet. The area became overwhelmed with the stench of the dead and dying. The occasional food was difficult to swallow combined with smells that seemed to pervade the entire world.

Carson joined several men in digging graves for the dead as well as pits for limbs and bandages. During times between the influx of misery, he read from the series of letters written over the past years by young Landon. As he read each letter from the first, he was deeply surprised at the ability and insight the boy had developed in reporting the news from Arrow House. Carson hadn't truly noticed until he read them in sequence, how each letter had become more attentively composed.

***

June 12, 1861
Dear Carson,
Everyone misses you. Momma says you mite come home next month. She says you mite let me go to the newspaper with you again. It was fun to write at a real newspaper desk. Come home soon.
Love,
Landon

December 20, 1861
Dear Carson,
I wish you would be home. Momma is very sad. She cries in her room all night. Bea says I should not worry but I can hear her through the door. Bea let me get in her bed last night because it was so sad. Bea thinks Momma is lonesome for my father since it's almost Christmas and he is dead.
Uncle Charles has been home from Washington. He starts his Senator job next month. Aunt Amanda is sad too. I think she feels bad for Momma. Grandmother says she just needs to take control. Bea says she needs to stop drinking wine.
I hope you get home for Christmas.
Love Landon

February 25, 1862
Dear Carson,
Uncle Charles and Aunt Amanda went to live in Washington last week. Everyone leaves me. First you and now Uncle Charles and Aunt Amanda. Momma cried a lot when they left but Aunt Amanda didn't even say goodbye to her. Grandmother said it was all for the best and Momma stayed in her room for two days and wouldn't let me in.
Come home,
Love,
Landon

September 14, 1862
Dear Carson,
Here is my report.
Today, Brighton McGuiness who works at Arrow House for the Flowers Family in New York asked Miss Bea Trudel in the chapel if she would marry him. She said she would. They plan on having a wedding in June next year.
How's that? Uncle II says he can print it in the paper with my name.
I hope you can get home to go to the wedding.
Love,
Landon

June 14, 1863
Today, Miss Beatrice Trudel and Mr. Brighton McGuiness were wed at Arrow Chapel at the Flowers home in New York. Mrs. McGuiness wore a beautiful white gown and Mr. McGuiness was very dapper, indeed. Though she would have liked Carson

Calahan to stand in for her missing father, he was away reporting the war for the Free Press so Mr. Richard Flowers II did it. The happy couple will reside and work at the Flowers resident as man and wife.

We wish you were here.

Love,

Landon Flowers II

January 29, 1864

Dear Carson,

I have bad news for you. I was at the paper with Grandfather yesterday. It snowed all day and when we left it was getting very deep. Laurence got us home but it was dark. Grandfather and I left the carriage and it drove off. As he stepped on the first stair of the porch, he slipped and fell and hit his head. I tried to lift him and I thought he was dead. I got to the door and yelled until Momma came. She sent me to get more help. I got Cleona and Brighton. By the time we came back, Grandmother and Momma had pulled Grandfather inside on a couch. The doctor was sent for and they said I had to go to the kitchen and eat.

I'm worried. They sent me to the paper today with Uncle Richard and grandfather is still home.

Love,

Landon

February 18, 1864

Dear Carson,

I have more bad news. I'm sorry to tell you that Grandfather contracted pneumonia while injured and it wouldn't be cured and

so he is now in a hospital. He just kept getting worse at home and they said he could maybe get better sooner if he was in a infirmary. Uncle Richard is going to run the newspaper until Grandfather is well and he said I could be his assistant. Momma said she would stay at the hospital with Grandfather so Grandmother can continue to run the house. Uncle Charles sent his love but said the war is taking all of his time so he can't come home. I wish you were here.
I hope this damn war is over soon so everyone can come home.
Love,
Landon

***

As Carson read, several riders approached, dismounted and spread word that the battle at Cold Harbor had concluded. The Union Army had amassed severe losses. Nearly 1,400 northerners were dead at the battleground or dying at Doggetts Fork. Hundreds more casualties were in transit to the field hospital.

Murphy was among those who arrived on foot, pulling a large wheeled cart he'd fashioned to transport his equipment. He had been a week at the front alone with his cameras. When he found Gonto still only minimally healed, he agreed to work with Carson on the burying detail. They dug and buried in three shifts for four days before the influx of wounded and dying began to decline.

***

Dibbins, totally exhausted, finally had a few moments to sit with Carson just before the war reporters were to leave. He looked sideways and stared into the sky as Carson sat across from him and explained his role as a war correspondent.

Finally the doctor spoke, "I hope you don't write about how noble and proper this war is." He slowly turned toward Carson, "I hope I didn't save you in Kansas so you could convince people that this lunatic Lincoln is righteous."

His eyes clouded and his stare glazed over, "The man is a tyrant and a butcher. These are his own people." He waved his arms toward the hundreds of graves surrounding the camp.

Carson sat silent as the doctor continued, "If that murderer is elected again, I simply hope some bold hand puts a dagger through his heart. I would consider that person a savior and a hero." They sat in silence a while, when someone screamed for a doctor's presence.

That evening, Carson joined his cohorts to return north. As they walked away, he glanced over his shoulder at the round, joyless man sitting at a wooden table, face in hands, sobbing.

A short time later, July sun filtered through the leaves as the three men made their way on foot, headed home.

35

They walked to Fredericksburg to issue reports about the Battle. The Union Army, although defeated at Cold Harbor, began to move into the heart of the Confederate homeland and word was that it would be a "total war" confrontation. Sherman was determined to destroy everything from Atlanta to Savannah. All reporters were forbidden access to the new operation and sent home. No one was permitted to report the "scorched earth" campaign.

Carson, Leak and Murphy rested two days in the captured town before making their way toward Washington DC.

August rolled in on waves of summer heat intensified by extreme humidity. Roads were lined with wounded boys and men doing their best to find their way home. Occasionally they found bodies molding in the sun at the edge of a lane where wounds had festered in the heat and men had succumbed. The smell was evident from a hundred yards away.

Survivors covered their faces and hobbled by, unable to do anything, lest they submit to the same fate. The task of clearing the roads was left to townspeople and farmers of the area who were still able. Elders, women and those too young for war, wandered their boroughs digging and filling graves with the newly fallen. The world had surrendered to a numb sense of defeat. Sadness, anger and hatred had passed and the people of northern Virginia seemed resolved to do only what was necessary for survival.

Sweat poured down Gonto's arms until the bandages covering his wound became damp. His hand had begun to throb an hour before and his breathing had become strained. He kept the fact to himself but as his head ached more and more with each step and he began to feel as though he might vomit, he stopped the trio, "My entire arm is burning. It seems to be getting worse. I thought it was just this air but it's getting worse. "

Flies that swarmed them appeared most intense around Gonto's hand.

"We need rest anyway," Murphy looked at his friend and noticed the strain on his face, "This damn heat is taking its toll. Don't want some farmer to come by and bury us if we pass out."

Carson led his friends off the road to a stand of trees. He and Murphy took Gonto's arms and helped him sit in the shade then joined him in the warm grass. "We might need to look at that. Are you up to having it unwrapped?"

Gonto spoke with shallow breath, "It might feel better without the dressing. Let it cool down and get some air to it."

Murphy stopped Carson as Gonto lifted his arm toward him, "It might be best not to remove the bindings until we have something clean to replace them. If we leave it open these flies might start eating their dinner."

As the thought registered, he lowered his arm to his lap and Murphy continued, "It's about two hours till sundown. We might have some breeze by then." He slapped his neck. "We'd be best to travel after dark when it cools. We should be able to get to Woodbridge by tomorrow afternoon."

Gonto placed his right hand on his left forearm and squeezed it. "This keeps throbbing like it is and I might not get all that far."

Mosquitoes had begun to swarm. "My stomach gets any worse and there'll be something else for all these vermin to concentrate on. Maybe if I just rest a bit?"

Carson watched as Gonto closed his eyes. The man already looked like one of the bodies they had passed and he didn't want his friend to die along this road. He was quiet a moment longer, then spoke, "There was a farmhouse across the field a short way back, I might see if they can spare some water and cloth." he paused, "They'll surely have something to clean that hand up."

He stood, "You rest here a bit and watch him, I'll be back before the sun sets." He spoke to Gonto who was already asleep, "We'll get you fixed up enough to get on to Woodbridge and a proper doctor."

Murphy watched from beneath the trees as Carson disappeared in the tall grass heading south and east. In his hands he held the half empty canteen that had been left to help with Gonto's fever. The shade created no divergence from the burning sun.

As Carson walked through the fields, sweat poured from him, but damp clothing couldn't offer any relief since no breeze was there to cool him.

The only movement came from waves of heat that rose up and carried a thick, rancid smell of body odor still blended with the stench that had become too familiar at Doggetts Fork. He believed the reek of death and rot would besiege him the rest of his days.

Before long, he saw the outline of a rooftop on the horizon. It appeared to his right. He realized he'd overcompensated and almost passed east of the house. The sun was still fairly high in the west so if he could get help he would have time to get back to Leak and Murphy before dark.

Carson approached the house from the rear and saw someone in the backyard. As he moved closer he noticed a large floppy hat on a woman working the dirt in the shade of the house. He decided to announce himself so he wouldn't startle her, coming from the fields rather than the approach out front.

He stopped, "Hello! Ma'am. Excuse me."

The woman froze on all fours and stared at him. At another time, he would have thought it humorous to see her there, motionless in the garden, like a startled rabbit. But this was not another time. He was sure she was terrified.

He hoped to calm her, assure her he was not a danger, "I'm sorry Ma'am, sorry to frighten you. I'm a friend. I just need to ask for some help." He stopped and raised his hands, "Might I come closer?"

She leaned up on her knees and said nothing.

Carson took a step forward, hands still in the air, "Ma'am, I truly need your help." He stopped again and they stared at each other in silence. The sun seemed to grow hotter on his face as she knelt there, barely more than a shadow in the shade.

"Ma'am, it's burning up out here, mind if I come closer so we can talk?" With that he took another step forward.

In an instant, the woman reached behind her, picked up a spade and rose to standing with the shovel in both hands. "You get yer Yankee hide out o' here, NOW!"

"I'm no soldier, Ma'am. Honest to God. I'm just trying to find help for a friend." He froze, eye to eye with her. She took a step forward and when she did, her eyes flashed beyond him and she shouted, "Kirkland!"

Carson turned to look when he felt a dull thud on his shoulder. Before he could fully turn back, the shovel made hard contact with the side of his face and everything went dark.

36

The sun had gone down when Murphy awoke. Gonto was still quiet and although a quarter moon lit the night, the air was still thick and hot. Carson had not returned and Murphy worried that something was wrong. He slapped at the swarm of mosquitoes that fed on him. His face and neck were covered in welts that burned when he rubbed salty sweat into them.

He checked Gonto for breath and was relieved to find his chest still rising and falling. He shook the man and called his name. Leak opened his eyes and in the moon's pale glow, looked around. "Where are we?" He whispered with a sandy voice, "Is Carson back?"

Murphy helped the man sit up and leaned him against a tree. "I'm afraid he hasn't returned. I don't know how long it's been but it's a lot longer than it should be."

He reached for Gonto's arm and brushed the bugs away to feel it. "The skin is hot. How's your head and your gut?"

The man sat up on his own and took measure. "My arm and my head are both throbbing bad."

Murphy looked around in the darkness, "I don't think we can wait, we need to get you to a doctor. Can you walk?"

Leak took a quick breath as Murphy helped him stand. "Doesn't look like I have much choice. We'd better move before you have to plant me here."

They started toward the road. "What about Carson? What's he going to think when he gets back and we're gone?"

Murphy tried to see his way and led Gonto by the arm, "He'll know we moved on. If we're not here, he'll find us on the road."

They reached the edge of the field. Leak draped his right arm over Murphy's shoulder and they shuffled north toward help.

***

Carson woke with an aching head. Alarmed, he opened his eyes wide to be certain he wasn't blind. Sun glow from a window confirmed he could still see. He attempted to sit up and discern where he was when he discovered he was lying on a feather bed under a cover but totally naked. Pounding in his head caused his stomach to turn and he dropped back down, squeezed his eyes shut and pressed on his temples. A cloth wrap encircled his head. As he traced the bandage the pulse pounded in his ears. He found a crusted area on the left side of his face and his blood pressure pounded even harder.

He heard the door open and tightened his aching muscles, forced himself up and prepared to protect himself. The woman from the garden entered, "Kirkland, you're awake." She had a pleasant smile on her face as she came forward. "I was getting' powerful worried. I was about to go get Missy Aubrie to come see to ya'."

She approached wearing a long flannel bed gown. Carson relaxed slightly and leaned against the headboard for support. He clenched his fists, both against the pain and to strike if necessary; although he worried he didn't have the strength to deal a proper blow if he should need to. His vision blurred and he found it difficult to focus through the headache.

She sat beside him and smoothed his hair above the bandage. "Those damned Yankees. Had it not been for me you might well be dead."

He tried to remember through confusion. She had attacked him. She'd struck him with a shovel. He swung his arm and pushed her hand away, nearly falling from the bed.

"Kirkland," she shouted, "Ya' need to be still so's them wounds kin heal." She bent down, and kissed Carson on the forehead. "After all I done to clean ya' up, don't dare start bleedin' again all over the good bed clothes." She reached for his hair once more and he cringed, "Sides, ya got to keep quiet so's the Yankees won't figger out yer here. It'll be alright now. I got ya home and everthing's gonna be just fine again."

Carson looked at her as though she was mad, "Ma'am, can you tell me where my clothes are?"

"Kirkland Macgregor! You worry 'bout sech silly things. Ya' bled all over so's I had to scrub 'em out. Got 'em hanging out back to dry off. It ain't like I ain't seen ya nekked afore. You'll have em' back soon's they're dried out. Momma's comin' by tonight an' it wouldn't be proper for ya' to be in yer altagether when she gets here.

The woman rose from the bed and pulled her night gown up and off. It dropped to the floor. "Meantime, I gotta get dressed an' get ya sompthin' to eat."

He watched her as she went to one of three trunks, knelt down and rummaged through for clothing. She was a sturdy woman and seemed about ten years his senior. Carson tried to evaluate her strength as she dressed. She was slender, well-muscled, and looked as though she had given birth a time or two. He gazed at her through his fog and despite the pain and situation he began to imagine being with her and bit his cheek in anger. Dressed, she pulled on a pair of high leather moccasins then took a straw hat from a nail near the door.

She finally spoke, "You rest an' I'll get somethin' from the garden." She smiled, "Sure is good to have ya' home again." Then left and pulled the door behind her.

Carson listened as her steps padded across the floor outside then another door squeaked open and closed with a muffled bang. He pulled the blanket back, moved his legs to the side of the bed and lowered his feet. He braced himself a few moments before attempting to stand. Throbbing increased until he felt he might vomit. Several deep breaths augmented his will and he pushed himself erect. He figured one of the three trunks might contain this "Kirkland's" clothing and although he didn't feel as though he could fight the woman off at this point, He knew he couldn't escape successfully while naked.

He used the wall to steady himself as he made his way to the trunks, reached to pull the lid of one when dizziness dragged him to his knees. He hit with a thud, stopped to listen and when he heard nothing, opened the lid. The trunk was filled with children's clothing, all meticulously folded and stacked conscientiously with a pair of child's shoes centered on top. He lowered the lid and shuffled to the next. As he struggled to open the second he heard the door squeak again then bang shut. Footsteps came toward the room so he scrambled on all fours to return to the bed. There were a few moments of hesitation as he forced himself up, sat back against the headboard again and straightened the blanket. Moments later the door opened and the woman entered carrying a tin plate. "Tomatoes aren't quite ripe but they'll do. Beans is all still flowers. If I knowed ya' was gonna get home I'd a saved some o' the rest of 'em." She sat on the bed and fed Carson slices of pinkish green tomato interspersed with sips of water from a tinny tasting cup.

"Got a surprise for tonight. I'm gonna cook up a right hearty supper for you an' Momma. We'll git ya' up an about soon enough."

Carson ate the tomato slices and his jaw ached with every chew, but he had to have something in his stomach if he were going to escape. He didn't know how long he'd been in this house. He was hungry when he'd gone for help. This could be the next morning or the following day, he wasn't sure.

"Momma's gonna be so happy to have ya' home again' she probly won't even notice what a sight ya' be." She ran the back of her fingers across his cheek, "Poor man, all black 'n blue, such as ya' are."

Carson turned his cheek away from her. Her smile diminished as though he'd slapped her. She bit her top lip, "Don't be that way, now. Ya' know it's been bad for all of us. Ya' can't know how much I been missin' you all this time. I thought I'd die bein' alone. Jus' give us a little time, it's gonna' be jus' like before. You'll see."

Tears welled in her eyes. She placed the plate on the floor, laid her head on him and began to sob.

Carson took a breath to say something but let it out and remained silent. He didn't know if he should confront or comfort the woman crying into his lap. It was apparent she was disturbed and he had no idea what might set her off. He decided to say nothing and hope she would become more complacent. He planned to wait until she slept and find some clothes when he had the strength to slip away. He placed his hand on her shoulder, as she cryed and faded to sleep.

***

Later, she brought his clothing as she'd promised, helped him from the bed and steadied him while he dressed. Although the nausea was gone and he'd regained some ability to focus, his vision was still hazy and he was exhausted.

Now fully dressed, he lay back on the bed with his eyes closed and for the first time, realized how sore his shoulder was as well.

She stood beside him and spoke with a soothing voice, "Kirkland, you'll be better in no time. Ya' just wait n see."

Without thinking he began to correct her, "My name is not..." But he caught himself and his voice trailed off.

Moments later, he looked to see her leaving, "You wait right here," she said, her voice more demanding, then pulled the door behind her and was gone.

Oh Dear God, he thought, *did she hear me?* He closed his eyes again when the outer door squeaked open and slammed shut.

Tonight, he thought, *tonight I'll escape this crazy house,* but despite his concern, he faded to a soft gray sleep for an undetermined amount of time.

He woke again to her standing at the entrance to the room. His every muscle constricted with terror when he saw her there, blood spattered, holding a large butcher's knife and beaming maniacally. His breath seized and he scrambled back against the headboard and part way up the wall.

Her smile all but evaporated. Crazed eyes grew large and confused as she watched his attempt to escape. She rushed forward and his breath failed completely. He rolled sideways, fell from the bed and struck his head again, hard on the floor.

The woman screamed and raced to him. From the floor, he watched her feet approach and heard her fading shriek as he passed out once more.

She dropped the butcher knife in her left hand and the beheaded chicken she had hidden behind her. She sat, grasped Carson and pulled his head to her lap, rubbed his face, smearing it with blood and began to rock back and forth and continued to wail.

***

Carson woke sometime later, still in the woman's lap as she rocked incessantly. Shocked to be alive, he tried to pull away but she held tight, with eyes squeezed shut, and continued to sway back and forth.

He had no idea how long they had been there but light was fading in the window. He heard what seemed a hissing sound emanating from her, over and over. It took several minutes before he realized she was saying something and a few more until he could understand her. A chill clutched his spine when he heard her constant repetition, "Don't die again, don't die again, don't die again..."

He smelled the dead chicken before he saw it. They had obviously been here for several hours. He realized she'd been trying to surprise him, not stab him.

He spoke softly, afraid to startle her. She too opened her eyes and looked directly at him but continued to rock and chant. His head ache was enormous so he lay back and let her continue for what seemed another hour.

Sunlight was nearly gone and still she rocked. Carson had actually dozed for a brief time but woke to what sounded like another voice in the house. The woman continued to sway and chant, unaware.

When the voice didn't repeat he wondered if it had been just ringing in his ears.

He breathed deeply and attempted to evaluate the situation. His headache seemed to have eased a bit and he decided to attempt to sit when someone appeared in the doorway and shouted, "Oh my Dearest Jesus. Rebecca, what have you done?"

An older woman rushed forward, took Carson by the hand and pulled him away from his captor.

Rebecca clutched tight, refused to let go and released a ghastly growl. Carson pushed against her and broke free as she clawed at his legs. The older woman helped him onto the bed and turned toward the younger woman, "Oh Rebecca, my dear Rebecca, Oh Lord, Rebecca." She sat on the floor next to her daughter, took her in her arms and rocked her just as Rebecca had done to Carson, "What have you done?" she sobbed, "What have you done?"

After a few moments she looked to Carson, "Dear man, are you alright? Are you hurt? Tell me she didn't do this." Carson lay silent, and just stared in confusion.

Rebecca finally spoke, "It's Kirkland, Momma, He's come home to me. Kirkland's home again, Momma. He's come back to me 'n Eldon. Did you bring Eldon with ya? "

Momma began to cry aloud, "My baby, my dear baby," rocked Rebecca and held her tight.

The room darkened completely before Momma spoke again. "Let's get you outta here and get some light." She found her way to the door and into the kitchen. Before long the faint light of fire edged the door and Momma returned with a lantern to help Rebecca from the corner where she lay curled in a ball.

"Mr., I got to get my daughter situated and try to explain things to her again. Soon as she's settled I'll come back and see what we need to get ya' right." She helped the younger woman stand and led her from the room, closing the door behind her.

Everything was quiet for a short time while muffled sounds floated through the door. Suddenly, Rebecca screamed, "NO, NO, NO, NO, NO, NO!" And the outside door screeched on its hinges. Footsteps faded and he could hear Momma's voice as it followed into the distance calling for Rebecca to stop and come back.

He decided this was the time to escape and pulled himself to a sitting position. His ears rang and he found himself lightheaded and nauseous again. He had to rest a moment if he were to successfully break away. Minutes passed; he took deep breaths to counter the dizziness. He was about to move his legs to the edge to see if he might be able to stand when he heard footsteps coming across the kitchen, toward the room.

The door swung open and there, with the lantern held low, stood Rebecca. She was filthy and disheveled but she smiled brightly. Illuminated from below, she looked evil and appalling.

Despite her presence, she spoke softly, with compassion, "Oh Kirkland, yer sittin' up. Ya' must be feelin' better. I was so worried my dear." She tilted her head to the side and continued in a kind voice, "I have a surprise for yer dinner. I'm putting it on the fire right now. You jus' sit back and rest some more and I'll come and get ya when it's ready." She stepped out and pulled the door behind her.

He could hear her sing softly as she moved around the kitchen. There was no sound of her Mother and he hoped she had gone for help.

When the smell of something roasting reached him he figured Rebecca would come soon. Since he no longer heard the mother and could not be sure of her assistance, he decided the time to escape was nearly gone, so swung his feet to the floor and tried to stand. Waves of nausea pulsed through him but soon passed. He heard the sound of tin plates and decided he had to go immediately and take his chances in the night.

He lowered himself to his knees and moved on all fours toward the window. His hand came down on something cold, soft and wet. He instantly realized from the smell he had found the dead chicken and he recoiled in disgust. It gave him determination to get away from this mad house and he pulled himself to the window.

He found a latch and opened the hook but the window wouldn't budge. There was clatter coming from the other room so he hit the frame hard to no avail.

The wood seemed swollen from the heat and humidity so he pushed again and the lower corner broke loose. He thought footsteps were coming toward the room and he had no time to return to the bed so he reached up and struck the top of the window frame as hard as he could with the heel of his fist. The window flew open and slammed against the outside of the house.

Carson looked toward the door and through the kitchen noise he could hear footsteps moving away. He took a breath and looked outside. In the darkness he could faintly see the ground below. His heart was beating hard and adrenalin surged. He grabbed the top of the opening and pulled his legs up and out of the window while he sat on the ledge. He could feel and hear every heart beat in his ears and knew he had to go.

He jumped out and his legs collapsed as he hit the ground a few feet below. Scrambling away from the house, he came upon the drive that led away to the road and began to move as fast as he could in the darkness, over crushed gravel. Larger stones tore at his feet but he continued without hesitation.

Stumbling and limping a hundred yards up the drive he heard Rebecca, distant and quiet at first. Her voice began to grow louder, though still muffled by the house. "Kirkland? Kirkland, where are you? No. Kirkland, NO!" The voice became more intense and Carson strained to move even faster on the uneven drive without falling.

When her voice became clear and crisp he knew she'd come outside. It sounded as though she ran around the house searching for him. He continued in haste. He had more than tripled the distance when her voice began to grow sharper and came toward him up the drive. In the dim starlight he could see a line of trees to the right. He stopped running and made his way through the brush toward the stand some 30 feet away. She continued closing the gap as he reached his goal, went to the far side and lay on the ground beneath some bushes behind the trees.

Moments later Rebecca approached, running and shouting, "Kirkland! Where are you?" she demanded "Kirkland, don't you dare leave me agin."

He buried his face in the crook of his arm to quiet his gagging breath so she might not hear. Just as she passed, he heard her fall hard on the ground, taking her wind. She was quiet for only a second and then she screamed at the top of her lungs; screamed as though someone was murdering her. The sounds echoed through the night. He heard her scramble up and continue running toward the road, demanding he return.

Several minutes later she came back, crying and chanting as she walked, "What am I gonna do now? Momma, I'm sorry, I'm so sorry. What am I gonna do now?" Her voice faded as she moved toward the house.

Carson lay still and tried to gather strength, blood pounding in his head. The screaming began again. As it did, Rebecca came closer, running at top speed toward the road. Again, she returned quietly sobbing and chanting.

This went on late into the night until Carson finally fell asleep from exhaustion.

He woke to silence when the sky became a dull gray, just light enough to see his surroundings, he made his was back toward the drive but stopped every few moments to be sure he was alone. When he found the way he rushed forward toward the road.

37

An hour later, as the sun broke full, the temperature began to rise and sweat poured down. The lingering headache combined with hunger, the aching shoulder, his torn feet and the lack of sleep took their toll. Carson decided he could go no further. He dare not stop on the road in case Rebecca had decided to search for him. In the distance was another stand of trees a few hundred feet into the grass. There was shade and a quiet place to rest, away from any eyes on the highway.

As he closed the distance across the field, he noticed movement. He stopped a moment to evaluate. Feeling there may be soldiers waking from a long night he continued. As he approached someone stood and came from behind a tree, "What you want here?" a voice demanded. Carson stopped again. The face of a black man was stoic but determined. Carson couldn't decide if the man was frightened or angry, so he smiled hesitantly and spoke through exhaustion, "I'm just a tired wanderer looking for shade and rest. I didn't mean to startle you."

He stood in the field while the sun beat down and his mouth was suddenly extremely dry. The two men stared off for several moments when another, younger man stood from behind the tree. "Come outta the sun an' have a rest."

The first man spun toward him and spoke sternly, "You crazy boy? We don't know dis place or dese people."

"Look at 'em Joseph he ain't in shape to do us no harm. Let the man get some shade. He cain't hardly stand." He looked back to Carson, "Come sit a spell, dis ol' hay cutter's jus' flappin' his jaw."

The older man retreated behind the trees uttering an unintelligible curse to the younger one.

Carson stepped forward cautiously and into the shade. It wasn't much cooler but it cut the glare in his eyes and allowed the droning headache to ease slightly. He sat in the grass and leaned against a trunk. "I truly thank you for your hospitality," he said softly. The old man snorted and turned his head. "Damn fool gonna have us kilt 'er worse."

The younger man looked toward the older one with derision. He sat next to Carson and offered his hand, "Name's Nathan," he said, "Nathan Grey, though soon's we get to New York I'ma changing' it to Nathan Blue." He chuckled and the old man snorted again. This here's Joseph, my woman's pappy."

"Carson Calahan," he reached for the other man's hand but it was withheld.

"Looks like ya got hit perty bad. Comin' from Cole Harbor? We heard da Rebs beat pants off the Feds, sompthin awful."

Carson spoke, "I was there but not as a soldier. I'm a reporter for the New York Free Press. We tell folks back home in New York how things are. Where are you coming from? You weren't caught in that mess were you?"

Joseph broke in, "You jes min yer business. An' you keep yer trap shut boy. For we all get round up an' put in chains."

The young man jumped to his feet, his hands curled into fists.

Carson rose to his knees between the two, "I'm sorry if I got into your business. If you'd like, I'll move on. I don't want to create any problems."

"Problems? My only problems come from dis ol man." He turned to the man sitting with his back to them, "You got to remember, it's me got us dis far. If it was you we'd been locked up in a burnt cabin, all dead. You give me respect old man an' keep yer own trap shut. We git to New York an' yer out on yer own. I ain't havin' nothing more to do wit' ya."

Carson was exhausted but he didn't want to be a wedge between these travelers so he stood to leave. "I apologize if I've caused a problem. You two relax. I'll move along and I'll leave you to yours. Thank you."

He turned and made his way back toward the road, limping severely. The two men continued to squabble and their voices grew louder. Carson looked back to see them grapple one another to the ground while the same time a young woman sprung from some bushes and rushed toward them.

Feeling responsible, he turned back to the scuffle. The woman pulled on Joseph's shirt, attempting to part the two men to no avail.

When Carson stepped up to intervene she backed off in fear and the two men, seeing him, stopped wrestling immediately.

The old man rose to his knees and spoke in anger, "Now see? Now ya got my daughter caught, too. At's what I been tellin' ya. Ya gonna git us all kilt. Dammit boy!"

Carson looked at the young woman. She stood in shock, as though she faced a firing squad. Her arms were bent with elbows back positioned as though she couldn't decide whether to fight or run. She looked from Nathan to Carson to her father and back.

Exhaustion overcame him and Carson fell to the ground next to Nathan. He laughed gently, "I'm hardly able to walk. I'm certainly not about to 'catch' anyone. Frankly, I think you've caught me, instead."

The three all stopped and stared at the broken man lying there laughing. The old man slowly shook his head. Nathan smiled and put his arm around his wife. "I think we alright for a time."

Moments later all four sat in the shade beneath the trees and tried to sleep.

When Carson woke the sun was going down. He looked at his companions and decided to leave them quietly. As he struggled to his feet, Nathan woke as well. He stood and helped Carson up. "Ya doesn't ha' to leave. Ya kin stay an' travel with us come nightfall. Moon's gittin bigger ever time. Gittin easier to see, faster goin'.

"Thank you Nathan Blue." He smiled, "When you get to New York find the Free Press and send word to me. Remember, Carson Calahan. Maybe I can help."

"Mr. Calahan, I cain't let you go off like dis. He reached into a bindle and pulled a worn rag, tore it in two and he helped Carson wrap his feet.

"I got some hard tack and dried beans I kin share wi ya. Ya ain't et since mornin. I'm hungry and I knows you gotta be." He broke a chunk of bread and found a handful of beans.

"I know they's hard to eat dry but iffin ys suck em fer a hour or two they get so's ya kin chew 'em.

Carson smiled as memories flooded back. "I think I can do that. I thank you for your hospitality. Much obliged." He took the gifts and turned to leave. As he made his way across the field back to the road he called over his shoulder, "You three be safe and take care of one another and I'll see you in New York." He continued through the weeds to the road north.

38

He came upon the area where he had parted ways with Leak and Murphy and although he didn't expect they would still be there, Carson searched throughout the field, calling them when he came upon the rancid smell of death. He froze with the fear he had left his friend to die. It wasn't hard to locate the body and he approached slowly, expecting the worst.

He followed his nose and broken grass when he found a soldier's hat, then a shirt. A few yards later lay a man with a huge gash in his shoulder covered by a brown, crusted bandage. It appeared as though he had succumbed to the heat and his infection and attempted to escape from the pain. He'd had torn much of his clothing in his fevered madness. It seemed he'd been running when he dropped and died.

Carson sat and cried as the pain of the past two days released and the realization this poor soul was not his friend Gonto.

He looked for something to dig with and bury the man but there was nothing in the field but grass. He made his way to the trees they had sat under two days before. They were leaved and healthy with large branches high above.

He returned to the man and tried to decide what to do. He couldn't imagine pulling the body back to the road, not knowing how it might fare. He eyed the man's boots and wondered if they might fit. He needed to protect his feet if he were to continue and the blanket rags were just not enough. It sickened him to rob the dead but drastic measures were a part of war. He finally pulled the boots off and gagged as he did.

They were near his size but he had to curl his toes a bit to fit.

Finally, with no other alternative, he spent half an hour pulling grass and weeds to cover the body. When he was done, the smell of nature softened the smell of death and he wondered if he would ever be able to smell grass again and not remember this day.

He wasn't one to say words over the dead so he sat until he could no longer endure the odor, stood and continued on.

***

Late the following afternoon Woodbridge came into view. He limped into the town and found the streets filled with broken soldiers. Everything seemed chaos.

He spent the evening searching medical tents, bars and boarding houses in hope of finding Gonto and Murphy. As he left yet another house in a fruitless search, he came upon the telegraph office.

"Why yes sir. There have been messages sent to the New York Free Press. Three since yesterday. The man looked at his records, "Two responses and in fact, I've got a message a sittin' here waitin' for pickup."

"Who is it addressed to? Can I see?" Carson reached toward the record book and the operator swiftly pulled it away and slapped it shut.

"Sorry sir, this here's private. I'm obligated to keep all information unrevealed to anybody but who it's addressed to." He smiled and pointed to a poster on the wall that stated, "Privacy is Paramount".

Carson glanced at the words then continued, "You don't understand, these are my colleagues. We're traveling together as employees of the Free Press. We were separated and I need to find them. There could be information in the messages." His voice raised and with the bandages and bruises he appeared overtly aggitated.

The operator reached under the counter before he spoke, "Look mister. I ain't gonna give you nuthin' so just calm down. I won't be fired 'cause yer bothered. Hell, everbody in this God forsaken town is bothered. Half is shot up an' the rest is crazy. An all of 'em wants somethin'."

Anger replaced the irritation on Carson's face. The man stepped away from the counter with a pistol in his hand. "I tole you to calm down." He began to breathe unevenly, "Get outta my office for I hafta do somethin' we neither want."

Carson's bruised eyes grew wide and he stepped back. His voice broke from exhaustion, "I need to find my friends. I've been looking all day." The pain in his voice diffused the situation and the man returned the gun to its place beneath the counter.

"I tole you, these here messages are private." His voice calmed as well, "Look, the guy is expectin' a message. Jus be patient, take a seat outside an' wait. Yer friend'll pobly be back here afore we shut the door tonight. You'll find 'em then."

Carson reluctantly retreated and sat on the filthy curb. Through the clamor of horses, carriages and foot traffic he waited. His stomach roiled as he smelled some type of roasting meat wafted through the stench of the city. It apparently came from somewhere up the street. He longed to search it out and supplant the dried bread and tasteless beans he had sucked on the road. Even more than hunger, he wanted to lie down and sleep. It had been a night and most of a day since he'd dozed under the trees with the Greys.

"You look a sight, Mr." A voice like soft ringing bells spoke through his haze. He glanced up to see a woman, not more than a girl, standing over him. "Need a warm place for the night? If ya' got a coin 'er two I'll take care of ya'." She smiled and fluttered her lashes. Carson sat and stared. Long brown hair was combed across half her face in an attempt to hide a large scar, apparently from a burn. He noticed her right eye was milky and partially closed. She apparently realized his discovery and her smile became even more forced. "You don't have to look, Mr. I won't even care if ya keep yer eyes closed. If ya come with me we'll have a real good night."

Carson just shook his head, side to side. He was overwhelmed by the wretchedness that had become Virginia over the past four years. He truly felt compassion for the girl standing before him. He was about to get up when the telegraph operator came from the door and shouted, "Tildy, dammit, I told ya not to do yer business in front of my shop."

The girl spun and her hair swirled revealing the extent of the scar. Carson noticed the side of her head was also burned. She was missing an ear and much of her temple hair. She looked back at Carson with fear in her eyes, realized he had seen what she'd tried to hide, then ran off down the street. He quietly watched her disappear into the expanding darkness.

"Damn shame bout that girl." The telegraph man spoke in a whisper. He went silent for a moment, wiped his hands on his pants and turned back toward the door "Hell, everbody's got problems these days," He sighed, "cain't help 'em all."

He looked back to Carson, "I just come out to tell you that I'm lockin' up in a few minutes. Ya might want to find a place for the night and come back in the morning. I'm a tellin' ya', ya' don't want to try to sleep on these streets. Ya' just might not wake up tomorrow. I'll be openin' at seven 'n if yer here ya could pobly find yer friends then."

Carson returned to the last house he had searched and offered to pay a quarter to spend the night on the floor, behind a locked door.

39

Noise rumbled from the streets all night. There were fights and nearly constant shouts that allowed only fitful rest. Once a piercing scream split the darkness and Carson found himself sitting upright, heart pounding and unable to determine where he was. Several moments passed before he remembered and lay back down on the rough plank floor to attempt to fall asleep once more.

He woke to a clock that chimed five times. His body couldn't tolerate the rigid floor any longer so he rose, made his way to the exit where he twisted the lock and unlatched the door. The street was virtually empty. Rabble from the night before apparently found places to light or had passed out. He made his way to the alley beside the building and relieved himself.

He wandered aimlessly searching for some place serving food that might be open at this hour. His stomach was empty and felt queasy. As darkness became translucent and the sun began to breach the horizon, a few bodies joined him on the street.

They were apparently working folk. As he approached a woman he attempted to stop her and inquire about an eatery but she became terrified, side stepped into the street and hurried on without responding.

A block ahead two men shuffled away from him, arms around one another. He picked up his pace to catch them, hoping against hope it might be Gonto and Murphy. As he closed the distance he realized it wasn't. One was filthy, caked in dried blood; the other wore a suit coat and was apparently in charge. As Carson approached they stopped and the man in the suit turned his head to see. "I don't want no trouble, now. No matter who you might be, let me get this man some help. He deserves at least that."

Carson stopped. The speaker sported horn rimmed glasses and a reverend's collar. He was apparently helping a victim to aid.

"No trouble, here." Carson spoke as the man struggled to hold the other up. "In fact, let me help." He went forward and took the injured man's other arm who collapsed as they held on and they dragged him half a block before either spoke. "You look a sight, yourself. If it ain't the war it's the robbers. Which got you?"

Carson smiled weakly, "Neither, it was a crazy woman with a shovel."

The man just looked at him as though he were mad.

After a few moments they came to a white building with a cross above the door. "This here's our church, help me get him in.

We'll get him cleaned up and see that he gets back to walking on his own."

They carried him inside and the Reverend shouted, "Violet, I need you. We got us another devotee."

They laid the man on a cot in the entry as a large woman in a grey gingham dress came through curtains from the back. Violet shook her head as she rushed to the wounded man and knelt down beside him. "Whew!" she exclaimed, and turned her face away, "this man ain't feelin' pain. He's already medicated perty good."

She looked him over, raised his arms and lifted each leg. He offered no assistance since he had evidently passed out. Carson watched as she managed the motionless body with ease and her large bosoms pressed against his filthy clothing. When she was satisfied she had identified his wounds, she pushed her bulk up from the cot. It tipped and groaned from the strain. Despite her size, she was very light on her feet as she disappeared through the curtains then returned a moment later. She held an earthen pot filled with water, knelt down and began to bathe the man's wounds. "Who's this other one, Reverend, where'd you pick him from?"

The Reverend stammered, "I...uh."

"Carson, Ma'am. Carson Calahan. I just offered to help. I was looking for someplace to get a bite when I saw the Reverend, here, look like he needed a hand."

The parson stepped forward, "I apologize, Mr. Calahan?" He reached out, "Kennedy, Reverend Kennedy. I thank you for your assistance." They shook.

As Violet cleaned blood and dirt from the injured man's face, Reverend Kennedy explained. "We used to have a quiet town, a Christian town before the war. It's not at all the same now."

Violet looked up at him as she dunked the rag in the water and squeezed dirt out. "Every morning I go out and search the streets for our brothers who've had an especially bad night." He tipped his head to the man on the cot. "This one ain't seen half what others have. Me an' Violet ain't been able to even save some, but we do what we can."

Violet looked up, "These boys seen some awful things in that war. Lots of 'em ain't quite right. They come back crazy and don't know what to do about it. We help 'em best we can. It's God's work, tryin' to help these boys."

Carson nodded. The two were both to be admired for what they were doing. War apparently hadn't hardened them. He could sense the hope and humanity in the room.

He smiled and tried to swallow but his throat felt like dust. "You wouldn't happen to have any drinking water in the back?" Carson hesitated, "I'm a bit parched."

Kennedy shook his head, "Oh my! I am truly embarrassed Mr. Calahan. You help me bring this man here and I forgot my manners." He turned to the woman, "Violet, kin you take a moment and get this man a cup of water?" He turned to Carson, "You said you were looking for something to eat and it went right past me. Violet, is there any more carrot stew from last night?"

The large woman pushed herself up again, "Still some inna pot. It's cold though, would that do?"

Carson realized how hungry he'd become, "That would be downright considerate, Ma'am. Cold or hot, I would be greatly obliged."

Moments later, Violet continued cleaning the wounds and bruises of the drunk while the men sat at a table and talked. Carson eagerly ate the stew and explained his dilemma at the telegraph office.

"I've not seen your friends that I could tell ya', but the town's filled with people we don't know. Not all are soldiers. Many came here when their farms were taken. We got a passel of people here in need. Keeps me and Violet perty busy tending to wounded bodies and wounded souls."

Carson pulled his watch and wound it, "It's almost time for the telegraph to open. I need to get there before they do in case my friends show up."

Violet, who had been quiet aside from grunts and 'tisks' made as she maneuvered the man to his side to sew up a gash on his shoulder. "Good thing he's as drunk as he is. He won't remember any o' this." When she had him propped against the wall, she looked at Carson, "Since yer friends are keepin' in touch with those in New York and you cain't see the answers, how come ya' don't send one back there yourself and ask where your friends are at?"

Carson froze with a spoon in his mouth. He rolled his eyes and slapped his forehead causing a sudden, sharp pain. He remembered the bandage and patted it. "Violet, you're absolutely right. Why the hell didn't I think of that?" He flushed at his own words and immediately apologized. "Guess the slap was prepay for what I was about to say."

He thanked them for their hospitality and rushed back to the telegraph office some time before the operator arrived.

40

As the telegraph operator walked toward him yawning, Carson greeted him. "I apologize for my attitude yesterday. This morning I bring you business."

The man opened the door and after settling in, took Carson's note and tapped the information onto his key.

Carson went back to the curb to wait for Gonto, Murphy or a response, whichever might come first. By nine o'clock neither Leak nor Murphy had returned to the office but a response to his wire finally came through.

He read it aloud to no one in particular, "Leak at Naples House Woodbridge, stop, Very ill, stop, Murphy wants you there, stop, Can't return until Leak recovers."

Moments later, Carson made his way through rambling masses toward the Naples House, per directions and strange caution from the telegraph operator.

***

He knocked on the dilapidated door to a shabby house that looked as though it had suffered from a battle itself. The door rattled on loose hinges and he feared it might collapse.

The entire building creaked as someone came to answer. A filthy old man dressed in nothing but overalls opened the door and stared through widely separated, jaundiced eyes, sunken deep within sallow, sagging hollows. His wrinkled flesh bristled with white whiskers that dusted his dirty face. He wore a hand carved wooden barrette that held his long gray hair in a bun at the top of his head.

"We don't got no rooms fer ya'. What ya' heard be wrong so's jus go away."

He slammed the door but it didn't latch and slowly opened as he shuffled back inside the hovel.

"Sir?" Carson said softly, "This is Naples House?"

The man turned back to look at him as though he were a trespasser, "I tol ya' we got no rooms here," and reached a bony hand to push the door.

"Wait, I'm not looking to stay, I was told my friends are here. I've come to find them."

The old man squinted from the light and let the door loose. It swung on its own volition until it was all the way open and rattled against the wall. He faced Carson full on and sneered, exposing rotting brown teeth. "You talking 'bout a man with a nasty hand and one haulin' fancy black boxes?"

Carson became animated, "Yes, that's them. I've come for them." He pressed inside the filthy room and was enveloped by the odor of decay. Can you take me to them?"

Ancient yellow eyes grew wide and the man's expression changed from irritation to fear. He backed away, his head began to quiver and he glanced down and to the right with a look of desperation. Still shaking, he spoke nervously, "Don't know. They's gone. Not here."

He wheezed a few times, gathered his wits and shouted, "Get outta my house," and quickly turned to shuffle toward a back room. As he slithered off he growled in a whisper, "Them two owes me two days let fer a room," He paused a moment, looked back and sneered, "an a dollar to have the damned body carted off," then tried to rush away.

Shocked, Carson watched the man escape and shouted, "Wait!" He went deeper into the filth and grabbed the old man by an arm and spun him around to the sound of cracking bones. It was as though the arm might break loose as he pulled the frail man toward him. "What are you talking about? Where are they?" He shouted.

The man pulled his other hand from a pocket of his overalls and pointed a small kitchen knife.

"One's dead and tother done disappeared afore payin' what's owed me. Iffin you don't want to join 'em you best let me be." He tried to pull away and escape.

"Wait a minute," Carson shouted, "You're going nowhere until you tell me what happened here."

The man raised the knife and thrust at Carson's chest. He grabbed the withered hand and squeezed until the blade fell to the floor and bounced away.

"You tell me now or I'll drag your scruffy ass to the street and kick your bones until you talk." He pulled the rickety body forward to the light when the man suddenly broke into a rattled scream, "Murder. Murder. He's got a knife to murder me. Heeelllppp!" He stretched his words out pitifully as he shrieked.

On the board walk, Carson looked around and saw someone nonchalantly glance and continue along.

"Apparently no one gives a damn if you die." He pulled the man close lifting him to his toes, "You're going to tell me what happened to my friends or the law will have to bury what's left of you."

The old man wriggled without hope. When he realized he couldn't escape he said, "Wait. Wait a durn minute. Yer a hurtin' m' arms."

Carson lowered him to his feet, "Tell me where my friends are and I'll let you go back and hide in your sty. Talk now or you'll never talk again."

He scowled for a moment, looked pleadingly to passersby for help and found none. Most turned away, while others never offered a glance. After a long minute, he sneered at those on the street, spit toward the gutter and stopped struggling.

Carson grabbed him by the straps of his overalls, pulled him close and demanded, "I said, tell me where they are!"

The man finally tilted his head in submission and spoke, "OK. OK. I guess they come to town late night an' found light at Mechell's."

"Who's Mechell?" Carson pulled him close again and sour breath made his eyes water. The man continued, "Mechell owns a bar. He sent them folks my way cause one was sick an it was late. I let 'em a room an next morning sent fer the doc. Doc come on to look at 'em, said he was surely bad off.

"T'other one went somewhere an' when he come back he got pissity cause doc wanted to chop a arm off. He said "No Sir you don't." and went out again."

The old man shrugged his shoulders, held out his hands and offered a weak smile, "Was two days ago an' he never come back. Sick guy up an' died."

His expression became harsh again, "Cost me a whole dollar to have 'em hauled off. A dollar o' MY money. I lost two days let an' a dollar o' MY own money on that lot."

Carson's wanted to crush the man into the wall. He took a deep breath and barely able to refrain, pulled him so close their noses touched. He spoke, "Tell me where the body was taken and I'll let you back to your rat hole. If you aren't straight with me, you best believe I'll come find you and I'll have no mercy."

***

"Why yes sir. We received the gentleman this way." The undertaker wore a tall black hat with strings of long greasy hair sneaking from the brim. He smiled his most sincere smile and exposed two missing teeth. Carson imagined the loss was from another meeting with a grieving relative. Red suspenders traced down a white blouse to hold up wool pants, shiny in spots from grease and wear. "I swear to you, he had naught but pants when he arrived at my door." The man looked down and shook his head, "They come that a way often. Lots o' desperate folk around here. Got no qualms to take what they kin get." Carson absently looked down at his boots.

"Have you seen anything of another man? Murphy is his name." He hesitated and continued, "They came to town together and ended at Naples House maybe two nights ago."

The undertaker looked up with a crooked eyebrow. "At's where we got yer friend, here. My boys carted him from there but never said about another." He shook his head and put a hand to his mouth, "Don't say I told ya, but if they was at old man Cory's place, I'd talk ta Mechell. He might know where the man ended. Won't say that's a fact but ya might just find yer friend. Them two are good boys. They take care of the invalids, but they do bring us a lot o' charity business."

Carson turned and rushed from the building. "If ya wanta spend time with yer friend," The undertaker shouted after him, "He'll be put down at night fall. Ya can say a word or two over him then." He turned back to Gonto's corpse and spoke softly to it, "An ya kin maybe pay me a couple dollars to cover cost."

***

It wasn't quite noon but Mechell's tavern was filled with clients. As Carson entered several people became quiet, many began to whisper and several hushed chuckles echoed throughout. Nearly all eyes followed him to the bar.

"New in town?" the bartender questioned. "Ya' come to the right place for what ails ya'." He looked at the bandage still wrapped around Carson's head. "What ya' be havin'?" He smiled a cagey sneer, wiped an empty glass with a filthy towel and placed it on the bar.

"I'm not interested. I'm looking for a friend." The small room became even more hushed except for one voice from someone evidently well on the way for the day. The bartender looked anxious and glanced at the drunk across the room before looking back to Carson who remained still.

"I'm told my friends came in here maybe two nights ago and the owner sent them to Naples House. One had a bandaged hand, the other pulling a cart. Is there someone here that might know about them?"

The drunk in the back slurred something and shook the table where he sat, knocking a glass to the floor, shattering it.

"Dammit Goldrick, I told ya' if you broke any more stuff I'd toss ya' ass outta here." The bartender threw the towel on the floor and came from behind the bar. The drunk tried to stand to defend himself but stumbled into another table and spilled more drinks. Three men jumped up, grabbed him, dragged him to the door and threw him in the street. The bartender followed the four and shouted out after the man, "Ya' keep yer drunken' ass outta my bar till ya' kin pay for what ya' broke. Don't even try to come back till then." He kicked at the air and closed the door. "Damn drunken pissant. If he ever pays up he'll drink from naught but a old tin can. Might cut 'is face off but he won't never break my glass again."

The three came back in, the mood lightened and conversation elevated. The bartender returned to his position, grabbed the towel from the floor and began wiping emptied glasses. "You boys need a fill up? I'll put it on Goddamned Goldrick." They laughed and the youngest one came forward carrying the empties. He looked to be no more than twelve or thirteen and stared at Carson as he set the glasses down next to him.

Carson turned to the bar keep, "So you must be Mechell. Tell me about my friends."

The bar tender pulled a large pitcher from under the counter, filled the three glasses and turned to Carson, "Cain't say as I rightly remember anyone like that. We get new people through here every night. Gets so I don't even notice no more."

The boy juggled the glasses spilling beer down his front as he made his way back to his friends.

"The old man sure remembers you sent them to him. He's telling me that you have more than a passing knowledge of where they might be." He glared at the bartender and waited. Mechell tilted his head back and looked around the room as if searching for help.

"That crazy old man don't know what he's talkin' bout half the time. Old coot's mostly teched."

"Everyone I've talked with seems to think the two of you are up to no good. A lot of busted up people come through here, easy pickings for the right team."

Carson glanced around the room then looked into Mechell's eyes, He spoke quietly, "My friends are well connected and we both know they were here. One is now dead and the other is missing. I intend to find out what happened."

The bartender raised his voice, "Don't you dare come to my bar to give me shit about nothin' ya' got no proof of. I'll ask ya to take yer lies outta here afore I have ya' thrown out in the street same as that damned Goldrick."

Carson reached out before the bartender could consider what had happened, took the man by the collar and pulled him forward. He spoke solemnly, "So are you going to remember or do we find another way to get the truth?"

Mechell moved to reach beneath the counter when Carson dragged him across the top of the bar. Several men jumped from their chairs as Carson bent down and moved in, face to face. He clinched the man's throat, cut off his wind and shouted, "Don't even think about it. You boys stand down while he still has breath to talk."

Mechell looked toward the room and shook his hand rapidly to wave the men off. They backed away but surrounded the two in a wide arc. Carson realized the odds were at least a dozen to one and knew there had to be several guns behind him. He loosened his grip and spoke, "I'm going to put you down now and I'll walk out of here." He lightened his grasp and Mechell gasped for breath.

Carson spoke softly into the man's ear, "I will be back in a bit, with better odds. I expect you to remember about my friends and I expect you'll help me find the one who is missing. He'd better still be breathing. Whatever condition I find him in, you can expect the same."

He squeezed the man's throat again, "Just know this; if his hair is even messed up, I'll show you no mercy. You best be full of information when I return or these could be some of your last breaths. You got that?"

The bartender nodded as Carson released him. He left him lying on the bar then spoke louder with absolute conviction, "Now you tell these boys to back off or some of them are going to die right here, right now."

One man moved forward and Carson spun on him, "If you think the hooch makes you faster, let's give it a try. I guarantee you won't see night fall."

The man backed off.

Carson left.

41

"I'm truly sorry Mr.," The sheriff, an overweight graying man with a large mustache, just sat in his chair as he rolled another smoke, placed it between his lips and struck a match.

"If I was to try and find everybody who comes to this town and disappears, that's all I'd do." He took a deep drag on the overly large roll as burning embers fell to his desk, which explained the numerous burn marks on everything.

"People come and go here and lots of them are pretty messed up. The war has wreaked havoc on more people than you can possibly know. I'm everyday being asked to find someone. Just can't do it all. There's just too many lost souls out there." Carson was visibly annoyed, "What about the bar tender and the old man?"

The sheriff took another deep suck from his cigarette when the seam split and dropped burning tobacco into his lap. He jumped up to brush everything off, stomping the fire out as it hit the floor. "Dammit all!"

When the embers were snuffed, he sat down and began to roll another while he talked. "There's rumors about Mechell and

Corey doing dirty work. Hell, there's rumors about lots of folks in this town. But they're just rumors. If you can find something that proves what you say, that there was bad business instead of just another dying soldier..."

Carson began to correct the man but he went on, "If you can prove something, I'll do what I can to find you justice." He placed the cigarette between his lips, struck another match and lit the small bush of tobacco sticking from the end. It flared up and he dropped the lit match and pulled it from his mouth until the flames faded. The match fell to his desk top, still burning and he slapped it out. The room suddenly reeked of burned hair and paper. He brushed his mustache then returned the cigarette to his lips and inhaled deeply. Before more could be said, he broke into a ripe, hacking cough, and waved Carson away.

"We'll talk again, Sheriff, I promise you that." Carson turned and left the office. He heard the man gagging and gasping for air as he walked up the street.

He wandered for a while attempting to determine his next step when he passed the telegraph office, stopped and turned back to talk with one of the few moral men he'd met in town. He went in.

"Howdy." The operator greeted him, "Didja' find yer friends?" His smile faded as he saw the look on Carson's face. "Guess maybe you did."

Carson stood silent for a moment, then took a breath before he spoke, "One is dead and the other is missing. No one will tell me anything and your sheriff is worthless. I don't know what to do."

"There's a lot of bad around here now a days. Old man Cory and that Mechell were already rotten before the war. They'd steal anythin' they could get their hands on, usually from drunks in the bar. But since this war it's said that lots of people Cory takes in to Naples house don't never come back. Don't seem no one wants to prove it. Most don't care."

Carson shook his head and closed his eyes. "One of my friends died there. The old man said he'd called a doctor but there was nothing that could be done."

The operator shook his head, "The only doctor that works with Cory is his cousin. And he's the undertaker too. The old man and Mechell seem to give 'em plenty of business. Him and Mechell's brother at the pawn."

***

Twenty minutes later Carson stood in the town pawn shop and surveyed Murphy's camera and Gonto's boots. The cart was already missing.

"Old man a town over was killed in fightin'. He had this new-fangled pitcher box. His widder brought it to me 'cause no one knows how to use it." He took the black box after Carson finished studying it and placed it back on a shelf.

"Pitchurs is a big thing comin' up. Iffin ya learn to work it you might could make a lot o' money." He smiled a big forced smile. "I could give ya a deal 'cause I don't think nobody round here might ever want it. The widder woman ain't comin' back, that's probably for certain." He smiled even larger.

"I'll have to think on that a bit. It certainly is curious how it got here."

The man's smile faded a bit before he forced it again.

Carson looked across the shelves, "No. what I'm actually looking for is a good side arm. It seems to be pretty dangerous out there at night, especially when you have no way to protect yourself."

The man perked up again and his smile became a bit more genuine, "I know just what you mean and I have just what you need." He pulled open a large drawer, "Why, we got some great pieces in from down south. Mostly rebel iron," he winked his eye, "they won't be needin' 'em no more, know what I mean?" he smiled an evil grin.

Carson walked from the shop with a heavy handgun in his vest and a pocket full of bullets. The afternoon was hot and muggy and the gun felt awkward and out of place as it bounced against his ribs. He made his way toward Mechell's bar to sort things out.

A block away the young boy from the bar stepped out from the side of a building.

"Mr." he said hesitantly, "I been sent to give ya' some news."

Carson stopped and looked into the boys eyes. He could feel the weight of the revolver drawing his vest down as an equal weight dragged at his heart. He wondered if he could actually shoot the boy let alone the man who may have killed both his friends, but he had to do something.

He looked down the street to the bar, "Don't think you can stop me. You might want to get away from here while you can." He started to walk on when the boy called after him. "No, Mr. It ain't what you think. It's yer friend. Mechell sent me to tell ya bout yer friend."

Carson stopped and turned back, "What about him? Tell me!" and he stepped toward the boy.

"Preacher Kennedy's got em'. Mechell found yer friend an' sent for the preacher. He's at the church gettin' help. He wanted you to know it warn't nothin' to do with him. He jus' sent some of his boys out and found your friend for ya. Said he did it 'cause it was right and cause he's a good man, not like people say."

Carson rushed in the direction of the small church and when he did the boy disappeared back into the alley.

When he arrived at the building adorned with the cross, he knocked and entered. Murphy lay on a cot while Violet hovered over him. She spoke before she looked up, "No need to knock, we're open to everyone."

When she saw who she was talking to, she smiled, "Sir, you must have a saint about you. You entered that den of evil and came back out again. On top o' that, you had this man delivered from their hands."

He walked to her side to see Murphy lying there, bruised and unconscious but still breathing.

42

"July 9, 1864, Woodbridge, Virginia
Byline, Calahan
It saddens this reporter to announce that his cohort throughout the hostilities of the past four years has passed from this world. Gonto Leak, a prize winning reporter for the New York Free Press and a wonderful friend, has died from wounds received at the battle of Cold Harbor. His name has been synonymous with honor and veracity for some twelve years and his dedication to truth and accuracy has given our readership a light within the darkness. Leak recently confronted grave dangers to inform the nation of events that are changing our country. With no apprehension for his own wellbeing he stepped into the agony of battle to report the horrors of this war. Three days ago Mr. Leak succumbed to the consequences of those dangers. He was placed to rest under the eyes of God at the cemetery of Woodbridge Virginia. His burial was attended by many friends and admirers and he will be sorely missed and long remembered.

***

Carson slowly made his way from the telegraph office back toward the church. The obituary seemed the final acknowledgment that he would never see Gonto again. The man had taken him under his wing and taught him to be who he was today.

He'd always remember Gonto, laughing heartily with a beer in his hand. There had been no one else other than the undertaker to see the man buried, however, Carson just couldn't let the world know that his closest friend and confidant had died and been entered into the ground nearly alone.

He slowed as he passed Mechell's and stopped to listen to the grating laughter from the drunks within. Mechell still refused to say where Murphy had been found and he and his cohorts denied any knowledge of even remembering either of his friends. Mechell claimed he had sent his "boys" into the streets to find the wayward Murphy out of the goodness of his heart. They had found him and saved him from certain death in some alley. When he asked none could seem to remember where that alley might have been.

He realized that his hands were clenched so tightly they were beginning to ache, took a breath and moved on. As he came upon the side street that led to the church he looked to the distance toward the sheriff's office. The man had been no help, even when presented with the evidence that Mechell's brother had possession of Murphy's camera equipment and Gonto's clothing. He wondered at how they might all be related in the plunder of strangers to this town. The sheriff had actually threatened Carson with jail and confiscated his pistol when they went to the pawn shop. The cameras and clothing were no longer there. Mechell's brother claimed Carson had been mistaken, there had never been any cameras and Carson had bought only a gun for revenge. The sheriff demanded Carson leave town the moment Murphy was able.

He stepped into the street, still looking toward the office, when a horse and buggy brushed by within inches. The driver didn't say a word, just continued on.

He reached the church and entered. There were three more cots in the front room with debilitated bodies.

Violet looked up, "Thank goodness yer back, I sure could use some help." She continued pulling one of the men over to access his wounds. "Either the reverends gotta stop findin' these boys or he needs to get me some assistance."

Carson stepped to her side, "Another possibility would be for the sheriff to do his job."

Violet laughed loud and looked up at him with a smile, "It would certainly be the day when that man got a backbone."

Carson joined her, rolled the wounded man over and held him while Violet stitched his cuts. When they were done he went to the back to the small room where Murphy was sleeping. Although not yet fully conscious, his friend seemed to be getting stronger. Next to his was another cot, offered to Carson for his ongoing assistance. Violet called from the front, "There's a satchel delivered. I put it on yer bed. Courier brought it when you was out."

Carson picked up and opened the leather pouch. He removed several newspapers from the New York Free Press. A large smile grew on his face as he read the headlines.

"Violet, can you come here for a moment? I need some advice."

***

With Reverend Kennedy and Violet's help, word of the headlines and the papers themselves spread throughout the town like burning tobacco in the sheriff's cigarettes.

Carson stood at the counter of the general store and shouted angrily as he read the paper, "How the hell did this get out? It wasn't supposed to be printed until next week. Damn it to hell, the soldiers won't even be here till tomorrow."

The entire town was alive from the banner. It read,

"Sheriff of Woodbridge, Virginia Arrested as Traitor."

The story went on to name four other members of the town, a bar owner, an undertaker, owner of a way house and the proprietor of a pawn shop, who were found to be in collusion with the sheriff, killing and robbing wounded Union Soldiers as they returned from battle. The article claimed the Federal Government had declared the five to be traitors to the Union and went on to say the five had been apprehended and tried swiftly by a squad of soldiers dispatched from Washington. Each was found guilty, and publicly hanged by the neck until dead.

***

Two days later, as they gently helped Murphy into a buckboard, Carson hugged Violet and Reverend Kennedy, thanked them deeply and wished them both health. He mounted the small wagon and waved as he drove off, past a boarded up bar and the sheriff's office with a large sign stating, "Sheriff Needed".

43

On the road to Washington DC Carson drove and Murphy began to explain what had happened.

"We traveled all day and most of the night to get Gonto help in Woodbridge. Arrived a few hours before sunrise and found the only light on the main street was in that bar; Mechell's."

He adjusted his seat and continued, "I helped Gonto in, explained the circumstances and asked for help. There were only a few people there, two passed out and the third seemed unable to even talk he was so drunk. The barkeep empathized with us and told me about Naples house. He explained the owner had a relative, a doctor, who could help Gonto right away."

He looked at Carson and shook his head, "I thought it was providence, He took me to the house, wakened the old man and helped us inside. Old Mechell actually helped bring my photo gear in. He asked me what I had in the cases. Carson, I should have known things couldn't be that easy."

He turned his head and was silent a moment before he continued, "The old man brewed us some tea then took us to a room in back. He said he would send Mechell for the doctor. That was the last thing I remember."

Murphy began to gasp for air so Carson pulled up, helped him from the wagon so he could grieve Gonto's passing. He cursed the war, the town that should have saved Gonto, then himself for being so blind.

Carson put an arm around the photographer and even though it was the peak heat of the day, he pulled a flask from his coat and they both swallowed hot whiskey to honor Gonto and the Free Press.

Murphy slept for the greater part of the remaining journey as they headed north toward Washington DC. To pass time, Carson read letters that had been delivered to Woodbridge before he left.

***

March 1, 1864
Dear Carson,
Things do not seem to be going well for Grandfather. They will not let me visit him any more at the infirmary. Grandmother goes every day and returns looking very sad. Mother says it will take time for Grandfather to get well and they are doing all they can do to make him better so he can come home. Uncle Richard, (he says I should call him Uncle Richard instead of Uncle II. He says I will understand some day since my name is Landon II), Uncle Richard

is running the newspaper now and he is always very busy. I go with him in the morning sometimes, but Mother says I have to come home at noon. Uncle Richard stops to see Grandfather after work and does not get home until after I am in bed.

He does not talk to me a lot but he gave me a desk to work at and asked one of the new ladies to help me with my writing lessons. I don't see Uncle Richard after we get to the paper because he is so busy but Shannon, the lady, is funny and she knows a lot about writing though she doesn't seem to know as much as you. There's something you should know about her but I'm not supposed to tell you.

I cannot wait until you can come home and help me write again. Mother says you, me and Mr. Leak can be a team.

I miss you,

Landon

May 12, 1864

Carson,

Uncle Charles was here last week. He spent some time with Grandmother and visited Grandfather. He could only stay overnight then he had to go back to Washington.

This morning Uncle Richard said they are sending you and Mr. Leak to another battle and you two are the only reporters who know. I told mother I was worried but she says you will not be harmed because you're a writer and not a soldier, but I could see she was worried too. Uncle Richard told her to come to the city today and he would take her to a special lunch so she would feel better. She left two hours ago and has not returned yet. This was my day to go work at the paper but I had to stay here because of the lunch. I don't think Uncle Richard likes me there. I think he takes me because you did. When he and Mother are together he never says anything to me. I really miss you. Please hurry and come home.

Landon

June 28, 1864

Carson,

Uncle Richard sent word home from the paper that they heard from you and you have been found. He said that you are with Gonto and Mr. Murphy in a town called Woodbridge. He said you are worse than ware but you are all right and will be coming home soon. I am really excited that you are coming back to New York. When you get here are you going to stay? Shannon says that since the war is not over you may have to go report on it again. I hope not. When will you come home? I can't wait.

Love,

Landon

July 5, 1864

Carson,

Mother says they have sent you the information about Grandfather. Everyone is very sad here. Grandmother has been crying since yesterday. Cleona takes her food to her in her room so she does not have to come to the dining table. I went to her room yesterday before bed and she hugged me really hard. I got into bed beside her and she just hugged me and cried. Lots of people have come to the house but only Mother and Uncle Richard talk with them, Grandmother says she is too ill to take visitors. Uncle Richard stayed home for the first time ever today and he and Mother have taken all the visitors in the parlor.

Bea and Brighton and me went for a walk on the grounds but Bea
cried a lot too so I went to the gazebo and sat by myself.
I wish you were here. Come home soon.
Landon.

He had the letters in order, first those from Landon then the

remainder from other members of the family. He found one from

Bonnie dated July 4 and read:

***

Dear Carson,
It is with heartfelt sorrow that I must inform you that Sir Richard
passed from the world this morning. He succumbed to a pleurisy.
The doctors did all they could for more than two months. Since
his accident he continued to decline. Each time it seemed he
would improve, another illness gave him a turn for the worse. I
will leave you with this sadness and tell you all on your return.
Sincerely,
Bonnie

***

Carson froze for several moments as the information

registered. Sir Richard had died! Richard Flowers, the patriarch of

the family and the head of the newspaper had died and he had not been there. He shuffled the remaining letters from the pouch and skimmed through them.

44

A month later, at the station in Washington DC, Carson stood with Charles as Murphy stepped onto the train for New York. With full recovery still ahead, Murphy was sent home. Charles convinced his brother it was in the best interest of the newspaper for Carson to stay in DC to work with him and report events of the upcoming vote. Senator Flowers had become the Washington director for Lincoln's reelection and it was determined that Carson, as respected as he'd become, should be the newspaper's voice to influence the country.

***

"Damn it Carson, I'm providing you with information no one else could even imagine. We need the headlines. I don't give a damn if it's happened yet or even if it's true. You're privy to these actions prior to the events." Charles pointed a large cigar at Carson's face while smoke blossomed just inches from his nose. The smell turned his head.

"I'm not only responsible for this reelection; I'm your boss. When I tell you to write something, I damn well expect you to do it, no questions! Understand?"

Charles shouted and spittle sprayed Carson's cheek with breath that reeked of whiskey and tobacco.

Suddenly the door opened, "Charles, dear. Your intensity is carrying into the parlor. Our guests are becoming concerned." Amanda spoke softly with an embarrassed wisp of a smile, to lighten her request.

He screamed at his wife, "Get the hell out of here. How many times do I have to tell you not to interfere in my business?"

Amanda cowered away from him and quickly pulled the door shut. Suddenly a crystal glass shattered against the wood followed by an even more intense shriek, "If those biddies don't like how I run my house they can get the hell out of here! I don't answer to them"

Carson was in a minor state of shock. He'd known fear on the battlefield as bodies collapsed in gunfire, however, this felt quite different. There he could retreat if necessary, find a safe haven. Here, there was no place to escape. He imagined what it might have been for the wounded to lie in a ditch as riflemen hovered nearby.

Charles spoke, "Have I made myself clear? You write what I say: no more, no less." He grabbed another glass from a tray, filled it and just as quickly drank it.

Carson offered a slight nod and stepped back to gain a bit of space should Charles continue his tantrum.

"Good! Now go write something for the world to see the moment Sherman reaches Atlanta." He turned his back to pour another whiskey. "I want mobs filling the streets to glorify Lincoln on Thursday. They need to believe this war is about to end and Mr. Lincoln's their holy savior." He emptied the contents and again poured another.

"Now get the hell out of my sight...And if my brother hears anything of this conversation or gets the slightest suspicion of your acts, I swear to almighty God, you'll be gone from the paper and I will see you on the front lines with an empty rifle in your miserable hands." He swung back toward Carson and part of his drink sloshed from the glass onto his sleeve. "God damn it!" He shouted, then threw that glass to the floor to join the shattered remains of the other.

Carson hastened through the doorway followed by curses and the sound of glass being kicked across the room.

He approached the parlor where Amanda and her lady friends sat together whispering. When he passed, they all fell silent. Amanda looked up, hands clutched in her lap and offered a smile. She tilted her head to one side as if to apologize. Her friends remained, it seemed, to provide support and they each huddled close for protection.

"I'll be off now, Ma'am. If you need anything…" and his voice trailed away. Feeling unwanted, and a possible hindrance, he bid them farewell and returned to his boarding house to follow the task laid before him.

***

September breezes breathed warmth as he left the telegraph office. His stomach became upset and he wondered what Richard might do if he discovered the information supplied these past weeks was based solely on speculation. If it proved incorrect or even false, where might that leave him? He wandered through evening streets and weighed the possibilities.

Indeed, Charles did possess access to inside intelligence and had manipulated information for the fabricated reports. His advance knowledge had so far come to pass, but it seemed a simple matter of time before things might go awry and all the lies would be discovered.

As he walked, he pondered what his future might while as the sun slowly descended behind the skyline.

In the quiet evening he heard his stomach grumble and became aware of how hungry he was. He pulled his pocket watch and was surprised to find he'd been walking more than an hour and a half. He looked around to see where he'd happened to, and realized it was a place he'd not been before.

The surroundings were rather unsightly. Streets of dirt rather than cobbles, were lined by disheveled buildings of faded grey boards. He glanced around, left then right, and found nothing familiar so turned around and wandered aimlessly in an attempt to discover a way back to the city.

Across the road, a block up, he spied a tavern. The smell of roasted pork drifted on the breeze and beckoned him.

As he approached, he was greeted by the sounds of laughter and joyous singing. Since the evening was growing dark, the lights, the sounds and most importantly the aroma of dinner drew him inside. "A few more moments to myself can't hurt," he thought, "Away from the lies and madness."

He entered the building through a bright red door. Few of the revelers even noticed and the merriment continued without hesitation.

He glanced around, stepped forward and took a seat at the bar.

"Good evening yer honor. What can I do ya' for tonight?" The bartender was a tall, muscular man with a balding head and huge mutton chops surrounding a welcoming smile.

"I'd like a large glass of beer and a hunk of whatever you're serving for dinner."

He nodded, filled a mug from his pitcher and placed the glass on the bar. Carson watched it foam over and grabbed it to catch the waste.

"I'll find what we mighten have left in the back. Drink hearty," even his voice smiled. He turned and walked away.

Carson took a huge breath and held it a moment before he released. As he breathed out, tension escaped and for the first time in years he felt he'd come home. A large gulp of beer softened the edge a bit more. By the third, the glass was nearly empty and the bartender returned with a plate covered by a huge chunk of meat. He placed it on the bar and reached below. The clink of silver rang when a fork dropped in front of him.

"Sorry, we're out o' potatoes but I threw some extra pork on the plate so's you'll get your nickel's worth" He looked at the near empty glass, "Fill 'er up?"

Carson smiled and nodded as he dug into the roast and began to devour it like a starving man. He washed down the pork before it was chewed.

The next beer warmed him, the roast filled him and singing from somewhere in the back offered a comforting peace.

His glass was refilled two more times while the bartender talked with him like an old friend and although it was just small talk, Carson felt at ease in this place.

As they spoke, a couple walked up arm and arm. She sat, back against the bar, on the adjacent stool. The bartender nodded to excuse himself, poured two beers and placed them in front of the pair.

Carson glanced toward the woman and watched as she flipped her hair and laughed. Something familiar drew his attention. Her scent seemed somehow memorable and welcome. He studied her at length until he realized her companion returned his curiosity with an intense annoyance.

Carson nodded and spoke with a slight slur, "Sorry, didn't mean to stare. Just thought I might know the two of you. I'm feeling pretty good here tonight," and he laughed.

The man quickly looked away as though to hide his face when the woman turned toward Carson. They studied one another for a moment in silence.

"Ruby?" Carson asked in shock. The woman's eyes grew large. She looked oddly frightened, jumped from the stool and rushed toward the door.

"Ruby!" he shouted again, and started after her, "Wait, it's me. It's Carson."

A hand grabbed his jacket from behind and pulled him around. He was ready to punch the culprit and follow the woman but he stopped in shock as he realized the bartender had seized him. He glanced around and the woman's companion was nowhere to be seen.

"You need to leave that lady alone, friend." He held tight, "You ain't goin' noplace." He spoke softly, "Trust me, you don't know her an, asides, you ain't paid your bill yet."

Through a beer haze, Carson attempted to figure what had just happened, or if it actually had happened. He was muddled and confused, in an unknown place. He thought he had found a long lost friend but he apparently frightened the person and was now being detained by a bartender. The tavern had quieted with all eyes on him. There was no indication of the woman or her acquaintance any longer. He'd watched her go out the door and no one else had passed since she left. The man had just disappeared.

It was as though the couple had never been there and Carson attempted to determine if it actually was Ruby or just a beer induced dream.

He spoke to the bartender who held him by the coat, "I thought she was an old friend of mine, Ruby. I haven't seen her in over six years. She disappeared back in New York and I let her go."

The bartender released his coat, brushed the wrinkles as though he were a valet, turned Carson back to his stool and helped him sit. Carson looked back in confusion then leaned on the bar. The barkeep went around to his normal spot and filled Carson's glass. "This one's on da house, friend. You look like you need it."

Carson took sip and spoke, "Do you know her? Ruby? I need to talk to her, to make things right for her again."

"Know the woman well my friend. Well enough to know her name ain't Ruby.

She's a sweet girl, grew up round here. Sorry, but she ain't who you think she was."

Carson looked around as the laughter picked back up and someone began to sing again.

"What about the man she was with? Where'd he go?"

The bartender looked at him with a crooked smile and shook his head side to side, "Weren't no man with her. She just come from the back to get another beer. I think you scared hell out o' her somehow."

Carson looked at him and puzzled for a moment. He reached into a pocket, placed two quarters on the bar, took a final sip and stood to leave.

"Wait a second son, that's too much for what you had an the last one was on me."

Carson waved a hand behind his head and stepped outside. The evening breeze was colder now with fall beginning to pass to winter. He took a few steps and pulled his jacket closed.

The bartended removed the plate and empty glass then wiped the bar clean. It looked as though no one had even been there that evening.   He turned to take the dishes away when the door opened and Carson stepped back into the room.

The tall man looked toward him, set his jaw and stiffened, waiting for what might happen next. Carson stepped up to the bar, leaned against it and with his fingers, beckoned the bartender who twisted his head to crack his neck then slowly approached and said firmly, "Yah?"

Carson leaned in and whispered, "Where the hell am I?"

45

Carson walked up the marble steps, through the massive opening and down a series of hallways until he came to a heavy oak door with a white enameled plate. It stated: "Senator Charles Flowers, New York"

He quietly stepped in to the soft buzz of conversations. Charles talked with two men while a woman in a gray felt skirt and high neck white blouse sat beside them and inscribed their words on a pad of paper. Another, a boy, stood as though he were at attention in the corner. The Page patiently waited for any request from the men.

Charles looked up, "It's about damn time you arrived. Who the hell do you think you are coming in here at this hour?"

Carson walked to the desk as the others watched. A slight ache filled him from the night before and he felt as though he'd been the center of too much attention lately. He glanced around and nodded to each pair of eyes as they concentrated on him.

"I apologize, sir. I had an unusual evening yesterday." A slight smile filled his eyes.

"I don't care an nth about your personal life. We are here to elect a president and you account for nothing if you can't attend to your tasks." Charles was beyond his normal unpleasantness. He looked back down at the desk and continued, "Now wipe that lazy smirk from your face and come over here. You'll have to gather information from the transcript for the time you've been absent."

Carson stepped forward and began taking notes. During the remainder of the meeting his mind wandered to the evening past. He was certain he actually had seen Ruby. He'd been a bit foggy but he remembered distinctly the look in her eyes when she saw him. She realized who he was. As he listened and noted arrangements agreed upon for the election, his anticipation grew as he came to realized that he might have Charles' resources to find the girl. He smiled at the realization that Ruby was no longer a 'girl' nor was he the boy that sat across from her in the coach on the way to the newspaper the day she left.

When the meeting ended, Charles spoke to the two men, "Horace, I'm counting on you to further the electorate's knowledge of what a derelict McClellan is. We want everyone to know just what a buffoon he's been during this war." He stopped, took a cigar from a box on the desk, bit off the tip and placed it between his lips. The Page jumped forward and struck a match to light it for him.

"You, Landers, dig deeper into the man's papers. Get more trash from his correspondence. Find who he's written and what he's had to say. I want to assemble everything negative we can muster this final month. I want to bury that man...deep!"

As the men left the room, he pointed his cigar at Carson, "Now you listen to me. I want you to absolutely scathe that man. Concentrate on his failures in the field. You won't have to embellish his ineptitude, the man's an idiot. He nearly lost this country to the rebels and now he wants to run it? An idiot and a jackass. And, dammit," he suddenly shouted, "I want this country to *believe* victory is near. If you can't get that across more clearly I'll have that blotched brother of mine find someone who will. You're not irreplaceable, you know. I don't give a damn if you did bring that woman and her child back from the Indians so my disfigured brother can replace my dead one. Fire must have baked more than his God damned face."

Carson took a breath and waited for the rant to end. When Charles finally sat, the Page served his morning whiskey. He poured it down and handed the glass back to the boy for another.

As Charles sipped his second drink and looked over papers, he spoke, "You have your assignment, take the transcript and draw what you need from it. You're excused.

Carson spoke hesitantly, "Charles, I need to tell you what happened last evening."

The man set his glass down and looked up, "Do you think I might actually give a damn?"

Carson smiled, "You might." He stepped to the front of the desk, "I found myself in a part of town I'd not been before. I stopped into a bar there and as I had dinner, I found Ruby Trudel, the girl who disappeared from Arrow House."

Charles dropped his cigar on the desk and stood up. The Page rushed to brush the burning ashes from the wood. Carson took a step back as Charles pushed the boy away and shouted at him, "You! Get out of here." He looked at the secretary and pointed to the door, "You too, both of you. Out! Now!"

As the door closed behind them Charles glared at Carson, "What did she say? What did that little tramp tell you?"

Carson gazed confused as Charles rose and came around the desk. "Is this blackmail? Is that what you two have planned?" His voice became louder, "What did that bitch say? What do you want, you little pissant?" He grabbed Carson by his lapels.

"I'm a married man with two boys. If you think I won't crush anyone who attempts to harm my family, you have much to learn."

The situation finally registered and Carson shook his head in horror. "What? For the love of God, what the hell have you done?"

Charles looked to the corner of the room, his eyes moved up and down rapidly as he thought. "Did she tell you about Bonnie too?" He let go of the lapels and his shoulders sunk for a moment as he stood in silence.

Carson stepped back, "We didn't talk. She saw me and ran off. I was hoping you might help find her so we could take her home." He stared at the man standing before him, "You knew she was here? And Bonnie? You've been with Bonnie?"

The man became rigid, his fists curled as he looked up, his face scarlet with anger, "I'm a man with great burden." He took a deep breath, "I carry the weight of the entire Flowers family on my shoulders. I also bear the responsibility of quietly running this entire country from behind the scenes. My father imposed this heritage, this liability on me. He demanded I manage the entire obligation after my older brother was disfigured and chose to conceal himself in the pages of the Free Press. My younger brother, jackass that he was, failed at everything he was ever expected to do and died shamelessly at the hands of savages. Then you brought back that ragged bunch of hayseeds and harlots home to try my soul." He turned his back and looked to the wall as he continued, "It wasn't supposed to be just me. We were supposed to share in this burden. Now it's my duty and mine alone. I need these jaunts, no, I deserve these jaunts. For everything I do, for everything I've done, I deserve to have what I need to keep me sane." He pulled his chair around, sat, looked at the wall and continued to talk in a quiet mumble.

Carson picked up the transcripts from the desk and exited.

***

September 30, 1864
byline Carson Callahan
The Battle of Chaffin's Farm
In one of the most heroic and surprising engagements to date, the African Division of the Eighteenth Corps offered their lives to maintain the sanctity of the Union in one of the best performances of the war. After being pinned down by Rebel artillery fire for more than 30 minutes, the Eighteenth Corps charged up the slopes of the heights. A negro soldier, Nathan Grey, who only months ago was an escaped slave, reported the African Division fought hard and many of their soldiers died in an effort to crush the rebels at Chaffin's Farm.

During an hour-long engagement the division suffered casualties but persevered by taking the field and defeating the enemy in their entirety. "The war is nearly ours" said Maj. Gen. Benjamin F. Butler. "The Confederate Army has been overpowered and will soon be vanquished."
President Lincoln sent his regards to the soldiers and spoke of his confidence that the end of this war is imminent with the Union being the victor.

***

Charles became a bit more complacent the following weeks. Although still disposed to effusive outbursts of cursing toward everyone he had contact with, he seemed assured that Carson was not intending blackmail. His security apparently intact, the threats of having Carson fired softened and became less persistent. As the election approached his determination intensified. He seemed not to sleep and indeed, did disappear on several evenings to places unknown, prior to reappearing at his office the next morning in the same clothing.

46

Carson began to frequent the bar where he thought he had recognized Ruby. During the following weeks he became firm friends with Dodd, the bartender; although he mentioned nothing about his interest during the time he spent in the establishment. It seemed many of the clientele were not daily regulars and they appeared to be much better groomed than the neighborhood. He noticed a few who attended more than once a week and their companions were seldom the same women. They always entered from the back or came down the stairs, rather than through the front door. The couples generally stayed to the shadowed corner tables, ate or drank and disappeared the way they came.

"Mighty pleasant place you have here, Dodd." The tall man poured another beer as Carson spoke, "My favorite pub in New York is twice this size and never has this much business. What's your secret?" Carson smiled and winked.

The mutton chops on the big man's face curled with his huge grin, "Just offer these folk a quiet place to have a bite of decent food. It makes them happy, I spose. I give them comfort an' a safe place. That's all most folks want, ya' know. That and a drink now 'n then."

***

A month later on a cold October evening, snow whipped the frayed streets on this end of town and burned Carson's face as he approached Dodd's. The red door shone bright against bleak gray landscape and beckoned him. He pulled it open and was accosted by bright lights, loud laughter and the smells of grease and beer. Carson smiled, loosened his scarf and proceeded to his favorite stool at the bar.

Dodd approached in an instant with his huge smile and booming voice, "Carson, my friend, where've you been? Gettin' perty dark out and we ain't seen you a couple days. Thought you might a gotten tired of the place and gone back to New York."

He was already pouring a beer, "Got some lamb left. Ya almost missed it, but I put a bite or two aside, just in case."

"Bring it on, Dobbs. I'm about to starve to death." He took a great gulp from the glass before he shouted after the retreating bartender, "Couldn't chase me back to New York in this weather."

He watched the big man disappear into the back when something caught his eye. A person in a cashmere coat hugged the shadowy side of the stairs, turned away from him and slipped out the back. It looked quite like Charles so Carson stood to follow until Dobbs appeared with his dinner.

"Where you think you're going? I just got your eats, I thought you were starvin'?

Carson looked over the barkeep's shoulder, "I think I just saw someone I know slip out the back," and began to move forward.

Dobbs sidestepped slightly and spoke softly, "Come an' eat. Don't give no never mind to who you think you saw." He tilted his head toward the bar. Carson took a breath and returned to his stool. Dobbs set the plate down, picked up a fork and waved it in front of Carson's face. "Look at it this way, whoever it was is long gone by now. Besides, it ain't none of your business."

Carson looked at the steaming lamb, breathed the aroma, then took the fork.

"I told you a long time ago, my place has good food, good beer and is a safe place for folks to be. Everybody deserves private time."

He stabbed a hunk of lamb closed his eyes and savored it then took a bite, looked up at the barkeep and said, "Damn, Dobbs, there's no better food in town, at any price." He took another bite, then emptied his beer and placed the glass on the bar with a thud. Dobbs filled it till foam rolled over the lip, "Your gonna need a few more of these to keep that cold out when you go home. Drink up, I'll give ya a couple on the house just because."

With the plate cleaned and another beer in front of him, Carson began to wonder if it had been Charles he'd seen or if he'd fantasized things again. He still wasn't absolutely sure his imagination wasn't being tested by Dobb's beer. After all, there were hundreds of well-to-do men in this town and many of them looked and dressed identically. To get elected to Washington they all had to conform.

He sipped the beer and mused about the secrets this place held.

He was feeling rather warm and it was getting late, so he prepared to leave. As he fumbled around in his pocket to gather some coins, a couple came through the back and went up the darkened stairway. He squinted to see, concluded it was no one he might know, and remembered what Dobbs had said about a safe place for privacy. He averted his gaze from the stairs, found some coins and counted them out on the counter. Half way through, he picked them up to count again. The beer was fulfilling its task. When he was satisfied, he pulled his coat tight, and stepped through the doorway. A razor wind whipped his face and he stopped and nearly turned back.

From within, a scream coursed through the opening, lingered on the wind and chilled his core. He turned, before the door slammed shut and rushed back inside. Everyone in the bar watched in silence as a woman rushed down the stairway screaming. She tripped the last few steps and fell to the bar floor. The man who had accompanied her followed just behind, gaited around her as he lifted a handkerchief to his face and ran to the back door. He left her splayed out and alone and disappeared into the night,

The woman was face down heaving great sobs. Dobbs went to her and helped her to her feet. She said something only he could hear. His eyes grew wide and he waved to one of the regulars who rushed over, covered the woman with a coat and led her out the back. Dobbs leapt up the stairs three at a time and disappeared into the darkness above.

A mournful "Oh dear God." echoed down the stairway and the entire bar seemed to freeze.

A heartbeat later people began to rush in all directions, some toward the front and several out the back. Few seemed confused and just sat, staring toward the stairway. Carson pushed through the crowd and up several steps when Dobbs appeared above in the shadows, with a woman cradled in his arms. Carson rushed to help him carry her down the steps before he realized both Dobbs and the woman were drenched, red with blood.

Carson sat on the floor while Dobbs laid her down to rest in his lap.

Dobbs said, "She's still breathin'. I'll get water and rags so's we kin find out how bad she's hurt." He rushed to the back and left them alone with those few remaining people gathered around to watch. As Carson held the bloody woman in his arms, fear took hold when her breath began to stall. Panic engulfed him and he looked at the empty faces for help.

Her blood continued to run and it wet and warmed his clothing. The sharp, metallic smell surrounded him and he wanted to wretch. He'd experienced it several times, far too many times in his life. He wasn't a stranger to death but this was the first time someone was about to die in his lap.

She was an innocent, not come to kill the enemy nor face her own end. This was desperately different. The woman in his arms had been brutalized. Despite what or who she was, this was wrong, this was horrible.

Dobbs returned with a pan of water and some rags. The few onlookers backed away to allow him access but as he knelt, water sloshed on both Carson and the woman, running down and across the floor mixed with her blood. He set the pan next to her and with a rag, began to wipe the damage from her face.

The front door burst open. All looked to see an old man in nothing but a coat, boots and long underwear standing with a gun in his hand. "What the hell, Dobbs? What's going on here?"

"Don't rightly know sheriff. Found this woman beat pretty bad, upstairs."

"She gonna be alright?"

"Damned if I know. I ain't no doctor." He looked toward the sheriff, "Know if anybody went for him? She's still alive."

"I just heard there was trouble here and come over. Had my pants washed and they was still wet. That's all I know." He turned to the door, "I'll see if I kin get the Doc over here. You know how he is this time of night," and he was gone.

Dobbs dipped the rag in the pan and rinsed thickening blood from her face. Her left cheek looked broken and both eyes were swollen. It seemed to Carson that her nose was out of place. Dobbs placed the warm cloth on her cheek and softly wiped away more blood when she moaned. She tried to move and moaned again. He rinsed the rag and the pan water turned scarlet. Carson swallowed heavily as Dobbs spoke, "Could you kinda turn her around a bit so's I kin look over back of her head to see if there's more cuts?"

Carson lifted her slightly and turned her. She screamed aloud. He loosened his grip and she nearly slipped to the floor before he tightened again. When he did, she screamed once more.

"Easy man. Ya don't want to kill her." They glared at one another for a moment and Dobbs continued to rinse blood from her hair as he looked for wounds.

When she screamed, Carson felt her breathing increase and become steadier. His anxiety slightly lifted. Dobbs soaked the last congealed blood from her face and Carson gently moved matted hair from her forehead. She took a sharp breath and her eyelids opened slightly. Beneath the swollen skin, he believed he felt a suggestion of recognition, and looked intently to distinguish who she might be beneath her battered face. He gazed at her for a moment then turned his attention to Dobbs, who, busy with his task didn't notice the question in his expression. He looked back to the woman and sensed from her glazed eyes that she, too, realized who he was.

"Ruby?" he asked, and her eyes slowly closed as she again released a pained moan. Dobbs ceased his effort, looked at Carson and spoke softly, "Let it be, friend." He offered, "Our charge is to be sure she makes it through this, not dig up her secrets." Carson gazed at him a moment then back to the woman. It was Ruby, he knew it was. A bit older and deeply bruised, but it was her. He could no longer see her eyes but with each passing instant he felt more certain. He wanted to hug her, to hold her near and tell her how sorry he was that they had all let her run away.

The door opened and a blast of cold air accompanied the doctor. Onlookers stepped back even further as this large basket of a man waddled across the floor to where Carson and Dobbs were nursing the broken woman. "What the hayells gone on here? Shit dogs, what one o' you is hurt? Ya's all covered in blood. Sheriff says it's only one."

He dropped his leather bag on the floor. The leather was as scuffed and bruised as Ruby. The large man hiked up his pant legs and nearly fell to his knees, puffing deeply as he hit the floor.

"What the hayell aire ya doing to the poor woman, Don't ya' know ya' ain't sposed to move someone's hurt bad?" He pushed Dobbs backwards and nearly fell on the woman. "You, you do this to her?" and he jabbed Carson in the shoulder three times with his finger.

"Dear lord, Doc. What the hell's wrong with you?" Dobbs pulled himself and stood towering over the round man as he rested on his knees. "She was found upstairs this way. We been trying to keep her alive till you got your fat butt here to do your job. Leave the man alone. You ain't the sheriff."

The doctor looked nearly straight up to see the bartender who was now standing over him, "I don't claim to be no sheriff but I'm tryin' to find what happened here to this woman, and who best to tell me but the one who did it."

"That one's long gone. We think he's one that ran out almost an hour ago." Dobbs looked around, "By the way, what'd you do with the sheriff?"

The doctor looked up and called to the lookers on, "All of you, get here and help get this woman up on the bar so's I kin stand up and check her. I'm about to pass out from bending down here on the floor." He looked at Dobbs, "Get me some clean water and dump these scabs out back for the rats."

Carson slipped out from under when the others lifted Ruby from his lap. The doctor looked like an egg rolling around the floor attempting to grasp a chair so he could leverage his bulk to his feet. He shouted to the back, "Get some bed clothes if ya got some back there. Might as well not cause her too much more pain on this here bar. Sides, it'll keep blood off so's yer customers won't gag evertime they sit here."

Carson stood next to Ruby as they laid her on some towels that appeared from somewhere. He took her hand and she moaned again.

"Get hell away from here. Ya look like the reaper himself. If she sees ya standing there you'll probably scare her to death afore I kin fix her."

Dobbs walked in with a pan in one hand and a bucket in the other, "There's a pump and draining sink in the kitchen. Go clean up and I'll be just behind you."

The doctor looked up at Dobbs, "You sure he didn't do this? I ain't never seen him before. Don't want him runnin' off afore the sheriff gets back."

"He was here with me you old cow. Didn't do nothing but help." Dobbs looked up, "Where is the sheriff anyhow?"

"Said he had snow blowin' in his flap and went to find him some trousers."

Carson moved into the kitchen, pumped the sink full and began to wash. The stove was burning red but he didn't take time to heat the water, he just wanted to get clean. Although it felt just shy of being ice, he took off his scarf and shirt, dipped them in the sink and swished everything around until they were only slightly pink. He drained the sink and pumped again.

Adrenalin from the events and the cold stinging his face had erased all indication of the beer he'd drunk. As he rinsed his shirt one more time he came to a conclusion: It *was* Charles.

47

Carson pushed on through an icy wind that cut through his coat. With each step, dry snow crunched beneath his soiled boots and enhanced the bitterness of the darkened streets.

For nearly three hours the doctor stitched Ruby's face and set her nose. They carried her back to the bloodied bed upstairs where she seemed to be restful. The doctor offered hope she would recover from the beating.

After being washed, his shirt had hung above the stove until it was warm and nearly dry but as soon as he stepped outside the lingering dampness became apparent. His wool scarf around his neck outside the collar of his coat was sure to be frozen solid by the time he reached Pleasant Plains. Despite the wind and snow, every step caused his heart to pound harder with anger and he began to warm from within.

Twenty minutes had passed unnoticed when he reached Church Street. The Flowers house came into view and his pace increased to a near run. At the front walk adrenalin took over and carried him up the steps to the door where he pounded hard with heels of both fists. Still early in the morning, the hammering echoed through the darkened streets and rattled the windows surrounding the door.

He stopped for a moment to hear if someone stirred but there was only silence so he pounded again.

With one last volley his right fist swung through air as the door was pulled open. In front of him stood Charles Flowers, hair mussed, a robe pulled hastily over his shoulders and a mix of fear and anger on his face. When he realized who was thrashing his door the fear dissolved and rage engulfed him.

"What the Hell?" He looked into the house, "It's just Calahan. Take the children to their room and you go back to bed, dear. I'll deal with this. "

Charles turned back to Carson, "What the hell do you think you're doing at this hour. Are you mad, or just drunk?"

Carson pushed the man inside, slammed the door behind him and shouted, "You ask if I'm mad? You truly have the countenance to ask if I'm mad. After what you've done tonight?"

Charles responded with a hushed demand, "Shut your mouth, Calahan. You're in my house. I'll not have your drunken shrieking in my very home." He grabbed the younger man by the shoulder and reached for the door to force his exit, but Carson pulled away, grabbed Charles' right fist and held it up to his own face.

"Look at these knuckles... Look!" He pushed them closer so he could see. "This is nothing to what that poor girl suffered. She nearly died at your hands."

"I told you to hold your tongue you son of a bitch."

Charles pulled free, pushed his assailant to the door, and leveled a punch meant to knock the man unconscious. Carson turned his head at the same instant and the fist cracked fiercely on hardened wood. Charles shouted in pain and grabbed his hand. Carson immediately swung and struck the man's jaw full force, knocking him backwards, to the floor.

He then pulled his foot back to level a kick when there came a scream from the stairway. Amanda stood in terror on the steps so he held the strike but finally turned back to Charles, balanced, and continued the kick to his midsection. Charles heaved hard, gasped for breath and blacked out.

Amanda screamed again, rushed to her husband and pushed Carson back. She fell to her knees, pulled Charles into her lap and rocked him as she sobbed quietly.

"If you knew what kind of man he is you'd not be with him. He has dishonored you and his family. On top of everything, he nearly killed Ruby Trudel tonight."

Amanda looked up through swollen eyes and spoke defiantly, "I know this man. I've always known this man." She placed her forehead against Charles' face, "He's my husband for God's sake. He's given me two boys and there is nothing," She looked back up with certainty, "nothing that will cause me to abandon him."

Carson noticed the boys at the top of the stairs. He took a breath and realized what kind of existence they must have. He spoke more quietly but firm, "Your father told you two to go to bed. Now! There's nothing here to see."

The two rose slowly and ran into the darkness. When Carson heard a door close he returned his attention to Amanda and spoke in an angry hush, "He apparently had a relationship with Bonnie behind your back..."

"Carson, stop!" She demanded, but he continued, "I believe he brought Ruby to Washington to use her. He's been seeing her for some time..."

"Carson!" She looked at him insistently, "I said I know my husband. I know all his strengths and I know, very well, his weaknesses. There is nothing you have to inform me of."

He stepped forward, knelt beside her and lifted Charles' hand, "Did you know this?" He held out the bruised and scuffed knuckles so she could understand. "He tried to kill Ruby tonight. He left her lying in her own blood to die."

He dropped the hand, took Amanda's shoulders and shook her gently, "He tried to kill her, Amanda. Who's going to be next? Another innocent woman, You? Your sons?" He released her and stood over the man lying there. "You don't understand, he holds the same hate his younger brother had. Something has to be done before he does kill someone. He can't be allowed to go on like this."

She laid her husband softly on the floor, stood, and face to face vehemently scorned Carson. "No! It's you who doesn't understand. This man is my husband and the father of my children. He is an essential element in leading this nation; for the sake of the country and the Flowers' legacy." She moved in closer and continued, "I will not let you or that harlot do or say anything to affect his position."

Carson took a step back as she continued, "Charles wanted you ostracized by the family and the newspaper. You were safe with Sir in charge, for some unknown reason he supported you. Just who do you think suggested you as the front line war correspondent?" She stepped closer again, "You were never supposed to return. You were suppose to die like the other one."

She looked toward the door and wrapped herself in her own arms, "Landon was gone but you brought his worthless boy and those vile women back from the frontier. You're the one who threatened this family's heritage."

She turned and looked to her husband on the floor. Her voice became louder, "Now you're threatening to destroy everything I've worked for." She glared back at Carson, "I believe it's time you left Washington. Do you understand me?"

He was dumbfounded as she stared directly into his eyes, "Charles has more influence in this city than you can ever imagine. If we choose, it will be you blamed for attempting to kill that tramp. It will be you charged with her murder next time when she's found dead. If that happens, I will watch as you're hanged in the public square."

Amanda became mordant and Carson's blood chilled as though he were naked in the snowy night wind, "If you take the first train back to New York, I'll allow you to return to the Free Press. Apparently II has some affinity for you as well, though I'll be damned if I understand what that might be. You will keep what you believe about Charles to yourself, now and forever. During this election, we don't need you to drag the Flowers name through the mud." She knelt down to help her husband as he began to cough and regain consciousness.

"He nearly killed Ruby and you want me to quietly sneak away? Pretend it never happened?"

She looked at Carson as she helped Charles to a sitting position.

"As far as that tramp is concerned, she's become too great a complication." Her face was bitter with hatred, "Don't even consider returning her to New York. I won't have her divulge any sordid lies."

Carson looked at the woman as though she were crazy, "If anything happens to that girl both you and your husband will see the inside of a prison cell for the remainder of your wretched lives." He pointed at them, "I don't care who you think you are or what you threaten, I'll do everything I know to destroy you."

Amanda knelt silent for several moments. Her eyes moved erratically as she assessed the situation. Finally she spoke, "She will not return to New York. As far as the family is concerned, Charles will heroically find her living in the streets. He'll restore her health and bestow upon her a proper education in Europe."

Charles coughed several times and rose to one knee. He started to shout but was consumed by another coughing fit, bent forward and hugged his stomach.

"It's done dear." Amanda helped him up and led him to a chair in the entry. "Everything is concluded, Carson will return to New York tomorrow. He understands fully and I've settled all concerns."

She looked at Carson, "Are we in agreement?" He looked blankly at her when she asked again, "Do you agree to my terms or shall Charles and I destroy both you and that tramp?" She helped Charles sit, "I assume your silence to be concurrence. You'll go now and prepare to meet the first available train for New York. Leave today, keep your filthy tongue and I promise the girl will be safe. Say anything or attempt to remain here and she will suffer the consequences. In God's name, I will see to that." She helped her husband stand and led him toward the stairway. As they ascended she turned, "Leave this house now and keep your tongue, Charles has a nation to guide."

***

Dobbs was congenial although distant when Carson stopped to tell him he was leaving. The bar was cleaned and polished and filled with several unfamiliar customers for an early afternoon.

I don't believe you're supposed to be here my friend. Weren't you to be on a train?"

Carson, shocked that Dobbs was already privy to the terms he'd agreed to spoke hesitantly, "I came to see Ruby. To be sure she's alright and let her know that should anything bad befall her to contact me." Carson moved toward the staircase when Dobbs took his arm.

"Don't you worry none, everything is good. And that woman who fell down the stairs yesterday is gonna do jus' fine. They took her to a real hospital this morning." He shook Carson's hand, "It's been good to know you and I hate to see you go but I'll watch for your name in the paper and tell everyone you were my friend." He continued in a muffled tone as he glanced around the room, "Now get the hell outta here for before somethin' bad happens."

***

That evening, the train pulled out of the station driving through a storm blowing up from the south. Bitter temperatures and snow were displaced by a cold, clammy rain. Carson stared out the window at the filthy, gray rail yards of Washington as the train passed through. The last several years welled up within him and he wanted to cry aloud.

48

All but the Mrs. met him at the station. She, still in mourning, seemed to be fading and refused to leave Arrow House. Richard had to physically restrain Landon as he rushed toward the cars before they'd stopped. Carson stepped to the platform and was greeted by Richard and Bonnie, the soon to be Mrs. Richard Flowers. The men shook hands and as Carson turned to hug Bonnie, was nearly knocked over by 11 year old Landon. The youngster's father-to-be gripped his arm and dug a thumb into the flesh, both he and Bonnie shouted in anger as the boy cringed.

"He's extremely headstrong." Richard explained as he pulled Landon back.

Carson implored him, "Let me see this young man. My God you've grown." He stepped forward and shook hands.

"I started to think I'd never see you again, Carson." and the boy hugged him like a bear. Carson stood a moment and smiled with slight embarrassment then looked around and despite the crowds, he reciprocated.

Standing in the rear were Bea and Brighton. He smiled tenderly at her and as soon as Landon released his grip, stepped forward to offer an embrace. As he hugged her he realized she was pregnant. With eyes wide, he reached one hand across and slapped Brighton on the shoulder.

"I'll be. Congratulations Papa."

The concerns he'd suffered for Ruby plagued him again and he hugged her sister tighter. He hoped against hope Ruby might find her station and attain the peace and joy that always seemed to elude her. He nearly whispered to Bea that he'd found her sister but in fear for her, he kept his pledge.

On the drive home, everyone talked at the same time, asking about the war, the election, Charles, Amanda and the boys. Word had proceeded that Carson had become quietly homesick and Amanda insisted Charles release him so he could return to New York. Carson shared what he could and bit his lip several times to prevent saying what he couldn't.

It was decided that Carson should take a few days to settle into Arrow house and reacquaint with family regimen prior to returning to work.

Landon, who now spent all of his week days at the office was thrilled and requested to stay home until the two could return to the newspaper together. He'd been expelled from school again when another teacher complained that the boy constantly focused elsewhere and was an irritation to others. Apparently, he continuously scratched and rubbed the back of his head whenever confronted, that being quite often since the other students mocked both his appearance and his actions. The school reported he was prone to constant outbursts whenever the instructors demanded his obedience, he rubbed his head even more until they demanded he spend each day with his hands firmly planted on his desk.

With few prospects left, Richard assigned a mentor at the newspaper, where the boy could not be expelled. The position had been conveyed to the woman who'd filled Carson's post in his absence since she had come with teaching credentials. Her relationship with the boy was cordial and Landon actually seemed to enjoy the arrangement. He cooperated and was finally beginning to catch up in his studies. It was decided he would complete his schooling at the paper.

Bonnie explained, "He's been a troubled boy. He's been teased unmercifully by the other students because he looks so different. He's quite clever but his only joy seems to be the written word. He's never as relaxed or agreeable as he is when he has a pencil and paper. The Free Press is like a tonic for him and indeed, for us. We offered Shannon the additional position as tutor and it seems to have been profitable all around. The boy is finally coming along."

For the next few days, Landon spoke incessantly of his new instructor.

Upon arrival, Carson was pleased to be reinstated at his original desk. It was near a window for light and just across from all the files. He settled in to his old quarters and began to organize. His personal items had been stored in a box and they were waiting for him next to his desk. The drawers were freshly cleaned but they carried a reminiscence of fragrance and as he arranged everything the way he remembered, he realized some items were missing.

He looked toward the files to see an attractive young woman as she entered several papers. She didn't seem aware of his observations as he watched her bend deeply at the knees and pivot to open the bottom drawer. In doing so her heavy skirt tightened and embraced her. At 25, after being engulfed in carnage nearly his entire adult life, the sight took his breath and he envisioned what she might look like beneath her jacket, her blouse and especially that which was hidden by the floor length wool skirt.

She closed the drawer, stood and turned toward him. When she caught his eyes she offered a wholly objectionable demeanor. He wondered how she could have possibly detected his thoughts. After all, her back had been to him. She spun decisively and walked off with her chin raised harshly.

A hand set upon his shoulder and he turned to see Richard. "There's apparently been quite a few 'suggestions' made to our lady employees since the troops returned." He smiled and winked, "On top of that, many have been displaced. They've had quite a hand in running this paper these past years. Several have written using male pseudonyms. Now, they're being phased out by the men returning to their rightful places. Many of these ladies are quite unhappy."

Richard patted Carson on the shoulder, "I imagine you seem a threat to what she feels she's earned. Let me introduce you. She's very amenable and a wonderful writer. In fact, she's kept your western byline alive while you were away. She is also Landon's tutor."

He smiled at me, "She's sat at your desk these past years so I'm sure she feels a bit put out. "

He proceeded in the direction she'd gone. "Come with me. I'll introduce you. I'm sure you two will hit it off." Carson hesitated a moment, realized he was standing alone, then followed.

***

A short eight months later Carson and Shannon walked arm and arm from the door of the Free Press out to the sidewalk. There was no longer a doorman and they had to make their way around a group of what many now called rabble. The entire city had changed. Everything was drastically different since the President had been assassinated. Mourning had come to an end and armistice was near. Peace accords were signed and thousands of wounded and disabled men returned to the city. The disposition of the nation had changed, especially on the streets of New York which were virtually littered with cast offs; men who had given so much to the effort only to lose their jobs, their homes and their physical essence and ultimately their acceptance. Crime had increased incrementally as troops returned and were abandoned without hope.

As Carson and Shannon walked to the tavern, She handed each beggar they passed a penny. It wasn't much but there were so many and she felt it better than the curses many New Yorkers offered. Carson appreciated the effort and many times had wondered what might his life might have been under different circumstances.

They entered the Rusty Peg and Charley came from behind the bar to greet them, "Hey Boyo, just read your latest." He nodded to Shannon, "Ma'am. Good to see ya' again. It's been a tad. What brings ya' in this afternoon?"

Shannon hugged the ageing barkeep, "As always, Charley, I came to see you." She winked, "Just don't let on to Carson. He can be the jealous kind."

He winked back and led them to a table. "Red!" he shouted and when there was no response he yelled even louder, "Persy. Da Calahans is come to see ya'. Bring da boy with ya' so's dey kin say hi an see how big he's got."

From the back room came a boy with sandy hair, He was somewhat large for a six year old. "Dare's da boyo. Come over an' give yer granda' a hug." The boy ran up to Charley who snatched him up and swung him around through the air. Both laughed cheerfully when Persy entered. "He just ate. You shake him to hard, you'll be wearing his lunch and I ain't gonna clean it up."

As she approached, both Carson and Shannon took turns hugging her.

"Let me have the boy. He needs a woman's touch." Shannon held out her arms and Charley passed the child to her.

Carson spoke to the boy, "Gonto, you get bigger every time I see you," and to Persy, "Good Lord, he looks like just his daddy." Persy offered a somewhat saddened smile.

"Ya gonna have some lunch? Red's got a great stew boilin' in the kitchen."

Carson answered, "Maybe. But first we have some sort of business. My Mrs. insisted we come by for reasons known only to her. I don't know what she has planned but she's been all giggles and whispers the entire morning. It's up to her."

Shannon handed the boy back to Persy and whispered something in her ear. Then to Charley she said through a smile, "You're going to join us today, 'boyo'. Take a seat."

Persy put Gonto down and he immediately started running circles around the table while she went to the bar as the others sat.

"Dat boy is bad as his old man was." He put his arm out and grabbed the child at full run. "Up here in my lap. How many times I tol you? No runnin' in here," then he bit him softly on the ear. The boy wiggled and laughed.

Moments later Persy returned with a bottle of champagne and four glasses. She sat down with them.

"Hey Red, dats one o' my last bottles of the good stuff. What goin' on here?"

She looked at him and handed him the bottle, "Just open it an' mind yer business." He popped the cork and filled the four glasses. Shannon led as they each raised one.

"I'm here to make a toast." Shannon looked around the table, "First, to you Charley, you've been a dear these past years." When he started to drink, Shannon placed her hand over his glass and stopped him, "Patience my friend, I'm not finished." She looked to Persy, "and to you Persy, and Gonto Jr. I don't know how I would have gotten along without your strength to keep me going." Charley started to lift his glass but Shannon kept her hand over it, "Not quite yet Bucco," and to my husband who had the good fortune to come back from the battlefield intact." Charley raised his eyebrows and tilted his head forward for permission to drink. "One more you poor man." She raised her glass high, "and to the new baby Calahan who's going to join us this winter!"

She let go of the bar keep's glass and drank hers down followed by Charley and Persy. Carson sat wide eyed as Persy kissed him on the forehead and Charley demanded, "Drink up boyo, dat ones on da house."

Shannon took Carson's hand as he sat nearly paralyzed, "My love, it's extremely rude not to drink to the new mother, especially when she's having your baby."

He looked around at the three of them, noticed his glass, tipped it up and drained the contents.

A grin grew on his face and he stood from his chair, tipping it over with a clatter. He pulled his wife in the air and swung her in a great circle and kissed her on the mouth.

Charley spoke, "Careful, dat woman is wit chile. You could break somtin."

He put her back on the floor and Shannon turned to the bartender, "Fill them up again. This is a celebration."

49

Landon did all he could to emulate Carson and spent most of his days at his side. The remainder of his time was shared with Shannon at their apartment to learn lessons and write in his journal. Shannon had been obliged to remain away from the newspaper since she was getting large and close to the birth of her child.

Richard explained, "I've kept you on since you're the only one who can seem to educate my stepson without a fight, and, because you're married to one of my lead reporters. However, I can't very well have you traipsing around this office in that condition. It's a distraction to the vitality of the paper."

Landon normally left the apartment for the office at six in the evening to ride home with his stepfather but often created a scene when that time came. To Carson's bother, each time Richard was required to work late or when Landon was too troubled, Shannon offered to let the boy stay with them. It was almost as though Landon had become her son rather than Richard and Bonnie's and

Carson felt a bit jealous at the amount of time the boy had spent with his wife.

Despite the annoyance, the three formed a keen relationship and Shannon, knowing the boy for several years, developed a motherly instinct. She seemed ready to love him as her own and often became agitated at the way Richard and Bonnie barely acknowledged him and treated him as a nuisance rather than their son. It bothered her that they accepted the amount of time he spent away without concern. When Landon spent the fourth day in a row at the Calahan's, Shannon confided in Carson, "I can see Richard's lack of concern. Landon is not his son, but Bonnie is his mother. It seems to me that even though she's found a new husband, she would want to spend more time with her own flesh and blood."

Carson took a breath and released it as quietly as he could. He so wanted to tell his wife the past he shared with Bonnie and the boy, but several years ago he'd sworn to keep their confidence until death to protect them both so they could each maintain the positions they'd come to know.

"We can't understand people's pasts, nor do we know the pain they were raised with. Rather than judge, we need to love our children and offer what we can to help guide Landon as well, so he doesn't become like his father and uncles."

Shannon looked at him and shook her head, "Carson, you constantly imply these are bad men. One a hero of the west, another a leader in Washington and the third a great business man. They've all earned success. I realize Richard wants more time with his wife and I question his actions, but I just don't understand your insinuations."

He looked deep into her eyes and longed to let the truth flow, to release all the secrets, lies and sorrows he held. He sighed again and spoke, "Those men have direction, success and money but are barren in purpose when it comes to others. They see the larger image but miss the foremost details." He looked at Landon, asleep with his head in Shannon's growing lap, brushed black hair back with his hand and spoke cryptically, "This is a boy my mother would have died for," then sat silent.

Shannon couldn't understand. He placed his other hand on her stomach, "I swear, both he and our baby will always know our love."

50

Fall entertained New York once again. Leaves turned spectacular colors, the air began to chill and the smell of winter breezed in from the fields each evening. After Sunday dinner at Arrow House, Landon had assumed what had become his usual practice and returned to the city with the couple. Carson, no longer annoyed by the boy's nearly constant presence, had become content to have him at the apartment to look after Shannon while he worked. She had grown huge in the past month and the doctor suggested a strong possibility of twins. The thought both excited and worried him and he was thankful to have Landon there to assist. In the meantime, the lessons Shannon provided for the boy kept her occupied as well.

Carson's serial about Horn had virtually come to an end during the war. Readers became less enthralled with the "wild west" and refocused on the exploits of the conflict, but since he had been in Washington reporting the election, he no longer covered the battles. With surrender at hand and the fight nearly over, the advent of Lincoln's assassination filled the news. Carson argued to return to Washington and report the event but Richard refused at Charles's insistence. It was agreed he should remain in New York to be near the very pregnant Shannon.

Carson became extremely angry but finally acquiesced when he realized where the request came from. He also welcomed the opportunity to stay with the mother-to-be.

In addition to the arguments, he received a private dispatch from Amanda explaining the significance of his minding his agreements, coupled with implied consequences to Ruby who was now alone in Paris.

He was given Gonto's former domain: crime and punishment. Although it was the gritty atmosphere Leak prospered in, Carson wasn't at all comfortable in New York police stations. He explained to Shannon, "I don't relish interviewing all the crooks and criminals, especially those on the police force."

His position brought him a distorted view of the city and everyone he spoke with. They were all associated with humanity's darker side so his own outlook began to reflect that and caused him anxiety in anticipation of the new baby.

Richard realized that something was amiss despite Carson's constant denial. To end the confusion, Bonnie suggested he speak with Shannon to find if she was aware of a problem.

He didn't see import in talking with his reporter's wives but since Carson refused to discuss what was bothering him and due to Bonnie's constant insistence, he finally agreed to meet with the woman.

The following afternoon he sent a messenger to verify she would welcome him and she quickly agreed.

Two days later, thrilled to find Richard at her door she invited him in and immediately stepped into the kitchen to heat water for tea. She pulled a chair from the table, while he in turn, looked at her with large eyes and insisted she rest and relax.

A short time later, as they sipped, she explained, "I believe Carson is becoming disillusioned by the crime scene. He's beginning to believe everyone in this city is evil and worries for our baby." She got up and offered more tea but he declined and waved her back into her chair.

"I certainly don't want you waiting on me. I've had my fill of tea, dear girl. It's news to me his assignment had become a burden, after all, Leak loved the position. I assumed your husband, as his dearest friend, would feel the same."

He was uncomfortable in her presence and with the information, quickly brought the discussion to an end. He rose to leave, hesitated a moment and spoke with a finger in the air, "A possible story was brought to me this morning. I intended to assign it to Halstaff but it might be a great fit for Carson. It takes place close to your apartment and it should last several months if not longer. He'll be available when your time comes and it will be a rather modern and thrilling experience. Yes, I believe I have the answer."

With that, he bid Shannon a good day and insisted she stay seated as he let himself out.

* * *

The following week, unaware of the discussion, Carson found the light he'd been hoping for. He was assigned to follow the well-known engineer, John Roebling.

Roebling had created huge projects across the country and built some of the greatest bridges known. He had just been charged with designing and building a new suspension to span the East River from Manhattan to Brooklyn and construction was just beginning. Carson was honored to have an opportunity to be on hand an report on such a significant project after wallowing so long in the city's underbelly.

He and John Roebling became quick friends and Carson was enthralled with the program. The two spent the following days reviewing and discussing John's designs and construction methods. Carson's demeanor improved quickly and his free time with Shannon became exceptionally enriched for the both of them.

But as construction surveys began, joy and hope were cut short when a horrible accident crushed Roebling's foot. He quickly succumbed to infection and died from his injury in less than a month. Carson was at the man's death bed and was devastated upon his friend's passing.

To keep the project on track, Washington, John's son and partner in his business took over. At the outset, Washington Roebling proved a condescending, eager upstart that grated on everyone around him. At the funeral he seemed almost joyful about his father's death, pulled Carson aside and announced, "All information about the bridge will be released only through my office. This project now belongs to me and I don't need a meddlesome newspaper man always on my doorstep."

Carson couldn't believe the audacity and left the funeral to escape the arrogance and file his friends obituary.

Carson's attitude began to waver almost immediately. The sudden loss of the man who had become his friend was aggravated by the son's brashness. He became deeply distressed and depression once again surrounded him like a shroud.

It was just 2:30 PM when he walked in a daze past the Rusty Peg. He stopped in the middle of the sidewalk, pondered a moment about the information in his notes and spoke quietly to himself, "Here's one for you, Gonto." He returned to the door, hesitated a moment, shook his head and entered.

Persy stood behind the bar, "Mr. Calahan. My, it's a tad early for ya, ain't it?" She came around to the door and hugged the man. "If I didn't know better, I'd think Gonto put ya up to comin' at this hour. It ain't even closin' time at the paper and it's far past lunch."

He returned her hug, kissed her cheek and stood back to look her over as he buried his sadness, "I now know why Leak was so fond of beer. I'm becoming more like him every day." He paused, "You'd just better watch yourself my dear."

She turned her head and gave him a frown, "Hey mister! And you with a wife at home carryin' yer twins. You better watch it or I'll tell 'er what ya' say." She pushed him along, "Get to yer table and I'll get you somethin' wet."

"Boy, "she shouted to the back. "Come here and say hello to yer uncle." She went to the bar to draw a beer.

Carson sat down as young Gonto dashed from the back, "Hey young man. How have you been?" The boy rushed forward, threw his arms around the man and hugged with all his strength. Carson hugged back and patted him on the head.

As Red brought the beer, Gonto released his grip and stepped back smiling.

Carson asked "Where's the boss? It's not like him to be away."

"He went to the market to get some fish for the meal tonight. Said he don't trust me after last I did it. Says I haven't a nose for good fish." She chuckled, "Personally, I don't think der is any good fish. I'm happy ta leave that stink up to Charley."

Carson was already on his second glass when Charley came through the door with a huge package wrapped in newspaper. He had a severe look on his face and when he saw Carson he threw the fish on the bar and hurried to the table.

Puzzled, Carson put his beer glass down, "Are you OK?" he smiled and continued, "Was the fish market that bad?"

Charley sat beside him and took his shoulders, "Dey been tryin' to find ya." He was stoic, "Landon come to da paper looking for ya, right scared. Its yer Mrs., she got problems."

Persy rushed over wiping her hands on a towel, "What Charley? What happened?"

"Don't know. Richard sent for a doc to go to yer apartment. The boy was too scared to tell. He just said Shannon was bleedin' all over."

Carson jumped from his seat, eyes wide.

"Go, man. Go now." And the bartender pushed him to the door.

"Don't just shove him out, ya old coot. Go with 'em." She hesitated a moment, "On second thought you watch Gonto and take care of the bar. I'll go. She needs a woman with her, not some old man who don't know nothin'."

***

Carson paced while Persy helped the doctor in the bedroom. She'd come out for towels twice and the second time Carson was marshaled to find help from neighbors and when they heard the situation, they all came. An elderly gentleman from 303 fetched a bucket of water while a woman scolded him for being too old and slow. While she waited, she built a fire in the stove to heat what he returned with.

Daylight passed into evening when the Mrs., Bonnie and Bea rushed through the door.

It was the first time the Mrs. had left Arrow House in more than a year. She took immediate charge and began to manage the scene. Someone delivered a basket of food and Bea prepared a meal for the crowd. Bonnie helped in the bedroom as needed and consoled Carson when she could. Time dragged on for what seemed an eternity.

Near 10:00 PM as the clock was striking the hour, Persy called to Bonnie who patted Carson on the arm, leaned in and hugged him before she stood. He rose to follow but she held out a hand to stop him before she entered the room.

Moments later the door opened. Carson stood silently and watched as Bonnie and the Mrs. whispered to one another. The Mrs. approached him, took him by the shoulders and pressed him hard into a chair. He couldn't believe the strength she exhibited. She then knelt before him and spoke directly, face to face.

"Now is not the time to lose strength. Your wife is extremely weak and you have to be here for her. The doctor has tended to her malady but she'll need you're support for her soul. You have to provide for her. She will require your care, now more than ever." She pulled back to look at him, "Do you understand?"

Carson's heart dropped and he wanted to scream but he shook his head, yes. His expression became harsh and his face ashen when Bonnie stepped through the door with a large bundle, wrapped in towels, and rushed past him. He attempted to follow her but the Mrs. held him in the chair.

The doctor emerged and looked around while he wiped his hands on a soiled rag. "I've done everything I can. The rest is up to God." He shook his head, threw the rag on the counter and returned to the room.

51

"It's good to have you back, my boy. How is your wife holding up?" Richard offered his hand as Carson stepped from the elevator.

Carson forced a smile. "She's doing better physically. She's finally come from her bed and spends some time in the living room, sitting in her chair each day. It's been an awful strain on her. The doctor told her he fears she'll never be able to have children now." He shook his head, "She rarely speaks and cries most of the time. Last two nights I've woke alone and found her in her chair weeping."

Richard patted him on the back, "We sent Beatrice to help. I understand that didn't go well."

Carson raised his eyebrows in a pained expression, "She brought her baby. That was something Shannon couldn't abide at this point. It only reminded her of her loss."

Richard placed a hand on Carson's shoulder and led him through the crowded room. As they walked the cacophony quieted and several employees stood to greet him.

"Back to work, all of you." Richard swept his free hand through the air. "Nothing to see here," and to Carson he said in a hush, "Sorry, my boy. They don't understand. They have no manners. Things will be back to normal by day's end. Take my word."

Richard led Carson into his office and motioned for him to close the door. He made himself comfortable in his leather chair, wriggling in to the hollow created by his time there. He lifted the top of a walnut box on his desk and removed a cigar. "Can I offer you one?"

Carson shook his head no.

Richard continued as he clipped the tip of the cigar, "We'd hoped Shannon would be soothed having Bea's little one around. I imagined it would ease her loss."

Carson stepped to the front of the desk and leaned on his fists, "It's not quite that simple, Richard. My wife is overwhelmed with bereavement. Rightly so. Another with a healthy child is not what she needs to heal at this moment."

Richard seemed quietly perturbed as he lit the cigar, shook the match dead and inhaled a deep breath. As he slowly released the acrid smoke he spoke, "I suppose I might have sent Bonnie to watch over her but she hasn't been available as of late. She's been tied up with that one of hers. She has no time for anything but to cater to his difficulties since Shannon's been ailing. That young Landon is a hellacious problem. He certainly is his father's boy." Richard shook his head, glanced down and picked up a note. He paused a moment to read, then spoke absently while still studying the paper in his hand, "Good to see you back. Work will bring distraction." He picked up another page, called into his tube for his secretary and ostensibly dismissed Carson.

***

Over the next several weeks Shannon regained her strength but her outlook seemed to diminish. She refused to go out or allow anyone into the apartment. When deliveries arrived, she demanded they be left in the hallway where they remained until Carson returned in the evening. He worried that their groceries would disappear before he could get home to take them in.

The most awkward situation was her refusal to see Landon. He traveled to the city with his step father on numerous occasions, only to end up at the newspaper when Shannon refused to open the door. Each time Richard became more bothered with the boy and on the seventh instance he called Carson to his office.

"You need to get control of this situation. It's neither good for your wife nor this boy." He glared at Landon who sat in a chair by the corner. "The boy was a problem when Shannon watched him but now, he's become insufferable."

Landon glared through nearly black, angry eyes while he rubbed the back of his head.

Richard continued, "Neither Bonnie nor I can deal with this situation. Each time he is scorned by your wife his insolence increases. He is causing pandemonium at Arrow House."

He took a cigar from the box on the desk, cut the end and lit it. This he time neglected to offer anything to Carson and slammed the box closed. "I hoped this would have been resolved by now. Bonnie is even taken to interviewing for a new governess. I've been charged to contact a woman from Boston on recommendation. It's said she can handle even the most difficult of boys." He frowned at Landon who crossed his arms and looked away.

"This woman," he searched his desk for a paper, "This Emily Whim, comes highly recommended but at an excessive cost. Money I shouldn't have to pay for my brother's son." Landon's anger faded to a pained gaze as Richard continued. Carson couldn't believe what he heard.

"You need to make things right with your wife. You have to bring her back to the fold, and soon. If this situation continues to deteriorate, I will be forced to hire this Whim woman."

Landon stood to speak and Richard shouted at him, "I told you to sit! I don't want a word from you," then he glared at Carson when he stepped toward the boy.

Richard suddenly refocused his wrath. "Stop, right there." He leaned forward on his desk as Landon began to cry. Carson ignored the order and continued to the boy. Richard fell back into his chair, took a forced breath and seemed about to burst into flames.

Carson reached out but Landon pushed him away and ran from the office.

With the cigar between his lips, Richard sneered, "Let him go. He needs to run off steam." He realized the cigar had stopped burning during his tirade so pulled another match and lit it once again.

Carson shook his head, astounded by what he'd just heard.

Richard looked at the cigar as he sparked it, then spoke sternly, "I might have been out of line but he'll be fine by dinner. Always is. Put food in front of that boy and nothing else matters."

He glanced up and continued, "In the meantime, if you can't get your wife sorted out you'll force me to hire this Whim to deal with that boy. If that's the case, I believe I might be encouraged to pay just a bit more and send him to her in Boston." He looked back down at his desk and continued, "There she might be able to improve her chances of breaking the little..." His voice trailed off as Carson proceeded to the door but he continued, "Don't dare go after him. It's a mistake to coddle that boy, he'll believe he can get away with this sort of thing."

As Carson pulled the door behind him, he thought he heard Richard mumble, "You should be damn glad yours died."

***

Shannon sat in her chair, curled into a ball and wept. Her body was stronger but she refused to care for herself. She hadn't bathed in some time and only ate when Carson made a meal for her and then, just enough to fill the emptiness.

Her life had come to a halt and she could realize no hope. Carson was a good man and a wonderful husband but she felt she didn't deserve his time. Losing the babies she had failed him as well as herself, and without worth she offered no value.

She wanted to end the burden, be released from the pain and provide freedom to Carson. So she sat nearly motionless but for the slight rise and fall of her chest from each shallow breath forced upon her. She waited for a divine end to her grief, an end to the constant throbbing of her heart and starvation of her soul. She simply closed her eyes and lingered quietly, awaiting fate to take her.

After a time, she actually felt her breath fade and her pulse weaken. At last her world seemed to ebb. Prepared for the end, she smiled, and patiently waited for release. She didn't need to say goodbye, they would all understand it had been necessary. So she waited.

But through the silence came a distant sharp crack. It drew her back with an intense gasp that caused her heart to hammer and her eyes to spring open.

It came again. Then once more and it became louder each time it repeated. The distant beat filled the room as a pounding thud. It rattled the door until adrenalin pushed through her veins and shook her alive.

She finally realized there was someone bashing against her door and wondered if providence had sent a messenger to help her on her journey. She laughed quietly to think she could will herself to die and so fate had brought assistance. Her end would finally come. She closed her eyes and hoped it would be quick and painless as she waited for the door to burst open and the assailant to proceed.

A voice came to summon her. It was harsh, broken and uneven. The sounds made no sense and she wondered if the envoy might be a guardian angel speaking in a hallowed language.

The pounding continued and the voice started to become intelligible. It called her name and began to plead, beg her to open up and let him in. The broken voice became stronger and more lucid when she realized it was simply someone who was hoarse.

The door continued to rattle and bowed until she thought it might burst. Her heart began to pound harder and she was overcome by fear. She laughed again as tears started once more. She thought, *I was just prepared to die and now the prospect frightens me.*

She rose and walked across the room, thinking, *If my death proves harsh, I might as well embrace it.*

She stood to one side, pulled back the latch and the door flew open. A body plunged in, caught her firmly and pushed her to the floor. She had closed her eyes again as the person grabbed her and nearly crushed her with his arms.

She saw the blood-black darkness of her eyelids. The pounding of her pulse was equally as loud as what she'd heard at the door. Breathing deeply, she lay quiet to let the attacker do his worst.

But he just laid on her and when nothing happened she noticed moisture dampen her chest and wondered if she might be bleeding.

Confused and without pain, she opened her eyes to see a head of black hair upon her chest. It was only then she realized that Landon was on top of her, sobbing with a damaged voice, crying into her night shirt.

She reached out to him and with both arms hugged him even closer. His tension released as completely as his tears. He collapsed against her like a soft, loving babe. Her tenderness and passion bloomed while feelings she believed had died with the twins flooded back and she whispered, "Landon? Landon, dear boy, what have I done?"

He lifted his head, confused. His eyes were haloed in scarlet and still dripped profusely.

Silence seemed to go on forever until he finally found strength to speak, "Shannon, they want to send me away." He sniffed loudly, "Shannon I don't want to be there anymore. They hate me. I want you for my mother. Please!" he implored. "I need you."

52

Shannon slowly overcame her constant depression when Landon moved in as her support, and to continue his education. He kept her occupied and allowed her to focus on someone else.

Richard was thrilled to let the boy live with them saying, "It will be good for Shannon, the boy and my pocketbook."

Carson consented when he arrived home that evening to find Shannon and the boy laughing. He decided not to discuss the young man leaving his family as long as his wife improved.

Although there were still nights of despair, and Carson occasionally woke alone while his wife curled in her chair, softly crying, those events grew fewer and further between.

During that time, it was announced that Amanda would be sent on a three month diplomatic tour of Europe to meet with wives of foreign heads of state in an attempt to gain underlying support for America from those countries. After several years of unrest and the assassination of President Lincoln it was decided a contingent of American women might be able to soften the country's image.

One evening in late November as Carson wrote in his journal, Landon helped Shannon prepare dinner when a rapid tapping at the door distracted them.

Carson closed his notebook and Shannon stepped next to him as she wiped her hands. "Who could that be this late?" But before he could reply, Landon was at the door and pulled it open.

There, hand still knocking on the air, was Bea. She was delightfully excited, rushed to Carson and hugged him while Brighton still stood in the hallway. He nodded to Landon in the doorway.

Carson held Bea at arm's length to ask what was wrong, but before he could speak, Bea cried out, "Ruby, Carson. We've found Ruby." She continued without pause, "Amanda came upon her walking down a street, and you'll never guess where." She took a quick breath and continued before he could respond, "Paris! Paris, France. Amanda passed by and didn't even recognize her but Ruby knew who she was and ran after to say hello. Can you believe it? Amanda and Ruby found each other around the world in Paris, France."

Shannon went to the hallway, took Brighton by the arm and pulled him in the room. She asked, "How in the world..." but was interrupted when Bea continued her monolog.

"The wire says Ruby has been living there for three years. She's a teacher now. After she left she was hired to teach English to French children. Amanda says she now speaks French as well."

Bea barely took a breath to continue, "Oh Carson, Amanda says Ruby is doing fine and sends her regrets that she did such a foolish thing when she ran away. She told Amanda how much she loves me and misses me." Her huge smile remained but tears gleamed in her eyes.

"Ruby said she is going to write me a letter. I'm going to get a letter from Paris, France. Can you believe it? A letter from Ruby!"

Brighton joined Shannon and Landon as Bea broke from Carson and spun around the room, nearly singing, "Ruby is the toast of Paris. My sister lives in France. She's going to send me a letter."

Brighton watched with joy as he spoke softly to Shannon, "She's been like this since we got da wire dis evening. I think Richard got fed up and told us to take the coach and come and tell you folks. I believe he just wanted a bit o' peace for dinner."

Bea took Carson by the hand during one of her circles and when he didn't join in her dance she rolled into his arms again and hugged him.

Shannon turned to Landon, "Do you remember Ruby? I understand you were rather young when she left."

Landon stood quietly a moment, searching his memories, "I can't say that I do, really." He looked at Bea's excitement and then to Shannon, "I know the name, of course, but I don't remember the person, other than from old photos."

She hugged the boy, "It certainly is happy news for Bea."

Brighton stepped forward and Bea turned to him and threw her arms around her husband. "She doesn't even know we're married or that she's an aunt. Oh Brighton, I have so much to tell her. I want to show her our son."

Bea stopped, pulled away and looked at Shannon in horrer, "I'm so sorry Shannon. I...I didn't..."

Shannon moved closer and took her turn at hugging the young woman, "Nothing to be sorry for, dear. You have every right to be excited about your sister and proud of all the wonderful things in your life." She held her tight, "Don't ever begin to feel bad about your wonderful son. I can't tell you how happy I am for you."

Bea's tears overflowed but didn't wash away her smile as she pulled Shannon even closer.

Carson, still by the table, watched the events unfold. A thousand thoughts fought to escape and he struggled to hold each back. Though he displayed a composed smile, turmoil filled him as he cataloged all the lies he held inside. *An English teacher?* He thought, *The girl I taught to read. They couldn't have fabricated something better than that?*

He watched Bea and Brighton and realized that over the years they had both gained so much, their part in the story had become their reality. The only memories they held of their childhoods were horribly traumatic. He couldn't find fault that they buried it all to become who they are today.

He looked to Landon, a misunderstood boy who was, at best, different and a hindrance to his parents without a thread of knowing why. Bonnie refused to even acknowledge the situation. She seemed to have succumbed to her lot in life and he wondered if she hadn't, conveniently, lost sight of her true past as well.

He watched Shannon laugh and discuss Ruby, the only one there, aside from Landon, not remotely aware of their collective past. She accepted the fiction as fact and it tore him apart. The woman was his heart, his foundation. Most of the time he could dismiss things past, but at times like this he was overwhelmed with guilt. It took every ounce of endurance to stop from admitting the lie they were living.

The woman he loved came forward and pulled him into the celebration. He let it all go and joined their delight well into the evening.

***

The letter arrived several weeks later. Bea's anticipation had grown with each day. The entire New York family, Carson and Shannon included, were invited to dinner so Bea could read the tome from her Parisian sister. Bea, who had studied the words enough to memorize them, stood to share the news with everyone.

She looked around the room with a smile and began:

My Dearest Beatrice,
It is with great excitement that I write this letter. I have missed you so much. I sincerely hope you have found it in your heart to forgive my reckless actions all those years ago. I do so apologize for not contacting you sooner, but I was afraid that you would no longer accept me. I have always regretted abandoning you at Arrow House although I did so knowing you were safe and loved by all around you.
I have no other excuse than I was an emotional young girl who needed to develop a direction. It has taken quite some time but I am now able to say I have come upon a comfortable and satisfying routine.

Amanda informs me you have kept me in your heart and are willing to hear from me again so I write this letter.

I must say, it was with complete shock that I passed Amanda here in Paris. She and I have had a wonderful time these past weeks. I will miss her when she continues her voyage. She has asked that you give her regards to Carson and tell him how she and Charles enjoyed his company in Washington. Thank him and let him know that all is well.

I understand congratulations are in order, you are now Mrs. Brighton McGuiness and the two of you have a child. I am so happy for you and so proud of whom you've become. Brighton is certainly a lucky fellow.

I must close. I have classes to attend to. Please thank Mrs. Flowers for all she has done to provide a home for both you and me. Tell her I sincerely apologize for leaving unannounced and for any concerns I may have caused.

Give everyone my love, especially little Landon. I miss you all.

Please, please, my dearest sister, please write back. I don't want to lose you again. I pray someday we will have the opportunity to be together once more.

All my love,

Ruby

The entire family applauded when Bea finished reading and curtsied.

"To Ruby." Richard raised his glass and everyone followed, repeating her name.

In turn, Carson joined and sipped as he studied Richard. He relaxed, satisfied he was alone in the knowledge of events in Washington and the hidden message from Amanda. She had apparently kept her word and he would indeed, keep his.

53

"Carson," Richard shouted to him and waved as he stepped from the lift accompanied by Shannon. "Both of you, come to my office so I can share the news." They made their way through the maze of desks and turmoil in the smoke-filled news room. Reporters yelled to be heard above one another systematically drowning each other's voices. Shannon absorbed it all as they passed though and in her heart, missed the days when she was there and the desks were staffed by women. This scene was a different chaos, but no more than it had been during the war.

"Come in, you two. Close the door behind you." Richard pulled a second chair to the front of his desk and motioned for the two to sit.

"I have something I'd like to discuss with the both of you. Can I get you anything, Shannon?"

She shook her head and glanced at Carson with concern.

"All right, I'll just get to the point." He took his place behind the desk, relit a cigar that had gone out in the ash tray, and continued. "Carson, on top of other duties, you've continued to follow this bridge story for nearly two years now. Am I right?"

Carson nodded.

"Now then, I've decided to remove you from the bridge coverage as well as all your additional responsibilities."

Carson's looked confused and shocked, "Have I done something wrong? I thought you were satisfied with my work. I've reported on both Roebling and his son and taken all other assignments you've given me. I've done my very best for this paper."

"Not the point, my boy. Ever since Washington Roebling's sickness and his wife's position as go between, progress on the bridge has faltered. Not your fault. But now it's announced his wife," He looked at a note, Emily, will take the reins of finishing construction and move the project forward with haste." He pointed his cigar toward Shannon. "My dear, I've asked you here to discuss something rather spectacular."

Carson and Shannon looked at one another. "I want you to oversee reporting of the bridge and weave Emily Roebling into the fabric. How about that?"

He smiled as Shannon took a breath and grabbed Carson's arm.

"Imagine, a woman reporter with her own byline, writing about a female engineer who's building the biggest bridge in history. What do you think?"

She looked at Carson, saw his concern before she responded, "But. What about Carson? If he's removed from the bridge and his additional..."

Richard laughed, smoke poured from his lungs, "That's the key to this offer, my dear." He faced Carson, "Information from the Midwest has begun to gather interest again. Our war is over and people are becoming bored. They want action and we can provide it. You, can provide it. There is a young officer who gained fast rank for his heroics. We have it from Washington, he's to be sent to quell the Indian problem and clear the area for settling."

He snuffed his cigar, stood and continued, "Carson, you have the background and the experience. You have the ability to paint the information bright red and grab our reader's full attention. We have correspondents already in place on those plains. They'll feed information and with your mastery, you will put the stories to paper. Your Horn stories were once the backbone of this journal, I believe you can offer that same excitement again. This will be the birth of the West and we are going to deliver it to our readers. You will gather the facts and fashion them into a new series somewhat like your former work. But this time, the Cavalry will win."

I have it on authority, this," He rummaged for another note, "this soldier." He found it and read, "General George Armstrong Custer, will give our readers all the adventure and thrills they can stand. In this time of peace and prosperity we need to report the unrest."

He reached for his cigar, lit it once again then pointed it toward Carson. It looked to be the glowing muzzle of a gun as he continued, "The west will finally become a safe place and we will be the paper that documents the rousting of those wild Indians. The New York Free Press will be responsible for our nation growing westward."

Shannon couldn't contain her excitement but when she turned to Carson, her smile faded. He seemed deeply disturbed. He spoke in anger, "Richard, this isn't Horn of the West. Horn fought the bad of both sides. That's what made him a hero, not this genocide."

Richard drew on his cigar, one eyebrow raised and he looked to Carson confused, "Times have changed since the Horn stories. This Indian problem continues to worsen. More and more settlers are being attacked and butchered. This Custer has vowed to take his Civil War experience and bring the difficulty to an end."

He flicked an ash and continued, "Hell man, these savages killed my own brother. You're lucky to even be alive. This closure is what our readers want and this is what we're going to give them. It will also offer excitement, adventure and, the elimination of the red threat. It will sell papers. I say, so be it. This nation needs to expand and we need to let people know it can be done safely. "

He came around the desk and looked down at Carson. "The war has been over for years now, people need something to believe in, to unite behind, and by God, this paper is going to give it to them. You'll place this golden haired General on top of a white horse and make him a giant whom our readers can idolize."

Angry, he pushed for agreement. "Do it for the nation, do it for the paper, hell do it for your job. "

He paused for emphasis, "You will work every angle associated with the surge west and tie it all to the termination of the Indian wars. That is now your purpose here."

Carson stared toward the window as if to find an escape.

Richard continued, "This is a combination deal. Imagine what this will do for your wife. She'll have her own byline. The bridge is being constructed and Shannon Calahan will become part of history. Is that why you're angry? I don't understand. I'll even offer you a raise if you do as well as I suspect you will, and your wife will have her own income. What more can I say?"

He spoke to Shannon, "Landon is nearly 21. He'll soon make his own way. To assist you in the transition, Charles and Amanda have agreed to take the boy for a year and introduce him to Washington. They've offered a room, training and work within the government"

He stepped next to her and placed a hand on her shoulder, "Shannon, you'll be free to become reacquainted with a work schedule, receive pay and the two of you will finally have your evenings together. I know how that can help a relationship. In addition, the boy will continue his education and see what it means to serve the government. It might just stimulate him to focus."

He turned back to Carson, "Shannon published for four years and never received credit. This is her time. Will you deny her that?"

***

An hour later the two sat with Persy at the Rusty Nail and relayed their forthcoming prospects.

"Does it mean we won't see ya around here as much?" She sounded concerned.

Carson chuckled, "Opposite problem, Red. You'll see the both of us that much more. This new position, for me, might make Gonto seem like he was a teetotaler. "

She laughed aloud, "That deserves a celebration." then shouted across the room, "Dear boy, bring the bottle I keep hidden behind the books and three glasses."

The boy put down the schooner he was drying and pulled the bottle from deep beneath the bar.

When he placed it on the table and set the glasses, Shannon stood to hug him. "Dear Lord, young man. If I didn't know you were just 15 I'd guess you to be nearly my age.

Red smiled, "I believe he's bigger n' his Da, and still growin'."

Gonto puffed up, "Charley says when he gets back to the bar, he's gonna make me his bouncer."

Carson chuckled, then looked to Persy in seriousness, "How is the old man doing anyway? Is he getting any better?"

Red sighed, "He seems to be growin' weaker every day. He just don't seem to care so much since his Sarah passed. Says the bar's goin to my Gonto, here, when the time comes. Says the boy's daddy nearly paid for the place, all the money he spent.

Gonto raised his head in pride though an underlying sadness surrounded him.

Carson reached across and slapped his shoulder, "Don't you worry young man. It'll be a long time coming. Old Charley has a lot of spunk left in him."

The boy filled the glasses and they raised them to the position.

54

Richard had been correct on one point, Carson enjoyed more personal time with Shannon, although the stories he was required to manufacture prompted additional anxiety. Every article promoting the war with the Indian nations caused him to become a bit more morose.

One morning Richard shouted and waved at him over the commotion of the office. He made his way through the confusion to the door where he was greeted, "Come in, come in and please close that door."

They both sat down and Richard continued, "Your articles have added quite a bit to our circulation. I'm grateful for that." He took a cigar from the box on his desk. "I think it's time to show my appreciations for all you've done. Both for my family and your work here at the Free Press." He stopped to light two cigars.

"Leak was destined to become a working manager here before his untimely demise, and I haven't truly considered any of these others." He swept his hand in an arc directing his cigar around the floor. "I realize that, for some reason, you have problems with this Custer business, however, you come through each time I need you. Just as you have from the beginning." He took a deep puff and released a stream of smoke as though adding suspense to his declaration.

"At this point, I would like to offer you the position of floor manager." He held his hand up beside his face, "Before you respond, I need you to know that you will have considerably more duties. We'll take some of western assignments away. I'll give Malcolm the pioneer accounts. He can do justice to the facts as they are. I'll still want you to follow this Custer business since you're narrative is generally written from personal experiences, distant though they may be. I don't feel anyone can be as believable, having not been there." He smiled at the man. "It will mean more work but the position will be coupled with greater pay." He hesitated a moment, "As well as the small office over there." He pointed toward a distant corner. "What do you say, my boy, are you ready to begin moving up?"

***

For the next two months Carson's attitude seemed to improve. He still had problems making a mad man sound like a saint. Reports and the photos filled his dreams but new responsibilities began to crowd out the anguish of attempting to canonize the General. Shannon was much more comfortable with her work and she seemed to talk of nothing but the bridge and the great Emily Roebling. Although they had more time alone now, their relationship seemed to be impacted by both her rapport with her new association and his increased despair coupled with the additional obligations.

However, they were both excited when told that Landon was on his way back to New York. Work had kept him thoroughly absorbed and the months had passed quickly. It wasn't until he heard of Landon's return that he realized that, although he had sent a few letters himself, the young man hadn't written at all after the first several days.

At the train, Landon stepped down from the car with a cheerful glow to find Richard and Bonnie waiting. Behind them were Shannon and Carson. He hugged his mother and Shannon, shook hands with Richard, then turned to Carson, paused, and hesitated. The atmosphere was at once cool and Landon's expression changed to utter disdain.

The carriage ride to Arrow House was filled with greetings sent from Washington, a letter to Richard and stories of the past months. While he conversed with Shannon and his parents,

Landon wouldn't address Carson directly and he only nodded yes or no to his questions. Shannon sensed something desperately wrong. She noticed her husband's anguish at being ignored and squeezed his hand. Landon's brow dropped in anger.

Carson could only imagine what damage the months with Charles and Amanda had done. He decided to speak to the boy alone and after dinner suggested the two go for a walk. Landon balked but upon Richard's insistence, they finally left the house.

"I have nothing to say to you." Landon stated the moment they reached the porch.

Carson strolled across the lawn to the gazebo and the young man reluctantly followed. At the steps, Carson gestured for Landon to enter first, followed him and sat on a bench. He motioned to the young man to join him but Landon refused.

Carson's fear was the boy had been abused and held him responsible for not offering a warning.

He decided to get things into the open and broke the silence, "What is wrong? What happened to you in Washington? Talk to me, please."

Landon paced a bit then turned away, "I have nothing to say."

Carson rose and grasped the boy by the shoulders. He pulled the young man around and was faced with anger and defensiveness.

"What did they do to you?" He pulled him forward but Landon pushed against his chest to keep a distance.

"Will you beat me too?"

Carson's hands dropped as he attempted to gather what he had just heard, "What the hell are you talking about?"

Suddenly the dam burst and everything poured from the boy at once. "I know everything. You and Ruby." his voice raised "You and my mother? I know what you tried to do to Amanda."

Carson's attempt to respond came out in a single, empty gust of air.

The young man continued his tirade, "You beat up Uncle Charles and threatened my cousins. Aunt Amanda swore them to secrecy."

Hatred creased his face, "But they told me what they saw. I wasn't afraid to ask. She took me aside and made me promise not to tell anyone. She's terrified of you, afraid you'll destroy the entire family, ruin Uncle Charles with scandal. You threatened them, blackmailed them so they would allow you to return and keep your position."

"No wonder Ruby ran away, escaped from you. And my Mother? I can't know how she even looks at you. How she's not told Richard. He would kill you with his bare hands."

Carson finally broke in, "Landon, none of this is true…"

The boy shouted, "She said you'd deny it all. This family puts up with you to save them from you, to protect their honor.' He turned away, "Don't worry. I agreed to keep their confidence and endure your presence if only for Shannon's sake. I won't stay around you any longer than I have to. Uncle Charles has procured a position for me at Brown. Next week I'll be away from here and rid of you."

He rushed to the lawn and shouted, "You no longer exist to me."

Carson stood in shock as Landon ran to the house. He felt numb as the young man disappeared from his life.

55

The entire world seemed destined for change. In the West, raiders gathered to end the "Red Menace". Horribly graphic reports continued to flood back to the Free Press. Photography had progressed with the times. Many of the accompanying pictures were far too horrific to print. Carson had to wade through pages of ghastly descriptions of the slaughter to glean any bits of supportive information that could bolster his stories. This Custer and his like appeared to make Captain Flowers seem nearly sane in comparison.

The job he loved became a daily laceration. Each myth he wrote pulled a fresh scab from his principles. He died a bit with each story crafted that portrayed these butchers as heroes. The only way he could cope was by capturing the truth in his journals.

He pleaded with Shannon, "If I pass, should you do nothing else, please read these journals and share them only with those who might profit. They are my life and my burden and as much as I regret passing the contents to you, it must be done. But please, cause no derision or pain to those we care about."

After years of requesting to read his journals and becoming offended by his secretiveness, Shannon agreed to keep the ever growing stack of chronicles safe and ultimately, honor his wishes.

Aside from complaining about the weight of his responsibilities and his aversion to being forced to manufacture lies about genocide in the west, Carson refused to discuss that which most deeply troubled him. He declined to share his demons or confide in anyone.

Even Bonnie claimed to have no idea what haunted him and neither Landon nor Carson would breach their concerns with her. Landon wouldn't face what he believed Carson had done to his mother and Carson couldn't share his pain if only to protect Ruby from reprisal.

Although bothered by her husband's constant distress, evasiveness and a growing sense of separation, Shannon gained some satisfaction in finally having her name in print.

Those mixed emotions caused pangs of guilt and in addition to his growing depression, further eroded her desire to be near him. Now, a welcome colleague of Emily Roebling, she shared increasing time away from home as the bridge grew across the river. Her reports were colorful and made the woman in charge seem greater than life.

The name of the new bridge had transitioned over several months from East River Bridge to her often reported Brooklyn Bridge.

As Carson became more and more involved in the horrors he read from the west, his attempts to codify the information and the lies that ate away at his soul made him increasingly resentful. With each lie he wrote, he withdrew even further from his wife and all around him. His growing detachment drove Shannon to spend incrementally more time with Emily.

When they were together she admonished him for being so preoccupied with situations he could not control. "Just let it be, Carson. It isn't as though you're killing these savages. You aren't responsible for their demise."

He looked at her, "You think not? You think that by demonizing these people I'm not somewhat accountable for their murders?"

She shook her head, "There is nothing wrong with what you're doing. It will all happen whether you write the stories or not." She hesitated a moment before she continued, "I truly don't understand how you can feel bad for these savages. Carson, they killed your family, Landon's father and all his soldiers. It's beyond me how you could ever have portrayed them with the slightest bit of humanity in the "Horn" stories. That was the most difficult thing I had to do when I took your pen name; pretend these Indians were somehow human. How could you ever write such…"

Carson jumped from his chair, arms raised, fists clenched and jaws so tight he felt his teeth would shatter. Shannon backed up in silent terror. He wanted release it all, tell her about the evil they were associated with; the bloodthirsty massacre of innocent people; the murder of his family; the hatred and the lies the Flowers brothers forced upon him and everyone else. He wanted to scream in her face, tell her who the real savages were.

He stopped when he finally saw her fear. She had backed into a corner and began to tremble at his anger. He stood over her with both fists raised and suddenly realized *he* had become the monster. *He* was the threat. He forced himself to stop. Guilt overwhelmed him and he turned and escaped from the apartment, his wife still quivered helplessly, in shock.

***

They rode together in silence in the Flower's coach. Since the night he very nearly struck her, Carson had become further and further withdrawn. He had returned late that evening to a still frightened Shannon but refused to talk about his reaction other than to say she had no idea of what life could bring. She attempted to discuss the incident but he felt more tightly cornered with each question so he opened a bottle and retreated to the kitchen, alone.

During the following days, although initially concerned, Emily assured her it was "Just the way of men," and convinced her to let him fume until his moodiness had passed.

Shannon, who was still deeply troubled, finally accepted the suggestion and began to share more of her life with her new confidant. The two commiserated about their losses and their loneliness. They continued to draw greater security and kinship through their experiences and accomplishments. She pulled further and further away from the man in pain who would not share any of it with her.

The woman who was building the greatest bridge the world had known, found support and friendship from the woman who kept account of all the details. They learned each other's strengths and shared each other's dreams. Their friendship and collaboration began to fill the vacuum that consumed Shannon since her husband's diminishing wellbeing.

Her new-found affinity helped fill the growing gap in her relationship but also added to the distance that emerged. Each day Carson seemed to grow angrier which caused her to pull further away and spend more time with her new friend. Their increasing separation only deepened his conflict and fed his depression. That in turn widened the chasm that lay open between them.

In the meantime, Landon interviewed and was hired at Brown University to work in the Humanities department. Carson and Shannon traveled to a celebratory dinner prior to the young man's entry into academia.

Richard decided with his continuing experience and education, Landon would accede to manager of the New York Free Press, displacing Carson. "Despite being my brother's son," Richard explained, "you are still blood, and you know what is said?"

As Bonnie explained in an aside, when presenting Shannon with the invitation, "Charles' sons are both finishing Harvard and will continue the Flowers' heritage in politics. After Landon completes his obligation at Brown, Richard feels he will make a great family contribution to the Times. Carson has been wonderful but how can one expect to pass the family business to someone other than family?

Carson and Shannon rode to the house in silence. She hadn't had the courage to tell him his position at the newspaper was now temporary.

Just prior to their arrival, Shannon thought out loud, "I was scheduled to join Emily in a meeting with corporate officers today but she understands family commitments. She said she would keep me informed if anything substantial arises." Carson quietly gazed out the window.

"We won't see Landon again for some time." she went on, "Richard has become so proud of the boy. It's about time he recognized his worth and I think we should support that."

Carson remained silent to prevent another argument. He bit his lip, aware from rumors at the paper that fate had provided him another devastating blow. He had protected so many members of this family, both actual and fabricated, and all his efforts had brought him nothing but pain.

He knew if either Richard or Charles found the truth of who Landon actually was, they would do everything possible to destroy both him and Bonnie as well. They would be thrown to the gutter without remorse.

Since the brothers and the paper had become so integral to her sense of wellbeing, it galled him that if he shared any of it with

Shannon, it would mean her downfall as well. She blindly and resolutely supported Arrow House in every conversation, even suggesting Carson was patently ungrateful. He was enraged that they held all the cards and he had no other option but to continue to be their pawn.

His growing anger and accompanied depression at his helplessness was a mystery to Shannon as was his escalated need to drink.

They arrived and his wife exited the carriage first and made her way to Landon on the porch to hug him. Carson delayed stepping down then waited in the drive until all had returned to the house.

The carriage moved off while he stood alone until, finally, Bea ran to him with papers in hand.

"Carson, I got another letter from Ruby." A smile radiated from her as she embraced him then whispered in his ear, "She sent a secret message and said it was for only your eyes."

He held her away and looked at her with surprise, waiting for the message.

Bea winked at him and said, "It's in my room, I'll show you later." They turned together, she took his hand and led him up the steps.

Later, at the table, Richard stood to make a toast, "We are here today to honor and bid adieu to our namesake; Landon Flowers the second. We only wish his father could be here to celebrate this day with us." He nodded his head toward his wife and continued,

"This boy came to us in desperate times of loss and deep sorrow. At that point we wondered if the Flowers line would continue." He smiled and nodded to Landon, "However, with the support and the foundation of our family members and dear friends," he tilted his glass to Shannon, "He has brought honor to the family name and today we celebrate his venture into higher education. We look forward to the time of his return."

Everyone clapped and began to talk when Richard requested a moment. I have another announcement I would like to make. Please stand up son"

Landon looked around and stood unknowing what was to happen.

Richard continued, "Tonight I'd like to announce, since my son has chosen to continue his education, as a member of this family, when he returns to Arrow House, Landon Flowers II will assume responsibilities of manager at the New York Free Press."

He raised his glass, smiled and said, "To our Landon Flowers, the Flowers dynasty and the New York Free Press."

The entire assembly stood and offered cheerful support to the dark young man at the end of the table. Carson clapped but his heart sank and Shannon held him for support.

***

He'd been quiet and detached all evening and just prior to boarding the coach, Bea hugged Carson and quietly slipped a folded paper in his hand, unseen by the others. He hugged her and placed the missive in his coat pocket. During the distressing stillness of the ride home, Richard's announcement coupled with the weight of the letter seemed to pull him further into the depths.

Shannon attempted to get him to discuss the event but all he said was, "My position at the paper is short lived now. All these years and all my efforts to be cast aside for a family member." At that he laughed and shook his head.

Shannon, equally in shock tried to soften the news, "You'll still be employed as a reporter and I have my position. We'll be fine."

He didn't respond and rode silent the remainder of the trip but fingered the note from Ruby and fought against pulling it out in front of his wife assuming it might bring more questions he would be unable to answer. He wondered what Ruby might say after all this time.

When they arrived home and Shannon prepared for bed, Carson sat in the kitchen, still in his coat, a drink before him. When she said her 'goodnight' and closed the bedroom door, he pulled the letter from his pocket, lifted it to the light and slowly opened the page. Before him was the reason Bea had not known the contents. The letter was scribed in French.

56

Two days passed before he could locate someone not associated with the Flowers family or the Free Press, who might translate the message Ruby had sent. Carson took caution to be certain that if there were any disparaging information, it would not find its way into the wrong hands. He feared for Ruby's well-being in addition to everyone else's.

Amanda's apparent financial support for Ruby would be terminated if she felt the least bit threatened. He wanted to be assured she was in a secure position before he did anything that might jeopardize her safety.

Referred to a French woman in Midtown, he interviewed her and was comfortable with her discretion. He still hesitated from uncertainty and fear but offered to meet with her the following day at the edge of Central Park. She seemed uncomfortable but finally agreed to his terms.

She was waiting on a bench when he arrived. He scoured the area to see if he might have been followed or if there were any familiar faces.

She smiled, took the note in one hand and waited as he placed a dollar in the other. He lingered to hear what was written when she suddenly put both in her jacket and explained she was late for an appointment. She offered to meet him there the following morning with a transcript. He reluctantly watched her rush off and his heart sunk as he imagined who her associations might be and what her motivations were.

***

That afternoon the lift opened to the normal confusion on the news floor and Carson saw Richard wave wildly through the window of his office. He acted extremely agitated, bouncing, almost jumping up and down waving a telegraph message in the air. Carson's heart sank at the thought the newspaper might have a wider reach than he anticipated.

He passed through the confusion to Richard's door when it flew open and the man shouted so he could be heard above the din, "It's about damned time you got here. You do work here, don't you?"

He went around his desk, shouted, "Close the goddamned door," and pounded his fist, still holding the paper. "Get over here!" he demanded and when Carson came close he pushed it in his face, "Read this and give me something as soon as possible."

Carson took the page and read,

"June 26, 1876- STOP- General Custer and nearly 300 troops found murdered by Indians in Montana Territory- STOP- Massacre of 7th Calvary by bands of wild Indians near Little Bighorn River- STOP- Five entire companies murdered in two days- STOP- More as we learn of it- STOP

Carson's eyes opened wide as he read and his spirits lifted. He and Ruby were not exposed and the General was dead.

Richard reacted immediately, "Get the hell out of here and get me something. This will lead in the evening edition."

Carson looked up and held up the four line message. "You want an entire front page from this?"

Richard came around the desk again, "No you imbecile. I want you to throw it out. What the hell do I pay you for? Find out where this river is, give me something about Montana Territory; the damn Indians in the area. Give me a rabid chief or some such thing. Be a goddamn writer for Christ's sake."

He turned Carson by his shoulder and pushed him toward the door. "Get Hanson to pull some file photos and have Portaco do some sketches."

He pushed him through the door and as it closed he shouted, "Make them bloody, damn it. I want 700 murdered heroes and I want crazy Indians, tell Portaco I said crazy!"

A short time later, after Hanson and Portaco had been set to task, Carson sat at the Rusty Nail to delve into pages of documents for bits of information to weave into a rendering of what might have happened near some river in the Montana Territory. He was impressed with the unusual name of the course and it became his title, *The Battle of the Little Big Horn: Custer's Last Stand.*

During the next hour and several glasses of bourbon, he wrote not one, but two descriptions of the events of The Little Big Horn; one for the paper and a second for his journal. Although there were few details, he allowed his imagination to fill in the spaces with past experiences. For each report, he reversed the qualities of the groups. For the paper, he made the soldiers to be champions. For his journal, he wrote what he knew tp be true.

At 1:30 PM he sent his story to the news room by way of young Gonto. He was in no condition to face Richard and with his belly full of courage, he felt he might tell the man the truth, so he sent the manufactured headlines to their home and retreated to his.

After two more drinks to mourn the stupidity of war, he withdrew to the couch in the living area and slept until the door opened.

Shannon entered with her back to the room and a package in her arms. She turned to see him as he sat up and yelped in surprise. She pushed the door shut with her foot and stared him as she placed the package on the table. "Carson, why are you not at the office? Richard was looking for you and he's angry as a bee. He said the piece you wrote was horrible, and he wants it fixed."

She stepped beside him, "You need to get back and do something. Richard is going crazy. He's assigned three people to rewrite for you because we're about to go to press. You can't be here, for God's sake, you need to be at the paper."

Carson sat up and stretched. He took a deep breath and the sour stench of bourbon hung over the room.

"You're drunk again, aren't you?" Shannon became annoyed, "Oh Carson, what is wrong with you? Renegades murdered hundreds of innocent soldiers and you sit here drunk? I'd think you'd want to be there to stop those animals, but you'd rather be drunk and write an incompetent article about it."

Carson tried to stand, to tell her how wrong she was, but as he did the room began to spin and he sat down hard.

"Carson, this has to stop." He couldn't determine if she was angry or concerned but he suspected it was a bit of both. She went to his side, placed a hand on his shoulder and spoke gently, "Emily assures me it will pass. She feels these stories are bringing your own losses to light again. I know how hard it must be, but excessive drink won't begin to help. Emily says..."

He jumped up, held his footing and shouted, "Emily has no goddamned idea what she's talking about." He pushed her hand away and weaved until he nearly fell.

"The Indians are trying to protect their families from crazy murderers. This country wants to exterminate them for sport. Writing stories that claim they're 'animals' incites the massacre and makes me responsible. Don't you understand, I might as well be the one holding a rifle to an innocent child's head."

Shannon stepped back in shock, "Emily says..."

He cut her off again and shouted, "Emily Roebling can go to hell and take her philosophy with her. I don't want any more talk about that woman in this house." He turned to her face to face, "This is my house, my life. She is not part of this family and I will not hear any more suggestions from her."

Both his words and his breath brought tears to her eyes. He shook his head and wanted to say more but the alcohol caused him to feel feeble. He stumbled to the table and picked up the bottle to pour another drink.

Shannon watched him spill the liquor as he negotiated the glass. Her silence broke in a flood of anger, "At least she has the decency to talk to me, to tell me when something's wrong. She doesn't cut me out and make love to a bottle."

He set the bottle down at an angle and turned toward her. It fell over spilling the contents as it rolled from the table and crashed on the floor. He swung back, picked up the glass and threw it down to shatter with the broken bottle.

Adrenalin seized her and she screamed back, "This obsession you have with the very people who killed your family is sickness. You are destroying yourself and you're destroying our marriage with this madness." She stepped toward him and softened her voice, "You need to face the fact that these savages murdered your mother, father and brother and sisters. You need to direct your anger toward those who deserve it. It's alright to hate them, to want them dead."

He took a breath, looked at the broken glass on the floor, then back to his wife.

Her anger diminished and anxiety began to grow as she looked into his eyes. There was an unholy glare surrounding him and she stepped back, fearing that he might finally release an entire lifetime of hatred. But he said nothing, staggered to the cupboard, pulled another bottle of whiskey and made his unsteady way toward the door.

Shannon cried as he opened it, "If you walk of here don't even think you can come back. You have ruined everything and brought nothing but pain and hatred to this family. "

He gazed at her through narrowed eyes, shook his head in sadness and left the apartment.

She feared she would never see him again.

57

A knock at the door startled her. She had spent the past several hours crying. Shannon wondered if he had sobered before he returned or if she would have to nurse and clean up after him again. She rose from bed and pulled on a robe. As the knocking became louder she hurried to the door in anger, opened it a crack and peeked through.

"Mrs. Calahan?" A man in a blue uniform spoke from the hallway. "Are you Mrs. Carson Calahan?"

Her heart stopped and she found it impossible to speak.

"Please open the door Ma'am, I got some bad news fer ya'."

***

The chapel at Arrow House was filled to capacity for the journalist. Carson Calahan had become renowned throughout the northeast. His work cultivated many followers over the years. Even Charles and Amanda felt it necessary to travel from Washington D.C. to present an appearance. Emily Roebling had been there from the first to offer comfort to Shannon. The only person noticeably absent was Landon, who claimed he was prevented from attending by his requirements at Brown at the close of the semester.

As the service ended and the Flowers family joined Shannon in the receiving line, a woman in a dark but flowered dress and veil stepped forward to offer condolences. When she approached Shannon she slipped an envelope in her hand saying, "I am so sorry I didn't get this to your husband before he passed." Then she disappeared as quietly as she'd arrived.

***

That evening Shannon sat crying in one of the many bedrooms of Arrow House. The Mrs. insisted she remain with the family for the next week to recover and recuperate. Emily had left for home earlier that evening, but before she went she removed a small package from her bag and covertly presented it to Shannon. She whispered, "It will help to ease your pain a bit, until you have your strength back."

Now alone in the room, she unwrapped the bundle to find a small bottle. She had no spoon to poor it in so removed the cork and sipped some of the bitter syrup. After several minutes, when nothing happened, she removed the cork and swallowed more.

Before long she realized she was no longer crying but heard an unusual buzzing in her ears. She stood and began to pace the room while thoughts of past years accosted her. She still couldn't believe Carson was gone, her babies were gone and now, she was entirely alone. Emily had proved a valued friend, however, that friendship could never counter her losses. She could only relive the past and had no vision of what the future might hold. She wanted to cry but somehow just couldn't. Every part of her demanded she scream at the top of her lungs but she still maintained the wherewithal to preserve her dignity there in the Flowers house.

She finally lay on the bed in an attempt to escape into sleep but her mind raced and her body had begun to tingle in an annoying manner. She rose. Picked up the bottle and stared at it, then decided the contents were a detriment so dropped it to the floor and searched the room for a distraction, something that might calm the feelings that now burned inside. As she continued to pace she remembered the strange woman and the envelope that she had been given earlier that evening.

She pulled it from the pocket of her dress that hung in the closet, sat on the bed and opened it.

There were two pages, the first written in a language she didn't recognize, so she turned the paper up and down to try and understand. That's when she noticed the second was written in English, inscribed with a handsome calligraphy. She dropped the first page to the floor and began to read,

My Dearest Carson,
I know this will be a shock, but I have decided I must let you know how I feel.
When the three of us left Pariah, my only hope was to die on that trail. I'd lost my child, my boyfriend, my father and my home. My only reason for living was to protect Beatrice until she could be safe. When we came upon you and the baby, alone in the wilderness, I fell in love the moment I saw you. You became my reason to go on.
On the train to New York I believed we were destined to be together and I knew then that Brighton would become Bea's savior. I wanted nothing more than to continue to live and be with you.
As time went on and we settled at Arrow House, everyone went their own way and I was abandoned once again.
I tried to care about the coach driver, but it just wasn't possible. When fate prevented me from being with him I realized I was wasting my time.
Charles had comforted me when he was there. He seemed the father I no longer had and when he paid my way to Washington I felt reprieved.

But you know what happened there. Life became a nightmare of an unprecedented nature. He kept me and used me at his discretion. When you appeared, I hid from you out of shame. I couldn't allow you to know what I had become.

That horrible night I pleaded with Charles to allow me to see you again. That's why he punished me.

I have only you to thank, a second time, for my life.

I realize you are married now, and the last thing I want to do is create tension between you and your wife. My world has become adequate since Amanda established the account for my welfare and silence. I will honor her wishes, however, I had to tell you, at last, that I love you with all my soul. With that, I can now let you go.

I send you my deepest and most humble gratitude for all the wonderful things you have done for my sister, Bonnie, Landon and especially me. It has been my greatest honor to know you and my only regret is that I was never able to show you the love that I will always hold in my heart for you and you alone.

All my love and thankfulness,

Ruby.

Shannon sat immobilized, unable to fathom what she had just read. Her mind raced over everything her husband had attempted to infer but avoided telling her until she realized all the "understanding" she'd believed she maintained was never even true.

She read the letter over and over into the depths of night.

***

465

Three weeks later Shannon and Landon met at a café in Providence. He seemed reluctant to look at her knowing what he knew and being absent from Carson's funeral.

She had insisted on the meeting and despite his hesitation, the young man finally agreed. He sat there, embarrassed, and waited for her to speak.

"I have something to show you. I have spent these past weeks getting to know who my husband truly was."

Landon reddened as he waited for her to pour out her pain, apparently now knowing of Carson's indiscretions with all the other women. His discomfort eased slightly as she gently smiled and placed a notebook before him.

He looked at the book with curiosity and then to her, his face transformed by question.

She slid it across to him. "I want you to read the passage I've marked. It's an enormous secret held by only a few. There is much, much more that you cannot yet know, however, I feel it's your right to understand this."

He picked up the notebook and looked at her in wonder.

"Just realize that Carson Calahan was a noble, wonderful man. The things he knew and the secrets he kept, ate him alive and destroyed his life. He did all this to save and protect you. You need to know this, but promise me, only you."

Landon looked at the book and began to read:

"August 18, 1856. Last night I woke in the darkness of the Kansas prairie to the wail of a tormented child…."

Photo by R Wooster

Libstaff lives and writes at the beach

of Puget Sound in Washington State

where he and his wife, spend much

of their summer at their retreat known as

"The Muse"